AUTHOR'S NOTE ON GEOGRAPHY

Please note, this book, although set in America, is written by an Irishman and so the spellings used are those his mammy considers to be the correct ones. If it's any consolation to you, she's not wild about the swearing but we left that in.

Also, while the author is rightly renowned for the gritty realism of his work, the area Coopersville that appears in this book, while based on several areas in New York, is actually fictitious. He did this as he didn't want to get slapped for inadvertently lowering the value of anyone's house.

PROLOGUE

"You may finish."

Bishop Ramirez gasped. He was kneeling beside his bed, praying alone – or so he had thought. He looked up at the stucco wall, its faded yellow paint, and at the crucifix that hung there. He could feel the hint of a breeze through the window, carrying the scent of flowers from the garden below. He blessed himself and resisted the urge to turn around and look directly at the man he now knew to be standing behind him.

Previous bishops had had guards, but Bishop Ramirez had endeavoured to make himself as different as possible from his predecessors. The last one in particular had been overly enamoured with the trappings of the office. His excess and willingness to forgive the unforgivable for the sake of convenience had led to his downfall.

Ramirez had joked, throughout his career as a priest, that for him to ascend to the role he now held, something very bad would have to happen. Something had. A scandal that had rocked the church to its very foundations. He was "a clean pair of hands", having spent all of his career outside the corridors of power, preferring the brutal honesty of the streets. He had only accepted the role on the understanding that he would be allowed to do it his way. His mission was to bring the church back to the people and restore it to the role it had always been intended to have: that of servant, not ruler. This approach had gradually started to win back public support, even as it angered those who had grown fat under the previous regime.

So no, this visit was not unexpected in the broader sense, although Ramirez would admit that he hadn't expected a man to appear, out of nowhere, five floors up in a locked room. It was probably just as well that he didn't have guards, as he would surely now be praying for the repose of their souls.

Ramirez nodded to himself. "And so it goes."

"Excuse me?"

"Never mind, my son. May I ask... I know I have angered many people in the last couple of years, but who in particular brought you to my door?"

"You did."

"And how did I do that?"

The man moved so that he was standing at the far side of the bed, leaning on the wall with the crucifix to his right. He held a gun in his hand – but casually. He had sandy hair that reached to his shoulders and looked maybe fifty, but with a lean, hard edge to him. A capable man, capable of anything.

"May I say, you are taking this well."

Bishop Ramirez shrugged. "We are alone in this room and, even on my best day, I don't imagine I could fight my way out of this if I wanted to."

It was the man's turn to shrug. "That is true."

"I knew when I took this job that there would be risks. It is the nature of these things."

"And besides," said the man, "this is not the first time in your life that you have had a gun pointed at your head."

It was not a question. They looked at each other for a long moment, neither man speaking. Finally, the bishop nodded. "I see."

"Yes."

"That was a long time ago."

"Not to me."

Ramirez blessed himself. "I am very sorry for the death."

"What death?"

The two men locked eyes again.

"I don't know what you..." started Ramirez.

The man laughed. "Please, you can stop the charade. I know the truth."

"In some ways, the man you knew did die that night."

"I raised him from a boy. He was my son."

Ramirez ran the back of his hand across his forehead, where a thin film of sweat was forming. It was a warm night, although he couldn't blame it on that. "Sadly, the world is full of bad fathers."

"Yes, many of them wear the same robes you do."

Ramirez nodded. "That is true."

"I'm curious, though. How did you do it? It was an impressive trick."

"There was no trick. I simply offered him the chance to confess his sins."

"I see."

"I would be happy to hear your confession too, if you so wish?"

"I'll pass. God turned his back on me a long time ago."

The bishop shook his head. "No, he did not."

"I didn't come here for a sermon."

"What did you come here for?"

The man raised the gun. "Apart from the obvious?"

"I could have been dead several minutes ago. You could have shot me in the street. They have repeatedly told me I am an easy target. I sense this is personal."

The man's face tightened. "You stole from me."

"No. Respectfully, I did not. People are not possessions. A man has the right to turn from the path he is on."

"Without me, the boy would have been dead a long time ago."

"But with you, the man had become death itself."

The man shrugged. "It's a living."

"Perhaps. But it is no life."

The man took a step forward, and for the first time, anger showed in his face. "You want a reason? Fine. I wanted you to know that I know. I didn't want you to die thinking you had beaten me."

"I had never met you until tonight. Do you truly believe I view it in those terms?"

"I am going to take him back."

Bishop Ramirez shook his head. "He is not the man you knew."

"We shall see. Any last words?"

The bishop blessed himself one last time, closed his eyes and spoke a prayer, his lips moving from muscle memory as the words formed in his mind. Then he looked into the hard eyes that were staring at him down the barrel of the gun. "I forgive you."

The man shot him once through the forehead. The bishop slumped onto the floor.

"The feeling isn't mutual."

CHAPTER ONE

"Bless me, Father, for I have sinned. It has been..."

Father Gabriel moved the rosary beads around between his fingers and did his best to stifle a yawn. It had already been a very long day and it wasn't anywhere near over.

Last night had been great – a rare victory. He had seen one of his kids win a state championship in the ring. The victory was nice, but it was what it represented that meant so much. Coopersville, when mentioned at all, was used as a cautionary tale about what happened when political neglect met chronic poverty. It was the bogeyman of the Bronx, the place parents warned their children they'd end up if they weren't good. And St Theresa's sat in the middle of a three-way gang war without end. Children were sucked in only to be spat out as young people with dead eyes and bullet wounds. Watching Bianca as she stood in the ring, the referee holding her hand aloft, so different from the withdrawn and distrustful girl who had slouched into his gym two years ago, had meant so much. He had been forced to fight back the tears.

His elation hadn't lasted long. He'd got the call at 2am, having just got into bed after dropping the kids back home. There'd been a drive-by over on Weston Avenue, in retaliation for one earlier in the week.

He'd gone to the hospital to give Little T the last rites and sit with his mother. The woman's grief was without bounds. Then he'd spoken to Razor, who'd been with him at the time and had taken two bullets. It was amazing: on the street they were hard men, brutal soldiers in a never-ending war, yet in a hospital bed they reverted to an almost childlike state. Gabriel had been here so many times over the last seven years. Each time, when the inevitable commitment to getting out had been made, he had to embrace it, to hope it would stick and the young men would stay the course. Invariably, they didn't. On the last Tuesday of every month, without fail, Gabriel took the bus upstate to visit with as many of the boys from his parish as he could during prison visiting hours. On the first Wednesday of every month, he visited graves.

The inside of the confessional was silent, except for the slightly laboured breathing of the man on the other side of the latticed wood divider. It was also unpleasantly warm, the church's heating system being blessed with only two settings – "sweltering sweatbox" or 'off'. In a New York January where the temperature was struggling to get anywhere above freezing, sweltering sweatbox was the better option.

The man on the other side of the confessional was mumbling to himself. Father Gabriel waited patiently. As it was in his nature to notice such things, he observed that there was a musty smell to the man, as if his clothing had got wet and not been allowed to dry properly. Father Gabriel took laundry seriously, it was the closest thing he had to a hobby.

The man on the other side coughed and said, "Sorry, I'll start again."

"Take your time, my son."

"Right. Thanks. Bless me, Father, for I have sinned. It has been…"

The man went silent again.

Gabriel wasn't great with people. It wasn't that he disliked them; rather, it was that he was an introvert in a job that all but demanded an extrovert. Other people just had that thing – the ability to effortlessly command a room and win somebody over. He had got better at speaking, particularly in the last couple of years. Still, he was a lot better one-on-one than addressing groups. It also helped that, in contrast to his first few years in the job, he had finally established relationships. It was easier to talk to people you knew than to strangers. This was why he liked the confessional. If you had to converse with a stranger, a predefined set of rules and the cloak of anonymity made it easier. He could just listen to the words and not have to worry about much else.

"When did Princess Diana die?"

"Excuse me?"

"Princess Di," said the man. "When did she pop her clogs? I'm trying to figure out when I was last at confession."

"I don't know that."

"Could you google it?"

"I do not have a phone."

"How do you not have a phone?"

"I own a cell phone, but I do not bring it into confessions, for obvious reasons."

"Ah right, I get ye – fair play. Although it must be tempting to sneak it in, play a bit of Candy Crush in the boring bits?"

"No, that is not— so, your confession?"

"Right, yeah. Sorry, Padre, I'm a bit out of practice on the whole confessing front. It's been... well, we don't know that. Hang on..." There was a soft thump, as if the man had slapped the wall. "Dolly the sheep! What year was Dolly the sheep?"

"I... I don't know what you're talking about."

"You must do. Dolly, the cloned sheep? They made a sheep out of the DNA of another sheep. It was supposed to be this amazing thing, and I remember thinking, if it was that clever, how come sheep have been doing it all this time?"

"An interesting point, but I am afraid that I don't know anything about this sheep."

"I suppose the Catholic Church probably isn't hot on all that stuff. Playing God and all that. Is there somebody we can ask?"

Father Gabriel was trying to decide if the man was drunk. His accent was Irish, which, even in the melting pot that was

Coopersville, was unusual, and he had a rather disconcerting stream-of-consciousness way of speaking. Normally in confession, Gabriel just let people talk, but he was aware that this conversation might need some directing, given the unusual path it was already taking. "How long it has been since your last confession is not important. What matters is that you're here now."

"Right. Spot on, Padre. Sorry, I'm rambling. Bit nervous."

"That's perfectly alright."

"Let's call it twenty-two years."

"OK."

"Give or take. Jesus, that's a long old time, isn't it?"

"As I said, you are here now."

"Right enough. By the way, can I ask – why are there big floodlights sitting in the church?"

Father Gabriel sighed; these were one of the biggest headaches he was currently dealing with. "We – actually, the diocese – hired building contractors, because our roof keeps leaking."

St Theresa's was a large church, built in a time when not showing up on a Sunday was considered scandalous. These days, regular attendance was the exception and not the rule, but the building hadn't got any smaller, only chronically in need of repair.

"So the big floodlights are here so they can find the leak?"

"Originally, yes. But the firm went bust, and despite extensive phone calls, nobody wants to come and take them away."

"Oh, right. That's a pain."

"Yes," agreed Gabriel. "These things are sent to test us."

Every day, Father Gabriel looked at the unsightly floodlights and resisted the urge to move them outside and let nature, or at least the larcenous tendencies of some of the locals, take its course.

"Anyway," said Gabriel, "back to your confession."

"Absolutely," said the man. "So, how do we start this? I mean, twenty-two years – that's a lot of sins."

"Where would you like to start?"

"Well... we could knock out the Commandments? Use them as a guide, like."

"If you feel that would be beneficial?"

"Well, 'twould be a good warm-up at least. I think I remember them. Christian Brothers properly battered them into me. First one – no false gods, right?"

"That is correct."

"We're grand on that one. One hundred per cent. Do you think he put that one first as it was the easiest one?"

"I think it was because it was important."

"Ah, well yeah, I suppose. They're all important though, aren't they? I mean, not the one about coveting your neighbour's ass. That feels like he had nine corkers and he wanted the even number."

"It is not our place to second-guess the Lord."

"No, you're right. You're dead right. Anyway – taking his name in vain? I'm scoring badly there, I'm afraid. I've always been shocking on that one. To be fair though, I'm Irish – that's just how we talk. 'Tisn't meant in a bad way. God is in the water over there."

"I see."

"Now adultery, on the other hand – gotta clean slate on that one."

"OK."

"I mean, don't get me wrong, Father, I'm just a man. I'm not immune to the urges. That Angelina Jolie, for example – I'd drink a tub of her bathwater if she wasn't a married woman."

"She is actually divorced now." It surprised Father Gabriel, who didn't read the papers or watch TV, that he knew this, but somehow, he did.

"Is she? Right, well, I'd better get a move on then. See you, Father!"

Despite himself, Father Gabriel smiled.

"Wait, does the Catholic Church still take a dim view on divorce?"

"It does, but I'm not sure that's your biggest obstacle."

"Ouch," laughed the man. "Low blow, Padre. Low blow."

Gabriel tensed. "Oh Lord. I am very sorry, that was completely inappropriate of me."

"What? Relax, Padre – 'twas a good joke. I was only messing with you."

9

Gabriel breathed a sigh of relief. "OK then." He had also never been very good at jokes. He had tried to learn that too, but levity, again, was not in his nature. "Let's get to your confession then, shall we?"

"Fair enough," said the man. "Where was I? Stealing – haven't done any of that."

"Good."

"Actually, well – now, let me think. I suppose technically I've, well – no, no. I think I'm alright. Don't mind me. Where was I?"

"I'm not exactly sure."

"Keep holy the Sabbath? Not great. I used to be a copper. Had to work it a lot."

"Working on Sunday is fine. All God asks is that you make time to come to Mass."

"Right." There was a pause. "I've not really been doing that either. Sorry, Padre."

"OK."

"Honour thy father and mother? That's a long story. Also – side note – I don't know if you can pass this up the tree, but I could really get behind a few additional Commandments."

"You would like to rewrite the Ten Commandments?"

"Not rewrite, just, y'know, add to them. Like, for instance, no littering. I think we could all get behind no littering, couldn't we?"

"It is very annoying."

"Right. And people with loud car stereos and the windows down, that annoys the bollocks off me. Oh, and adults riding their bicycles on the pavement – sorry, 'the sidewalk', as you call it over here – that drives me fecking spare."

"Yes. I think perhaps we should get back to your confession, don't you?"

"Right. Sorry, Padre. Sorry." The man's voice lowered in tone and became quieter. "Thou shalt not kill." There was a long pause. "That's a tricky one."

Father Gabriel sat back in his seat; this had taken an unexpected turn. "How so?"

"Well, there're justifications, aren't there?"

"Are there?"

"Like in a war, soldiers have to do what they have to do. I mean, within reason."

"Have you fought in a war?"

"No."

"Did you say you used to be a policeman?"

"That's right."

"Well, deaths in the line of duty, while unfortunate... If you were acting to protect others, those are not a sin."

"Yeah."

"Provided there was no other option. As the Bible says, vengeance is the Lord's."

Gabriel, his ears ever alert, heard a rustling sound from the other side of the latticed wall and, on instinct, his left hand slid down to the small blade strapped above his ankle, hidden under his sock.

"Right, yeah. The vengeance thing, that's tricky. First time I killed someone was – well, whenever Princess Diana died."

"Ah, I see."

"Oh God, sorry – that sounded wrong. I mean, not her. That wasn't me."

"I didn't think..."

"Right. Good."

The silence hung between them. Gabriel pulled his left hand back to his lap, holding the rosary beads as he worked them through his fingers.

"He was... If you know a man is going to kill – going to kill again – then ending him is sort of justified, isn't it?"

Gabriel pushed up his glasses and pinched his nose between his fingers. "This man – could he have been brought to justice?"

"No. It wouldn't have been possible."

"I see."

"Here's the problem though. A part of me was glad about that."

"Ah."

"Yeah. That was the first time I ever..."

"There have been others?"

"Oh God, I'm not some serial killer or something. I mean, I killed somebody last year, but they were trying to kill me. That was one hundred per cent self-defence."

"OK."

"Two other people died too, but technically I only wounded them, and they were all there to kill me. I mean they were properly assassins, like."

"I see." Gabriel slid his hand down towards his ankle again. "And why were these people trying to kill you?"

"Well, ah… Now, this is going to sound bad."

Gabriel said nothing, deciding to let the man say what he needed to.

"They were trying to kill me because I'd killed somebody about twenty years ago."

"Was this the person you mentioned previously?"

"No, somebody else."

"Right."

"But, again, that was in self-defence. Not lost a wink of sleep on that one. That fella was a monumental prick – pardon my French."

"Do you consider yourself to be a violent man?"

There was another pause. "Well now, I'd… You'd have to say that, I suppose. Thing is, with all due respect, Padre, I've seen a different side of the world than you probably have. I've fought for what I believe is right and I'd like to think I've been on the side of the angels. I've tried to protect those that needed it and stop those that needed stopping."

"I see."

"If you don't mind me saying, you say 'I see' a lot, Padre."

Gabriel shifted in his seat. "Well, you see…" He grimaced. "I mean, it is not my job to judge you, my friend, it is God's. I am here to simply connect your call."

"Right, yeah. Course. Sorry. Although, speaking of that, that's sort of why I'm here."

"I don't know what you mean."

"I think you might be able to help me."

Gabriel slipped the blade out this time.

"You see," continued the man, "this guy from twenty years ago. He had taken a friend of mine prisoner – a good friend of mine. A woman. Well, we were together, if you get my meaning."

"Sure."

"And he was going to kill her. She was an American who'd been snuck out and brought to Dublin for her own protection. A lot of bad stuff had happened to her."

"And she needed protection from this man?"

"Yeah. Him and his 'fellow travellers', if you like. The woman, her name was Simone and... I loved her."

A silence descended again, as if the other man was lost in thought. Gabriel decided to give him time. Eventually, the other man coughed, bringing himself back from wherever he'd gone. "Sorry, Padre, I just... Y'know, I don't think I ever said that out loud before. I said it to her once, and that went badly. Still. It's the truth. Most everyone who knows me thinks I'm dead. I left behind my whole life in Ireland – the world I'd built for myself and everything else I love – because this woman, Simone, is in trouble and I had to come here to try to help her."

"I see."

"Maybe she doesn't need it. Maybe what I feel isn't what she feels. Regardless, she has a lot of people after her. Although, d'ye know, it weirdly only occurred to me last week... Twenty years. She could be dead from natural causes or... y'know. I could be over here like Don Quixote, tilting at windmills. But still, for all that, the woman is in danger and bad people are looking for her. If she's alive, I've got to find her first."

"If what you say is true, I wish you luck, but I do not see how I can help."

"Well, funny you should ask. A few days ago – Christmas Eve, to be exact – well, myself and a couple of friends, we try to help out women in need of assistance. Y'know, dealing with violent partners.

And we helped this woman, Helena. Her ex-husband had tracked her down."

"Do I want to ask how you 'helped' in this situation?"

"Actually" – the man's voice brightened – "you can. I didn't even punch anybody, 'twas all non-violent."

"That is good."

"Yeah. I mean, there was a bit of Tasering and a pinch of tranquillising, but very little actual violence. The fella and his helper got arrested."

"So you worked with the police?"

"Not exactly. The point is, it was handled in a mostly – almost entirely – non-violent way."

"Good."

"We even broke into an orphanage and left presents."

"That was you?" Father Gabriel had heard about that; Rosario had shown him an article at the time. The paper had called it a Christmas miracle.

"Yeah, that was us."

"How does that relate to this woman?"

"Ah, it's a long story. Point is – stick one on the good deed column. Now, where was I? Right – this woman, Helena. She knew someone who knew someone. Said a friend of hers had heard about a Father Gabriel in the Bronx and how he'd helped a woman escape from a bad situation by putting her in contact with a group of nuns."

"I don't know what you are talking about."

"With all due respect, Father, I think you do. You see, my Simone, how she got out of New York was with the help of a bunch of nuns. The Sisters of the Saint."

"I have never heard of these sisters." Gabriel winced; he had said it too fast.

"They're not proper nuns. I mean – well, they are – but they're excommunicated or something. I dunno, nobody ever explained the exact details. What I do know is that they help women who need help and they fly so far below the radar they're almost impossible to find.

I've been in New York for nine months, Padre, and you're the first decent lead I have."

"I cannot help you."

"Respectfully, Father, I don't believe ye. All I'm asking is that you contact them. Bernadette. Assumpta. They know me. Tell them it's Bunny McGarry, and that Simone is in danger."

"I am sorry, sir, but I do not know these people. Is there anything else I can do for you?"

"That's like telling a man in a burning building that no, you can't have the water, but how are you for marshmallows? Here."

A piece of rolled-up paper was pushed through the slats in the wood. "That's a number that I can be reached at. I'll have it on twenty-four hours a day. I'll be waiting for your call."

"Please, sir, you need to listen. I cannot help you, because I do not know these nuns of which you speak."

"I really hope that isn't true, Padre, as you might be the only thing standing between an innocent woman, a good woman, and a pack of evil bastards who will stop at nothing to get what they want."

Father Gabriel sat in silence as he listened to the man stand up at the other side of the booth. "Now if you'll excuse me, I've got a long walk and they say it might snow."

Father Gabriel sat and looked at the piece of rolled-up paper, stuck between the slats.

CHAPTER TWO

B danced along the edge of the world and threw punches at the sky.

"S... s... stop doing that."

She executed a neat pirouette and worked her way back along the two-foot-wide stone wall. "Float like a butterfly, sting like a B!" She threw a five-shot combo and then raised her hands above her head.

Emilio rolled his eyes. "You'll drop like a st... st... stone if you're not careful."

"Not even gravity can defeat me! You feel me?"

Trey sat on the edge, his chin resting on the barrier's thick metal bar, and let the bickering of his two closest friends wash over him. He watched the streets, eight storeys below, through a pair of old binoculars with a cracked right lens. He had spent a lot of time up here over the years – they all had – but he still found it mesmerising. "B, gravity can definitely defeat you. I mean, I know you're still buzzing from being the state champion and all..."

"Undefeated!" she hollered at the top of her lungs.

"But think how sad a pancake you'll make on the sidewalk. All that wasted potential."

B pouted and stepped back onto the roof. "You two are downers. I need a couple of real hype men. Just for that, I ain't gonna let you carry my belt to the ring."

"Y... y... you don't got a belt. You got a cup."

"I don't got a belt yet – yet! You heard that man last night, I'm gonna go to the Olympics, baby!"

"Where you get a medal," said Trey. "Not a belt."

Despite having taken up boxing only twenty-three months beforehand, Bianca had made all-state as of last night, when she won her match in the first round. In amateur underage bouts, stoppages were a rare occurrence, because of the thick headgear and padded gloves, but it hadn't been much of a contest, in truth. It turned out that the girl Trey had known since she was two had grown into a fifteen-year-old with what one organiser described as "some of the fastest hands he'd ever seen on any boxer". They'd gone back to teasing her relentlessly since then, but last night, he and Emilio had been hugging each other in the bleachers and hollering in delight.

Emilio was over by old man Dianelli's pigeon coop, industriously scooping seed out of a bag and placing it in the feeder. His Dolphins cap, like always, was firmly on his head. Trey suspected he slept with it on. The only time he took it off was when forced to do so in school, and even then it went back on as soon as the bell sounded. A Dolphins cap was a ballsy move in New York, representing a rival football team that was in the same division as the Jets. Trey was one of the few who knew the truth. Emilio didn't care for football, but the dude really loved dolphins.

"C'mon," said B, "let's go do something."

"I gotta f... feed the pigeons."

"Man, why do you spend so much time on them racist birds?"

Unnoticed, Trey rolled his eyes. They had gone around this loop a lot – pretty much every day for a month, ever since Emilio had taken responsibility for the pigeons.

"B... b... birds aren't racist!"

"Those birds are owned by a racist. He used to always be talking to them. I bet he told them all kinds of messed-up shit."

"Mr D is just old."

"Yeah. Racist and old. Old racist honky."

Bianca had a love of the word honky, despite being white herself. While they'd never discussed it, it was noticeable that, despite Emilio being of Puerto Rican descent and Trey being black, it was the white girl who got all fired up on the subject of racism. Trey supposed it made sense, with the weird way their tight little group worked. The three of them had been inseparable since damn near birth. Trey had got into it with Darnell Wilkes last year, when he'd been making up those lies about B; and B had gotten into more than a few fights over the years, if anyone dared to mock either Emilio's stutter or his lack of a working right arm. A broken neck suffered as a child meant he could barely move it. It had also led to him being raised by his grandma. His parents had gone to jail, and that was the last he'd seen of them – except for a card that had turned up three months after his twelfth birthday.

"Grandma says Mr D is alree... r... right," said Emilio.

"That's only because she's too deaf to hear everything he says."

That was true. Mrs Fuentes was deaf and getting deafer, although she seemed to always understand Emilio, even if everyone else had to shout.

B noticed Emilio's glare and backed off. He was sensitive on the topic of his grandma. She held her hands up. "I'm just saying. C'mon, let's go!"

Trey caught B's eye. "Stop busting his balls, man. You know he's gonna do the thing until it's done. My boy ain't never left anything unfinished. He is fastidious in his duties."

"Yo, Emilio," Bianca said around a toothy grin, "Einstein over here just called you a fast idiot."

"Cool. I n... n... never been called f... fast before."

Trey surveyed the area around them. Even on an overcast winter's day, he could see the whole of Coopersville from up here. They'd come joint last in a "desirable places to live in New York" article in the paper last year. A run-down island of poverty in the Bronx that had so far withstood every wave of urban gentrification. Rich folks might always be looking for their next cheap property investment, but not in an area known for poverty, gang violence and drugs. Their building stood right in the middle. To his left was the Philpott housing project, Los Diablos Rojos territory; to the right, Bleacher Street marked the start of C-Boys territory; and behind them, that was New Bloods. Trey found it depressing that, despite the warfare that had raged as a permanent backdrop to his life, nothing ever really changed. It was like the trenches he'd read about in World War One – only here, whole generations had run into the machine gun fire, for no discernible ground gained.

"Hey, Trey," said Bianca, "if you want to come back to school with us, I'd happily jab you a couple of times, see if I can knock some points off that monster IQ of yours?"

"I dunno," said Trey. "If talking to you my whole life hasn't done it, pretty sure nothing will."

Trey didn't look around as he felt the air move. Bianca had recently taken to throwing volleys of punches at his head, close enough that he could feel the breeze on his skin. Despite his instincts, he studiously ignored it. He knew that if she found out it annoyed him, she would do it a whole lot more. It was also noticeable that she never did it to Emilio.

"Hey, E," said Trey, "you near done?"

"Nearly."

"Only, you know them animal shows you like?"

"Yeah. *Animal P… Planet* is my jam!"

"Well, one is about to kick off right in front of your very eyes." Trey felt the air stop moving as Bianca leaned over, curious to see what he was looking at. "You know how animals limping out on the African plains are in for a world of hurt?"

"Yeah," said Emilio.

"Well, we got one. Least the Coopersville equivalent."

"What are you talking about?" asked Bianca. "I can't see."

Trey held out the binoculars to her and pointed. "Look. There's some old white dude walking down Bleacher and – oh damn! He's reading a map!"

"For real?" said Bianca.

"Yeah, and the wildlife has just noticed."

CHAPTER THREE

Marcus sat on the stoop and watched, a wide smile on his lips. He heard the door behind him open as Sergio stepped out.

"OK," said Sergio, all business, "I got it. Let's go."

"Hold up, brother, hold up. Take a look at this."

Sergio looked across to where Marcus was pointing. An old white guy with a thick beard was standing in front of the alley beside Wong's, holding a fold-out map in his hands. "Damn, *ese*, that old white dude looks a long way from home."

Marcus clapped his hands together. "I know, right? I feel like it'd be our civic duty to help him out."

Sergio shook his head. "Nah, come on, homie, we gotta get this done. You know how Santana feels about people going off schedule."

Marcus waved his hand dismissively. "Fuck that, off schedule. We're independent contractors. I ain't passing up easy green. This'll be done in like five minutes. We can get about his business once we've handled ours."

"C'mon, man, let's just do what Santana wants. You know how he gets."

Marcus was getting annoyed now. "You too much of a pussy. I'll do

21

it myself. Santana got where he is by taking what's his – I'm just doing the same."

Marcus stood up and strode across the street. Sergio watched him go, then felt the weight of the packages he held in his coat pockets. There was nothing about this that he liked. Marcus stopped in the middle of the street and looked back at him over his shoulder. Sergio scrubbed at his goatee, and then, with a sigh, he followed Marcus across the street.

"Excuse me, sir, are you lost?"

The man looked at Marcus over the map and gave him a broad smile. "To be honest with ye, I am. 'Tis embarrassing. I found the church fine, but then I must've been distracted when I came out as I seem to be on the wrong street now."

"Ahhh." Butter wouldn't have melted in Marcus's mouth. "No problem, sir, we'll get you where you need to go."

"Well, that's very kind of ye, lads. Much appreciated."

"No problem at all, sir," said Marcus, winking at Sergio as he spoke in his most polite voice. "Happy to be of service, although I'm afraid there is a charge for our directional assistance on this fine winter's day."

The man looked between the two of them. "Ah right, I was afraid of that."

Marcus nodded.

"Would the charge by any chance be all the money I've got on me?"

Marcus nodded again.

"And your phone," added Sergio.

"Yeah, your phone too."

The man slipped his hand into his pocket and pulled out a phone of a type Marcus didn't recognise. "This phone? Believe me, lads, you don't want this phone. It doesn't have maps or email or any of that. Ye can't even get the scores on it. Plus – fair warning – it's the property of a shadowy organisation within the American government and they will probably take a very dim view of you half-inching it."

"Half what?" said Sergio.

"Half-inching," repeated the man. "Pinching. As in nicking, stealing, absconding with. Sorry, I don't speak the local variation on the lingo. Speaking of cultural misunderstandings – can I just clarify, you are definitely mugging me?"

Marcus laughed. "Check this motherfucker out. You English dudes are funny."

The smile fell from the man's face. "English?" He shook his head. "That's one."

"You threatening me, old man?" Marcus took a step closer. "This can go one of two ways. Do you want the hard way?"

This was greeted with a disconcerting grin from the man, who looked over Marcus's shoulder, directly at Sergio. Now that he saw him straight on, there was something weird about the dude's eyes. They didn't look in the same direction. Come to that, he seemed way too happy about things. Maybe he'd escaped from some institution or something?

"Well, seeing as you're offering – I'll take the hard way." He turned and nodded towards the alley they were standing in front of. "Shall we take this somewhere a bit more private? Don't want to unduly upset the locals."

Without waiting for an answer, the man turned and walked into the alley, folding the map as he went. Suddenly, this all felt very wrong to Sergio, in a way he couldn't give voice to. "Hey, Marcus, c'mon. We should…"

Marcus turned around. "What? You scared of some English dude?"

"We should…"

Marcus turned and followed the man down the alley. Sergio was seriously beginning to regret agreeing to team up with him.

The man stood calmly with his back to a dumpster as they approached him. The alley was a dead end. He was trapped, at least in theory. In reality, he was calmly pulling a thermos flask from his pocket and unscrewing the cup from the top.

"Does anybody mind if I finish me soup before we get down to business?"

Marcus laughed. "Man, this dude is too fucking funny. He got mad jokes."

Sergio watched as he calmly poured thick green liquid into the plastic cup.

"I tell ye, lads, I'm a demon for the soup these days. I noticed I was putting on a bit of weight, what with eating in restaurants over here all the time. I mean seriously, boys, 'tis a fine country you've got here, but two words: portion control. I'm amazed any of ye can fit through a door. So anyway, my friend Cheryl – lovely girl – she got me this soup maker for Christmas. I buy a load of veg that's on the turn – end of the day you can get it fierce cheap, and I'm on a budget since the previously mentioned shadowy organisation cut off my allowance for refusing to give updates – then throw in a bit of stock, some water and voila! Twenty minutes later – soup. Thermos keeps it warm all day too."

The man blew on his cup and then drained it in one before calmly screwing it back onto the top of the thermos flask.

Marcus cracked his knuckles. "Give us your money, that phone and your coat, and we'll let you keep your motherfucking soup."

The man smacked his lips. "I've not got much money, the phone doesn't actually belong to me and the coat... I'm afraid the coat has tremendous sentimental value." He rolled his head around his neck. "My lady gave it to me, you see."

"Well," said Marcus, "you gonna have to ask her to buy your ass a new one. I don't even want it, I just don't want you to have it."

"That's two. I can't ask her to do that as, y'see, I've not seen her for twenty years. 'Tis a long story."

"Bitch bought you a shitty coat and then left you. Pretty short story."

The man's smile faded and was replaced by a look of cold steel. "That's four."

Despite himself, Sergio asked, "Wait, what happened to three?"

The man ignored the question, not taking his eyes off Marcus. "She also didn't buy it."

"No?"

"No. She pulled it off the body of the man I'd just killed."

Marcus pulled the gun out of the back of his pants. "I'm bored of this, old man. Give me your money."

"Come and get it."

Marcus advanced quickly, holding the gun out in front of him as he walked. He'd expected the man to react how anyone would when a gun was pointed at their head. He'd expected him to flinch. Instead, he stood stock-still. Marcus placed the tip of the weapon directly in the centre of the man's forehead.

"You gonna run your mouth now?"

"Feck it. Didn't know you had a gun. That's impressive."

"Give me your shit."

The man wrinkled his nose. "What? Like my poo?"

Marcus pushed the gun forward, pressing the barrel into the man's forehead, forcing him to take a step backwards.

"Ouch, that'll leave a mark."

"I'm gonna shoot your ass."

"That'll leave a bigger mark."

Sergio stepped forward. "Marcus, we drop a body, Santana gonna be pissed. He said—"

"I know what he said."

"S'alright, *ese*," said Sergio, "be cool. I'll go through his pockets."

Sergio moved behind the old guy and started patting him down. He felt a wallet in his inside coat pocket and went to get it. "OK, I got..." There was a loud snapping noise and Sergio screamed. He pulled his hand back out and held it in his other hand. "Mother—"

Marcus watched him dance around. "What the fuck, man?"

Sergio held his hand up and yowled. A large mousetrap had snapped shut around his fingers. "You broke my finger, you..."

The old guy shrugged. "My hotel is on the lower end of the scale. It's got a slight rodent problem."

Marcus pulled the gun back, ready to slam the butt down onto the old guy's head. As it was making its descent, his hand was met by the flask, which was travelling a beautifully judged arch that caused it to smash directly into Marcus's wrist. The gun flew from his hand as he yowled in pain.

"One."

The old guy had thrown his whole weight behind the swing, his momentum causing his body to twirl around, which he followed through by driving the point of his left elbow straight into Marcus's face.

"Two."

Sergio, having managed to prise the mousetrap off his shattered finger, lowered his shoulder and charged, intent on tackling the old dude to the ground. Instead, like a bullfighter, the man sidestepped gracefully, extending his left foot as he did so and sending Sergio tumbling headfirst into the side of the dumpster. Pain flashed across his eyes like sheet lightning as his head slammed into unyielding metal. He found himself on his hands and knees, the foul stench of rotting food filling his nostrils as mushy, wet cardboard squirmed under his fingers.

Sergio turned around just in time to see the old man connect with a left hook to Marcus's jaw.

"Three."

He followed this up with a swift kick to the right knee that caused Marcus's leg to twist at a sickening angle as he crumpled to the ground.

"Four."

Sergio wasn't packing, but he scrambled for the blade that he always carried inside his jacket pocket. He got messily to his feet, a ringing in his ears as he swayed slightly. He brandished the knife in front of him, his back pressed against the dumpster.

"I'll cut you, old man."

The old man smiled. "Your choice." He raised his right hand. "Do you want the flask?" He raised the other hand, which now held Marcus's gun. "Or this."

Sergio considered his options briefly before holding his hands up in surrender.

"Toss the knife."

Sergio looked at it.

"Do it, and if you don't hit the back wall with it, I'll shoot you and make you do it again."

The knife hit the back wall.

"Nice throw. Now get down on the ground, face down, arms spread."

Sergio looked at the muddy ground, covered in the kind of unpleasantness that life left behind. "Aww, man."

"Would you like to hear your options again?"

With a grimace, Sergio did as instructed.

The man walked over to Marcus, who was groggily attempting to get back to his feet, stumbling like a newborn deer while holding his shattered wrist to his chest. Their tormentor slammed the flask into the side of Marcus's head, causing him to slump to the ground again, unconscious.

"And that's five. You got an extra one because I'm not having the best of days." He turned back to Sergio. "Now that he's having a nap, I think it's time you and I had a chat."

"Look, man, I'm sorry."

"Yeah, I'd imagine you are alright. Empty your pockets."

Sergio's pulse raced. "I swear, man, you don't want what's in my pockets."

The man leaned over and looked into Sergio's eyes. "Well, if you say so. I mean, you seem trustworthy."

The man shoved the flask back into his coat pocket and took a few steps towards the mouth of the alley. Sergio's whole body relaxed.

"Although..."

Sergio watched the man turn and walk back to stand in front of him again. "You did get my nationality wrong, and I am a bit sensitive about that."

"That was him!"

The man used the barrel of the gun to scratch his beard. "Oh yeah, 'twas. Well spotted. Still though. I just wanted to check you'd not got a gun, so I didn't get shot in the back, but now I really am curious as to what's in your pockets."

"Look, man – we're Diablos Rojos, man. You don't want none of this, believe me."

"You're what?"

"Diablos Rojos. This is our territory."

"Di-ab-los Ro-jos..." The man sounded the syllables out slowly, as if savouring them. "D'ye know, one of my big regrets – and I've got many – is I don't know any Spanish. They taught us French in school. Fecking French? I mean, sure, the women are fantastic, but I can't stand the food. Too much butter on everything. And pain au chocolat? For feck's sake, you can't start the day with chocolate. Chocolate is something you build up to. 'Tis a treat. What the feck did you do while sleeping that deserves a treat? 'Tis excessive. I much prefer Mexican food."

Sergio looked up at the man. Even if he weren't concussed, he reckoned he probably wouldn't have understood what was happening now.

"So, Diablos Rojos, what's that stand for? I mean, in English, like?"

"Red Devils. We the red devils, man."

"What the—? Are you a Manchester United supporters' club or something?"

"No."

"Well, I don't want to add to your troubles, but I'm guessing they've trademarked that, and they are notoriously litigious."

Sergio shook his head. This was all starting to feel like some messed-up dream.

The man moved behind Sergio and started unzipping the left pocket of his jacket.

"Aw, man – don't."

He felt the package being removed; this was swiftly followed by a boot connecting with his ribs.

"Oof!"

Sergio didn't need to see to know what the man held in his hand. It was a Ziploc bag full of tiny baggies, all labelled "Red Devils". Santana said it paid to advertise.

"I'll be honest, this was a bit of stress relief for me up until now, but I take rather a dim view of drug-peddling scum."

"You—"

Sergio was interrupted by another boot to his ribs, unerringly hitting the same spot as last time and redoubling the pain. Then he felt his other pocket being unzipped.

"How much is this?"

"You don't—"

"I can boot your ribs again if you'd like."

"It's five G."

"OK. Well, I'll put this to good use. I've seen a self-cleaning soup maker advertised. I might get one of them."

"Seriously, man, I ain't playing. You take that – you a dead man. Santana will find you."

"The guitar lad?"

"What?"

"Plays guitar in the band called – actually it's called Santana, now I think of it. Never liked that. Like Bon Jovi. 'Tis fecking cocky naming your band after yourself."

"No. Santana, he runs the Rojos, man. He'll kill you. He'll kill your family. The dude don't play."

"He also has a shocking understanding of trademark law. I'm smelling two lawsuits – and counting." The man came back around to stand in Sergio's eyeline. "Now, you tell whoever you like that I'm confiscating all of this. I'll destroy the drugs and we'll say the cash is for covering expenses and emotional hardship."

Sergio shook his head furiously. "No – no, no, no. He'll kill me, man, he'll kill me."

Bunny glanced over at the still unconscious form of Marcus. "Well, not to sow disharmony in the family, but if I was you, I'd strongly consider blaming him. Right, one last thing, then I'll leave you in peace. Could you tell me... How do I get back to Cypress Avenue Station from here?"

CHAPTER FOUR

Smithy sighed.

Whoever had said that if you expect the worst from people, you'll never be disappointed definitely had a point. What they had failed to mention, though, was that you could still be incredibly irritated.

He had more than enough self-awareness to realise he had an anger management issue. His experiences, up until this point in life, had provided ample evidence of it. Even if they hadn't, the court-mandated anger management course was a pretty big clue.

He slammed the cab into reverse.

Overall, he enjoyed driving the taxi. His friend Marcel owned it. Thanks to the proliferation of app-based ride services, the medallion for a yellow cab wasn't worth as much as it once had been. Smithy was sure he'd heard they once went for a million bucks, but he reckoned it was still pretty valuable. How Marcel, a French-Canadian dwarf who wrote poetry in between pickups, had come to own one was a mystery, and any and all efforts made by Smithy to find out more had been met with the kind of oblique answers that only a poet writing in their second language could come up with.

Smithy didn't spend much time hanging out with the little people's community. It just wasn't his thing – he'd never been much of a joiner. In fact, Marcel was Smithy's only similar-sized friend in New York, and even then, he wasn't someone you met up with regularly. He was the kind of guy who turned up at your door stinking drunk, bleeding or once, rather memorably, carrying a bust of Jimmy Carter. Smithy hadn't received a coherent explanation of how Marcel had come to be in possession of that either. Smithy had first become aware of Marcel's existence when some guy had tried to beat him up for sleeping with his wife. The only way Smithy could explain to the big drunken idiot that he'd got the wrong dwarf was to win the fight first. Then they'd had a heart-to-heart during which the man had realised that he was angry more at himself, for having been a bad husband, than he was at Marcel. This had led indirectly to Smithy meeting Marcel. Despite their rocky introduction, they had become friends, because while he could be accused of being many things, Marcel was never dull.

Still, the man was a mystery wrapped up in an enigma and wearing a beret. Despite their long association, Smithy still couldn't tell if he wore it ironically or not. And he didn't know how Marcel had come to own a New York taxi any more than he knew how Marcel had managed to move to Tahiti with his current boyfriend. All he knew was that he had gifted Smithy the use of the cab for an indeterminate amount of time. He'd only found out about it when the barman at a bar they both frequented handed Smithy an envelope containing the keys along with a poem that Smithy had yet to decipher.

If history had proven anything, it was that Smithy was not predisposed to having a boss. He'd tried to work it out recently and he reckoned, best guess, he'd quit more jobs than he had been fired from. The final tally really depended on things like whether you considered setting the boss's desk on fire to be officially handing in your notice or not. The idea of driving a cab, therefore, and being his own boss, had its appeal. What he was currently doing would almost certainly have lost him his licence to do so, except the Taxi and Limousine Commission hadn't actually finished processing his application yet and you can't lose what you never had.

With a squeal of tyres and a cacophony of honked horns, Smithy hurled the taxi into a reverse U-turn that ended with the car facing the correct direction in the right-hand lane, having narrowly missed taking out the wing mirror of a parked sedan. He slammed the vehicle into drive and jammed his foot on the gas.

He'd used the taxi for a few weeks before Christmas, up until he'd stopped to help Bunny with that thing on Christmas Eve. Overall, the job had many plus points. Nobody met a more diverse cross section of the world than a New York taxi driver. Smithy had stalled in the first act of the play he was writing, but his time in the cab had given him a hundred new ideas. Every passenger was a story, and he'd taken to furiously scribbling notes when stopped at traffic lights. In the three weeks prior to Christmas, he'd met a lot of people. Some had spoken no more than a couple of terse words; some had poured out their souls. One night, he'd turned off the meter and sat in silence while a man who had recently been widowed sat in the back seat, looking up at the Brooklyn Bridge, and talked himself out of a bad decision. A broken heart was laid bare, and he saw the man's love for the woman who had completed him and then his realisation that she would hate what he was considering. Men being men, the U-turn of his intent had been justified when Smithy opined that the Knicks might not suck this year and that he knew a guy who knew a guy who might be able to get tickets for *Hamilton*. He'd really wanted to see that show.

Smithy had driven a pregnant woman to the hospital, which had been kind of cool. He hadn't charged her, figuring that it was good karma. But thanks to the Christmas party season, he'd also had to clean up an unacceptable amount of vomit – none of which was his.

On top of all that, he may well have been an unwilling observer to the conception of a child. It was surprisingly hard to stop two people having sex if they seemed to be getting off on your admonitions. Still, "Big Daddy" and "You Bad Girl" had seemed very much in love and were probably well suited for each other, in their own messed-up way. That was the night Smithy had started paying for someone else to valet the cab.

Neither the vomit nor the unwanted voyeurism was what had annoyed him the most though. No – not by the longest of long shots. Lots of people had questions when they noticed that he was a dwarf. He wasn't wild about it, but as long as they were asked politely, he didn't mind them in his current circumstances. The way he saw it, he was driving a vehicle that people were passengers in, and they had the right. So yes, he had extensions to the pedals, and the seat was specially customised. Nope, it wasn't hard – he could drive as well as anyone else, due to the cab's modifications.

So today, this guy – the douchebag who was currently hurrying around the corner of East 121st Street and Third Avenue – had asked the usual questions. Smithy had seen the expression on his face as the douchebag had made his calculations. He'd learned to recognise the look after it had happened the first couple of times. What was it they said? Most people avoided engaging in criminality only because opportunity never presented itself. Besides, skipping out on a fare wasn't really a crime, was it?

This time, enough was enough. The anger management course, the books, the Tony Robbins seminar he'd signed up for at a particularly low moment – they'd all said the same thing. Count to ten, take a deep breath, realise that you are losing control. As Smithy threw the cab around the corner of 121st and Third, the little voice in his head was counting to ten, but it was doing it sarcastically. Smithy was really calm right up until the point he wasn't, and try as he might, when the levee broke the levee broke. This douchebag was circling forty in a charcoal grey suit and a cashmere overcoat – he wasn't anyone's best guess at what a criminal might look like, but Smithy saw it differently. He'd seen the look and the sweaty palms rubbing together, the licking of the lips in nervous anticipation. As soon as the cab had pulled to a stop, he was out the door like he'd been shot out of a cannon. The door was still open – swinging around wildly as the car veered back into the lane it was supposed to be in. Smithy really needed to get that central locking thing fixed. The guy had just started to slow his run, no doubt thrilled with himself at having skipped out on a $23.50 cab fare, when he turned at the sound of squealing tyres. At almost 9pm, the sidewalks were only sparsely occupied, which was just as well, as the cab – with a shuddering jolt and a burst of sparks – mounted the kerb and blocked the guy's path.

Why does a guy who can clearly afford it decide to skip out on a fare? Midlife crisis? The thrill of the chase? Something to liven up a life that had fallen into a rut? That would certainly explain what happened next. Smithy had half-assumed that the guy would reverse course and run back the way he'd come. Instead, he'd gone for the leap onto the hood of the car and the slide over, like Steve McQueen in *Bullitt* or one of the *Dukes of Hazzard* boys. It was a trickier manoeuvre to pull off than the douchebag had anticipated: his knee hit the side of the car, leading to an ungracious face plant on the hood followed by a messy landing in the doorway of a trophy store that had its metal barriers down. A homeless guy who had been lying there in a sleeping bag broke his fall.

Smithy didn't like talking about his past, for many, many reasons. Still, it had been colourful. It had also left him with some useful skills – for example, the ability to flip himself out of a car door and onto the roof, and from there to leap into a perfectly executed elbow drop from height onto an opponent's back. When he'd learned this skill, the hardest thing had been to make it look convincing while not actually hurting your opponent. Thing is, if you knew how to produce an excellent fake, the genuine article was easier. Even as he came in for a landing, a tiny part of his mind, the part not shrouded in red mist, was marvelling at how his form was pretty good for someone who hadn't executed such a manoeuvre in over a decade. The face of the man in possession of $23.50 that didn't belong to him made a satisfyingly unpleasant sound as it hit the sidewalk. Smithy then flipped himself over to land on the guy's back, pinning him while knocking any wind the douchebag had left firmly out of his body.

"Hi there – quick customer feedback survey. How would you rate your ride in my cab? A) excellent, B) average, C) the reason you now have a broken nose, bruised ribs and a life expectancy that a mayfly would consider brief?"

In lieu of an answer, the man made a gurgling sound as he attempted to catch up with the latest developments in breathing in a world where noses were broken and dwarves were riding your back like you were a birthday pony ride.

"What the fuck?" Those words came from the sleeping bag. Smithy turned to see the bearded face of the homeless guy peeking out from his cocoon and felt instantly guilty.

"Oh – sorry, man. I was apprehending a fare-skipper."

The homeless guy sat himself upright. "I'm just, y'know, trying get some sleep. Don't need dudes falling on me."

"I know. I apologise."

The homeless guy looked down at the fare-skipper. "Maybe he can't afford it? Times is hard."

"Get the fuck off me," whined the passenger. "This is assault."

"Citizen's arrest." Smithy shifted his weight and reached around to grab the guy's wallet from inside his coat.

"Hey! You can't—"

Smithy used his free hand to slap the back of the guy's head. "Yes, I can."

Smithy flipped open the wallet. "Well now, what have we got here, I wonder?" He looked at the driver's licence. "Nathan Perriman. Hi, Nathan, delighted to make your acquaintance." Then Smithy pulled out the banknotes. "I make that about... what? Over six hundred bucks."

The homeless guy gave a disapproving shake of the head. "Nathan, man, not cool."

The invective Nathan issued in response was met with a wallop on the earhole from Smithy. "Now, Nathan, it feels like you're just not learning your lessons regarding proper social etiquette." He turned to the homeless guy. "What's your name, brother?"

The homeless guy looked slightly taken aback. "They call me Fudgy."

"Cool. I'm Smithy. Apologies for, y'know, this."

Fudgy shrugged. "Hey, man, nobody likes getting ripped off. I feel you."

Smithy gave him a nod. "Appreciate it."

"Get off me."

"No, Nathan. I'm afraid this experience isn't something you can skip out on."

"You can keep the money, just—"

Smithy slapped the back of his head, slightly harder this time. "No kidding."

"Please, I'm sorry. Oh God, I peed myself."

Smithy looked down. He had.

"Hey, man," said Fudgy, "it happens."

Smithy continued his examination of the wallet. "Let's see: credit card, credit card, Starbuck's loyalty card. Damn, someone likes to stay caffeinated. And..." He found the baggy in the zip pocket. "Oh my, I'm guessing this is some of that cocaine I've heard so much about. So, has that misplaced confidence worn off yet?"

"Keep it."

Smithy shook his head. "The dude is unfailingly generous."

"Hey, man, could I have that?"

Smithy looked into Fudgy's eyes. "Ah, sorry, brother – no offence, but it doesn't seem like the cool thing to do."

Fudgy nodded sagely, clearly used to not getting anything in this life for free.

"On the upside though..." Smithy flipped through the notes and pulled out a ten and a twenty. "I'm taking thirty bucks. That's the $23.50 you owe me, Nathan – plus I'm guessing you're a big tipper."

Nathan said nothing.

Fudgy's face lit up as Smithy wordlessly handed the rest of the notes to him and then put his finger to his lips. "The rest of your money I'm giving to a worthy cause, because, y'know, we're all in it together."

"That's stealing," said Nathan in a less conciliatory tone.

"Wow, you've suddenly developed a finer sense for that concept than you had in my cab. This is progress. Look on the bright side: you can have your wallet back."

"Alright, fine."

"It'll be under a rock in front of the Alice in Wonderland statue in Central Park."

"Aw, come on!"

"Life ain't fair, Nathan," said Smithy. "In fact..." Smithy lost the train of thought as the Bluetooth headset in his left ear rang. He hated the thing on principle, but he'd reluctantly bought one for when he was driving, as – despite the dramatically contradictory evidence of the previous few minutes – he actually took road safety very seriously.

Smithy tapped his finger to it to answer. "Yeah?"

"Howerya, Smithy, how's it going?"

"Hey, Bunny. Oh, you know, the usual."

Nathan used this opportunity to make an ill-judged attempt to throw Smithy off his back. Having been anticipating it, Smithy leaped up nimbly and, placing his hand on the hood, landed a couple of feet back, from where he was perfectly positioned to deliver a swift punch to an area that would make Nathan's evening all the more memorable.

Fudgy sucked in air and winced sympathetically. Some experiences traverse class, race and, well, everything except possibly gender.

"I need your help," continued Bunny. "You got time for a drink?"

Smithy accepted Fudgy's fist bump and then patted Nathan, who was engrossed in a very personal pain, cordially on the cheek as he walked by his prone body.

"Yeah, sure. A drink sounds good."

CHAPTER FIVE

Jackie watched the door expectantly while Paidi and Donal, the Porterhouse Lodge's two most regular of regular customers, pretended to read their newspapers. In fact, the term "regular customer" didn't really do the two men justice. For as long as Jackie had managed the place, both men had spent six to eight hours of every day sitting at either end of the bar, like the sentinels from a Ken Bruen novel. Jackie would have thought that the greatest plus of being retired was that you didn't have to turn up to the same place day after day, but apparently not. The two old duffers were here come rain or shine – and even when there had been several feet of snow. Jackie lived in the apartment upstairs with his wife, so he had opened the pub for them because, well, what else was he going to do? Just because the old lunatics had walked there in the middle of a blizzard, it didn't mean he could feel right sending them back home in it. They'd spent so much time in the place that they'd worn grooves into their stools. You couldn't refer to people like that as 'customers'; they were more like family.

And not unlike family, they could also be intensely annoying. The only thing the two men ever agreed on was that things were getting worse, and the reason they were both pretending to read the paper today was because they had found a new argument to have. It was Paidi's contention that the Porterhouse Lodge had gone unforgivably upmarket – serving the besuited work crowd rather than the everyday working man that used to be its clientele. Donal entirely disagreed, saying they got more casually dressed wasters in the doors than ever, and that was what was sending the pub to hell in a handcart. Jackie had made the terrible error of being dragged in as judge in this latest dispute. To get a proper sample size, it was decided that they would monitor the people coming through the door for the entire day, business wear versus casual, and count which they got more of. Jackie had been the one who'd decided that the winner would be the first to make it to fifty. It was currently poised at 49–49, and it had been for ten minutes now. The tension was becoming unbearable.

Jackie drummed his fingers on the counter. Sod it, he was getting himself a whiskey – this was getting to be torturous. He was just turning towards the optics when the door slammed open and a six-foot-tall fox staggered in. Jackie recognised it instantly. It was Funtime Frankie from the hit kids' TV show of the same name. His grandson loved it. His granddaughter had too, until the day she'd announced that it was "for babies" and she now hated it. It was hard to keep up.

Donal dropped his paper and pumped his fist. "Winner!"

Paidi waved his hand in disgust. "How are you getting that? Winner? That's not casual attire."

"Well, it sure as shite isn't a business suit!"

The head of the costume was pulled off to reveal someone else Jackie recognised: Jackson Diller. It was definitely him, although he didn't normally look this sweaty and frantic. He leaned on the bar and panted heavily.

"Hey, Diller, how you doing?"

"Hey... Jackie... I'm... long story."

Jackie smiled. "It always is with you guys. Smithy and Bunny are in the back."

Diller nodded. "Could you hide me?"

"What?"

"I need to hide."

"If you don't want to see them, you could just not come here. I mean, while we appreciate your custom and all, we'll survive without that lemonade sale." Diller was a non-drinker, which had also led to a debate between the sentinels as to whether he should be allowed to use the pub. Donal had made a firm ruling on that – he'd always liked Diller. Speaking of which…

"He doesn't count," said Jackie in his best stern voice. "It's still 49-all."

This was met with outraged grumbles from both ends of the bar, which Jackie waved away. "Judge's decision is final."

Diller looked confused and then gave Jackie a pleading look. "Please, Jackie, I'm being chased."

"Let me guess," said Jackie. "Bunch of posh dudes on horseback with a pack of dogs?"

"Good one," said Paidi.

"No problem, Dill," said Jackie, raising the hinged bar flap and letting Diller in behind the counter. "You can just sit in the back hall there."

"Thanks, Jackie."

As Diller disappeared, Donal shook his head. "This is how it starts."

"How what starts?" asked Jackie.

"This'll be a furry bar in a week, you mark my words."

"What are you on about?"

Paidi nodded in agreement. "Yep. Happened to Gallagher's over on Clayton. Place is full of them furry fuckers these days."

"You two are making even less sense than usual," said Jackie, "and that's really saying something."

"Furries," said Paidi. "Weirdos who dress up as animals and then have sex with each other."

"That's not a thing," said Jackie.

"Oh no," said Donal. "It is alright. They'd a big write-up on it in

41

the paper. They call having sex 'yiffing' – after the sound that foxes make when they're on the job."

Jackie considered himself on the more liberal end of the scale, but this horrified him – his grandkids watched that show. As if on cue, Diller stuck his head out the door. "I'm not one of them. I'm working as a mascot up in Times Square."

Jackie nodded, relieved. "Yeah, that makes sense." It was a New York institution – out-of-work actors in costumes charging tourists five bucks to get their picture taken with Darth Vader or Elmo or Pocahontas. "By the way, Dill, you never said, who is—?"

In answer to the question Jackie hadn't finished asking, the bar's double doors flew open again and two more foxes stumbled in.

"Told ye," said Donal.

"Gallagher's all over again," agreed Paidi.

"Both of you shut up."

The two foxes pulled the heads off their costumes to reveal two sweaty men. One of them had shaggy blond hair, the other was a couple of eyebrows away from being an egg. The bald one looked around. "You seen a fox come in here?"

Jackie stopped to think. "Could you be more specific?"

The blond pulled a face. "Very funny. A guy in a costume like ours?"

Jackie shook his head. "Doesn't ring any bells."

"We saw him come in here from down the block," said Baldy.

"Is that right?" said Jackie. "Well, I ain't seen him. What about you, fellas?"

Both of the sentinels shook their heads before Paidi added, "How come you're wearing the heads?"

"What?"

"You ran in here and then you took the heads off. Would it not have been easier running about with the heads off?"

The blond guy looked genuinely appalled. "We can't take the heads off outside. It'd ruin the magic for the kids."

Donal nodded. "Method acting. Fair play."

"We're gonna take a look around," said the bald guy.

Jackie shook his head. "I'm sorry, gentlemen, but this here establishment exists for the purchase and consumption of alcoholic beverages in a convivial atmosphere. I'm afraid you turning it into the *Animal Farm* remake of the *Diary of Anne Frank* is not going to be conducive to the aforementioned objective."

"What?" asked Baldy.

"He says feck off," said Paidi.

The blond guy took a step forward. "Shut up, old man."

"Ohhh now," said Jackie, taking a baseball bat from underneath the bar in as casual a manner as it was possible to do so. "Paidi is a loyal patron of this here watering hole. Nobody tells him to shut up."

The bald guy tried to stare Jackie down.

"Is there a problem here, Jackie?"

Jackie turned to see Bunny standing in the archway that led to the back room, two empty glasses in his hands.

"Nah, Bunny, everything's fine. Our furry friends were just leaving."

The blond guy pushed the other towards the door. "C'mon, Stevie."

Stevie seemed to have as little sense as he did hair. "You tell your friend – we own Times Square."

"Is that right?" said Jackie. "Congratulations. That's a prime bit of real estate. You should spend some of that money on getting your suits dry-cleaned."

The two foxes departed.

"What in the feck is going on here?" asked Bunny, placing the glasses down on the bar.

"Place is becoming a furries bar," said Paidi.

"Shut up, Paidi," said Jackie. "You can come out, Dill."

Diller emerged from the hallway looking sheepish. "Thanks, Jackie."

Bunny stared at Diller, confusion writ large on his face. "What have you come as?" Then his body language changed. "Wait – were them lads looking for you?"

"It's alright," said Diller. "Don't go getting involved."

Bunny looked towards the door. He wasn't used to not getting involved.

"Usual?" asked Jackie.

Bunny nodded.

"One lemonade, one whiskey and one Guinness coming up."

Diller, Smithy and Bunny sat around their usual table, although Diller wasn't dressed as he usually was.

"I don't get it," said Bunny.

"What do you mean?" asked Diller.

"You dress up as, like, a fox?"

"Not just any fox. Funtime Freddie."

"Right, yeah. And then you just hang about in Times Square looking for business?"

"You're making it sound a lot more hooker-like than it is," said Smithy. "Tourists love it. They get a picture with their favourite character from whatever."

Diller nodded. "You could make a fortune being the dude from *Game of Thrones*, Smithy."

Smithy shook his head. "No, thank you. I've had enough looky-loos to last me a lifetime."

Bunny slapped the table. "You could use your thing! Ye know – your thing." He pointed at his head. What he was referring to was the fact that Smithy, as an after-effect of getting run over in a convenience store parking lot, occasionally heard in his head what could be considered "the voice of God". At least, Diller believed it to be that, Bunny seemed undecided and, most importantly, the voice itself seemed utterly convinced of it. Smithy tried to rationalise it away as some form of post-traumatic stress, but that argument had so far failed to work on the voice.

"How could I use 'my thing'?" asked Smithy, in a tone of voice that made it clear he didn't think there existed a sensible answer.

"Easy," said Bunny. "You get yourself a little booth and a sign that says, 'I hear the voice of God in my head. Five bucks – you can ask him anything.'"

"It doesn't work like that," said Smithy. "And even if it did, I think I'll stick to driving a cab rather than being a freak show for tourists, thanks all the same."

"Fair enough," said Bunny. "How's that going by the way?"

"The cab? Fine," said Smithy, with a nod. "Great. No problems. Can we get back to Diller? These guys are after you because...?"

"Because, one of 'em works one side of the street and the other does the other. They are trying to suppress my right to engage in free competition. I mean – there's four Darth Vaders."

"Hey, wait a second," said Smithy. "You told me you were going to be the dude from *Star Wars*."

"Lando Calrissian," said Diller with a nod. "Yeah, I tried that. Not enough people knew who I was. A few Korean tourists asked to get their picture taken with me and I'm pretty sure they just wanted a picture with a black guy. That was weird."

"Hang on, hang on," said Bunny, knocking the bottom of his pint glass on the table for attention. "Them two pricks chased you all the way here?"

Diller nodded.

"What were you doing hiding behind the bar? Me and Smithy would've taken care of it for you."

Smithy nodded.

Diller looked embarrassed. "Well..."

"What?"

"I mean, no offence, guys, but I'd rather handle it my way."

"What's that supposed to mean?" asked Smithy.

"It's just that – y'know I love you both – but when you get involved in stuff, it has a tendency to get a bit... violent."

"Ah, here now!" said Bunny, who'd been in a violent clash with two drug dealers just that afternoon.

"That's not... that's..." said Smithy, who'd come there directly from nearly hitting a fare dodger with his cab before landing an elbow drop and a cock punch on the dude.

The table descended into a rather frosty silence as everyone took a drink.

Diller pulled the collar of his suit out again, trying to circulate some air.

"Have you not got a change of clothes?" asked Smithy.

"Nah. My stuff is in a locker at the bus station. I need to go back later and get it."

Smithy nodded. "Right."

"So," said Diller, turning to Bunny, "what is this about?"

"Well, as it happens, I'd like to engage your services. I need your help following a priest."

"Cool," said Diller, looking at Smithy excitedly. He'd been trying to convince him that they should start their own private investigation business for quite a while now.

Smithy grimaced. This was why Bunny had insisted on waiting for Diller to get there before explaining the nature of his latest emergency. He thought Smithy would have tried to talk him out of it and he was right. Smithy loved working with Diller, but he wanted the kid to go and be the actor he was destined to be. He didn't want to look back on it twenty years from now and regret that he'd turned a really good actor into a gumshoe.

"By any chance," said Smithy, "would this be the priest you were going to see about finding the sisters?"

"That's right. He says he's never heard of them."

"So why are we...?"

"'Twas the way he said it," said Bunny. "He knows them, I'm sure of it. Ideally, we should've started the surveillance before I asked him, but que sera. If he's not contacted the sisters already, I bet he will. He knows what I look like, so..."

"I'm in," said Diller.

"Hold up," said Smithy. "I'd like to help, but this sounds like it could take quite some time. I've got the cab and Diller's got his job."

"I'd rather do this," said Diller excitedly.

"Yeah, but we gotta pay the bills."

"Oh, sorry," said Bunny, "did I not make it clear? I'm hiring you – on a proper rate, too."

Smithy furrowed his brow. "You had to get a loan of fifty bucks off me last week. Has your magic bank card been turned back on?"

Bunny shook his head. "No, I ehm... I came into some money." He pulled a wad of notes out of his pocket to emphasise his point. Then he peeled off a fifty and pushed it across the table to Smithy.

"Thanks."

"This is great," said Diller. "I'm gonna get one of those fancy lemonades to celebrate."

"Hold up, hold up, hold up," said Smithy. "Where did all this money come from?"

"'Tis not important," said Bunny. "So, are you in?"

"Yes," said Diller, unnecessarily.

They both looked at Smithy expectantly.

He sighed. "Alright, fine."

All three men suddenly looked towards the front of the bar, where a great deal of shouting had broken out.

"Stay here," said Smithy to Diller, before getting up and moving across to where he could see around the corner.

"What is it?" asked Bunny.

Smithy stood there watching.

"Smithy?"

Smithy turned back. "I have no idea. A guy in a suit and a dude in a hoodie walked in and now Paidi and Donal are losing their collective shit."

CHAPTER SIX

"OK," said Father Gabriel, "first things first: show me your hands."

Bianca obediently held her hands out in front of her, and the priest examined them carefully, turning them over and back. He looked at them like he was expecting to see the face of God. The man was pretty intense about everything he ever did.

"And you iced them when you got home, like I told you?"

"Yes, Father G."

"And you've not had any aches or pains in them?"

"No, Father G."

"And you got a good night's sleep?"

"Three bags full, Father G."

He looked at her, his round frameless glasses making his eyes look somehow bigger. Trey had once described him as a Latino John Lennon. Bianca hadn't understood the reference, but then he'd shown her the picture and she'd got it.

"Oh, I see," he said. "That's how it is now. You win yourself a title and suddenly you're giving me attitude?"

She smiled back at him. "Can I see my trophy again?"

He gave her a stern look, mostly to keep from giving her the smile she wanted. "No, you can't. You said you wanted to train, so we train."

He'd taken the trophy back to the church last night, as per her wishes. She hadn't had to say why. Something nice like that – if she took it home, it might disappear.

"Maybe I could practise holding my trophy up? I'm worried my swagger game is off."

Father Gabriel let go of her hands and gave her a playful tap on the cheek. "I think your swagger game is just fine, Señorita. What we have to work on is your humility."

"Ohhh." She grinned. "He talking smack now. You gonna get in the ring with me, Padre? Teach me a lesson?"

This was a recurring riff in their conversation, the joke being that Gabriel was so small and slight of build, he wasn't that far out of her weight division. In reality, despite being a sprightly thirty-four years old, he never boxed in the gym he had built. That a Franciscan priest was training fighters had been met with a lot of disapproval in some quarters as it was. The gym was not about him. It wasn't much of a gym, truth be told, but he was proud of it.

The idea had come to him one morning as he sat eating his breakfast after another long night administering last rites and offering ineffective comfort to relatives in the ER. He had been working in the parish for nearly four years, and in that time, he had mostly met his congregation at funerals. He would inexpertly deliver impassioned sermons he had spent all week crafting, only to see blank faces interspersed with occasional snoring. It had felt like there was an impenetrable force field between him and his congregation and try as he might, he couldn't find a way through. Night after night he had prayed for inspiration, for the Lord to show him a way to make a connection. He'd been tired – tired of simply praying for the dead and offering cold comfort to the living. He'd wanted to find a way to fight back. To stop children becoming soldiers in the war that the gangs perpetually fought, with Coopersville as their battleground. So, without asking – for fear someone would say no – he'd taken the modest bungalow next to the church, where he was supposed to live, and knocked down the internal walls. He'd done the first one there and then in a fit of zeal and then he'd had to pay one of the local men to come in and fix it, as he knew nothing about working construction. He had moved his bed into the church's basement; it would be fine for his needs.

After a few false starts, St Theresa's boxing gym had been born. To begin with, the ring was a square marked out in chalk and there were some basic weights and a heavy bag. He'd scrounged some gloves and put up a notice on the door: "All welcome. No weapons. No gang colours. All disputes left outside or settled in the ring."

A couple of young kids got sent there by desperate mothers looking for anything to keep them off the streets. Father Gabriel had got himself a book from the library. His one advantage, at the beginning, was that the kids didn't know enough to realise he was making it up as he went along. It had happened gradually – kids drifting through the doors in ones and twos. From little acorns... It turned out, he had found a way in.

Now, the gym's biggest problem was space. They had to work out schedules so that everyone could get in and still there was not enough room. They'd rigged up a second shower, but they needed more. Around him right now, a dozen kids trained, the older ones helping the younger. In an hour, another dozen would replace them. Later that night, the women's self-defence class would be filled to capacity – taught by Gina Marks, a nurse originally from the Philpott housing project. She'd got out and now lived in Brooklyn with her husband and three kids, but wanted to give back. They also had a couple of hours of women-only training on the schedule. Bianca wasn't bothered by the boys so she trained whenever she could. In this gym, she got respect. Only a fool could see her work and not realise that she was something special.

"I'm not getting in the ring with you, Bianca, but don't go thinking a trophy made you a champion. It's training. Discipline—"

"And determination," continued Bianca, who knew this speech well. "That's what makes a champion."

"Just because I've said it before, it doesn't make it wrong."

Bianca raised her hand into the air theatrically. "Preach, Padre, preach."

He cracked and gave her the smile she was going for. Gabriel tried not to play favourites, but given Bianca's journey from a lost and angry little girl to the powerful and confident woman she was growing into before his eyes, it was hard not to. He had also found that, put in the context of the gym and training, communicating with the kids had become so much easier. Everyone was there for a purpose and talking was secondary. Somehow the pressure was not as great. He simply spoke better from behind a heavy bag than a pulpit.

Bianca turned and pointed at the far corner, near where Darrell Wilkes was ineptly but enthusiastically losing a fight with the speed bag. "I was thinking we could put my trophy over there."

Gabriel shook his head. "This is a gym, not a trophy room."

Bianca gave a mocking pout. "But we got yours up?"

Gabriel turned his head to follow her point and his heart sank. The framed article from the newspaper was back up on the wall.

Rosaria Annabella Montoya, the parish secretary, was part force of nature and part gift from God, but she was also the bane of Gabriel's existence. He'd taken it down twice now, and argued his case for why it shouldn't be up there, but Rosaria was immovable on this point. It had been she who had contacted the paper. They'd all known that they needed money from somewhere if they were going to expand, and they definitely needed to expand. That kind of donation wasn't going to come from Coopersville – Gabriel had been very insistent on not taking money from the gangs. Still, the gym couldn't fulfil their needs – and that was just in the training area. The club had expanded beyond its initial remit, becoming more of a community hub than a boxing club. Kids had needed somewhere to do their homework and so they'd curtained off an area at the back of the church and put tables in. Mrs Welpes from down the block was keen to create an amateur dramatics club, but they had nowhere to rehearse or perform. And then there was the works programme for the older kids. It had started with Father Gabriel needing jobs done about the place last summer and it had just grown and grown. He'd gotten Fred Daniels to give a carpentry class and that had gone well too. Every success led to another problem, though. Soon, Gabriel had found himself with more eager hands than he'd known what to do with, the church only needing so many odd jobs done, even in its dilapidated state. They had gone around to anyone they could think of, trying to find work for the young men. Gabriel's logic had been simple: put 'em in a job, keep 'em out of the gangs. Society told these kids they were worthless, and the gangs fed off that, offering a sense of belonging that was otherwise missing from their lives. If you wanted to break the cycle, you needed to find opportunity and pray to God they took it. Gabriel was a realist – he'd lost an awful lot more fights than he'd won, but he still had to fight every one. So, yes, he had agreed to the article, but only on the condition it was about the kids. That was not how it had turned out. "THE PUGILIST PRIEST" was the headline. It made him out to be a combination of Mother Teresa and George Foreman and he couldn't look at it without cringing. He'd been so careful with the photographer, or at least he thought he had, always making sure there were boxers between them. He'd told them he didn't like having his picture taken. The photo showed two kids sparring, their bodies a blur of motion in the foreground, while it picked him out in the background, standing perfectly still, looking on intently.

"Alright," said Gabriel, clapping his hands together, "you go warm up – and then shadow-boxing. Three rounds. And what is our focus?"

"Fundamentals, fundamentals, fundamentals," finished Bianca.

"That's right, champ." He threw it in to see the grin spread across her face. "Let's get to work!" He turned around. "Darrell – feet, look at your feet. You aren't painting a wall, son, you're boxing."

Darrell looked down and then up again, giving Gabriel a big thumbs up. He then repositioned his feet and went back to losing on points with the speed bag. The kid had plenty of enthusiasm. They were due a sit-down; he'd been having trouble at home which had resulted in him sleeping rough a couple of times. Gabriel tried to make a mental note. As he walked by, he took the framed article down off the wall and stepped out the door into the brisk afternoon. Though brisk didn't do it justice; it was below freezing the last time he'd checked. His brown Franciscan robes were comfortable but not the best for the cold.

"Father Gabriel!"

He turned to see Rosario, hands on hips, her face all scrunched up in a picture of outrage. "I caught these two vandals looking at the wall outside the gym, all suspicious."

Gabriel smiled and moved towards her, in the forlorn hope that this might result in her lowering her voice. Standing beside her were Trey and Emilio, looking truly terrified in the way that only teenage boys can when faced with a tornado of outraged middle-aged female.

"Ah, Rosario, I was just coming to see you. I forgot to tell you: the boys and I had an idea last night and they're going to do a little work for me."

"But they do that vandalism. I seen 'em about the place."

Father Gabriel put his hand on the shoulder of Emilio, who despite the temperature had a full-on case of the terror sweats. Rosario could have that effect on a boy – or, indeed, a grown man.

"Yes, the boys expressed their art in some places without asking permission first" – he gave them a stern look – "and we had a long talk about that. But this time, they are doing a commissioned piece for the church, as have many of the world's greatest artists throughout history. Michelangelo—"

"They ain't no Michelangelos."

Gabriel smiled. "Now, Rosario, art moves on and the boys have talent, when it is applied in the right areas."

That statement had the bonus of also being true. Primarily it was Emilio – or OAB, aka the One-Armed Bandit, to give him his full street tag – who was the artist. Trey was his assistant in these matters, or so Trey had explained to Gabriel in one of their long heart-to-hearts. Despite his handicap of only having one arm of much use, Emilio had an undeniable artistic flair. If Gabriel had a rule, it was to find the spark and fan it into a flame, then all you could do was hope that it was strong enough to stay lit when real life came to inevitably rain on the kid's parade. This was Emilio's spark.

"I don't know art," continued Rosario, "but that kinda thing ain't it."

"Respectfully, Rosario, I disagree. This wall here is looking pretty grim; I think it could do with something special."

"No gang nonsense!"

He nodded in agreement. "Don't worry, I have agreed a specific brief with my artists."

The boys both nodded in insistent agreement. This was technically true. They had decided it last night when he'd taken the kids out for pizza, while Bianca had been in the restroom. Neither of the boys were gang affiliated either. Emilio, in the unspoken rules of the jungle, seemed to get a pass due to his arm and stammer. Trey... Trey's situation was far more complicated.

"Well, I suppose..." Rosario gave the boys the kind of look people normally saved for unexploded ordnance. "But I'll be watching you!"

This was as close as Gabriel ever came to getting agreement out of Rosario on anything. Technically, as the parish's one and only priest since Father Martin had retired, he had final say on things such as this, but nobody, least of all Rosario, acknowledged that. She was the queen bee and woe betide anyone who crossed her. He had gotten better with dealing with her over time. It helped to realise that her heart was always in the right place, even if her nose could often be where it didn't strictly belong.

"I was just coming to get you. There's a phone call for you in the office."

"Could you take a message?"

"It's a man from the diocese. He says it's important. The man was very insistent."

"OK."

That was probably bad news, but at least he'd got her off the subject of the boys. He could sense them physically relax now that they were out of the path of the Rosario Express.

She looked down and Gabriel's heart sank.

"What you doing with that picture, Father?"

And now it was heading straight for him.

"I, um..." He glanced around, trying to find an escape route. Trey and Emilio gave him looks of sincere sympathy, having just been where he now found himself. "I just, I... I'm worried somebody will knock it off the wall in there." He'd previously convinced her out of hanging it in the actual church on religious grounds, but he couldn't stretch that to cover the gym, much as he'd like to. "Maybe we could hang it in the office?"

That morning, he had been to visit the middle school, and he'd a rather stilted discussion with the kids about the importance of always telling the truth. In truth, it was a little more nuanced than that. This lie was necessary – possibly life-saving.

Rosario gave the kind of frown that was more than just lips – she threw her whole face into it. It was really quite something. "I think it should be where everyone can see it."

"I just think, when we're in the office working, it's the best place for it."

Rosario's face brightened. "We could get two of them? I got a dozen copies of the paper."

Gabriel's heart sank, and then he snatched at the only lifeline he could see. "This person is still on the phone waiting?"

"Yes, but—"

"Thank you."

He turned and headed for the back of the church, resisting the urge to break into a run.

The office was a cramped little storeroom they'd converted. It had a filing cabinet and one and a half desks. Gabriel had the half. He placed the framed article on it, sat down in his squeaky chair and picked up the receiver that sat atop a pile of bills he needed to get to soon.

"Hello, Father de Marcos speaking."

"Hi, Gabriel, it's Phillip."

"Oh, Phil, hey! Sorry, I didn't know it was you. Did you hear? One of our boxers won the state championship last night. They say she might go to the Olympics – wouldn't that be something?"

"Gabe..."

Gabriel's heart sank as his mind registered the tone of voice, his breath catching.

"What is it, Phil?"

"I'm sorry, it's... it's Bishop Ramirez. He's... he's dead."

"Oh."

"I'm sorry. I know you two were close. I only heard this morning. We got an email from the diocese of São Paulo. It will make the news soon. I thought you should hear it from me."

"Right. OK." Gabriel stared at the tabletop in front of him, the wood pockmarked and uneven from years of use. He thought of Bishop Ramirez and how he had saved him, given him his chance in life. "May God have mercy on his soul."

He was lost in thought for a few seconds as his mind filled with memories of his mentor. He had meant to find the time to call him. How long had it been? Amidst the recollections, he was dimly aware of an alarm bell ringing in his own mind. The death of a bishop in Brazil would not normally make the news, unless...

"How did he die?"

There was a pause before Phillip spoke. "They found him in his room this morning. He'd been... he'd been shot in the head."

"Oh."

Gabriel looked at the framed article again, at himself staring back. He'd told them he didn't like having his picture taken.

CHAPTER SEVEN

"I spy with my little eye…"

Bunny stopped talking as he noticed the thumping noise coming from the front seat of the cab. Smithy was headbutting the steering wheel repeatedly.

"Are ye alright there, Smithy?"

"No. No, I'm not."

Smithy liked Bunny – he did, he really liked Bunny. If you'd asked him to list the people he liked seven days ago, Bunny would definitely have been on that list.

Bunny was his friend.

Bunny was his friend.

Bunny was his friend.

The problem was that over the last seven days he had spent an average of seventeen hours and thirty-six minutes a day in Bunny's company. He was now ready to kill Bunny.

The first couple of days had been alright. The downside of Bunny's current soup kick was that he was a frequent and robust passer of wind. The temperature had struggled to get above freezing all week and the cab's air con was poor at the best of times. Being trapped in the company of Bunny McGarry's ass was nobody's best of times. So, there was that. They had also run out of conversation. In hindsight, that should have been predictable. Neither man was big on talking about their past, so they didn't have an awful lot of anecdotes they could swap. And, possibly most importantly, Smithy hadn't realised just how mind-numbingly boring surveillance work was. Father Gabriel was a machine. The man barely seemed to sleep but what he did do was work. And work. And work. He also had a schedule which he stuck to religiously, no pun intended. This made him tedious to follow. That and the fact that there wasn't a great deal of following to do, as he hardly went anywhere. They'd followed him to the hospital a couple of times, where they'd figured out he was visiting local gang kids. He had also spent a couple of evenings dropping in on old or otherwise infirmed parishioners in the nearby projects. Coopersville, if the press was to be believed, was one of the most dangerous areas in New York, yet Father Gabriel de Marcos walked through it as if he were untouchable. Everyone seemed to know him, and those who didn't stayed well out of his way.

In seven days, there hadn't been even the slightest hint of a nun. What there had been were a couple of terse exchanges in the cab. Smithy was a man who liked his own space, and he guessed Bunny was too. If their confinement together in this vehicle went on much longer, something would be said that couldn't be unsaid. Nerves were frayed. Part of the problem was that neither of them could leave. Smithy had to be in the cab as he was the only one who could drive it because of the modifications. Sure, you could take the extensions on the pedals off and remove the custom seat, but by the time you'd done that, whoever you were trying to follow would be out of sight. So, Smithy couldn't leave the cab. And for reasons he seemed unwilling to explain, Bunny wouldn't leave the cab. He sat slouched down in the back seat, his face obscured from view by a baseball cap. When queried, he'd explained that he didn't want the priest to catch a glimpse of him, as that would give the game away. The only time he'd looked up was so that he could engage in a game of I Spy, one in which he fundamentally misunderstood the rules. That had been yesterday, and it had by far been the ugliest of clashes in what was an already tense week. Not that everyone felt that way. The third member of the team, Diller, had no such problems. He took the early shift, cycling out to watch the padre from just after 6am every day. Any concerns about Diller in his current role had long since been dismissed. In hindsight, they'd been ridiculous to begin with. He had grown up in Hunts Point, an area as bad as Coopersville, and he had survived there. It was quite something to watch. He managed to disappear in plain sight almost effortlessly. Any time a local noticed him and engaged him in conversation, they left smiling, like they'd just caught up with an old friend. Only Jackson Diller could be a young black man standing in the middle of some of the most contentious gang territory in New York and make himself nobody's concern.

So, between them – Smithy and Bunny in the cab and Diller on his bicycle or on foot – they had the priest well covered. They'd accounted for everything, except for the possibility that Smithy would find himself one particularly soupy fart away from beating Bunny McGarry to death with his own flask.

"Are you seriously still upset about the last game of I Spy?"

Smithy tried to count to five in his head. "I just… Let's talk about something else."

The incident had occurred when Bunny spied something beginning with O. Smithy had spent nearly two hours on it. He had been determined to get it. Finally, he had given in. Oxygen. It had been goddamned oxygen!

Smithy had lost his shit. You could not see oxygen. It was invisible. It was part of the air. In the Bronx, probably not that much of the air, but still. If oxygen was allowed, then so should be the chemical make-up of whatever was in glass or asphalt or that weird dude who stood on the corner talking loudly to nobody. Of course, it might have been the case that he was standing there talking to the oxygen. Readiness to react be damned – after that incident, Smithy had gone for a walk around the block.

"Alright," said Bunny, "we won't play it again so."

"Good idea."

"I was just—"

Bunny interrupted himself, hunkering down further in the back seat as two guys, one black and one Hispanic, walked by. They had got the occasional long look from the locals – cabs didn't spend a great deal of time in Coopersville, and they were even less likely to stop, but enough passed through on their way to somewhere else that their presence wasn't overly noticeable. They changed spots regularly to various locations on the block to minimise suspicion too. Still, as the two guys walked by, Bunny ducked right down.

"OK," said Smithy, "enough is enough. You're going to tell me what happened."

"What?"

"Don't 'what' me. Those two dudes – one of them had his arm in a sling and the other had a bandage on his head. On the one time you visited this area prior to this week, did you get into a fight or something?" Smithy watched Bunny's reaction in the driver's mirror. "You did, didn't you? Unbelievable!"

"Alright there, Judgey McJudgeface, wind your neck in."

"Wind my what?"

"Never mind."

"Wait a second. The money you're using to pay us – where did that come from?"

Smithy watched as the two men crossed the street further down the block. "Oh my god, did you rob drug dealers?"

"No, I didn't. I mean, technically..."

Smithy shook his head. "You are unbelievable."

"If you must know, they tried to rob me! I just defended myself."

Smithy nodded. "And the money?"

"Well, I mean, 'tis just common sense. If somebody tries to rob you, you taking what they have on them – that's not robbing, that's a valuable lesson."

"Right. And who are these guys?"

"I didn't get their names. I was a bit busy."

"I don't mean their names. This place is New York's version of South-Central LA, so I imagine they're in a gang."

"Oh right, that – yeah. They called themselves the... the something diablos. The Red Devils."

Smithy shook his head. "Unbelievable."

"That's what I said. That must be a registered trademark. They're asking for trouble."

"What are you talking about? Did you even read those articles I printed out for you?" Smithy had done some research the night after he'd met Bunny in the Porterhouse and agreed to help him. He had found the article about Father Gabriel's boxing club that had been in the *Times* a couple of weeks ago, and he had discovered an academic paper some NYU postgrad student had written on Coopersville's gang problem and how nothing had been done about it. The New Bloods, the C-Boys and Los Diablos Rojos were the three main gangs and they ran the place. Drugs, prostitution, protection. Everything. A young man in Coopersville had a twenty-five per cent chance of being involved in a violent shooting by the age of nineteen and that figure was just based on confirmed incidents. Police called it a war zone. The paper was a couple of years old now, but it presented the New Bloods as the biggest and baddest of the gangs. Weirdly, if one were to look for an upside, it was that the gangs had evolved to be remarkably diverse – location trumping ethnicity. They were almost entirely male though, the barrier of gender remaining intact.

"Of course I read the articles," said Bunny. "That's why I'm trying to be all incognito and that, like."

"Great. Well, if I die in a hail of bullets, at least I'll know why."

"Ara, don't be so dramatic."

"You know, Diller had a point about you."

"How's that?"

"When he said you have a tendency to try to solve your problems with violence."

"Hold your horses there, cowboy. If my memory serves, he said we both did that."

Smithy ran his hands over the wheel. "Yeah, he did, but I mean, c'mon..."

Bunny sat up and leaned forward. "You think you're less violent than I am?"

"Well…"

"You do!"

"I mean, you said it yourself, Bunny. You were in an altercation with those guys just last week."

"They tried to mug me!"

"And you ended up with a wad of their money."

"I didn't say it had gone well for them. A man is entitled to defend himself."

"I'm just saying."

"Alright then, Mahatma fecking Gandhi – honestly, when was the last time you were in a scrap?"

"That's not important," said Smithy.

"Really?" replied Bunny, gleefully. "I bet it is."

"My point was, overall, you have a tendency to get into more fights than I do. That's all."

"Right," said Bunny, "let's settle this." He extended his hand through the open partition. "A bet. First person to use violence to resolve a situation loses."

"Are you expecting me to give you odds?"

"No. Evens."

Smithy whistled. "I hate taking your money. Or rather the money of whoever you took it off."

"Who mentioned money?"

"Yeah. Probably best not to."

"No," said Bunny. "I just mean we should really make it interesting."

"OK."

"Cheryl," said Bunny.

"Woah," said Smithy, holding his hands up. "I'm confident of winning, but I'm not betting my girlfriend. I mean—"

"Would you shut up? You know that's not what I mean. What I'm saying is the loser, whoever he may be, has to perform at her club."

"When you say 'perform'?"

"I mean do some of that pole dancing – spangly outfit, the lot."

"I'm not sure they'll have something in your size."

"Well, I doubt they make them outfits in children's sizes for you either, but we'll have to find out."

Smithy narrowed his eyes and gave Bunny a hard look. There were some buttons you didn't press.

"What's wrong?" asked Bunny, all mock innocence. "Are you losing that temper of yours? Thinking about smacking me a wallop in the chops?"

Smithy took Bunny's extended hand and shook it. The handshake was as relaxed as an Israel–Palestine peace conference at a BBQ Shack. "It's on."

"Great."

"Fantastic."

"Superb."

"Amazing."

"Tremendous."

"Monumental."

"Magnifi—" Bunny was interrupted by Smithy's phone chirping – just in time, as he was running out of adjectives.

"Hey, Dill," said Smithy, putting the phone on speaker. "Perfect timing. Bunny and I are having a bet and—"

"He's on the move," interrupted Diller. "He's just exited the church and he's heading south."

"OK," said Smithy, starting up the engine. "He might be going over to see that old lady on Roper again."

"Probably," agreed Bunny. "But keep your eyes open, Diller."

"We'll sweep around the block and pick him up at the crosswalk," said Smithy. "You hang back and—"

"Holy shit!" yelled Diller over the phone.

"What?" said Smithy and Bunny in unison.

"A van just pulled up and then – this guy was walking down the pavement, and he – I saw him earlier, but I didn't—"

"Diller," said Smithy, "tell us what's happening."

"Happening? That's what I'm telling you – somebody's just kidnapped the priest!"

CHAPTER EIGHT

With a squeal of tyres and a loud honk from a car they pulled recklessly in front of, Smithy had the cab out of the space. It was just after 3pm, so traffic was reasonably busy but moving, people pushing it to get wherever they needed to be before the rush-hour gridlock.

"Where are they now?"

They lost whatever Diller said under the engine noise. Smithy tapped the button to send it to his Bluetooth headset while using his other hand to guide the cab around a truck that had double-parked outside a store to make a delivery.

"Dill, say it again – where are they?"

"They're on Weston Avenue – about fifty yards ahead of me."

"OK," said Smithy. "We're a couple of blocks away. Keep 'em in your sights but stay back."

Smithy swung a sharp left, which caused Bunny to tumble across the back seat and two lanes of traffic coming the other way to slam on the brakes.

"Jaysus!"

"Put your seat belt on."

"What's Diller saying?"

"Not much. Panting. Sounds like he's pedalling hard."

"I am," said Diller. "They just took a right. Onto – I don't know the street name."

Smithy tried to construct a map of the area in his head. "OK. Tell me what you see, Dill."

"We're passing a 7-Eleven."

"Too generic."

"There's a club – Gossip."

"Cool. I got you." Smithy had passed that on the drive over.

"Take a right," said Bunny.

"Shut up," said Smithy. "I know what I'm doing. No backseat driving."

Smithy took the right – which he was going to take anyway.

"Tell him to describe the van."

That was actually a good idea. "Dill, what's the van look like?"

"It's a white panel van."

"Anything written on it?"

"No."

Not good. That was the most generic of vans, picked to fade into the background.

A thought struck Smithy. "How are they driving?"

"What?" asked Diller.

"Are they running lights or anything?"

"Oh. No."

"Good. That means they don't think they're being followed."

They might just have a chance to catch up.

"Traffic's heavier here," panted Diller.

Smithy pulled a sharp left and… "Damn it!"

He punched the wheel in frustration. They were on a road with cars parked either side, leaving just enough room for two cars to pass – or for one large garbage truck to block all traffic in either direction.

Two garbage men were lackadaisically picking up trash cans and lobbing the contents into the compactor at the back of the truck. Smithy laid on the horn, which only had the effect of getting a broad smile and a flip of the bird from one of the garbage men.

Smithy checked his rear-view. Three cars were now backed up behind them.

He tried to reverse but the VW Beetle directly behind them wouldn't play ball, its owner laying on her own horn instead and adding to the hand signals.

"Shite," said Bunny. "We're fecking screwed."

"Hang on."

Smithy jerked the car left, losing a Camry its no-claims bonus as, with a screech of metal, the cab managed to squeeze between two cars and up onto the pavement.

"You're paying for any damage."

"Fine," said Bunny.

A mother and young child dived into a doorway in front of them. As they passed the garbage truck, a trash bag landed on the windscreen and burst open.

"Oh, for...!" Smithy turned on the wipers, which only had the effect of distributing the garbage more fully over the windscreen. A diaper, banana skins, potato peels, cardboard packaging, wet kitchen roll and magazines cluttered up his view, then jammed under the wipers to leave them stuck halfway across, juddering and whining in protest.

Smithy bobbed his head up and down, looking for a gap. "I can't see a thing."

Behind him, Bunny stuck his head out the window, like a dog excited to be going to the beach. "You're OK. Keeping going straight."

Smithy resisted the urge to mention backseat driving again.

"Keep going straight," shouted Bunny.

Smithy kept going straight.

The car hit something.

"That's just a trash can."

Someone screamed.

"Nowhere near her."

A loud scraping noise as something gouged the left side of the car.

"Just a scratch. Ah, for fuck's sake!"

"What?!" Smithy slowed down.

"Keep going," said Bunny. "I just got some of the garbage in my mouth."

The whining noise stopped as the wipers gave up the fight.

While primarily focusing on trying to see around the debris, Smithy couldn't help but notice that the magazine jammed under the wiper appeared to be gay porn. It was the twenty-first century – what kind of weirdo didn't just get their pornography online like everybody else?

"Right, we need to get back on the bit for cars. Get ready to go right," hollered Bunny.

"Say when."

With a crunch of metal, the cab came to a juddering halt.

"When," said Bunny, sounding sheepish. "It was only a tree. Back up."

Smithy did as he was told.

"Now go right."

The car bounced as they made it back onto the road once again.

"Assholes!" hollered a voice, which may well have had a very good point.

"What's going on?" asked Diller.

"Never mind," said Smithy. "Where are they now?"

"They took a right; they're on Bleacher."

"OK."

"I think they're heading for—"

"Stop!" yelled Bunny.

Smithy slammed the brakes on. The back door opened and Bunny clambered out. He grabbed the magazine and a few of the larger chunks of garbage from the windscreen, revealing a woman pushing a stroller, standing in front of the car, her eyes wide and mouth hanging open in a picture of inexpressible rage.

"Jesus!" said Smithy.

Bunny gave her a wave. "Sorry about that, love, we're on a mission from God."

Bunny got back into the passenger side, and before he'd even closed the door hollered, "Floor it!"

The mother rushed out of their way and Smithy did as instructed. They were coming up to another big junction.

"Oh shit," said Diller in gasping breaths in Smithy's ear. "I think they're heading for the on-ramp to the freeway."

"Damn it," said Smithy. "They get there, they're gone."

"What'd he say?" said Bunny.

"Seat belt," said Smithy in lieu of an answer as he pulled the car into the left-hand lane, the one traditionally reserved for traffic heading in the other direction. One such vehicle turned the corner and made the wise decision to pull quickly out of the way.

The traffic lights hanging above the junction were red, which was why the lane they had just departed was full of stationary traffic. The junction controlled the flow of vehicles onto a street that had three lanes of traffic in both directions.

"Red light," said Bunny.

"No shit," said Smithy. "Hang on." And then he floored it.

There was a logic to it. If you were going to attempt to cross a road where six lanes of unsuspecting traffic were going about their business, you would want to do it at the highest speed possible, so that you were in any one place for the least amount of time possible in order to minimise the already high risk of something hitting you. That was just physics, probably.

"SHITTING NORA!" screamed Bunny.

Smithy kept his eyes forward, as there seemed no point in looking at what was about to hit them. Better to focus on the prize, which was the other side of the junction, where the crosswalk was blissfully free of pedestrians.

In his peripheral vision there was a blur of movement and then something clipped the rear bumper of the cab. Smithy tugged the wheel right with all his might to correct their course. A couple of cars zoomed past in front of them and then, incredibly, they were through.

"Jesus!" said Bunny.

Smithy's heart was playing a Ginger Baker drum solo in his chest and he felt the irresistible urge to giggle. That had been spectacularly stupid – he couldn't believe he'd done it. He also couldn't believe it had worked.

"I think I've pissed meself," said Bunny.

"Then you're paying for the valet too." Smithy raised his voice. "Diller?"

"They've stopped at the lights and then they'll be at the on-ramp."

Smithy pulled a sharp left too fast, the back end of the car sliding out of control temporarily as it fishtailed right before correcting.

"The junction is up ahead, I think," said Smithy.

"I've got an idea," said Diller.

"What kind of idea?"

"A really bad one."

Smithy saw a white panel van turning left at the junction in front of him, about to get on the freeway.

Smithy assumed it was the van they were after.

This was confirmed a second later when it collided at speed with a figure on a mountain bike. Smithy watched in horror as Diller slammed into the windscreen and then rolled over the top of the van, landing in a messy heap on the road behind it.

CHAPTER NINE

Marky got out of the van because, firstly, if you're trying to keep a low profile, you can't just drive off when your van collides with a cyclist, and secondly, even if he'd wanted to drive off, there was a mountain bike jammed under the front wheels. They'd been hired for this job through the usual sources and it had seemed straightforward. Three of them to snatch one priest – how hard could that be?

Of course, as with anything, you couldn't legislate for stupidity. He was looking between the bike at one end of the van and the unconscious figure at the other end, trying to work out what to do. A lot of people had stopped to watch, and a couple had come over. A morbidly obese man was leaning over the body.

"We need to put him in the recovery position."

"No!" screamed a middle-aged woman with tightly cropped hair who was hurrying over, laden with shopping bags. "Don't move him – he might have a head or spinal injury."

"Seriously," said the man, "I watch a lot of ER shows."

"Yeah, well I work in one. Get away from him."

She glanced at the line of stopped traffic behind them. Most of the drivers were out of their cars, looking on. "Can someone call 911?"

Sensing which way the wind was blowing, Marky moved over towards the unconscious man. "He... he came out of nowhere."

The nurse ignored him, placing her bags down and leaning over to try to get a look at the cyclist's face without moving him. "Honey, are you conscious? Can you hear me?"

"I gotta get going."

This last remark earned Marky a glare from the nurse. "The hell you do."

A cab screeched to a halt beside them.

"Diller!" A dwarf leaped out of the driver's side and ran over to the prone body. "Diller, you OK?"

Marky felt something jab into his back. "That's a gun – don't say a fecking word." A large man was standing behind him, a meaty hand laid on his shoulder.

The dwarf bent down. "Jesus, Dill, are you...?"

The nurse and the fat guy both gasped as the man on the floor turned over and gave a big thumbs up. "Hey, Smithy. It worked."

"It...? It worked? You stupid... I'm gonna run you over myself!"

The cyclist, who had miraculously recovered, got to his feet gingerly, the dwarf helping him up.

The gun jabbed into Marky's back again. "Open the back," said the voice.

"I can't, I..."

The hesitation was met with another jab. "Do it – or I'll shoot you and then I'll do it."

This was going to get ugly.

Marky grabbed the handle of the sliding door and pulled it across – ready to hit the deck to avoid the inevitable hail of bullets.

He stayed on his feet. Stephen and Clark were unconscious. The priest, his hands cable-tied together in front of him, was kneeling over their bodies. The priest looked over Marky's shoulder at the large man behind him for a long moment, and then he nodded. "Let's get out of here."

CHAPTER TEN

Smithy took a corner a mite too fast.

"Alright, Speedy Gonzales, ease up there," said Bunny. "We don't want to look like we're fleeing."

"But we are."

"All the more reason not to look it."

Smithy took a breath and eased his foot off the gas. They were a few blocks away now and, seeing as they'd tossed the van's keys, it was unlikely anyone was in hot pursuit. Bunny was in the passenger seat while Diller and the priest were in the back.

"I don't understand what just happened," said Smithy.

"Which part?" asked Bunny.

"All of it! Are you OK, Diller?"

"A few bruises, but I'll be alright."

"But you were hit by a van moving at speed!"

He watched Diller nod and smile happily in the rear-view mirror. "Yeah. I performed a Wandinky roll. The trick is to jump up at the right time. Had to get my feet free of the bike, hit the windshield and roll."

"How the hell did you know how to do that?"

"I read it in a book."

"What?" said Bunny.

"The library had it. It was a book written by this old Hollywood stuntman, Carl Wandinky."

"Let me get this straight," said Smithy. "You cycled into the path of a moving vehicle because you thought you knew how to get hit in the right way so that it probably wouldn't kill you because you read it in a book?"

"Well, it sounds stupid when you say it like that."

Smithy was nearly beside himself. "It sounds stupid whichever way you say it! Jesus, Dill!"

"It worked, didn't it?"

"I just... I can't... I... I..."

Father Gabriel turned to Diller. "Thank you for taking that chance to help me."

"No problem."

"Which brings me to the next thing I don't understand," said Smithy. "Why were those guys trying to kidnap you in the first place, Father?"

"I'm afraid I have no idea."

"Really?" said Smithy, not trying to hide the disbelief from his voice. "You've no idea who's so pissed that they sent a snatch team for you?"

Father Gabriel shrugged. "No."

"And," added Bunny, "how come the two guys in the back of the van were unconscious?"

"Yeah," said Smithy.

"They were both standing up when the van came to a halt." He turned to Diller. "I assume that was when you..."

"Makes sense." Diller nodded. "Yep."

"Then they both fell forward and hit their heads," finished the priest.

Smithy had stopped at a set of traffic lights, because he was now once again driving like a relatively sane person. This allowed him and Bunny to exchange a highly sceptical look.

"Right," said Bunny. "And you have no clue who they were?"

"Well, in hindsight," said Father Gabriel, "I think they've been following me for a couple of days. They were probably harder to spot because you were so obvious."

"You made us?" asked Diller.

"I'm afraid so. Did you think a cab parked around the neighbourhood wouldn't attract attention?"

"Well..." said Smithy, feeling a little disappointed. He thought they'd been doing quite well.

The priest turned to Diller. "If it's any consolation, you were much better than they were."

Diller, diplomatically, didn't comment on this.

"By the way," said the priest, "if you can get your bike back, I know someone who might be able to fix it for you."

"Nah," said Smithy. "We ain't going back. Bunny, you owe Diller a bike."

"Fair play."

"Not to mention all the repairs on the cab."

He shrugged. "Easy come, easy go."

"May I ask a question?" said Father Gabriel.

"Yes."

"Where are we going?"

Smithy wasn't driving anywhere other than "away". He looked across at Bunny.

"I dunno. Back to the church, I s'pose?"

"Thank you," said Father Gabriel. "I appreciate it."

"So you've no idea who those men are?" asked Bunny.

"As I told you – no. I'm just a simple priest."

"Yeah," said Bunny. "Here's the problem I have with that. A simple priest doesn't a) get kidnapped and then b) get the hell out of there before the cops show up because he doesn't want to answer questions. Come to think of it – c) doesn't sit there calmly after he's been kidnapped and then rescued. You should be freaking the fuck out! Look at you, you're calm as can be."

"Perhaps I'm in shock?"

Bunny turned in his seat and looked long and hard at Father Gabriel, who said nothing and just looked back.

"Can I ask a question?" said Diller, who did not like tension.

"What?" replied Smithy.

"How come the cab's covered in garbage?"

"I don't want to talk about it."

"Actually," said Bunny, gleefully, "that was caused by Smithy's violent driving."

"You can't call it violent," said Smithy.

"I can think of several people who'd disagree."

"It was reckless. Reckless – I'll give you that. But there's no way it counts as an act of violence."

"Reckless counts."

"No, it doesn't," said Smithy. "Leaving your front door open or having unprotected sex or bluffing an ace – those things are reckless too, but none of them are violent. However, pulling a gun on somebody – now that's a violent act."

"No, it fecking is not. I didn't shoot the fella; I just *threatened* to shoot the fella."

"It still counts."

"It definitely does not."

Diller turned to the priest. "Do you understand this argument?"

He shook his head.

Bunny touched Smithy on the arm and pointed at a space. "Pull over a second."

Smithy did so.

Bunny unclipped his seat belt and turned around. "Alright, let's stop playing pretend. Whatever is going on here, Padre, if you don't want to tell us, that's up to you. Thing is, though, whether you like it or not, we saved you."

"I didn't ask you to."

"No, but we did it anyway, because you seem like a good man."

The priest said nothing.

"But a good man, when someone puts themselves at risk" – he

pointed at Diller – "nearly gets themselves killed, in fact, all to help him – a good man would want to repay that kindness."

"While I am thankful for this man's bravery in helping to save me, he did not do it for me. He's never met me."

"That's true," said Diller. "I did it for Bunny, but ask yourself, would Smithy and I be putting ourselves through all this if he wasn't somebody seriously worth helping?"

Smithy nodded. "The guy literally threw himself in front of traffic."

Gabriel looked out the window for a long time before he spoke again. "They will not be happy with me for this. There are very strict rules."

Bunny held his breath.

Father Gabriel rubbed his hands over his eyes and sighed heavily. "Fine. Head towards Brownsville in Brooklyn and I'll direct you from there."

Bunny, his eyes wide with excitement, turned to Smithy.

"Alright," said Smithy, "but I'm starting the meter."

CHAPTER ELEVEN

"Please?" said Bianca, giving Trey the same pleading tone and hands-clasped-together entreaty she'd been using on him since they were five.

"No," said Trey. "I'm not doing your homework for you."

They were taking their usual route home and they were late, at least as far as Emilio was concerned. Bianca's dad didn't care what time of day it was, beyond bar opening and closing times, and Trey was going home to an empty apartment. Still, they ran by Emilio's clock. Most days, he fed the pigeons before school, but he still liked to check in on them every night before dinner. His grandma had strict rules on what time he was allowed to get home. More than anything, Emilio did not like to see her upset, so the trio effectively ran on a schedule dictated by an old lady and a coop full of potentially racist birds.

It was getting dark, and the wind whipped around the buildings. No matter how long Trey lived here, it always caught him by surprise.

"I'm not asking you to do it, Trey. I'm asking for your help with it."

Trey turned to Emilio. "You got your book report done?"

Emilio nodded. "D... d... d... done and dusted."

"See, E got it done."

"Yeah, but he ain't got my distractions to deal with."

"You don't know that. Hey, E – you spending much time standing in your room shadow-boxing with a poster of Dwayne Johnson?"

"Every night."

"Aw, come on, Trey."

"Mrs Marshall knows my writing style, B. She'll know you didn't do it right away."

"You could dumb it down."

"Not that much!"

Bianca shot a dirty look at Emilio, who quickly suppressed his snigger. "Besides," she added, "you know Mrs M misses her favourite student. It'd be a nice trip down memory lane for her."

Mrs Marshall had been Trey's English teacher. It was she who had put him forward for the scholarship to Waldorf. She'd started the ball rolling and then his older brother, John, who everyone – including their mom when she'd been alive – called Pocket, had picked it up and run with it. Trey hadn't wanted to move schools, but his brother and Father Gabriel had sold it as his way out of Coopersville. His big chance. He'd gotten the tuition scholarship and Pocket had found the money for everything else. So every morning at 6:30am, Trey got on the first of two buses, changing into his Waldorf Academy school uniform in the toilets of a McDonalds on the way. He didn't want to be seen in that damn stupid blazer in Coopersville. Then he attended classes where he felt incredibly out of place before returning home via the same route and routine. He liked Mrs Marshall, but he spent a lot of time wishing she hadn't liked his writing so much.

"Have you read the book?" asked Trey.

Bianca fiddled with the hair behind her ear in the same way she did every time she was about to lie. "I am familiar with it. I have, y'know, read it, but I'm finding it hard to put my feelings about it into words."

"OK," said Trey. "Well, just give me a real rough summation."

"If I could do that, I wouldn't need your help."

"Just the basics. What is *Of Mice and Men* about?"

"Well..." She paused and looked from Trey to Emilio and back again nervously. "There's this mouse."

Bianca's face scrunched up into its typical pout of pinched anger as Emilio and Trey howled with laughter. "There's this mouse!" repeated Trey.

"Both y'all better shut up. I can knock you both out, y'know?"

Trey rubbed tears from his eyes as Emilio gasped for breath beside him. The angrier Bianca looked, the funnier it made it.

"Man, fuck y'all. I don't need you."

"Ain't that the truth."

All three of them straightened up, and the laughter died as they turned to see the source of the voice. Three older kids were hanging out in a nearby doorway. Marlon Bryson was only a couple of years older than Trey and the others, but he stood at six foot five. He'd been on the school basketball team before he'd been expelled, and he still hung out on the half court outside their building most days. Trey recognised one of the others as Rico, but the third guy was a stranger to him. Marlon favoured Bianca with a smile.

"You alright, champ?"

"Yeah, I'm fine, thanks."

"These two bothering you, champ?" He emphasised the word champ playfully every time he said it.

"Nothing I can't handle."

"Well, you let me know, champ. Can't have our local celebrities being bothered while they go 'bout their business," he said, emphasising the Z in business.

Bianca went to walk around and Marlon stepped into her path. "Whoa now, champ, what's the hurry? Ain't you gonna show us your belt?"

"No, it – it was a trophy, and it's over at the gym."

"That right?" Marlon ran his finger under his nose. "Y'know, you need anything – money, equipment – you let us know. The New Bloods are happy to provide."

"I'm good, thanks."

Bianca went to walk by again, but Marlon shifted his position, laughing. "Hold up, hold up now. Let me talk to you for a little bit. How about you and I go grab a slice?"

"I gotta get home," said Bianca.

"You can spare a few moments now – I seen your pops heading down to Dasey's, I reckon he'll be propping up that bar for a while. We got time."

"She s... s... said no."

Marlon didn't turn his eyes from Bianca as he spoke to Emilio. "Who the fuck's asking you, retard?"

"Don't call him that," said Bianca, a low growl in her voice.

"OK," said Trey, "we gotta get going, so we'll see you."

"You can leave, but me and the lady are having ourselves a tête-à-tête."

Marlon reached out to grab Bianca's arm, but Emilio slapped it away.

Marlon shot a hand out, catching Emilio in the chest and sending him staggering backwards.

Bianca pushed him back. "Fuck you."

Trey quickly placed himself between the two, extending his arms out to separate them. "Everybody chill. Just chill."

Marlon pushed Trey. "Get out of my way, fucking midget."

Rico, who had been watching on, stepped forward. "Yo, Marlon, that's Pocket's little brother, man."

"So?" said Marlon. "Don't mean he can step to me."

Rico looked concerned. "I know – just relax. You know how he is."

"Shut up, Rico." Marlon glowered at Trey. "Fine, you can go."

"We're all leaving," said Trey.

"Fuck no. I ain't having that retard disrespecting me." He jabbed a finger in Emilio's direction again.

"He didn't mean nothing by—"

"Shit," said Rico, taking a step back.

Trey heard the screech of tyres as the SUV came to a halt beside them, having seemingly appeared out of nowhere. Pocket was out of the passenger-side door in one fluid movement. He'd always been a good athlete, short and stocky but blessed with an economy of movement. He was nineteen now and looked every inch a fully grown man. He had an air of certainty about him. Marlon stumbled as he backed up, stopping when his back reached the wall. Pocket stood inches away, calmly looking up into Marlon's eyes as he spoke.

"You OK, Trey?"

"We just—" Marlon stopped talking when Pocket moved his head just a fraction.

"I don't recall speaking to you."

"I..." said Marlon, before leaving it at that.

"Trey?"

"We're alright, bro, I'm just going home."

"Sure. Hold back a second – I need to talk to you. But first..." Pocket moved himself a little closer and looked into Marlon's eyes. "I need to check my boy Marlon here's clear on a few rules we have."

Seeing Marlon so terrified gave Trey no vicarious thrill of victory. Quite the opposite. Despite Pocket's best efforts to keep it all away from him, Trey would have to be deaf and blind not to know who his big brother was – one of the shot-callers in the New Bloods. Pocket had worked his way up, with a reputation for being a cold-blooded killer. He was Ice Redmond's number-one trigger man and he had made it very clear that his brother was untouchable. The New Bloods respected that and so did the other gangs, once it had been made known that non-compliance was a death sentence. There had been one time that someone from the C-Boys had come at Trey when he was younger. Pocket had exercised a policy of disproportionate response. After the ensuing tit-for-tat bloodshed, the other gangs had agreed to an unofficial understanding that anyone touching Pocket's kid brother was bad for everybody's business. Trey had heard about it all second-hand, mostly from Emilio. More than anything, he wished that it wasn't like this. Pocket was a smart guy and a loving brother. When their mother had gone, he had taken a long, hard look at their lives and found the best way he could to protect his little brother. Love could be a truly terrible and terrifying thing.

"I meant no disrespect, Pocket," said Marlon. "I just... The retard was mouthing off."

Pocket put a finger under Marlon's chin. "You don't call him that."

"I just…"

"Emilio and Bianca like family to us. You know how I feel about family."

"Sorry, I…"

Pocket looked at Rico and the other guy. "And how do you two feel about this situation?"

Rico held his hands up. "I tried to tell him, Pocket. Didn't I try to tell him?"

The other guy nodded furiously.

Marlon looked desperate. "I was just, y'know… playing."

"Oh," said Pocket. "Alright then. So you're saying I'm overreacting?"

Marlon stood there with his mouth open, overwhelmed by the deluge of wrong answers falling around his ears.

Trey rubbed his hands together nervously. "We gotta go, Pocket. I'll see you at home."

Pocket glanced over at him. "Yeah, sure, bro. One sec." He turned back to Marlon. "We'll finish this later."

Marlon nodded gratefully and then stood there looking at Pocket, frozen in place.

"So, you can get out of here right the fuck now."

Pocket took a step back and Marlon and his friends hurried past, not making eye contact. The word "friends" might no longer be applicable, though. From the corner of his eye, Trey caught Rico throwing a hard slap at the back of Marlon's head as they moved quickly away.

The three of them removed, Pocket became Trey's big brother again, that huge room-lighting smile returning to his face. "Sorry 'bout that. Hey, B, Emilio, what's up?"

"Nothing," said Emilio.

"We good," said Bianca. "Thanks for, y'know…"

Pocket waved her thanks away. "Don't you three worry about those assholes. I'll set 'em straight later."

"No, don't…" Trey started, and then he stopped. Pocket wasn't the easiest to talk to these days, and Trey knew that contradicting him in front of others would not be appreciated.

Pocket placed a hand on Trey's shoulder. "You OK, little bro?"

"All good."

"Mrs Barnes dropping over dinner, OK?"

"Yeah. I told her to skip a couple – we got lots. You back home tonight?"

Pocket glanced at the SUV's tinted windows. "I'm not sure. You got money?"

Trey nodded.

"You need anything?"

"I'm fine."

"OK, Einstein," he said, giving Trey's hair a playful ruffle. "I'll catch you later. You call me if you need anything."

"Sure."

"Alright then."

He turned and tossed a playful feint in Bianca's direction. "And congrats, B. We all proud of you. Representing Coopersville."

Bianca gave him a big grin. "You know it!"

He bumped fists with Emilio and then hopped into the SUV. It pulled off and headed back down Bleacher.

"Man," said Bianca, "having your big brother is like having your very own fairy godmother."

"Yeah," said Trey without enthusiasm.

Emilio said nothing. He and Trey had talked about Pocket long into the night on more than one occasion.

They continued their walk, nobody saying anything for about half a block, until Emilio touched Bianca's arm. "Hey, B. Brothers can be c... complicated. You know any b... b... books 'bout that?"

CHAPTER TWELVE

Father Gabriel rang the doorbell and then glanced up at Bunny. It was noticeable that, for a man who had remained remarkably calm through the ordeal of being kidnapped, the priest seemed extremely nervous now. Bunny wasn't without sympathy. He'd met Sister Bernadette twenty years ago in Dublin, and though he'd helped her out several times over the years, the woman had never lost the ability to put the fear of God into him.

"Let me do the talking," said Father Gabriel.

"Right."

Bunny was equally nervous – the two of them standing there like young lads picking up their dates for a dance. He'd been looking for the Sisters of the Saint for nine long, gruelling months, and now he was finally on the doorstep of the women who could hopefully lead him to Simone.

This was the first time Bunny had stood beside the priest. The man was five-eight at best and slight of build, with round framed glasses that made him a prime candidate to illustrate the dictionary definition of the word "bookish". And yet Bunny had opened the back door of a van to discover two unconscious men while the padre kneeled there calmly, as if praying for their souls. Try as he might, Bunny couldn't get a read on the guy.

The building they were standing outside appeared to be an abandoned school. Carved from an unwelcoming grey granite that gave it an air of foreboding, it was four storeys high and in a state of disrepair. It looked like it was waiting for a wrecking ball to put it out of its misery. There were bars on the lower windows. Those that weren't boarded shut were the kind of translucent glass that educational institutions of a certain era specialised in, designed to let light in but not allow any young imaginations out. Bunny was glad they hadn't had that in his day. It was a long time ago now, but the strongest memory he had from school was the entire class sitting through a maths lesson while surreptitiously watching two dogs shagging on the lawn outside. As far as the Christian Brothers went, it was the closest thing they'd ever had to sex education.

The surrounding area looked like what Bunny now considered typical working-class New York. Ethnically diverse, rough around the edges, but nicer than Coopersville, where Father Gabriel's church was situated. Admittedly, Bunny was mainly basing that on the fact that they'd been there for several minutes and nobody had tried to mug him yet.

Father Gabriel looked at the doorbell, considering if enough time had passed for a third ring.

"Are you sure they're in?" said Bunny.

"They're in."

"It doesn't look like anyone's here."

"They're in," he repeated.

"Fair enough."

The whole place looked deserted to Bunny.

Father Gabriel reached his hand out towards the bell and then pulled it quickly away as he heard a bolt being slid back on the other side of the door.

The door opened just enough for a woman in a wimple to stick her head out. Bunny was taken aback – he didn't know what he'd expected, but she was maybe in her forties and strikingly beautiful, with piercing blue eyes. She looked like the nun you'd expect if the role had been cast by someone whose only experience of them had been watching *The Sound of Music*.

"Hi, Father Gabriel."

"Hello, Sister Dionne."

"Is everything OK?"

"Yes, fine."

The nun looked Bunny up and down. "How is Father Martin over at St Justin's?"

"Still dead, God rest his soul," responded the priest.

Dionne nodded. Bunny guessed the question was a test, a chance to signal if something was wrong. Satisfied that Gabriel was at least not there against his will, Dionne relaxed slightly. "We're not accepting visitors right now, Father."

"I wouldn't be here if it wasn't important."

"I appreciate that but I'm afraid your timing isn't great. We're not open for business."

"Please," said Bunny, who shut up after Gabriel laid a hand on his arm.

"Please," said Gabriel. "I need to speak to you, and this man... He has helped me out with something. He has been looking for you."

"Yes," said Dionne, "we're aware of him. A large, bearded Irishman has been looking for us for quite some time now."

Bunny raised his eyebrows. "You knew?"

She turned to look directly at him. "That you have been looking for us? Yes. Knowing who's looking for you is a large part of being good at not being found. Or at least that used to be the case." She looked pointedly at Father Gabriel.

"Please, Sister, he says he has information you need to hear, and..." Gabriel hesitated. "I will vouch for him."

She shook her head. "I'm sorry, I'm under strict instructions."

Dionne disappeared from view and the door started to close. "Please," said Bunny. "What about Bernadette?"

After a moment, the nun stuck her head back out and eyed Bunny suspiciously. "What about her?"

"Can I talk to her? She knows me. Bunny McGarry. Tell her it's important. Simone is in danger."

"How do you know her?"

"Simone?"

"No," said Dionne. "Sister Bernadette."

"They used to have a house in Rathmines in Dublin. Twenty years ago, now. Simone lived with them for a bit and then, after she left Dublin, I helped Bernadette out with a few things. I know Assumpta too!"

Dionne eyed Bunny. "You've spoken to Assumpta?"

"Yeah – well, no – well…"

Father Gabriel gave Bunny a quizzical look.

"It's sort of a trick question," said Bunny. "Assumpta never spoke much."

Sister Dionne looked at Bunny for several seconds, clearly internally debating something. "Oh, damn it – hang on."

The door closed and they could hear chains being removed. It reopened again and the two men stepped into a long, dank hallway with a marble floor. At another time, a small part of Bunny would've been mad keen to slide along it in his socks.

"I'm going to regret this. Are you armed?" asked Dionne.

Both of them shook their heads. Bunny had stashed the handgun he had recently acquired in the glove compartment of the cab.

"Good," she said, closing the door behind them. "Just so we're clear" – Dionne raised her hand to show them the Glock 9 she was holding – "I am."

She led them up two flights of stairs and into a classroom. On the walk up, Bunny changed his mind – the place could never be demolished, it was far too valuable as a set for horror movies. At one point they passed a wall which had a mural that might once have depicted Jesus meeting a joyous group of children. Unfortunately, time – and a leak somewhere in the roof – had made it look like Jesus was a demented psychopath who was melting children with his superpowers while beaming a happy grin.

Dionne instructed them to wait in the classroom and then

disappeared. The room was lit by one buzzing fluorescent light on the ceiling, which flickered on and off occasionally, and the waning sunlight from the end of a New York afternoon coming through the dirty windows. Bunny made the mistake of cramming his bulk into one of the all-in-one wooden desks, just to see if he could. He quickly came to deeply regret this decision, as he was pretty sure he was unlikely to get out of the desk without leaving a pile of kindling in his wake. Father Gabriel stood at the window, looking out the top half, which was clear glass, lost in his own thoughts.

"So," said Bunny, "how long have you known the sisters?"

"A while."

"How'd you meet?"

The priest didn't answer. Bunny nodded to himself and drummed his fingers on the tabletop. Between the limited time he had spent in the priest's company and the seven days he had spent trapped in a cab with Smithy, he was getting royally sick of the strong, silent type.

Fifteen minutes later, Bunny was halfway through trying to subtly slide himself out of the desk when the door opened and Dionne walked back in. She didn't look any happier with her lot in life than when she had left them.

"Sister Dorothy will see you now."

The priest nodded and moved to follow Dionne back out of the room. They both stopped to look at Bunny. Dionne raised her eyebrows. "Will you be joining us?"

Bunny fell to the floor in three embarrassingly ungraceful stages and then managed to wriggle his way out of the table. Dionne turned to look at Gabriel, who shook his head.

"Sorry about that. Seems I might have put on a bit of weight since the last time I was in one. 'Tis the portion sizes in this country, I'm telling everyone."

Dionne led them down the hall and into what appeared to be the principal's office. A nun sat behind an imposing wooden desk. Bookshelves and filing cabinets lined the walls, with another door at the back of the room. The woman – Sister Dorothy – spoke in a West

African accent that was both melodious and authoritative at the same time. "Hello, Father. It is always nice to see *you*."

The message wasn't exactly subtle.

Dionne moved to stand behind Dorothy, leaning against the other door.

"I'm—" started Bunny, but he stopped as the nun glared at him. He reckoned she was probably well into her sixties, but she was reaping the benefits of all that clean living. She didn't have any laughter lines, although that may have been because she wasn't much of a laugher.

"I know who you are," she said. "We have been following your efforts to locate us." She looked pointedly at Father Gabriel. "We thought we had assured that you finding us would not be possible."

Father Gabriel looked uncomfortable again. "I am sorry, Sister. He heard of my connection to you because of the situation you helped me with last year."

"A strict proviso of which was that you forget we existed. Did we not make that clear?"

Father Gabriel nodded. "You did. When he first approached me, I denied all knowledge of you."

"And yet here you are."

"The situation changed."

"How exactly?"

"Bishop Ramirez is dead."

For the first time, the woman's visage of cool and certain anger cracked. "I had not heard that. I am sorry. He was a good man and I know how much he meant to you."

"Yes, but..." Gabriel glanced at Bunny. "Perhaps we could discuss that later?"

She looked at him for a long moment before nodding and then turning her gaze in Bunny's direction. "Mr McGarry." She enunciated each syllable of his name as if they were three separate words.

"Hello, Sister. Sorry to barge in."

"Yes, well – I will say this for you, you are persistent. How long have you been looking for us? Six months?"

"Nine, Sister. It's important."

"It always is."

Bunny looked confused.

"Do you honestly think you are the only man looking for us? For a group of celibate women, we have no shortage of male pursuers."

"It's not like that."

"Isn't it?" she said, raising her eyebrows. "Let me guess exactly what it is like. There is a woman, important to you, who disappeared with our help and you want to find her?"

"It's not like that. I mean – alright, it is, but not how you're making it sound. She's in danger."

"I don't doubt that."

"Not from me. She's... People are after her – serious people. They won't stop until they find her, if they haven't already."

"Yes," she said. "Speaking of which, may I enquire how you are not dead?" She turned back to Father Gabriel. "Are you aware that the man you brought to our home has risen from the dead? I have read his obituary in the newspaper; it seems he had quite a... colourful life. It concerns me that a man who is supposed to be dead and buried in Dublin is alive and well in New York. I wonder what kind of assistance he has been given in order to make that happen."

"OK," said Bunny, "I can see how it looks. Can I just take a minute and explain, please?"

Sister Dorothy nodded.

"The woman I'm looking for is called Simone Delamere. She was in Dublin twenty years ago – because you helped her escape from New York. She was living in a house in Rathmines with Sister Bernadette and Sister Assumpta. The reason she had to get out of New York was..." Bunny hesitated. He found this part hard to explain. "There existed a certain tape of her with some powerful bloke and, well, certain people wanted it gone. She killed a man in self-defence. Self-defence," he repeated.

"I am aware of all of this."

"Right. Well, they found out where she was and a man came

looking. I was able to help her but... the man and his associate ended up dead as part of the deal. Simone had to run again."

"Yes, we are aware."

"Alright," said Bunny, "well, are you also aware that they came looking for Simone last year because the bodies of the two aforementioned dead guys were found? It turns out a lot of people want the tape they think Simone has. Powerful people in the US government."

"How badly do they want it?"

"Well," said Bunny, "let me put it this way: one side sent a team to follow me, in the hope I might lead them to her or the tape; and the other side faked my death to get me here to find her."

"So, you're working for one of these 'sides'?"

Bunny shook his head emphatically. "No. I used them as a means to an end. I'm working for me. Actually, I'm working for Simone, so please, for the love of God, can you let her know that she's in danger?"

"We do not have any way of contacting the woman."

"Well then, could you give me a clue as to where she was when you lost contact? Any ideas on where she might have gone?"

Dorothy shook her head. "No. We are not going to give that information to someone we don't know."

"But... ye do know me. Ask Bernadette. We've had our differences, but she knows I wouldn't lie about this. Not this."

Dorothy shook her head again.

"Or Assumpta? She'll remember me – probably." Sister Assumpta was... odd was a kind word for it. She barely seemed conscious of her surroundings at times.

Dorothy shook her head again.

"Ah, for – please? I demand to speak to Bernadette."

"You demand?"

"Please, I'm begging you?" To emphasise his point, Bunny fell to his knees – a dramatic gesture that he instantly wished he'd made on a non-wooden floor. "I'll do anything."

"Get up. I am unimpressed by histrionics. You have made your point."

"But—"

"You have made your point," she repeated. "Please wait outside."

Bunny got himself back on his feet, and after a look around the room, as if trying to find something else to say, he turned and left.

He stood outside for ten minutes while Gabriel spoke to Dorothy. Dionne stood awkwardly nearby, keeping an eye on him.

Bunny leaned against the wall. "Honestly, Sister, I'm just trying to—"

She held her hand up for silence, but when she spoke her tone was almost sympathetic. "Really, there is no point appealing to me. Sister Dorothy is the head of the order and I can't go against her wishes."

Bunny sighed. "No disrespect, but your order seems to specialise in recruiting women who are tough as old boots and stubborn as fecking mules."

Dionne gave a sad little smile. "You really have met Bernadette."

Bunny nodded.

"I wouldn't judge Dorothy on today. It's been a rough few weeks. I'm afraid your timing sucks."

"Story of my life, Sister. Story of my life."

"Look," said Dionne, "I'm making no promises, but leave me your number, and if Dorothy changes her mind, I'll give you a call."

Bunny gave her the number of his burner phone and then they waited in awkward silence until Father Gabriel emerged.

"Well," said Dionne, "if that is all, I shall show you gentlemen out."

When they got outside, Father Gabriel bade Bunny a terse farewell and left. Bunny walked back around the corner to where the cab was parked. He'd hoped for so much more when he finally found the sisters, but still. There had been that moment, that single moment... When he had asked if they could give him a clue to Simone's whereabouts, Sister Dionne had given a subtle involuntary head movement. She had looked in the direction of the filing cabinet in the corner.

Smithy and Diller were leaning up against the cab, having taken the time to clean the remains of the garbage off it.

"Well?" said Smithy. "How'd it go?"

"Not great," said Bunny.

"Could you define 'not great'?" asked Diller.

"Let me put it to you this way: how would you two lads feel about helping me break into a nunnery?"

CHAPTER THIRTEEN

Father Gabriel jumped when the bag lady touched him on the arm. She pulled back, shocked by his instinctively defensive posture. He stared up at her like a man just coming out of a dream or, to be more accurate, a nightmare. She was well into her sixties and had been trundling by with a shopping cart containing all of her earthly possessions.

"What?" said Father Gabriel.

"Sorry," she said, already regretting getting involved. "Your phone is ringing."

"Oh."

Gabriel noticed that the phone in his inside coat pocket was indeed ringing. He'd been ignoring it, lost in his own thoughts. Embarrassed, he reached in to pull it out.

"Sorry, I'm... I was miles away. Thank you."

The woman nodded and moved off quickly, the wheels on her cart squeaking as she trundled off down the path.

Father Gabriel glanced around him. He was sitting in a park. He couldn't have said exactly which one though. After leaving the sisters, he had walked and walked, trying to process what had happened and what it all meant. There was really nothing to be figured out when you got down to it. His past had finally caught up with him. He had lived with the Sword of Damocles dangling over his head, sure that this day was coming. There could be no doubt. Abraham was certainty and this was certainly Abraham.

Father Gabriel glanced at the screen and saw that he had twenty-six missed calls. Most of them would be from Rosario – as this one was.

"Hello."

"Father – gracias a Dios – you're alive!"

"Sorry, Rosario, something came up."

"Something came up? Something came up, he says! We been looking for you everywhere!" He could hear the relief in her voice turn to anger. "You been missing for hours. I called the cops. I got Gina Marks checking with all the other hospitals. You missed training at the gym. You missed the meeting with that guy from the diocese. You had Mrs Darnard waiting for an hour. We were worried sick!"

"I'm sorry. It... it was an urgent matter."

"You gotta tell me where you goin'. Remember, you agreed to that. I gotta know. I gotta know."

To someone on the outside, Rosario would come across as a stereotypical mother hen, worrying needlessly. He was a grown man, after all. But Gabriel knew the whole story, which had poured out of her over a couple of days not long after they'd first met. A mother's grief was unlike anything else. The pain, the wrenching pain, was so excruciatingly intense. That, and the sense of overwhelming, crushing guilt. It didn't matter how many times you tried to take it away, you couldn't lift the burden. Mothers never truly bury their children – they carry them on their shoulders for the rest of their days. In Rosario's mind, her son would still be alive if she had known where he was and who he was with. It didn't matter that he had been fifteen and making decisions for himself. His death was her failure.

"You need help, Father? Where are you?"

Now he was present again in his own life, Gabriel noticed how cold he was. He hadn't taken his gloves when he left the church, not expecting to go far. "I'll... I'll be back soon."

Rosario, going through her own series of emotional responses, now that relief and anger had at least been visited briefly, landed on concern. "You OK? If you want, I can come pick you up? I got my car back from the shop – I can come get you."

"Honestly, there's no need. Thank you, Rosario, I'll be back soon."

He would be. He couldn't walk away from this life or from the consequences of the last one.

"OK. Did it work out alright?"

"I'm sorry – what, Rosario?"

"The thing. Y'know, the thing that came up?"

Gabriel stood and pulled his coat more tightly around himself. In the distance, he could see the old bag lady looking through the contents of a trash can.

"It's... it's too early to tell."

CHAPTER FOURTEEN

Diller and Bunny sat in the cab.

"Jesus," said Bunny, "'tis brassic. It'd take the bollocks off a brass monkey."

Diller rubbed his hands together and looked out the window. "I don't know what the hell you said, but if it meant it is cold then you're right, it's cold."

Diller pulled his most prized possession, the oversized duffle coat he'd found in a thrift store a few weeks before, more tightly around him. He loved it. Even on a night like tonight when the temperature was well below freezing, it was like walking around in his own one-man tent.

Bunny rubbed the condensation off the window and looked out into the night. "D'ye think he'll be much longer?"

Diller shrugged. It wasn't a question that anyone could give a meaningful answer to. The clock on the dash now said 2:14am – Smithy had been gone for almost twenty minutes. Diller had never "cased" a building before, or been there while anyone else did it, so he had no frame of reference for when the third member of their team would return.

Bunny turned around in the passenger seat and looked at Diller.

"Thanks again for doing this, Dill. The pile of favours I owe yourself and himself are really mounting up."

Diller waved his concerns away. "Happy to help, and besides, you hired us for the week and getting paid for doing actual investigative work was pretty cool. Now this is over, I'm going to have to find something else to do."

"Are you not gonna go back to being the mascot thingy in Times Square?"

"Nah. Too much hassle."

"Seriously," said Bunny, "I'd be more than happy to help out with that. I wouldn't – I could just have a quiet word with them lads."

Back in Dublin, Bunny had been a grandmaster in the art of the quiet word. Admittedly, his hard-fought and well-established reputation for being willing to go considerably beyond a quiet word meant he almost never had to. He'd been thinking about that a lot recently, between Father Gabriel asking him if he was a violent man, Diller's remark about his method of problem resolution and then his bet with Smithy, it was – though he wouldn't admit it – starting to bother him. As silly as it sounded, he had never thought of himself as a "violent man". He considered himself someone who dealt with the problem of violent men. It was a distinction that was at the core of his self-image.

"Forget about it," said Diller. "Standing around in a silly costume all day wasn't exactly a lifelong career goal. I'm happy to help out. Besides, if I wasn't doing this, I'd be home alone, struggling to keep warm. This is way more exciting."

Bunny nodded. "Still – thanks. By the way, how is your ma getting on?"

"Mom is doing good. I'm gonna see her Tuesday."

"Great."

They lapsed into silence again. Bunny pressed his face to the window and looked out into the night. Despite having been expecting it – waiting for it, in fact – Bunny still jumped when the driver's door opened and Smithy climbed in.

"Jesus," said Bunny, "you're a sneaky little sod. I never saw you coming."

Smithy shrugged. "We're supposed to be staying unseen. Always a good idea when you're trying to break in somewhere."

"Fair point. So, how's it looking?"

Smithy furrowed his brow and nodded. "It should be relatively straightforward. There's an alarm box at the back of the building but it isn't connected to anything. I spotted two cameras, both of which are clearly broken. There's a door out back with a lock that looks pretty basic, but they might bolt it from the other side. I suggest we try that first and then if it's a no go, there's an outside fire escape we can reach and we can find a window to jimmy."

Bunny nodded. "Sounds like a plan."

"OK," said Diller, "let's go!"

"Whoa, whoa, hang on," said Smithy. "Did you not tell him his role in this escapade?"

"No," said Diller, "don't make me wait in the car again. I can do stuff."

"You're not waiting in the car," said Smithy.

"Good."

"You're protecting the car while also keeping a lookout for cops."

"You're kidding, right? This area ain't as bad as Hunts Point, but it ain't far off. At night, I guarantee the cops only come through here if they're chasing somebody or shots have been fired. They're not cruising around the area checking everyone's tucked up in bed."

"Which is exactly why I need you to keep an eye on the cab," said Smithy. He handed Diller a walkie-talkie. "We're on channel three. Let us know if you see anything suspicious."

Diller shook his head. "Suspicious? Everything that happens around here after dark is suspicious."

"You know what I mean."

"Man, I am sick to death of being the junior partner in this crew."

Bunny shrugged. "Sorry, Dill."

Smithy and Bunny had an unspoken understanding: Diller could help out with their "situations", but only on the strict proviso that he didn't commit any actual crimes, and he wasn't put in harm's way. Seeing as he'd already thrown himself at a moving vehicle that day, Smithy had been unsure about even letting him come. The thought of having to explain to Marcel that his taxi had been stolen was the only thing that'd brought Smithy round. Then again, that would save him having to get all the damage from the earlier car chase fixed. Bunny was paying, but Smithy disliked mechanics with the kind of pure, intense energy you typically only found at the heart of a star.

Bunny opened his passenger door. "Right so, let's kick this donkey in the knackers and see if he dances."

Smithy placed his hand on Bunny's arm to stop him. "Look, are you sure about this?"

"What's there to be sure about? I asked them nicely and they wouldn't play ball. I don't enjoy breaking in there any more than you do, but you both know why I'm doing it. I've no choice."

Smithy nodded. "OK, it's just... I dunno. I have a bad feeling about this."

"You always say that."

"Yeah," said Smithy, "and I'm always right. When has anything we've done ever gone to plan?"

"But you said yourself, 'tis an easy target."

Smithy picked up his tool belt from where it lay in the side pocket of the door. "Yeah, I know. That's what worries me."

"Ara, what's the worst that could happen?"

Moments before, on the second floor of the supposedly abandoned school, Sister Zoya, aka the worst that could happen, had been watching the three men sitting in the cab on one of her monitors. The door behind her opened and Sister Dionne walked in.

"Well?"

"It's exactly as Dorothy predicted. They triggered the alarms fifteen minutes ago."

"They already tried to break in?"

"Negatory, big momma. My system picked them up through facial recognition."

"Oh. I see." Dionne really didn't, but experience had taught her that any questions put to Zoya regarding technical matters only resulted in a lot more confusion.

Dionne pointed at the spare chair and Zoya nodded. The girl was nervous about her personal space and Dionne always asked as a matter of course before entering it. She sat down and looked at the feed showing the three men sitting in the car, talking animatedly. "Damn. I was really hoping Dorothy wasn't going to be right – just for once. Who's with him?"

"The tall drink of hot chocolate and his vertically challenged sidekick – they stayed outside in the big yellow taxicab earlier."

"I see."

Sister Zoya's vocabulary was becoming an increasingly odd hybrid. She was from Pakistan, and when she'd joined the sisters several years ago her English had been basic. She had added to it primarily by devouring YouTube videos and TV shows. Not liking to leave her room had left the woman with an unhealthy amount of time on her hands. She was still only nineteen, but Dionne was pretty sure most nineteen-year-olds didn't speak like her.

Dionne glanced at the other screens. Zoya had over a dozen cameras that were all but invisible to the naked eye stationed around the property, not counting the two decoys. Zoya liked her security to be discreet, as that way the criminally inclined were not deterred from attempting to break in. She viewed such opportunities as a wonderful way to test her toys in the real world. The woman was a genius – although you couldn't use that word within her earshot – and she had proven invaluable to their organisation. Still, Zoya's presence there made Dionne sad. When they'd agreed to rescue her and her mother all those years ago, it had been for the express purpose of giving them a fresh start. Instead, her mother hadn't made it out of the Gomal Pass and the trauma had left Zoya with agoraphobia and other issues. She had become a sister by default – the lost child with nowhere else to go.

Dionne took her eyes off the screen and noticed that Zoya had a large new poster of one of those Japanese comic book characters she liked up on the wall. Dionne found the overly large eyes disconcerting.

"Where did that come from?" she asked.

"It's new," said Zoya, using the joystick on her desk to move one of the cameras around.

"Exactly my point."

"I got it delivered."

"What?"

"Not to here. Calm down."

"But you... How did you?"

"I got it dropped off somewhere and then my little Birdie picked it up."

"It can do that?"

Zoya beamed a wide smile. "Yeah. Easy-peasy."

Birdie was the drone that Zoya had designed. It ran almost silently and had other features, all of which Zoya had explained to Dionne and none of which Dionne understood. It was the reason they had a crystal-clear shot from above the cab full of three men about to make a big mistake. Through a friend of a friend, the sisters had patented several of Zoya's designs, and a couple had been sold for quite a lot of money. Dionne and Dorothy had tried to convince Zoya to take the fruits of her labour and leave, start a new life for herself, but the girl was insistent on staying. She had requested that all the money from her work go back into financing the order. All she asked was that nothing be sold that could have military applications. So, she stayed, and the sisters sourced the parts she needed through various methods that avoided detection. All of which meant that the sisters had a young woman who was possibly one of the world's greatest engineers living with them, and they couldn't persuade her to step outside into the big bad world.

Dionne was drawn to movement on the screen. The doors of the cab were opening.

Zoya clapped her hands excitedly. "Looks like we got ourselves a ball game, folks – batter up!"

CHAPTER FIFTEEN

Smithy and Bunny tried to look casual as they crossed over. At this time of night, the streets were largely deserted, save for the occasional low-rider cruising by with its stereo on too loud or the odd homeless person wandering around, looking for warmth where none could be found. It was past 2am now, and while New York may have been the city that never slept, the suburbs dozed from time to time. With a quick glance around to confirm they weren't being observed, Smithy and Bunny slipped into the alley at the side of the school.

Smithy wordlessly led the way, using the torch on his phone to navigate the broken and cracked paving stones. They came to a wooden door with chipped paint which was half-covered by some very unimaginative and anatomically impossible graffiti. Smithy slipped a thin leather case from out of the tool belt hidden under his coat and selected what looked to Bunny like a scalpel and a long, thin bit of metal.

"Here," said Smithy, handing Bunny his phone, "keep the light on the lock."

Smithy set to work. It had been a while since he'd worked a lock. While a part of him was keen to see if he still had the skills, another part had hoped he'd never use them again.

"Hold the light straight."

"Oh, sorry, I just..."

Smithy looked up to see Bunny staring into the sky. "What?"

"Ah, nothing. I just had this weird feeling we were being watched."

Dionne shifted backwards as the infrared image of Bunny seemed to look directly into the camera. "Can he see Birdie?"

Zoya shook her head. "Not possible. My little Birdie has this radical mesh screen. You look at her from below, all you see is a HD rendering of the sky above her. Next best thing to invisible. Uh-huh, oh yeah. Sweet as."

"Right," said Dionne, feeling only slightly more assured.

"Besides" – Zoya's fingers flew across the keyboard and a couple of command windows opened up on the central screen – "if it's a weird feeling they're worried about..." She laughed maniacally.

"What in the...?" said Smithy.

"What's up?" asked Bunny.

"There's something wrong with..." He stood up and tugged on the long, thin bit of metal. "It's stuck. How can it be stuck?"

"Did you jam it in?"

"No." Smithy let the tool go and it flipped instantly to stick firmly to the door. "What in the hell?" He looked around. "It's like the door is magnetic or something."

Zoya laughed. "I like this guy. He's real quick on the uptake. Do you want to see something really fun?"

Dionne rolled her eyes. "Oh, go on then."

Zoya giggled again. "Let's crank it and spank it."

· · ·

Bunny and Smithy stared at the door.

"What in the shittin' hell is going on?"

"I have no idea," said Smithy. "It doesn't make any sense."

With a soft tinkle, the two tools suddenly detached themselves from the door and fell to the doorstep below.

"Crap, give me the light," said Smithy. He took the phone and bent down, only for his tool belt to slam into the door instead. "Jesus."

"Stop pissing about."

"I'm not. It's got me. It's got my belt."

"Oh, for..." Bunny grabbed hold of Smithy and attempted to pull him away from the door. "I got ye, I got ye..."

"Let me just untie the belt."

"No, I..." Bunny placed his foot against the wall and proceeded to try and heave Smithy off the door with all his might. Just as he did so, the force holding him was released. Both men flew backwards, landing messily in an icy puddle behind them.

Despite herself, Dionne smiled as Zoya slapped the desk. "Yes. Yes. Yes. That was so sweet!" Zoya unexpectedly tossed her hand up for a high five. Dionne looked at it uncertainly. While on one hand it represented a step forward for Zoya and her personal space issues, on the other, Dionne really hated high-fiving.

"It feels like you're not embracing the good times, Sister Dionne."

Dionne attempted a begrudging high five that was really more of a pat, and she cringed while doing it. "Just focus, Zoya. Don't underestimate them. Don't forget – this man was clever enough and persistent enough to find us."

"Yeah, and I'm going to make him regret that."

Bunny picked himself and his now cold and soaking arse off the ground. "Right, feck this. I'm shoulder-charging the fecking thing."

Smithy stepped in front of him, stopping Bunny before he could get started. "Don't!"

"But—"

"Seriously, think about it. Whatever kind of security that door has, if it contains a strong enough magnet to grip metal like that, it'll be thick. You ever shoulder-charged metal?"

Dionne glanced at Zoya, who nodded.

"Little dude isn't wrong. The Irish fella would have Wile E. Coyote-ed himself there."

"So, what happens now?"

"Well, personally, I'd love to see them try to come in the front door."

"What happens when...?"

Zoya turned to Dionne, an alarmingly excited look on her face. "Oh, it is really good!"

Bunny and Smithy stood in the alleyway, Smithy readjusting his tool belt while Bunny tugged at the back of his trousers, hoping to prevent them freezing to his arse.

"This is messed up," said Smithy. "I don't know what the hell just happened, but it is my considered opinion we should get the hell out of here."

"Oh, for feck's sake," said Bunny. "So they've got a security door. Big deal."

"A security door? That's not like any security door I've ever seen."

"Fine," said Bunny, "if you don't want to do it, just give me a crowbar and I'll get myself in."

"I'm just..." Smithy shook his head. "You can be really annoying, you know that? Follow me."

·   ·   ·

"Ahh," said Zoya. "They're going for the fire escape. Well, never mind."

"OK," said Dionne, "I should wake Sister Dorothy."

"Wait, wait, wait – there's loads more coming first."

"Just give me a hand moving this, would ye?"

"It's on wheels," replied Smithy.

"It won't budge."

"Have you released the brake?"

"What b...? Oh, right."

Bunny released the wheel brake and trundled the blue plastic dumpster over towards the fire escape. He positioned it carefully under it and then, once he'd re-engaged the brake, tried to climb on top of it. Smithy jumped towards the wall and used it as a springboard, grabbing the lip of the dumpster and pulling himself up.

"How in the feck did you do that?"

"I went to the Olympics in the dumpster jump. Come on." Smithy assisted Bunny and the big man stood unsteadily on the thick plastic of the lid, testing his footing.

"Right," said Bunny, reaching for the bottom rung of the ladder, now just within his reach. "D'ye know, we don't have these in Ireland."

"Dumpsters?"

"No. Fire escapes. Like outside ladders like this."

"What do you do if there's a fire?"

"I think we just put it out."

"Revolutionary," said Smithy. "Well, come on then – pull the ladder down."

"I'm trying," said Bunny. "'Tis stuck."

"Give it a tug."

"What do you think I'm doing?"

"Put your weight into it."

"I fecking am!"

Bunny took a firm grip of the bottom rung in both hands and, for the second-ever time in his entire existence, he attempted to perform a pull-up.

Zoya turned to Dionne. "Do you want to press the button?"

"What button?"

"It's a surprise."

Dionne rolled her eyes. "Zoya, this is a tad sadistic."

Zoya reared back, looking genuinely offended. "No, it isn't. I am defending the castle."

"Well, get on with it then."

"Fine." She pressed a key on her keyboard and the ladder, previously stuck solid, suddenly came loose.

They watched as it descended rapidly, slamming the Irishman into and through the top of the dumpster as his colleague dived off it just in time.

Zoya folded her arms. "That wasn't sadistic; it was essentially just gravity. Mostly."

"Remind me," said Dionne, "to never get on your bad side."

"Bunny?"

Smithy didn't get a response, but he could hear movement from inside the dumpster.

"Bunny?" Smithy repeated. "Are you OK?"

"I got smashed through a dumpster and, for the second time today, I have a face full of garbage. In fact, I'm near drowning in the stuff. Does 'Are you OK?' really strike you as a sensible question, given the circumstances?"

Smithy looked around. While Bunny's dumpster dive hadn't exactly been graceful, it hadn't been that loud.

"I told you—"

"And it's definitely not the time for I told you so's."

"Alright," said Smithy. "Point taken."

The walkie-talkie strapped to Smithy's belt beeped. "Diller to Smithy. Over."

"Yes, Dill?"

"Is everything OK? Over."

Smithy looked up to see Bunny dragging himself out of the dumpster, the sourest of expressions on his face and a banana skin dangling off his shoulder.

"Well," said Smithy, "the operation has not been without its issues, but morale remains high and we are striving onwards."

"Sarcastic little bollocks," muttered Bunny.

"What was that? Over."

"Never mind. We're cool, Dill. All OK your end?"

"Yeah. Over. By the way – you keep forgetting to say over. Over."

"OK," said Smithy, as Bunny stumbled out of the dumpster and did a little jog of disgust to get various bits of garbage off himself. "Thanks for checking in, but this conversation is now..."

Smithy clipped the walkie-talkie back on his belt.

Bunny took off his coat and made a retching face as he removed a particularly unpleasant item from the pocket. "I'm going to need a month's worth of showers to get close to feeling clean again."

"Wow," said Smithy. "Two showers."

Bunny spat onto the ground. "I need to get rid of the taste." He pulled a hip flask from his pocket and took a long pull on it. Then he held it out to Smithy, who shook his head.

"I'm good. I try not to get too loaded while committing B and E."

"Suit yourself, although there's been feck all entering yet and the only breaking has been done to me."

"I think you might need a new coat."

"That ain't happening," said Bunny, putting it back on. "C'mon, let's get moving."

Bunny lifted the ladder out of the dumpster to allow Smithy to move it and then lowered the bottom rung carefully to the ground.

"I'll go first," said Smithy.

"You sure?"

"Absolutely. You stink, and I'd rather be upwind of you."

"Thanks, Smithy, you're all heart."

"I'm quite pleased with the next one," said Zoya. "It's real subtle."

Smithy reached the first landing and looked at the window. It was boarded over with thick wooden planks. A glance upwards revealed that the one on the next floor up was uncovered and would be the easier and quieter option. He turned to continue up the stairs when the fire escape shifted slightly, causing a gutter above him to move.

Smithy shoved his fist in his mouth to stop himself from screaming as about half a bucket's worth of ice-cold water landed on his head.

Bunny reached the landing and stopped. "What's wrong with you?"

Smithy turned around to face him, his body still shaking from the shock of the ice-cold water.

"How'd ye get wet?"

Smithy looked upwards suspiciously. "Fuck. Cold. So cold."

"It'll be warmer when we get inside."

Smithy put his hand out to stop Bunny moving. "Are you familiar with the film *Home Alone*?"

"Course. Is that relevant?"

"I'm beginning to believe it might be."

Bunny looked up and then back down at Smithy. "Ara, you're getting paranoid. So they have some kind of weird security door. The rest was just bad luck."

"Really?" said Smithy. "How come that water wasn't frozen? Should have been ice."

Dionne looked across at Zoya.

"He's good," said Zoya with an appreciative nod. "I have a little heater on the pipe, keeps it just above freezing."

110

"Don't take this the wrong way, but you really do scare me."

"You're overthinking it," said Bunny.

Smithy shook his head. "From now on, we go slow and you do exactly as I say."

"Alright," said Bunny, raising his hand, "you're the expert."

Smithy gingerly made his way up the next flight of stairs, looking up, down and every other direction on every step. Eventually, while ignoring Bunny's none-too-subtle mumblings from behind him, they made it to the next landing. He looked at the window. It looked relatively normal.

"Right. Let's jimmy the thing and get inside. My arse is starting to freeze and that isn't one of them figures of speech."

"Slow and steady. Slow and steady."

"Jesus. One go at that ice bucket challenge and now you're a fecking Buddhist monk."

Smithy ignored him and examined the window. "I can't see any wires. The glass looks relatively normal."

"So let's—"

Smithy shushed Bunny and then pulled his 3-in-1 stud finder from his belt and held it to the frame. It beeped immediately.

"Aha."

"What?"

"I can't see any wires, but this is detecting electricity running around the whole frame. This window has some kind of alarm on it."

"Can you get around it?"

Smithy shook his head. "I probably could, but I bet whoever secured this place is banking on someone going for the seemingly easy option. I say we leave it and head for the roof."

Bunny rubbed his hands together. "Jesus, Smithy, you're a cute hoor!"

"I'm a what now?"

. . .

"He's a what now?" asked Zoya.

"It's an Irish phrase," said Dionne. "It means 'smart cookie', I guess. I only know that because I dated an Irish blackjack dealer for a while."

"Really?" said Zoya.

Dionne shifted in her seat, embarrassed. "Another life. If they're heading for the roof, I really am going to wake Sister Dorothy."

"OK."

Dionne got out of the chair. "Oh, and check the other guy is still at the cab."

CHAPTER SIXTEEN

Diller hugged his arms around himself more tightly. He could have sat in the taxi and waited, but he was getting bored. He considered using the walkie-talkie in his pocket to ask for another update, but he guessed Smithy wouldn't appreciate it. After this, he was going to refuse to get involved in stuff unless it meant he was actually involved in stuff. OK, Smithy and Bunny in their own distinct ways were badasses, but Diller had skills too. He knew a lot of useful information. Hell, it was only about twelve hours since he'd cycled in front of a speeding van and executed a flawless Wandinky roll. Well, nearly flawless. While he hadn't admitted it, he had a rather big bruise blossoming up on his ribs. Still, it was pretty cool. Honestly, Diller felt like he really hadn't got enough credit for that.

He jumped as a voice emerged from the alleyway behind him, singing.

"Oh say, can you see..."

Diller turned to look down the alley. He could make out a shape moving back there in the darkness. It was hunched over in a shambling walk. Once he'd gotten over the shock, he had to admit that the voice, a deep baritone, had a certain quality to it.

"By the dawn's early light, what so proudly we hailed at the twilight's…"

The figure slowly emerged, his head down towards the ground as if searching for something. He was an older guy, his hands shoved into the pockets of the ragged hoodie he wore, his jeans held up by rope. The man shuffled slowly as he sang, oblivious to being watched. Only when he reached "and the rockets' red glare" did he look up and notice Diller. He halted. The light caught his yellowing scattershot teeth before he lowered his head and took a step back.

Diller put his hand out. "Hey. It's OK. You're OK. I mean you no harm, sir."

The man eyed him suspiciously but stayed where he was.

"You got a fine singing voice there."

The man gave an uncertain, lopsided half-smile and nodded, still wary but relaxing a bit. "Thanks. Apologies. Didn't mean to disturb."

"Oh, you didn't. You helped warm a cold night."

The man nodded again and shuffled forward once more. Now he'd pulled them out of his pockets, Diller noticed the tremor in the man's hands. He looked to be in his late fifties, his hair thinning but his thick, unkempt beard stretching down to his chest. It was hard to tell if the shake in his body was for medical reasons, through dependency or just from the bitter cold. The man wore only the hoodie and jeans over boots.

"Hey," said Diller, "if you don't mind me saying, aren't you cold?"

The man nodded, still slightly wary. "Yeah, happens I am. Bitter night. Bitter, bitter night. What you doing here?"

Diller smiled. "Oh, I'm just waiting for a friend."

"You drive a cab?" he said, jabbing his chin towards it.

"Nah, it's my friend's."

"Ahh, OK, well…"

Diller rushed forward as the man stumbled, catching him before he fell. "Easy there. Are you OK, sir?"

"Sorry, son. I'm a little dizzy. Took a few shots to the head earlier."

Up close, Diller could see the bruising on the man's skin and the swelling under his right eye that was half closing it.

"Oh dear," said Diller. "If you like, sir, when my friend gets back, we could bring you to the hospital?"

"Nah, no hospital. I got no use for no hospitals."

"Honestly, sir, it'd be no trouble."

The man pulled back slightly and Diller released his arm.

"Why you keep calling me sir? You being sarcastic at me?"

Diller stood back. "No, not at all. I mean no offence. I just don't know your name."

The man looked at him for a long moment, deciding what he thought of this answer. Then he gave a curt nod. "OK then."

"In fact," said Diller, extending his hand to shake, "I'm Diller – Jackson Diller, but everybody just calls me Diller."

Diller stepped back as the man pivoted and snapped off a salute. "Corporal Arnold Williams, 18th Engineers, reporting for duty!" For a moment he stood proud and still, and Diller could see the younger man he'd been. Then the man lowered his hand and the fleeting moment of transformation had passed. He became smaller again before Diller's eyes.

"You see much action, Arnold?"

"Yeah, I've seen plenty. Too much."

Arnold nodded at Diller and started shuffling away. "You have a good night now."

"Hey, Arnold," said Diller. "Seriously, we could take you to a shelter or something. It's really cold tonight."

"Nah," the man said, with a shake of the head. "Gotta keep moving. Can't give 'em a stationary target."

"Well – we should see about getting you a coat, maybe?"

Arnold looked down at the ground again. "Had a coat. Good coat. They stole it. That was what the fight was about. Three on one, sons of bitches."

"Oh," said Diller. "Did you call the police or..."

Diller saw the look in Arnold's eyes and stopped talking. "They don't care none about some old homeless dude."

Diller thought for a second and then took off his duffle coat. "Here, Arnold, you take mine."

Arnold pushed it away. "Nah, man. Nah. You need your coat."

"Honestly, I have a wardrobe full of 'em at home. You take it."

Arnold looked at the coat and Diller could see need triumph over pride. "If you're sure?"

"I insist."

Diller held it out and Arnold put his hands through the sleeves. Once inside, he hugged it to himself. "Damn, that's good. So good."

Diller smiled. "I'm glad you like it."

"Thank you, son."

"You're welcome, Arnold. You stay safe now."

"Much obliged." With a wave, Arnold walked away.

"Hey, Arnold."

He turned to look at Diller again.

"Thank you for your service."

Arnold gave a more casual salute and then turned to continue walking away. As he did so, he began singing quietly to himself again.

"O'er the land of the free and the home of the brave."

Unbeknownst to Diller, thirty feet above him floated a silent observer, beaming pictures back to a room that sat a couple of hundred more feet away. Zoya stared at the screen, alone in the room. She watched as the old man shuffled off and Jackson Diller rubbed his arms up and down himself, trying to keep warm.

When she spoke, it was only to herself. "Dude gave the man his coat."

Then her attention was attracted by a flashing red light. Jackson Diller's two amigos had finally made it to the roof.

CHAPTER SEVENTEEN

Smithy took a long, hard look at the door.

"So," said Bunny, "are we dancing or what?"

Smithy tapped the screwdriver he'd taken out of his belt against his chin. He didn't need it, but he felt the tapping on some level helped him think. "Well, there's no current going through it. I'm not detecting any metal, so it is just wood."

"Right," said Bunny, "so after fifteen minutes of prodding and whatnot, we've discovered the door is definitely a door. Time well spent." They were standing on the roof of the school, and at this height, the sharp winter wind whipped around them.

Smithy turned around, feeling his temper rise. "I'm telling you – this place is not what it seems."

"And I'm telling you, Smithy, you're overthinking it. They have a security door downstairs, sure – that makes sense. This isn't the nicest of areas. But we're up on the roof now and I don't reckon the pigeons are that larcenous."

"And the other stuff?"

"What other stuff? I fell into a dumpster and some cold water splashed on your head."

"It wasn't like that."

"'Twas exactly like that. You're paranoid. I told you about smoking that wacky tobbacy stuff; it makes you go loopy."

Smithy took a deep breath. He would have to try counting to ten again. "OK. I need to do a couple more checks on it and then..."

Bunny shook his head. "Nope. 'Tis cold, my arse is literally freezing and at this rate it'll be dawn soon. Stand back – I'm smashing the fucker in."

"That's a terrible idea."

Bunny walked over to the other side of the roof and did some basic stretching exercises.

"What this needs is the application of a bit of honest-to-God Irish beef."

Smithy held his hands up. "Fine. For the record, I am against this."

Bunny nodded. "Noted. If I get blown to smithereens by a landmine or thrown through a portal into another dimension, feel free to take the piss at my funeral."

"We can't give you a funeral. You're already dead."

"You can never have too many funerals." Bunny waved his hand for Smithy to get out of the way. "Shift over there. Dead man running here."

Smithy shook his head and moved away from the door. "Fine."

"Here we go." Bunny swayed back and forth on his heels, like he was about to go for a world record in the high jump. "One... two... three!"

He had always been a deceptively good athlete, in the sense that, to look at him, you wouldn't have thought he was any kind of athlete at all. His speed and agility had surprised more than a few miscreants in their time. None of them, however, had been as surprised as Bunny was now. Shoulder lowered as he charged forward, he experienced the sickening sensation of the door flying open before him as he was about to make contact. His momentum carried him through, and there was a notable lack of floor on the other side. Such was Bunny's velocity, he didn't even have time to get out an expletive as he fell. He landed about twenty feet below in darkness, a couple of mattresses taking the worst of it.

Smithy ran over to the open door. "Bunny? Are you alright?"

Bunny's voice emerged from the darkness below. "What in the shitting hell just happened?"

"Well, the good news is you didn't damage the door."

"Now is not the time for sarcasm."

"How far down are you?" asked Smithy. "Are you OK? What can you see?"

"To answer your questions in order: feck knows, no broken bones and I can see feck all but... Ah, shite."

"What?"

"I... Yeah, I appear to be behind bars."

"Like... you're in a cage?"

"You could say that."

"Feels like now would be a good time to reassess how crazily paranoid I am."

"Nobody likes a gloater, Smithy. Take the win with dignity."

"Right. There's rope in the back of the cab. I'll get Diller, we'll pull you up and then we're out of here."

"Fine."

Smithy turned around and gave an involuntary yelp. This was initially out of shock, as a tiny UFO appeared to be floating a foot from his face, but it became one of pain as the UFO squirted pepper spray into his eyes.

He stepped back, reflexes trumping the certain knowledge that there was no floor behind him. To his credit, he at least managed to yell an expletive as he fell – a really good one too.

CHAPTER EIGHTEEN

Bunny's fall into the abyss had been broken by the mattresses at the bottom of it. Smithy's fall had been broken by Bunny – specifically his face, which had been looking upwards at the time.

The door above had then slammed shut, leaving them in total darkness.

"Diller. Diller, can you hear me?" said Smithy.

Nothing.

"Nada. I'm guessing something is blocking all signals."

"Yes," said Bunny. "I figured that out from your first six attempts to raise him."

"What in the hell are you getting snappy at me for?"

Bunny took a deep breath. "I'm sorry, Smithy. You're right. This is all my fault. You were helping me and I didn't listen to you. I guess I was so desperate to finally get a lead on finding Simone, I wasn't thinking straight."

Smithy put his walkie-talkie away and sat in the darkness, his back to the bars. "Forget about it. I know how much she means to you and everything you've gone through to find her."

"Yeah," said Bunny. "If only I could convince certain other people of that."

"Not for nothing but... these nuns, I mean seriously, what in the hell? Who has this kind of security?"

Bunny shrugged. "I told you they're not exactly like ordinary nuns but they were never known for their technical prowess. I guess they must've learned some new tricks. You've not got a tissue, have you?"

Smithy opened one of the pockets on his tool belt. "I got wipes."

"Yeah, anything to stem the bleeding."

"You're bleeding?"

"Ah, only a nosebleed."

"Here."

Smithy held out the packet of wipes in the direction of Bunny's voice and, after some wafting, found Bunny's extended hand.

Smithy sat back. "Sorry about... y'know..."

"What?"

"Landing on your face."

"Ah, 'twas my own fault. Standing there like a divvy, all but asking for somebody to land on me. I should be the one apologising – dragging you into this."

"Forget it. Do you think they'll call the cops?"

"I doubt it. They're fierce keen on keeping a low profile. Can't see them filling out a police report."

Smithy felt relieved, not least because he hoped that, somehow, he would not have to explain this to Cheryl. His girlfriend was an understanding woman, but they had held previous discussions about his tendency to make bad decisions.

"So, they'll let us go then," said Smithy. "They're not going to harm us. I mean, they're nuns."

"Jesus. You can tell you've not had the benefits of a Catholic education. Violence isn't off the table, but to be honest, if given the choice of a severe clipping around the earhole or a talking-to, I know which one I'd take."

Smithy chuckled to himself. "You mean *Sister Act* lied to me? Say it isn't so! Oh, not to pile on, but you know how you tried to smash that door in?"

"Yeah?"

"Violent act. I win the bet."

"No fecking way. I didn't even—"

They were interrupted as the lights came on. Both men put their hands to their eyes. Maybe the lights were extremely bright, or maybe it just felt that way after sitting there in the pitch dark.

It turned out their cage was in the middle of a long passage. It looked like two sets of metal bars had thunked down to trap them in an otherwise perfectly harmless hallway. While Smithy thought the light was, overall, an improvement in their situation, it meant he had to look at walls painted a vomit-like shade of green only ever found in institutions.

Bunny watched as Sisters Dorothy and Dionne came around the corner. When they had met earlier, he'd been busy unsuccessfully pleading his case, but Bunny didn't think Dorothy had been in a wheelchair. She was now. An electric one that glided soundlessly towards them.

"Howerya, sisters," said Bunny. "I apologise for dropping in unannounced."

Dorothy stopped a few feet from the bars, with Dionne standing beside her. "That is alright, Mr McGarry. Sadly, we were expecting you."

Bunny pulled the wipe away from his nose and looked at the blood on it. "I'd apologise but I think that'd ring hollow."

"It would. I am afraid you have failed the test as to whether or not we can trust you."

Bunny could feel his anger rise. "A woman is in danger and you're playing silly buggers. Your organisation ain't what it once was." He looked up at Sister Dionne. "Fair play though, you sold it well. That little look over at the filing cabinet? I swallowed the bait right up."

Dionne had the decency to look uncomfortable. Maybe she hadn't liked this little trap idea. Then again, she could be faking him out again.

"I'm a desperate man," said Bunny. "That's all your test proves. Yes, I tried to break in, but like I said, a woman is in danger. If you'd just let me talk to Sister Bernadette, we could straighten this out."

"You are in no position to be making demands," said Dorothy.

"Ask her. Ask Bernadette. I helped her out plenty of times back in Dublin."

"Why is it, then, that she didn't leave you a way to contact her when she left Dublin?"

Bunny looked away. "We didn't leave things on the best of terms. A difference of opinion. Still though, she knows I only want the best for Simone."

"We will pass your message on," said Sister Dorothy. "But can we now assume that you will leave us be?"

"No," said Bunny. "The woman I love is in danger, and come hell or high water, I will find her."

"Why is it you men are always so convinced women need saving? In our experience, they mostly need saving from men."

Bunny held his hands out. "Not from me. I'm a flawed man – Lord knows I've made plenty of mistakes – but go ask Bernadette. Go ask Assumpta. I am on the side of the angels."

Dorothy's eyes widened. "Really? Does that normally involve breaking and entering?"

Bunny shrugged. "Desperate times. I'm fairly sure your lot haven't always stayed inside the lines of legality. Don't forget, I first came into contact with you after you smuggled a wanted murderer out of the country."

"If we let you go, are you going to try this nonsense again?"

Bunny gave a mirthless laugh. "Let me go? I'm refusing to leave until I speak to Bernadette."

The two nuns exchanged a look.

"Fine, have it your way." Dorothy turned her chair to go back the way she'd come.

She stopped as Smithy cleared his throat pointedly. "Excuse me – hi. I'm Smithy, co-conspirator. Firstly, kudos to whoever you have in charge of security." He noticed Dionne's eyes flick up to a smoke alarm on the ceiling, which he guessed wasn't really a smoke alarm. Dionne looked back down and blushed as she realised Smithy had caught her.

He stood and waved at the smoke alarm. "Love your work. Very impressive."

"So," continued Smithy, turning back to Dorothy and Dionne. Before he could speak, a female voice from an unseen speaker filled the hall. "Thanks, dude. Sorry about the pepper spray."

Dorothy looked annoyed at this. She glared at Dionne, who offered a shrug.

"Don't worry about it," said Smithy loudly. "It was actually a pretty mild solution, as those things go."

Dionne looked down at him. "You really do have to question your life choices when you've been pepper sprayed enough times to be able to compare."

Smithy shrugged. "As it happens, my girlfriend makes her own and gives them to people as gifts. I've been a guinea pig a couple of times." He raised his voice again. "Speaking of which – a little tip: she says just a hint of paprika gives an extra kick."

"Ohhh, thanks," said the disembodied voice.

It was Sister Dorothy's turn to cough pointedly, in a way that even the person who wasn't there couldn't miss. "If we're all finished?"

"Sorry," said Smithy, "I just have one question. Why don't you tell Bunny the truth?"

"Excuse me?"

"Look, I'm an interloper here. I've known him for under a year and, well, he's annoying as hell, but he's a good man."

"You'll forgive me, but your reference doesn't carry much weight."

Smithy held his hands up. "Sure, I get that. But my point is, I'm not as close to it as he is. The guy is desperate. He'd do anything to protect this woman, and because he's so desperate, he can't see it."

Dorothy said nothing, just raised her eyebrow, as if to wordlessly say, "And?"

"Every time he says Sister Bernadette's name, you two get a little more tense and a little more peed off. You can see it in your body language. If I was a betting man – and sadly I am – I'd bet the reason that Bunny can't speak to this Sister Bernadette is because you can't speak to her."

The two women said nothing, but they both glared at him. Direct hit. "I'm right, aren't I? She's not dead, because that's a whole other reaction. It's something else."

Dionne looked down at Dorothy, who glared at Smithy for several seconds. If looks could kill, he would have been a smoking pair of sneakers.

When she finally spoke, her voice came out as a monotone. "She is currently... temporarily unaccounted for."

"What?" said Bunny. "The woman must be banging on the door of eighty by now. Has she wandered off or something?"

"No," said Dionne, sounding angry. "She has not. If you must know, she was last seen in Colombia a few weeks ago, and since then she has gone off the radar."

"What was she—?" started Bunny.

"That is none of your business."

Bunny flapped his arms out. "Oh, for God's sake, why didn't you say so? Let me out; I'll go find her."

"Really?" said Dorothy. "Are you familiar with Colombia, Mr McGarry? Are you fluent in Spanish? Do you have contacts in law enforcement down there?"

"No on all three, but at least I'd be looking and not sitting up here on my hole."

Dionne took a step forward, her face clouded with anger. "How dare you!"

Dorothy placed a gentle hand on Dionne's arm.

"Every available member of the order is currently out trying to locate the sister. It is a very difficult situation. The last thing we need is you charging in there like a bull in a china shop."

"But—"

"But nothing, Mr McGarry. If you don't speak Spanish... How is your Latin?"

Bunny gave her a confused look. "'Tis alright. I have a bit from me schooldays."

"One of my colleagues came up with an official Latin motto for our order: *non opus est virum*."

Bunny scratched at his beard. "No man, no cry?"

"There is no need of man. In short, we do not need the assistance of you or any man. Get to the root of most of the world's problems, Mr McGarry, and I guarantee that you will find a man with what he is sure is a good idea."

"Well, you can't stop me looking for Bernadette myself and that's exactly what I'm going to do."

The McGarry stare was a legend among the Dublin criminal fraternity for its ability to transform hard nuts into jelly. Sister Dorothy locked eyes with him, and they stayed looking at each other for a very long time. Smithy was tempted to wave a hand between them just to break the tension, but the odds were good that it would burst into flame.

"Err, Sister," said Dionne, before bending down and whispering something in Dorothy's ear.

Dionne looked at Dorothy expectantly, but the older woman didn't budge. She paused for a moment and then whispered something else in her ear.

Sister Dorothy pursed her lips. "Alright. So be it."

Dionne stood and gave a tight smile. "Great. Seeing as you are so keen to help, Mr McGarry, you can prove yourself by assisting Father Gabriel with his problem. If that goes well, then we will consider helping you – or, hopefully, Sisters Bernadette and Assumpta will be back with us by then."

Bunny scratched at his beard. "Ehm, I don't know what the good padre's problem is."

"Well, you should go and ask him."

"Alright. It's a deal." Bunny moved forward and offered his hand through the bars to shake on it.

Dionne gave him a smile. "That will not be necessary."

Dorothy waved her hand in front of her face. "You stink."

Bunny took a step back. "Yeah, sorry about that." He looked up towards the smoke alarm. "I got slammed into a dumpster."

Sister Dorothy started to move away, Dionne following in her wake.

"Hey," said Bunny, "hang on. How're we supposed to get—?"

He was interrupted by a rope ladder descending from the ceiling and whacking him in the head.

"Ouch. I had to ask."

Bunny looked up. "Right so, let's get out of here."

"Whoa there, cowboy," said Smithy. "I'm going first." He grabbed the ladder and started to climb. "And they are not wrong. You really do reek!"

CHAPTER NINETEEN

As far as anyone else was concerned, the next morning he was back to being the Father Gabriel they expected, only more so. A whirling dervish of energy, determined to get as much done as humanly possible. Never the greatest talker but always a man of action. He explained his mysterious disappearance the day before by saying he'd had to deal with somebody in a lot of trouble. It technically wasn't a lie, apart from the omission that the person in question had been him.

When Rosario came in at 8am she found him in the office, having nearly got the parish's accounts up to date. She looked at him in disbelief. Father Gabriel was a diligent worker, but his one area of weakness was paperwork. But he had been unable to sleep and so he'd thrown himself into the most mind-numbing of tasks he could find.

Once that was done, he rang Danny Clarkson. Danny had his own scaffolding business, and he owed Father Gabriel a massive favour. Gabriel had called in a little bit of it by asking Danny to lend him some scaffolding for a week. Danny had not been keen but he had eventually cracked and sent a couple of guys over who got the scaffolding erected by midday. Now Emilio could get started on his end of the bargain.

Then Gabriel sat down and wrote letters to a half-dozen boys from the parish who were currently over in Horizon Juvenile Center. While he couldn't admit it to himself, he was giving what he thought might be his final words of encouragement. He knew that, for some of them, he had been the only steady influence in their lives, and that him being gone would not be good.

He then visited a few of the older parishioners, all but jogging between visits. That took him up to the time the kids got out of school and training began. He made sure to work his way around the room, checking in on everybody in each session. He pulled Darrell Wilkes aside and had that chat about school and what was going on at home. It was what he expected – Darrell's mom had a new boyfriend, and they were not getting along. They talked it all through, Gabriel giving the kid the chance to vent, and then decided that Darrell would come to the church a couple more evenings a week to get his homework done. Early on, one of the moments of breakthrough for Gabriel had been the realisation that nobody actually listened to most of these kids. Problems left unaired would fester until eventually the kid became the problem, and then it was almost always too late to separate the two. Gabriel may not have been the most natural of talkers, but listening was only about listening.

Having done his rounds, he treated himself to thirty minutes working with Bianca. The girl didn't need encouragement so much as she needed restraint. Having seen real success, she was understandably ravenous for more. It was his job to pump the brakes – remind her that everything would happen in time and that more training wasn't the answer. She had a long career ahead of her and it could take her to a lot of amazing places, but she had to be smart. She nodded and smiled and appeared to listen, but even as he spoke, Gabriel knew that the words were bouncing off that force field that only youth and true passion could create. It was like young love, in its way. Still, that was another lesson he'd learned: even if the words didn't sink in at the time you said them, they would still be there, floating around. When the right time came, all you could hope for was that they'd land and make a difference.

After that, Gabriel stepped outside into another bitterly cold day and surreptitiously slipped around the corner for another meeting. Emilio stood looking up at the scaffolding, looking more emotional than any man should at the sight of rusted metal and dilapidated brickwork. Trey stood grinning beside him, enjoying his friend's excitement.

Father Gabriel put his arm around Emilio's shoulders and looked up at the scaffolding with him. "So, Michelangelo, are we good?"

"This. Is. A... A... Awesome!"

Gabriel grinned. "What it is, is thirty feet of canvas for you to express your talent on. You earned it." Gabriel turned to Trey. "Did they do it like I asked?"

Trey nodded and stepped over to release the rope. A thick white sheet came down, concealing the scaffolding and the wall behind it. "They sure did."

"Excellent," said Gabriel. "You two work behind that, and remember, if anyone asks, it's getting treated for damp and you're painting it for me."

Both boys nodded.

"Rosario has agreed that you can leave the ladder and your other stuff in that big cupboard down at the back of the church – and in the name of all the saints in heaven, do not let a drop of anything hit the church floor on your way through or else that woman will have all three of us hanged, drawn and quartered."

Both boys nodded again.

"Well then," said Gabriel, pushing Emilio gently forward, "get going!"

Emilio took a few steps and went back to gawping.

Trey moved to join him, but Gabriel stepped forward and lowered his voice. "Not so fast, young man – you and I need to have a discussion."

Trey's face fell. "OK, before you say anything—"

"Oh no," interrupted Gabriel, "before you start with excuses, let's get our facts right, shall we? You got into a fight in school?"

"It wasn't much of a fight."

"Trey!"

"He started it."

"Oh, come on now, son – you're a man of words. You telling me you couldn't find some for this situation?"

Trey looked down, his chin tucked into his chest. "He's some rich asshole. He was mouthing off."

"And what do we say?" Gabriel moved closer and picked Trey's chin up, forcing him to look at him. "We are not defined by how others see us. We are defined by how we choose to see ourselves."

Trey nodded.

"Now, how's everything at home?"

Trey shrugged. "It's... y'know."

Gabriel did. Pocket had been one of his earliest members at the gym. He and Trey had been inseparable, the younger brother following the elder like his shadow. Good kids. Then when their mother had passed, Pocket had gone from older sibling to de facto parent and things had changed. Technically, they were in the care of an aunt, but the reality was that it was just them. Pocket had taken command of the situation. They didn't get visits from Family Services anymore, because Pocket had seen to it. Of the many who had either fallen by the wayside or simply fallen, Pocket had been one of the hardest for Gabriel to take. He had tried to talk to him, and still he went over it again and again, wondering if there was something he could have said or done to make it different. The equation, as Pocket had seen it, was simple. There was a lot of evil in these streets and the only way he could make sure Trey got out was to control the evil. And so Pocket gave himself to the gang life on the understanding that Trey would remain untouched. He had been a young man consumed with anger at his mother's passing and love for the little brother she had left in his care, and Gabriel hadn't been able to show him any other options. He knew what Pocket had become, and it broke his heart. Few would understand it as Gabriel did. If the mother had lived, if there had been enough support – if, if, if – the boy could well be heading to college now. He certainly had the brains for it. Instead he was a gangbanger with the dead eyes of a man who has taken life. Father Gabriel knew better than anyone how human lives were products of circumstance. All that separated Pocket from any of the kids sitting in a classroom at NYU was the hand dealt and cruel chance.

Still, despite all of that, they had worked together when Trey's opportunity to gain a scholarship to Waldorf had come up. The boy had talent; the piece he had written describing his mother's last days had brought tears to his eyes when he'd first read it. It wasn't that he used flowery language – it was the raw simplicity of it that cut to the quick. A teacher had submitted it without asking and it had blown away the committee. Then there had been paperwork to complete, which Gabriel had readily agreed to help Pocket with. He had tried to use it as a chance to reach the good kid still inside, but the angry young man had shut that down fast. The love he held for his brother was all that remained of the goofy kid with the quick wit that Gabriel had first met.

"Has Pocket been home much?" asked Gabriel.

He knew the look in Trey's eyes all too well. He'd rather die than give the slightest hint of betrayal of his brother. "Yeah, he's been around. He got Mrs Barnes across the hall making dinners for us and taking care of the apartment. It's as clean as it was when mom was…"

He didn't finish.

"Father Gabriel?" the shout came from Rosario at the back door.

"I'll be with you in a second, Rosario," he replied, before turning back to Trey. "What are you up to tonight?"

"B is coming over. I'm helping her with… something."

Gabriel smiled. "Well, our champion can try to do her own homework for a little while. You can drop over to see me at, say, eight o'clock?"

Trey started to object. "Well, I don't…"

"Eight o'clock, Trey, no excuses."

Trey nodded.

"Father Gabriel!" came the holler from Rosario again.

"I'm in trouble," he said with a smile. "Now, you go help Emilio with his masterpiece."

Trey nodded.

"Father—" Rosario stopped mid-holler when she saw him walk around the corner. "There you are."

"Y'know, Rosario, you could come looking for me rather than shouting."

"I'm a busy woman and you got a guest."

Gabriel stopped walking. "What?"

"Yeah. There's a man outside, and he refuses to leave until he sees you."

"Oh."

It wasn't that he wasn't expecting it; he'd just hoped he'd have more time.

CHAPTER TWENTY

"Oh," said Father Gabriel, letting out the breath he hadn't realised he'd been holding. "It's you."

Bunny looked up from his seat on the church's stone steps. "'Tis indeed. Why? Were you expecting somebody else?"

Father Gabriel stepped out of the church's main doors. "I thought we were finished with..." He stopped talking and reflexively put his hand up to his nose. "What is that smell?"

Bunny shifted. "Sorry. I ended up going for an inadvertent dip in a dumpster last night and the coat hasn't quite recovered. I gave it a wash in the sink, but that wasn't cutting it, so I went to town with a shitload of air freshener. I might just have overdone it."

Father Gabriel nodded. "Yes. I think it is safe to say you did."

Bunny looked up at the sky. "Don't worry. They say it'll rain later – I'm sure that'll take the sting out of it."

"We have some clothes from Goodwill inside. You're welcome to see if you could find a replacement."

"No," said Bunny firmly, "this is my coat."

"As you wish. Which does rather bring us to the question of what you and your coat are doing here?"

Bunny nodded. "Good news. I've come to help you with your

problem."

"What problem?" asked Father Gabriel.

"I'm not exactly sure, but it involved you getting a free ride on the not-so-fun bus yesterday."

Father Gabriel glanced around. "That has been taken care of."

"All due respect, Padre, no it hasn't. I saw your face. You were relieved to see me – that's never a good sign."

Father Gabriel looked around. "Where are your two friends? Have they got better at hiding?"

Bunny shook his head. "Nah, their work here is done."

Bunny had insisted on giving them the remainder of the money he had "acquired" earlier in the week, despite their protestations. He hoped it would be about enough to get Diller a new bike and Smithy's taxi looking like it hadn't just lost a fight with one of those Transformers that somebody kept insisting on making films about.

"The two lads did the job I asked of them. They followed you and got me to the sisters. Admittedly, the route from A to B wasn't quite what I had envisioned, but, y'know, sauce for the goose is sauce for the gander. All worked out fine in the end."

"I am glad. So, I am of no further use to you and you do not need my help."

"I'm afraid 'tis not that simple, Padre. You see, Sister Dorothy has instructed me to prove my worth by assisting you with your issue in order to, how to put it, prove I'm not some kind of shite-sipping gobshite."

Father Gabriel wrinkled his nose. "I am going to guess she didn't put it in quite those terms."

"I'm paraphrasing," admitted Bunny.

"And... wait. You left the sisters when I did yesterday. When did this conversation occur?"

Bunny could feel his face redden. "Well, let's just say I dropped back in for a visit."

It was Father Gabriel's turn to shake his head. "You seem to make rather terrible decisions, Mr McGarry."

"Yeah. To be honest with you, I'm not on a great run of form in that regard. But I mean well."

"I'm sure you do. Still, I do not require any assistance."

"I thought you'd say that," said Bunny.

"And yet you came anyway?"

"I did." He kicked the duffle bag that sat at his feet. "And what's more, I'm not leaving."

Father Gabriel descended the steps to look Bunny straight in the eye – as much as such a thing was possible with a man who could not look himself in the eye in the mirror. This also had the advantage of getting him upwind of the Irishman, which meant his nostrils felt less like they were going to shut down in protest at the olfactory assault. "Listen to me: I do not need your help."

"You did yesterday."

"I would have handled the situation in my own way."

Bunny gave him a funny look. "I'm sure you would have done too. I mean, assuming the two armed men holding you captive hadn't – what was it? Oh yeah, banged their heads and knocked themselves unconscious when the truck stopped suddenly."

Father Gabriel looked around. The very last thing he needed was somebody overhearing this conversation and asking questions. "What exactly is your intention here?" He nodded at the duffle bag. "Are you intending to move in?"

"As I see it," said Bunny, "some bad people are after you. It seems unlikely they will restrain themselves to trying to grab you between the hours of nine and five so, with all due respect to the wonder that is Dolly Parton, I'm not working those hours. Consider me your twenty-four-hour security detail for the foreseeable."

"Absolutely not."

"I won't need to follow you into the shitter or anything. We can have boundaries."

Father Gabriel stood up. "If you come within ten feet of me, I'm calling the police."

"As Bobby Brown once sang, that's your prerogative. I'll just tell them I'm concerned about the nefarious characters trying to kidnap you and you can explain the rest."

Father Gabriel took a couple of deep breaths. "Has anyone ever told you you're intensely annoying?"

"D'ye know, it's never come up before."

Father Gabriel stomped back up the steps. "The answer is no. You are not coming in."

"Fair enough," said Bunny, stretching himself out on the steps, his head resting on his duffle bag. "I'll be right here."

Father Gabriel stopped and looked down. "You can't stay there. It will be bitterly cold tonight. There is talk of some kind of winter vortex hitting us."

It had been on the news. He hadn't seen it, but Rosario had made a point of recounting it to him and they had started making plans to check up on vulnerable parishioners if it was as bad as predicted.

"Don't worry about me, Padre, I've got a nice flask of soup. I'll be grand."

Father Gabriel gave him one last long look before turning away. "Fine. Have it your way."

"Tremendous."

Father Gabriel slammed the door behind him, which earned him an admonishing look from Mrs Wu, who liked to drop in to pray at this time of day.

One hour later.

Rosario had been leaving for the day, but she came back in to find Gabriel. "Father – that man is still outside on the steps."

"Yes," he said, not looking up from doing a very bad job of trying to balance the church's chequebook, "I am aware."

"But," said Rosario, "he says he is waiting to talk to you."

"I understand. I am dealing with the situation."

"OK, only…"

Gabriel looked up. "What?"

"You're not though, are you? He's sitting out there in the cold and you're balancing the chequebook."

"It is a very complicated situation."

"It doesn't seem that—"

"Thank you, Rosario. Have a good night."

Two hours later.

Father Gabriel tried to peek out the front door without being seen.

"Howerya, Padre."

He opened the door fully. The street was dark now but still busy with foot traffic.

"Do you have nowhere else to go?"

"I wouldn't say that so much as I have nowhere else I'm willing to be."

"I already told you, I don't need your help."

Bunny nodded. "You did. And I told you that you were going to get it anyway."

"The answer is no."

"There wasn't a question there."

Two more hours later.

Trey had been and gone. Gabriel had talked to him about the importance of maintaining focus. Ultimately, Pocket's choices were Pocket's choices, and while Trey might want to help him, first and foremost Pocket had to help himself. Though Trey hated to hear it, he had God-given talents, and if he wanted to make the world a better place, he owed it to himself to take the opportunities he had been given. The kid had mostly stayed silent and nodded through the talk. Then, with tears in his eyes, he had spoken of his mother, and it had been Gabriel's turn to shut up and listen. There was nothing new in the conversation, but its purpose was not the imparting of new information – the idea was to re-bandage wounds and reinforce resolve.

Speaking of resolve, Trey had asked about the man lying on the steps outside too. Gabriel had told him to ignore him. The truth was,

Gabriel was failing to do that himself. He stared up at the ceiling of his office, looking for divine inspiration in the damp patches. He checked the weather app on his phone. It was only getting colder. He reluctantly stood up and walked through the church. Mr Noon nodded at him as he passed.

"Oh, Father, there's a man outside who says—"

"Yes," said Gabriel, with a tight smile, "I'm aware of it."

Yet another hour later.

Father Gabriel opened the door again.

"Howerya, Father."

"OK. I will go back to see Sister Dorothy in the morning, and I will explain to her that I don't want your help."

Bunny sat there, visibly shivering. He blew into his woollen gloves. "You can try, but she strikes me as the stubborn sort."

"*Mãe de Deus*! If that isn't the pot calling the kettle black. Look, I will talk to her tomorrow."

"Grand."

"So you'll leave?"

"Nope. I'm staying here to protect you whether you like it or not."

Gabriel stepped out and looked around. "And exactly how will you protect me when you're dead?"

"Well," said Bunny, "that's really more of a metaphysical quandary, Padre, so of the two of us, I'd imagine you're best placed to answer it. Oh, and when I freeze to death, feel free to stick a red suit on me and pretend I'm a statue of Santa Claus – I've got some form in that area."

"I will not give in to emotional blackmail."

"Right," said Bunny. "Well, speaking as the blackmailer and the hostage, that's unfortunate. The poor bastard is going to freeze to death, but I admire your firm stance."

"You are unbelievable."

"And coming from a man who works for an invisible bloke in the sky, that's really saying something."

"Do you think this is funny?"

"'Tis hard to tell. I think whatever bit of my body is used to determine what is and isn't funny has shut down because of the cold. 'Tis like one of them government shutdowns you're always having over here. My unnecessary services are sending the staff home."

"You need to go."

"'Tis funny you should mention that. I don't suppose you'd let me in to use the bog?"

"The what?"

"Sorry. The bathroom."

"No," said Father Gabriel, rather more loudly than he had intended.

Bunny waved at a woman who was walking by with her dog in tow. She looked embarrassed to be caught looking. "I'm not one to be judgey, but this could start to look a smidge unchristian pretty soon, Padre."

"For the love of God, I am pleading with you to leave."

Bunny shook his head. "And for the love of a woman, I'm afraid I can't do that."

One hour and twelve minutes later.

While there had been the tiniest glimmer of hope for it being otherwise, Father Gabriel was not in the least bit surprised to find Bunny lying down on the steps again.

"Howerya, Padre." His teeth were chattering as he spoke. "Don't worry about the needing-the-bog situation. Let's just say that resolved itself."

Father Gabriel looked up at the sky and then back down. It was then that he noticed the figure standing across the street in a puffer jacket with the hood up, watching them intently. "Who is that?"

"What, across the street? Well," said Bunny, jiggling his legs to try to keep the blood flowing, "I'm not on a first-name basis, but I'm pretty sure he's a member of the whatchamacallems – Red Devils gang."

"And why is he watching you?"

"He and his pal noticed me about fifteen minutes ago. I'd imagine his job is to make sure I don't move while the other lad goes and gets his gun."

Father Gabriel gave the man at the far side of the street a long, hard look. "There is no violence around my church; the gangs know this."

"When they shoot me full of holes, you can send them a strongly worded memo."

Father Gabriel pursed his lips and breathed out through his nose. "Alright. Fine. Have you still got that gun?"

"No."

"Do you really think now is a good time to lie to me?"

"I think the bit that decides that is frozen too."

Gabriel said nothing, but he held his hand out.

Bunny looked up at him. "I appreciate the gesture, Padre, but I am not willing to be put out of my misery just yet."

The men locked eyes again. After glancing around, Bunny slipped his hand into his coat pocket and handed him the gun, which Gabriel concealed within his robes.

Bunny laughed in a way that sounded rather unhinged. "Jesus, Father, while I appreciate the sentiment, it feels like you've left me at a distinct disadvantage in the forthcoming gunfight."

"No guns in the church. Ever."

"OK, but..." Bunny looked up, his alarmingly red face filled with hope. "Does that mean...?"

Gabriel nodded. "C'mon, get up."

"I can't."

"I'm letting you inside."

"I know that, but I think my arse may've frozen in place."

Father Gabriel swore to himself and then reached down and grabbed Bunny's arm.

"Count of three," said Bunny. "Actually, make it two, I think yer man's friend might be back."

CHAPTER TWENTY-ONE

Zoya jumped in her chair and let out an involuntary yelp as the door behind her opened.

Sister Dionne stuck her head in. Seeing as Zoya's room doubled up as her workshop, it paid to be cautious when popping in. "Are you alright?"

"Yeah, yeah," said Zoya. "Cooler than a polar bear's icebox. You just startled me."

"Really? I'm literally the only person who ever comes in here. How big a surprise could that have been?"

Zoya felt herself blush. "Sorry, I was zoned out."

"Right. So, anything happening?"

"Absolutely nothing."

"So Father Gabriel hasn't let him in yet?"

"Oh, that? Yeah, yeah, he let him in about twenty minutes ago."

Dionne opened the door fully and stepped inside. "Why? What else are you watching?"

Zoya hit a key and her screens shut off. "Nothing, *nada*, *nyet*. In my head, that was over – the priest sitch – and I'd moved on to other things. I'm like a shark, y'know..."

"You never sleep?"

"I was going for I gotta keep moving forward, but sure, your thing works too."

Dionne nodded and then put her hand on her hip in a sign that Zoya knew meant she was going into "talk" mode. "Are you OK? You're acting a bit... weird?"

Zoya would bet that Dionne had originally constructed that sentence with "even for you" tagged on the end but diplomatically omitted it. People often think weird people don't know they're being weird. They do. What makes weird people weird is they don't care, as they find "normal" to be, in itself, weird.

"Yeah, I'm fine. Too much caffeine maybe, but other than that – cool, cool, cool, Daddyo."

"Right. I have warned you about those awful energy drinks."

Zoya rolled her eyes. "Ten-four, big momma. Roger Wilco."

It had recently dawned on Zoya that she had started saying a lot of stuff ironically in conversation and then it had crept in and just stuck. Now even she wasn't sure where she stopped and the ironic techno-geek image she liked to project started.

"Actually," said Zoya, stilling Sister Dionne's hand as she reached for the door handle, "can I ask... why are we keeping an eye on the priest and the Irish dude? I mean, everybody we have except us is out looking for Bernadette and Assumpta, so if anything happens, it ain't like we could try to intervene."

"Yes, but at least we can keep an eye on them, and things might change. Bernadette might walk through the front door tomorrow."

Zoya tried to smile back encouragingly at this. She didn't pretend to understand much that went on around her – at least not in the human world, which she found confusing at the best of times. Still, she knew some bits of the Bernadette-and-Dionne puzzle, although she couldn't fit them together. The two women seemed to share a great deal of history and didn't appear to like each other at all. In fact, their bickering had been an almost ever-present background noise in the hustle and bustle of the order. Then Bernadette had defied Sister Dorothy and gone off with Assumpta on some mission. That had been weeks ago, and since then there had been no word. It had only dawned on Zoya, in Bernadette's absence, that to argue so much, she and Dionne must have sought out each other's company. It was a big building, after all.

Zoya, as well as monitoring all communication channels, had alerts set up should any of the aliases previously used by Bernadette or Assumpta pop up anywhere. Sister Dorothy had sent the entire order out to try to find them. So far, it was like they had disappeared off the face of the earth. It also appeared to be tearing Dionne apart that she had been forced to stay behind. Dorothy was sick and Dionne, despite her own protestations, had been voted in as their next leader. It surprised Zoya to realise she missed the bickering – the big old place seemed so quiet and empty now with just the three of them in it.

Dionne seemed to want to talk. "So, did you use Birdie to keep an eye on them?"

"The priest and the Irish dude? A bit, but there's a traffic camera that, after a little encouragement, now catches the church, so we got 24/7 eyes on the front. I'll use Birdie to drop in some of my remote cams tomorrow to cover the back."

"Great. If nothing else, those two should make for an excellent reboot of *The Odd Couple* franchise."

"The what now?"

Dionne sighed. "*The Odd Couple*," she repeated. "It was a film? And a TV show, come to think of it." She shook her head. "You really do make me feel old."

"Sorry," said Zoya. "Hey, Dionne? What was it like in the good old days, when the internet ran off steam and the only way you could send an email was to print it out and staple it to a pigeon?"

Sister Dionne laughed and pulled a face as she stepped out of the room. "Don't forget to actually go to sleep at some point, missy."

Zoya saluted. "Aye aye, oh Captain, my captain!"

"And don't pretend to have never heard of *The Odd Couple* one minute and then quote from *Dead Poets Society* the next."

Zoya waved and then pressed the button she had installed under her desk that caused the door to slam. She knew that Sister Dionne would have a big smile on her face as she walked down the hall, laughing to herself. The reason she knew that was because there was a camera covering the hall. As she turned the corner, Dionne waved at it and pulled the face again.

Now she was gone, Zoya could get back to what she had been doing before Dionne had interrupted her – due diligence. She was really just following orders. Three men had tried to break into the school, and the sisters had instructed her to keep an eye on them. Admittedly, she may have gone above and beyond on that score. Through a combination of traffic cameras, licence plate recognition on the cab and judicious use of Birdie, she had followed them home the previous night. She had watched as the Irishman was dropped off at a crummy-looking hotel in Queens before following the cab as it stopped at an all-night valet place, presumably to wash out the smell of the Irishman following his dumpster dive. Then she'd followed them to Hunts Point and watched as the little guy had dropped off Jackson Diller. He had moved quickly and quietly through the streets for a couple of blocks as Birdie flew silently overhead. There were no cameras here. He'd reached a row of houses with boarded-up windows, nipped down an alley and clambered up and into a second-floor window. Any thoughts that he might have been breaking in were dismissed as Birdie's sensitive mic picked up the sound of him checking on someone called Mrs James.

Zoya had spent today doing her job: checking for any communications from the sisters out in the field; running her sweep of media, message boards and law enforcement bulletins to see if anything had turned up that might be of interest to them; and finally, tweaking the school's defences after last night's "live test". After all that, and only after all that, she had checked in on Jackson Diller. The night before, Birdie had laid an egg – which is what Zoya had nicknamed her remote monitoring cameras. There was no mission-critical reason for it; she just found him... interesting. It seemed he had left early in the morning and returned at about 6pm. If that surveillance was in any way justified, Zoya knew the next bit wasn't – although, if pressed, she could pass it off as a 'test'.

Birdie already far exceeded the capabilities of any commercially available drone. Through a combination of clever battery design, solar panel recharging and improved aerodynamic performance, she could stay airborne for longer and travel further distances than anything that wasn't owned by the US military. Zoya had also come up with the idea of using "nests", which meant that Birdie had deposited a few of her own batteries in discreet locations dotted around the city. Her dual-battery design meant that she could swap out a dead one for a live one while maintaining operation. It was a design that would probably be worth a lot of money, but Birdie was Zoya's favourite and she wasn't giving it to anyone.

Still, this test – which she had put into her notes as "Christmas 2.0" – was something different. She had waited for the cover of darkness, as delivering this large a payload would increase Birdie's visibility. She flew in the 500-metre above-ground zone and took a route that avoided tall buildings to minimise the chances of being spotted. She also monitored police bands for any reports of an unexplained flying object.

Acquiring the package itself had been tricky. Normally, she would have had it delivered to one of their dummy addresses and had one of the other sisters pick it up for her, but the only person who could do that was Dionne and she hadn't wanted to bother her. She also hadn't wanted to explain what she was doing. Instead, she bought it herself and then contacted an independent courier to deliver it. The great thing about New York bicycle couriers was that they were all far too busy to care about your weird request – a big enough tip and they'd deliver a baby to a pack of wolves. She'd watched from a distance via Birdie as the Lycra-clad woman dropped the parcel in a remote spot in Pelham Bay Park and then sent the text message confirming receipt. The courier had shaken her head and pedalled off to the next job. Then Birdie had swooped down and retrieved it. Zoya was very pleased with how effectively Birdie's clamps had worked on a non-standard-sized package.

Given her precautions, the only difficulty in the flight had been the unexpected, in the form of a seagull who tried to take an interest.

A blast of AC/DC from the internal speakers had warned it off. She had delivered the package forty-five minutes ago and now she was just waiting. The test was already a success, and she had logged it as such in her records. That was the important thing. That was all that mattered. Everything else was scientifically insignificant.

She watched as Jackson Diller climbed up to the second-floor window and then stopped as he noticed the package sitting there. He looked at it warily and then glanced around. He touched it and moved quickly backwards, as if expecting it to blow up. But curiosity triumphed over caution, and he untied the string that held it together. Then he ripped through the packaging. Zoya zoomed in on his face as he opened it. She watched as the wide smile spread across his lips. Her heart pounded in her chest.

She pulled back as he stood up and put the coat on. It was a puffer coat in classic black with a feather down interior, featuring a double-layer design with a funnel neck, a classic collar, buttons over the front zip fastening, long sleeves, side slit pockets and a quilted exterior. She didn't really know what most of that meant but it had sounded impressive on the website. Jackson Diller seemed to like it. He put it on and hugged it to himself and beamed a smile into the cold winter's night. Unseen, several miles away, Zoya beamed back.

CHAPTER TWENTY-TWO

Father Gabriel handed Bunny the cup of hot cocoa.

"Thanks very much, Father."

Gabriel couldn't quite bring himself to say the words "you're welcome". Bunny wasn't. For better or worse, it appeared that he was stuck with the Irishman, which, given his current situation, was the last thing he needed. He would try to make time to go talk to the sisters tomorrow and see if he could resolve the matter. Given that Sister Dorothy had been furious with him for breaching protocol and bringing McGarry to see them in the first place, he was not optimistic. And there was no dissuading the man himself from following what he considered to be his orders.

They were in the storeroom that formed the main part of the basement. Broken furniture, boxes of old hymn books and trash bags full of donated clothing filled most of the space. Bunny sat on a battered armchair which had been there since before Gabriel's time. Normally the place had a damp, musty smell, but the Irishman's coat was dominating in that area – even from across the room.

"I see you found dry clothes that fit you?"

Bunny nodded. "Yes. Thanks, Padre. There's a load of stuff over there in those orange bags that seems to be my exact size."

"I see. Mrs Washington donated those. They belonged to her former husband."

"Bitter divorce?"

"Terminal heart attack," said Gabriel, blessing himself.

Bunny looked down at the hooded Yankees sweatshirt he was now wearing. "Jesus, if that isn't a wake-up call to lose a bit of weight, I don't know what is."

"Indeed. Very sobering." A thought struck Gabriel and he held his hand out. "Speaking of which, no alcohol of any kind is allowed in the church."

"What! It's been a while, but is the blood of Christ not represented by wine anymore?"

"That may be the case," said Gabriel, "but we do not have a policy of bring your own."

Bunny looked up at him, his eyes filled with outrage. "Technically, this room isn't in the church, is it? 'Tis more below the church when you think about it."

Gabriel said nothing, he just looked pointedly at his extended hand.

Bunny pulled a flask from the back pocket of a dead man's jeans and handed it over with a petulant look on his face. "A nip against the cold never hurt anybody."

Gabriel opened the flask and took a smell before pulling his head back in revulsion.

"What is that?"

"Poteen."

"It smells like gasoline."

"Now let's not be insulting to a national treasure. That's made out of sugar beet and malted barley, and aged in virgin Irish oak."

"Well, no drinking on church grounds."

Bunny shook his head in disgust. "Is that a new commandment? Because I've drunk on church grounds several times in the past."

"And what did the priests think of that?"

"Who d'ye think I was drinking with?"

Gabriel put the flask into the pocket of his robes. "It is not a Church rule, but it is a rule in this church."

Bunny took a gulp of cocoa. "I don't suppose you'd consider letting me use a drop of it to liven up this cocoa?"

"No."

Bunny mumbled over the mug, which he cupped in two hands. "Hospitality ain't what it once was."

"You are not a guest. You are an imposed inconvenience."

"I will quote that in my TripAdvisor review. You can expect a harsh rating."

Gabriel pointed over at the corner. "There are a few mattresses over there, from when we provided shelter from the 2016 blizzard, and there's bedding in the closet." He indicated the door at the far end of the room. "Through there are my private quarters, with the emphasis on private. Please respect that."

"Sure – I won't touch any of *your* stuff. Did I mention the EU has given poteen geographically indicative status?"

Gabriel looked down at him and puffed out his cheeks. "I don't know what any of the words you just said mean."

"It's like champagne. Something can only be called that if it comes from the right region. It also means that taking it off an Irishman is basically a hate crime."

"Do you think you might have a problem with alcohol, Mr McGarry?"

"Well, I do now." Bunny slurped at his cocoa. "And seeing as we'll be spending a lot of time together, you might as well start calling me Bunny."

"No, I won't be doing that. In fact, seeing as you are so insistent on staying, you will be Brother McGarry, a visiting Franciscan monk."

Bunny looked up in surprise. "How in the fecking hell am I going to pull that off?"

"Firstly, by not speaking like that. There will be no swearing. I have spare robes that will probably fit you from when Brother Dominic stayed."

"Let me guess, did he have a heart attack too?"

"No. A stroke."

"Oh."

"They did say it was brought about by his weight issues."

Bunny nodded. "I had to ask."

"In fact, let me lay out the rules specifically. While you are 'staying' here, you will keep a low profile. There will be no drinking, no swearing, no smoking—"

Bunny looked offended. "Who said I smoked?"

"I just assumed you had all the bad habits. There will also be no womanising."

"Shame. I thought the robe and sandals would really help me pull the chicks."

"No sarcasm."

"You show me the bit in the Bible that bans sarcasm? The good Lord gave us freedom of expression. Sarcasm is a legitimate form of communication. You can't take that away from me."

Gabriel shrugged. He was aware he was just being childish now. "OK. But the other things, those are sacrosanct. I have worked too hard to establish myself here. I want you to be respectful of where you are and the work we do."

"Not a problem at all. I am happy to help any way I can."

"Yes... And most importantly of all – no violence."

"I'm not a violent man."

Gabriel took a half step back, slightly surprised by the ferocity of his tone.

Bunny looked down into his near empty cup of cocoa as if embarrassed by his own response. "I only ever use it when the situation requires it."

"Do you remember the chat we had when we first met?"

Bunny glared up at Gabriel. "I forget the rules – are priests normally allowed to throw confessions back into somebody's face?"

Gabriel bit his lip and looked up at the ceiling. Then he took a deep breath and returned his gaze to Bunny. "I apologise, that was inappropriate of me. It will not happen again."

Bunny nodded, looking at least mollified. "Fair enough."

"I will take your coat."

"You're not throwing that coat away," snapped Bunny.

"No. But I will wash it."

"Oh. Right. Thanks."

Bunny stretched his back out and rolled his head from side to side. "So, when are we going to talk about the other thing?"

"What other thing?"

"Who is after you and why?"

"That's none of your affair."

"'Tis literally the reason I'm here."

"No, no, it isn't. You are here because you refused to leave, and I could not let your stubbornness result in you freezing to death on the steps of my church. Now come on, follow me. We're going to the gym."

Bunny put his mug down and clapped his hands together. "Alright. Now you're talking. If I win, I get my poteen back."

"We are not going to box, *Brother* McGarry. But you will be taking a much-needed shower."

CHAPTER TWENTY-THREE

Bunny put the mop back into the bucket and looked down at the floor. He was pretty sure this was the first time in a long time, possibly ever, that the storeroom of St Theresa's had been mopped. The basement had a permanent smell of damp that, instead of being removed by the disinfectant, now seemed to form a heady cocktail with it. Over in the corner, the boiler made all manner of clicking and whirring noises and then occasionally juddered in a disturbing manner. There were oil stains on the floor, but despite his best efforts, Bunny could not find one that resembled the face of Jesus. He'd really hoped to proclaim a miracle and take the rest of the day off.

His limbs ached, but other than that, Bunny was showing no ill effects from having spent a large part of the previous night on the church steps. That morning, Father Gabriel had brought him a bowl of warm porridge, and once he had established that Bunny was fully fit, had set him to work. Bunny was aware he was being punished, but he was fine with it. He had to keep an eye on Father Gabriel, and once the padre had promised not to leave the church grounds without him, Bunny was more than happy to take his punishment.

Bunny had known a fair few priests in his time – even been friendly with some of them. Gabriel, however, was something different. There was a touch of the zealot about him, even for the Franciscans, who were traditionally at the more ardent end of the scale. Gabriel had been up at 5am and working. Bunny knew his type – the fella had the relentless motor of a little guy who could spend the first fifteen minutes of a game getting run over by his opponent only to grind the guy down by the end. Bunny could respect that. However, Gabriel also seemed to have the sense of humour of a bulldog who'd been booted in the knackers. Bunny had tried to lighten him up a bit with a splash of verbal jousting, but there was simply no craic to the man. No swearing, no drinking, no violence – what kind of rules were they? Did he think Bunny was some primal animal who couldn't control himself? Having said that, he'd fecking kill someone for a decent pint right about now.

The one upside of his new religious rebirth as "Brother McGarry" was that he enjoyed the robes. Sure, based as they were on brown sackcloth, they may not set pulses racing at New York Fashion Week, but they were very freeing. Bunny enjoyed the airflow downstairs immensely. He wondered, when exactly did trousers become the one and only option for men? It felt like they were really missing a trick here. He was less keen on the sandals, not least as it'd meant having to cut his toenails, but the robe definitely had something.

He had tried to engage Gabriel in a discussion on the propriety of going commando, but the prissy little sod had just given him a stern "no" and walked out. While Bunny was none the wiser as to who was after the priest, or why, he was beginning to wonder if it was somehow related to his deficient interpersonal skills. He'd had a nose around Gabriel's room – although the word "cell" seemed more appropriate. He had a bed with the hardest mattress known to man, a chest of drawers containing a spare set of robes, some underwear, one set of street clothes and two Bibles. There was a total lack of any personal mementos. The man didn't seem to have been born. It was like they'd made him by melting down some old priests and pouring them into a younger man's body.

"Brother McGarry!"

Bunny nearly dropped the mop as he turned to find Gabriel standing behind him. "Shitting hell!"

"Language!"

"Sorry, Padre."

"What exactly happened between you and Los Diablos Rojos?"

"Ah, nothing much. We had a discussion about copyright infringement. I wouldn't worry about it."

"Really?" said Gabriel. "Because their leader and two of his goons are outside my church, demanding to speak to you."

Bunny propped the mop up against the wall. "Don't worry, I'll sort it."

Gabriel stepped in front of him, placing his hand on Bunny's chest. "No, you will not. Remember our agreement, *Brother* McGarry – no violence."

CHAPTER TWENTY-FOUR

Gabriel stood inside the large double doors of the church and looked at Bunny. "Whatever happens, stay here."

"But—"

"No buts. I will handle this." Gabriel pointed over to the rack of yellow beeswax prayer candles to the right of the door. "If you want to do something useful, you can grab a scraper and take the wax from those up off the floor."

"You're going out to handle three gang members and I will be scraping wax? This feels like we're not using our resources to maximum efficiency, Padre."

Gabriel grabbed Bunny's arm and guided him towards the candles. "Let us be honest, *Brother* – you have not proven yourself to be a resource. You are currently more of a liability. If you step outside this door, our deal is over. Are we clear?"

Bunny turned his eyes to heaven and then begrudgingly nodded. "Fine."

Gabriel paused with his hand on the door handle. He had to remain calm. Calm could defuse most situations; one of the books he read had said that. He couldn't remember which one.

Gabriel took a deep breath and then opened the door.

"Hello, how may I help you?"

Three men stood there, looking impatient. To the left stood a man wearing a coat that identified him as the one who had watched them from across the street the night before. To the right stood a bigger guy with the hood of his coat up. Gabriel recognised neither of them, but he knew the man in the centre, more by reputation than through any other means. He wore a designer suit under an expensive-looking coat, and shoes you could probably see your reflection in. While the others scowled, he wore a bright smile and a relaxed demeanour. "Father, we are sorry to disturb you. My name is Alfonso Santana."

"I know who you are. You run Los Diablos Rojos."

Santana nodded. "Good. I am glad to see my PR team are doing their job." He gave Gabriel a large smile, which was not returned. "My two associates here are Marcus and Sergio. It appears they had an... unfortunate run-in with a gentleman last week. They inform me this individual entered your church last night and has yet to leave."

"What does this man look like?"

Santana turned his head towards the man standing to the left, who he had identified as Sergio. "He was an older guy, big dude – had a beard."

"Yeah," chimed in Marcus, "and he had a fucked-up eye."

Santana turned his head sharply in the other direction, giving an admonishing look.

"Sorry, but he does."

Father Gabriel nodded. "I see. I believe you are referring to Brother McGarry."

"Excuse me?" said Santana, surprised. "This gentleman is a priest?"

"No, not all Franciscans are priests. I am, but he is a brother in our order, having taken a vow of poverty, chastity and obedience."

Santana looked at each of his colleagues in turn. Both men squirmed with embarrassment under his glare.

"He wasn't dressed like no priest!"

"Yes," said Gabriel. "Occasionally when we travel, we have to wear civilian clothes." This was not the case, but Gabriel was confident these men would not be au fait with the intricacies of Franciscan travel practices.

Santana shook his head in disbelief and turned back to Gabriel. "Well, it appears your brother got into a violent altercation with my two associates here."

"That is regrettable."

"It is."

"Yes," said Gabriel. "It is a sad indictment of the lawlessness of Coopersville that a man of God cannot walk the streets without being set upon."

"They claim it happened the other way around."

Gabriel looked at each of the men in turn. "Really? They claim a Franciscan brother, an older gentleman who has taken religious vows, attacked them unprovoked? Does that strike you as likely, Mr Santana?"

"Well, why don't you send him out and we can discuss it?"

"No," said Gabriel, "I will not be doing that. Brother McGarry was very shaken up by the experience."

"Really?" said Santana. "Because, leaving aside what started this sorry affair, it seems your associate acquired a quantity of money from these two, and a... package."

Father Gabriel nodded. "I know nothing about that, although we did receive a large anonymous donation to the church's roof repair fund recently. Perhaps somebody found this money you mention on the street?"

Santana's smile cracked. "It's still my money."

"I'm afraid we have no way of knowing that."

"And the... other matter?"

"As a prominent local businessman, Mr Santana, I am sure you are all too well aware of the scourge drugs are to our community. I know that, personally, if I found such substances, if that is what this was, I would immediately destroy it, or hand it in to the police."

Santana moved forward and lowered his voice. "I'm done playing, Father. Send the man out or we go in and get him."

Gabriel took a deep breath. "I am aware of what you deal in, Mr

Santana. I don't pretend to understand how such matters work, but I do have one question for you: how will it look if it gets around that two of your men not only attacked but were bested by a frail old Franciscan brother?"

"Frail!" started Marcus, but a slight turn of Santana's head silenced him.

"I would imagine something like that would involve a great loss of face," said Gabriel, "which would be bad for business, would it not?"

"Are you threatening me, Father?"

Gabriel forced himself to maintain eye contact. "No, Mr Santana. I believe you were threatening me."

Sergio tapped Santana on the shoulder and pointed at the police patrol car that had just pulled up across the street. Gabriel was relieved; he had told Rosario to call them.

"And," Gabriel continued, "if anything were to happen to Brother McGarry or this church, imagine how badly that would play in the press?"

"Who gives a fuck?" said Marcus.

Gabriel looked directly at him. "Mr Santana does, because some things get big headlines, and big headlines mean that even the city fathers, who we all know are shamefully content to ignore the crime epidemic in Coopersville, will not ignore that. There would be demands for action, task forces, crackdowns. I would imagine such a state of affairs would be very bad for business. But I could be wrong. I have the number of the journalist who gave us a big write-up in *The New York Times* recently; I could ring and ask her, if you like?"

The two patrolmen had now exited their car and were crossing the street, their hands nervously resting on the handles of their holstered service revolvers.

Santana gave a big smile and laughed. "I like you, Father. You're quite a man."

"I can't say the same."

"Your friend, though – he can't stay in there forever, and hey, accidents happen."

"Father," said one of the patrolmen, "is everything alright?"

Santana turned, his hands held mockingly in the air. "Everything is fine, officers. I was just enquiring about making an ostentatious contribution to the church, but thankfully it seems my money is not needed."

Santana and his two men walked down the steps, Santana keeping his eyes fixed on Gabriel the whole time. "We'll be seeing you real soon, Father."

Father Gabriel made the sign of the cross. "I hope the good Lord shows you the error of your ways."

Santana turned away, "Likewise, Father. Likewise."

CHAPTER TWENTY-FIVE

Trey heard the key turn in the lock and was out of bed before the front door opened. He stood in his bedroom doorway and watched as the figure tried to sneak in unheard.

"Hey, Pocket."

Pocket flinched and then relaxed, favouring his brother with a smile. "What's up, little bro? You should be asleep."

"Yeah, I was," lied Trey. "You know me – always a light sleeper."

"True dat." Pocket came over and gave him a hug. Trey returned it, holding it a second longer than perhaps his brother had wanted. He could smell something sweet and sickly on Pocket's breath.

They disengaged.

"You want something to eat?" asked Trey. "We got plenty of meals in the refrigerator. Mrs Barnes keeps bringing 'em."

"Yeah, I'll grab something."

"Let me get it." Trey pushed by him. "It's no trouble. You don't know which is which. Let me..."

Trey hurried into the kitchen and opened the refrigerator. "Let me see: we got linguine, we got rice and beans with some kind of fish thing or we got some of them chicken enchiladas with roasted tomatillo chilli salsa."

Trey looked back into the living room where Pocket was now sitting on the couch, looking for the TV remote. "Yeah, whatever's easy."

"Or," said Trey, waiting for his brother to look in his direction, "we got mac and cheese?"

Years fell away and the two brothers smiled at each other. It would drive their mother to distraction that, whatever she cooked – and the woman could cook – Pocket was always happiest with mac and cheese.

Pocket clapped his hands softly together. "Ha, you know me so well, bro."

"Mac and cheese coming up. Juice too?"

Pocket nodded.

Trey threw the dish into the microwave, turned it on and filled two glasses with juice.

"Hey," said Pocket, "you catch the Knicks result?"

"Yeah," replied Trey, "nothing good."

"Damn."

"They're taking a run at the record for worst losing streak in team history."

The two boys had been Knicks fans since before Trey could walk – literally. There was a picture on the wall of a toddler Trey wearing his older brother's Knicks cap, far too big for him.

"Hey though," said Trey, rushing into the room with excitement. "Did you…?"

Pocket, thinking his brother was busy, was sniffing something from a tiny silver spoon. Trey knew enough to know what it was, but he turned around, trying to not be seen seeing. "Did you hear? They're saying we might sign Kevin Durant?"

Pocket wiped a finger under his nose and shoved something quickly into the pocket of his jacket. "For real? Man, that'd be something."

"Right?" agreed Trey. "Maybe we could go catch a game soon? See how bad they suck."

"Yeah," said Pocket. "Totally."

"They're at home this weekend."

"Oh, yeah, just – now ain't a great time for me."

"Sure," said Trey, brushing it off. "Whatever."

"Soon though. We definitely gonna do that."

"Cool."

Pocket drummed his fingers on his knees, looking oddly out of place in his own home. "So, how's school?"

"Yeah, y'know, OK. Mostly."

Pocket raised an eyebrow. "Mostly?"

Trey waved it away. "Don't worry about it. Some of these rich kids are a little much."

"Don't let them give you no shit, little brother. You want, I can roll up and..."

"No, no," interjected Trey. "Honestly, it's fine. Are you kidding? I can handle that with my eyes closed. It's just funny is all. I'm from Coopersville – no Brad from the Hamptons is gonna bother me."

Pocket nodded. "Represent. OK, then. Hey, you seen any more of that Marlon fool?"

"Yeah, we cool."

Marlon had found him the day before and issued a grovelling apology for his behaviour. Trey hadn't failed to notice that three fingers of his left hand were held in place by a bandage wrapped around a splint. There had been an alarming desperation in his tone.

The microwave pinged and Trey placed the plate of mac and cheese on a tray with some cutlery and a napkin.

Pocket threw his coat off and retook his seat, MTV now playing low on the TV in the background. Trey placed the tray on his knee and sat down beside him.

"Oh yeah. Mac and cheese!"

"Line up, ladies, because we aim to please!" finished Trey with a giggle.

"Mac and Cheese" had been their name when the two brothers, all of nine and twelve at the time, had decided they were what the rap world was waiting for. Pocket laughed uproariously and threw an arm around his baby brother. "I forgot all about that! We were something."

"Mom thought we were good."

Pocket shovelled macaroni into his mouth. "Bless her, the woman was a saint, but she didn't know music!"

"Oh, come on now," said Trey, laughing, "those moves we had were tight!"

They both did their head nod routine in perfect unison, two to the left, two to the right, followed by a shoulder roll left and a slide right.

Then they both fell into fits of laughter again, and Pocket grabbed his plate to stop it crashing to the floor.

"I still don't know why our routine was all upper body."

"Sure you do," said Trey. "Mom wouldn't let us move the table, so we couldn't do any fancy footwork."

Pocket chuckled away to himself again as he returned to his meal. "That's right. It was just after we decided we were gonna be wrestlers and you broke her chair."

"Me?" said Trey. "You were the one who told me to go up top and drop the elbow on you."

"Well, I had to find some way to make it believable that you could take me."

Trey slapped his brother's shoulder. "I could take you easy. You're big and slow."

"That right?"

There was a moment's pause before the brothers launched into each other, the plate going flying for real this time. Trey managed to get on top and wrap an arm around Pocket's neck. His big brother picked him up and play-slammed him back into the couch, but Trey maintained his grip. "Yeah. Can you smell what the Mac is cooking!"

Pocket waved his arms around, making a show of it but letting his little brother win, same as he always did. "I was Mac; you were Cheese!"

"Never," said Trey. "I'm not having the whack name."

A couple of bars of a song Trey didn't recognise issued from Pocket's jacket. "Let me up."

"Never," said Trey with a giggle. "Not until you admit I'm Mac!"

Pocket's voice dropped. "I ain't playing." He put his hands up and broke Trey's hold effortlessly, before hustling to the coat stand and pulling his phone out. "Yeah?"

Trey watched him from the couch. Watched his body language change.

"I'll be right there."

Trey must have done a bad job of hiding his reaction, as Pocket grimaced when he looked at him. "I gotta go."

"Sure."

"It's... important."

"Cool."

Pocket put his coat back on.

Trey hesitated, and then... "Are you going to be back Saturday?"

"I don't know. Things are a little... intense right now."

"OK, only—"

Annoyance flashed in Pocket's eyes. "I'll try. You a big boy now, Trey, don't be relying on me."

"Alright," said Trey. "Whatever."

Pocket moved towards the door. "You good for money?" He turned when Trey said nothing. "Are you?"

"Yes!" said Trey, picking the plate up off the carpet. The cheese was going to leave a stain.

"Alright then."

Pocket opened the door.

"It's her anniversary."

Pocket froze.

"Saturday. It's three years."

Pocket lowered his head and stood there for a long moment. "January 11th, of course it is."

Trey stood there, the plate in his hand. "I thought we could go down to the graveyard."

Pocket nodded.

"You still haven't been, have you?"

"Ain't my thing."

"OK."

Pocket looked back over his shoulder. "We could do something else though?"

"That'd be cool."

"Alright. I'll holler at you."

Pocket took a step out and was about to close the door when he stopped. He didn't look back as he spoke. "You know... anything happens to me, you're taken care of. I made sure."

Trey didn't know what to say to that. His mouth felt suddenly dry. "Something gonna happen to you?"

"Nah, man – I just... You'll be OK."

"I'll have nobody. Money can't buy that back."

Pocket stood there for so long that Trey wondered if he would speak at all. When he did, his voice came out soft and low. "Life ain't easy, ain't fair. You got the golden ticket though. You take your smarts and go out there and do your thing. You leave Coopersville and you never look back."

"I like it here."

Pocket turned now, anger in his eyes. "No, you don't – you just don't know anything else. Soon as school is done, you get out and never look back. Ain't nothing here for you but pain. Find something better."

"Maybe there isn't somewhere better."

Pocket grabbed the door. "That better not be true."

He closed the door and Trey stood there, the plate in his hand, looking at the space where his brother had been.

CHAPTER TWENTY-SIX

Father Gabriel felt his eyelids sag and then jerked himself awake, experiencing an awful moment of social awkwardness as he wondered just how noticeable it had been. They were sitting in the curtained-off area on the balcony of the church, which served as a meeting room due to the lack of any other usable space that could fit more than two people.

Mr Grassam, who worked for the diocese, was rambling on and appeared unaware of Father Gabriel's momentary dip. In Father Gabriel's defence, the man was a terrible droner. He was every unfair cliché of accountants wrapped up into one dandruff-coated stereotype. Gabriel had noticed that if you listened to the first two sentences of what he said, regardless of how long he spoke, you got all the relevant information. What's more, if you somehow missed that, he would helpfully recap in the last two sentences before he finally stopped speaking. The headline here was that the church didn't have enough money. They had nothing saved and little coming in. None of this was news to Father Gabriel. While he feigned concern and tried to nod in all the right places, his attitude was that there were things that needed to be done – in Coopersville the list was pretty much infinite – and what money there was should be spent immediately and then more found.

Sitting next to Mr Grassam was Lorraine Wynns, the poor woman who was primarily concerned with the "finding more" part of the equation. Father Gabriel had all the time in the world for her, and she was, happily, the case that disproved every accountancy stereotype. She was a volunteer who had moved across from a Manhattan parish when Coopersville had nobody with any financial expertise to help them. She had met Father Gabriel at a diocese meeting two years ago. He had summoned up all his courage and recruited her over a slice of apple pie and a cup of near undrinkable coffee the following week. The poor woman had probably said yes just to stop the garbled fifteen-minute speech he had launched into. She had been giving one night a week to a well-to-do area, until his desperate pleas had convinced her of how much someone with her skill set would mean to St Theresa's parish. Now, she worked part-time, and had her husband, her neighbour and two people she played tennis with trying to help out too. Father Gabriel had made sure to invite the Wynns family to Bianca's fight, and he had sought them out afterwards. They got so few victories and he wanted them to taste that one. It had been a wonderful, if small, moment.

Lorraine, showing greater resolve than he, stayed focused on Mr Grassam as he spoke and was even taking copious notes, which meant she hadn't noticed Father Gabriel's "long blink" either. Rosario, despite also taking notes, clearly had noticed Father Gabriel's dip. She was looking directly at him. Despite having known her for so long, he couldn't say with any certainty how much her expression was sincere admonishment and how much was playful mockery. The woman still scared him a little, which, given his life up until this point, was really quite something.

Gabriel tried to tune back into Mr Grassam, who he hoped might be coming in for a landing soon.

"... having already exceeded this year's budget, and given the overrun incurred last year, we cannot allow this fiscally irresponsible trend to continue. While we no doubt all appreciate the good work done, we must also appreciate sound financial planning—"

Mr Grassam was interrupted by a roar of approval which was not in support of the concept of sound financial planning. Four heads turned toward the window, which faced onto the gym.

"What is that?"

Father Gabriel felt himself redden as he turned back. "Apologies, Roger, it appears that the evening training session is a little more lively than normal."

He and Rosario shared a look. The session was under the control of Brother McGarry – or Bunny, as now everyone but Gabriel referred to him. It had been eight days since Gabriel had introduced him into the running of the church, and it had been disruptive, although not in the way Gabriel had expected. Bunny was everything that Gabriel was not. While Gabriel was all about quiet asides and preaching self-control and discipline, Bunny was the fun uncle who came in and shook the place up. He had won over the kids in less time than Gabriel would have believed possible. They couldn't understand half of what he said, but they responded to his energy. He'd done in a matter of days what it had taken Gabriel years to achieve. Even Rosario – who had reacted firstly with disbelief upon learning that the smelly drunk on the steps was apparently a visiting Franciscan brother, and secondly with horror when Gabriel had explained that he would be staying for a while – had been won over. Bunny had managed to charm the fearsome woman. She feigned outrage at his line in flirtatious banter – Bunny regularly told her that she was in danger of stealing him away from his vocation with her "fiery Latin loveliness" – but Gabriel noticed that she regularly sought out the Irishman's company. So did everyone, to be fair. Bunny was undeniably popular and, Gabriel had to admit, he had proven himself invaluable. He had boxed in his youth and had helped a lot with training. He had even managed to get Darrell Wilkes to understand that his feet were for more than standing on. Bunny had refereed the light sparring rounds they held between boxers of similar stature on Wednesdays and Saturdays and he had, in all honesty, done a better job than Gabriel of making it fun. And his running commentaries had been enjoyable enough that kids had hung around to watch.

"To your point, Roger," said Lorraine Wynns, getting the meeting back on track, "rest assured we are fully aware that we need to secure additional funding, both for the operational budget and for the longer-term desire to build facilities here that are fit for purpose."

Gabriel wasn't jealous of Bunny. He was... It was just that... Well, OK, maybe he was a little jealous. He had started to feel like the warm-up man who had thought he was doing OK until the star turned up. Gabriel, with the help of people like Rosario and Lorraine, had built this place up into something special. He had worked his fingers to the bone and begged and borrowed to make a run-down house into, well, a run-down gym. One that hummed with activity most of the day. Still, with the arrival of Brother Bunny, it had more energy flowing through it. He was probably being oversensitive. He had slept even less than normal since last week, waiting for the next move, which was surely coming. Abraham was not the kind of man to make one attempt at something and leave it at that. He was being toyed with. All Gabriel could do was wait.

He noticed that nobody in the room was talking and that, worse yet, everyone was looking at him. This felt like that recurring dream where he was giving a sermon only to discover he was doing so naked. He gave an awkward smile. "Absolutely." It seemed as safe a statement as possible in the circumstances. He caught a hint of an eye roll from Rosario.

"What the father means to say," she began, "is that thanks to our recent media coverage" – Rosario said it with obvious delight at having been proven right – "we have a gentleman from The Regency, a Wall Street charitable fund, coming in to meet with him this evening. They are looking for New York projects to offer significant long-term backing to, and they have been very impressed by what they have heard about our work here."

"Yes," said Gabriel, picking up the baton he had dropped. "Rosario has spoken to the gentleman, and God willing, this might be exactly the kind of support we were hoping for." Rosario and Lorraine had been positively giddy with excitement. Even Gabriel had allowed himself to hope. Whatever was coming, maybe he could leave here knowing that all he had worked for could be carried on. That truly would be something.

All four heads turned as there was another loud roar from the direction of the gym.

Gabriel stood up. "Excuse me for a moment, please. I'm just going to check on that. Make sure nobody is getting carried away."

Before Rosario could protest, Gabriel was through the curtain and hopping quickly down the stairs. Mrs Wu gave him a disapproving look as he walked through the church, towards the cheering which had now been supplemented with rhythmic clapping.

Trey was sitting up on the ropes in the corner of the ring, cupping his hands around his mouth to be heard over the clamour of the crowd.

"In the red corner, the punching pride of Coopersville, the lay-me-out lady, the knockdown queen, the one and only Bianca, the New York state champ-ee-on!"

This was met with a roar from the crowd.

"And in the blue corner, from Ireland in the United Kingdom..."

Bunny, still wearing his brown robes, turned around from the comically OTT stretching exercises he was engaged in, looking genuinely outraged. "What in da feck are you talking 'bout? Ireland is not part of the UK! What do they teach you at that fancy-arsed school?"

Trey gave Bunny a grin, having correctly guessed exactly how to irritate him.

"Why I oughta..." Bunny backed into Darrell Wilkes, who was acting as his corner man, and pretended that he was holding him back while the crowd laughed.

"Seconds out," hollered Trey. "Round one! Ding ding!"

Bianca moved to the centre of the ring, laughing as Bunny – hamming it up like a two-bit wrestling heel – ran forward and bounced off one set of ropes and then the other. She stood in her perfect defensive stance as Bunny clambered up on the second turnbuckle in his corner and hollered, "I must be the greatest!" This was met with a good-natured mix of cheers and boos from the crowd.

Bunny hopped back down onto the canvas and moved towards Bianca, arms extended and crooked at the elbow, his fists rolling in front of him like the technique seen in black-and-white photos when boxing appeared to solely be the pursuit of bald men with handlebar moustaches. "Put 'em up, put 'em up!" he lisped, before lowering his gloves and sticking his chin out in an Ali-like taunt, pulling his head back in just in time to avoid a lightning jab from Bianca.

"Ye can't touch me," he shouted, "I'm too beautiful! I must be—"

He was interrupted by a flurry of punches from Bianca, getting his hands up just in time to avoid a direct hit but still being sent backwards by the barrage.

"BROTHER MCGARRY!"

The room turned as one to see Father Gabriel standing in the doorway, his face a picture of rage. Bunny dropped his gloves like a guilty schoolboy caught cavorting around by the teacher. Everyone stopped what they were doing – everyone, that is, except the one person in the room who had the laser focus of a champion. External noises did not distract her. Which was how fifteen-year-old Bianca Jones knocked Bunny McGarry out cold.

CHAPTER TWENTY-SEVEN

"I am so sorry," said Bianca, not for the first time.

"Stop saying that, Bianca," said Gabriel, "you have nothing to be sorry about."

Bunny nodded his head as much as he could while holding a wad of tissue to his nose. "He's right, you've nothing to be sorry for. That was a ferocious right hook."

"Actually," said Trey, "it was a left jab."

Bunny pulled the tissues away from his nose. "That was a jab?" he said, too loudly, looking up at Bianca with a look approaching awe. "Jesus, girl, I pity the lad who forgets to buy you flowers."

Bianca blushed.

"Keep your voice down." Gabriel glanced around. They were standing in the corner of the gym, Gabriel having ordered those who were supposed to be training to get back to it and those who had finished to clear out. Still, he knew that all around him, kids were going through the motions while keeping one eye on the melodrama unfolding in the corner.

"What I would like to know is what exactly you two were doing in the ring sparring." Gabriel was trying and failing to keep the anger from his voice. He had been very clear with Bunny about this kind of thing.

"They weren't really sparring," said Trey.

"No," agreed Bianca, "it was just a demonstration."

"A demonstration of what?" Before Trey or Bianca could say anything, Gabriel raised his hand. "And if you don't mind, I would like to hear from the supposed adult who was present."

Gabriel glowered at Bunny, who looked at the wad of tissue and then tossed it in the trash can beside him. "I was showing the lads about keeping their guard up, like you asked me to. And I thought a good demonstration would be using Queen B here to show them what'd happen if even a much bigger opponent, i.e. me, didn't keep his hands up and defend properly. I wasn't throwing any punches. I was basically a volunteer punchbag."

"And," said Bianca, "I was holding back."

Bunny's eyebrows shot up. "I got floored by a jab from a fifteen-year-old girl who was holding back? Well, that is certainly a moment to give a man pause for thought."

"Your wounded pride aside, *Brother*," said Gabriel pointedly, "I don't think this kind of thing is appropriate for a man in *your* position to be doing, is it?"

Bunny nodded, receiving the message loud and clear. "Sorry, Father, it won't happen again."

"I should hope not."

Bunny gave a sly smile and poked Bianca in the ribs. "At least not against this monster anyway!"

Bianca giggled.

"Right, well, you should get changed, Bianca, and Brother McGarry, you and I will discuss this later."

"Oh dear," said Bunny, "that's me to bed without me supper."

Annoyed as he was, it took Gabriel a couple of moments to spot Trey gesturing at him from his position behind Bianca. When he finally noticed, he looked over in the direction of the doorway, where Emilio was standing, looking very nervous. Oh yes! He had been so distracted with Bunny's tomfoolery, it had completely slipped his mind. Today was to be the grand unveiling. Gabriel glanced at his watch. He should have just enough time before Mr Green from that Regency fund turned up.

"Actually, could you all come outside with me for a minute?"

"Oh God," said Bunny, "I thought he was joking about starting a firing squad." This comment earned him an admonishing look from Gabriel.

As they headed towards the door, Bianca looked confused, but she was the only one. All pretence that anyone was doing any form of training stopped as everyone followed them. Trey looked excited while poor Emilio looked like he was about to throw up. Father Gabriel gave him a pat on the shoulder. The poor kid was sweating profusely and looked in serious danger of fainting.

"What's going on?" asked Bianca.

"It's a surprise," said Trey.

"I hate surprises."

"Yeah," said Trey, "sucks to be you."

Gabriel turned the corner and noticed that Rosario and the other members of the committee had joined the gathering crowd. The scaffolding had been removed, but a white sheet still covered the wall. The great advantage of Bianca's training schedule was that it had given Emilio and Trey a window each day to come and work on it. Then Emilio had spent the last few evenings out here in the bitter cold, putting the finishing touches to it, while Bunny held a torch for him.

The crowd formed a semicircle. Danny Clarkson, the scaffolding king, nodded at Gabriel from his position at the side of the sheet, where he was holding a rope expectantly.

Gabriel looked around. "Right, what should we do now?"

"Speech!" barked Bunny, which resulted in Emilio's legs all but going from under him. Bunny gave him an affectionate wallop on the back. "Don't worry, Picasso, I didn't mean you."

Bunny looked at Gabriel expectantly, and he self-consciously stepped forward and stood in front of the sheet. Last night, he had written some notes in preparation for this moment. Actually, while he'd hate to admit it, he had spent quite a lot of time on it. He had even come up with what he was fairly certain was a joke. Maybe he was a tiny bit jealous of Bunny.

He cleared his throat and took a deep breath. "Ladies and gentlemen, I have a confession to make. I know I urge you to always tell the truth... Well, I am afraid I may have told some of you a little white lie."

This was met with mocking gasps and laughter. Gabriel smiled as he held up his hand. Mission accomplished. "But my intentions were good. You see, this wall does not actually have a problem with mould."

"It's the only one we got that doesn't," said Rosario, who was taken aback that this entirely serious remark was met with laughter.

"That is true," said Gabriel. "Recently, as you all know, our humble gym produced its first champion."

This was met with several voices shouting encouragement and cheering Bianca's name. The girl herself looked suddenly embarrassed.

Gabriel smiled at her and continued. "And I – I mean we, the committee and I" – he pointed at the other three members, two of whom had no idea what this was about – "thought we should commemorate this achievement. And what better way to do so than by using the talents of another of our equally gifted Coopersville prodigies..."

Emilio really did look like he was about to lose his lunch.

Trey covered his mouth with his hand and shouted, "One-Armed Bandit in da house!" which was met with some more cheers and laughs. "So, like many popes before me, I commissioned a piece of art to grace the wall of our unassuming gym. I haven't yet seen it and, like all of you, I'm curious – so without further ado..."

He nodded at Danny Clarkson, who released the rope, causing the white sheet to flutter to the ground.

Gabriel stepped back. There was total silence as the crowd stared up at the wall. Honestly, he hadn't known what to expect, but what he saw took his breath away.

Eventually it was Rosario, of all people – who had been horrified by the very idea – who started the applause. The rest of the crowd joined in enthusiastically. Up on the wall, Bianca stood in the middle of a boxing ring, looking almost angelic as her smile beamed for all the world to see, her hand held aloft in triumph. Emilio had managed to capture something of her essence that Gabriel would have never believed possible with spray paint. There was something in the face – the mix of pride and fragility in the smile, the eyes didn't follow you across the room so much as force you to look up to the sky as they did. At her feet, the skyline of Coopersville stretched out beneath her, and written in dark colours were the words POVERTY, DRUGS, CRIME and GANGS, formed into snakes. But Bianca's head was tilted upwards, and above her head were the words that Trey and Emilio had spent hours obsessing over. In bright blues and yellows, colours of hope, rang out the message: *WE ARE STRONGER THAN ANYONE IMAGINES.*

The applause built and built as the crowd began to whoop and holler. People were rushing forward to pat Emilio on the back. In the clamour, Gabriel looked at Emilio's face – the terror now replaced by relief at the rapturous reception. Gabriel looked back at the wall and noticed the words TRAINING, DISCIPLINE and DETERMINATION on the band of Bianca's shorts. He turned to smile at Emilio, touched by the detail, but despite being surrounded by well-wishers, the boy's face had dropped. Gabriel followed his eyes, and he saw Bianca quietly slipping away, back into the gym.

He was about to turn back to Emilio to offer some words of reassurance when Rosario grabbed his arm.

"Father, Father – Mr Green from the fund is here."

"OK, I..." Father Gabriel turned and saw his past smiling back at him from the doorway.

Abraham.

CHAPTER TWENTY-EIGHT

Gabriel was back in the meeting space on the balcony. It had taken a bit of doing, but he had politely made it clear to Rosario that she was not needed in this meeting. He would speak to Mr Green in private. "Mr Green", for his part, had cheerfully chimed in that yes, he would prefer to speak to the father "mano-a-mano". They had walked through the church in silence, Gabriel's mind a writhing mass of emotions. Here it was, the day, the moment, when his old life came crashing down onto his new one. Part of him wanted to scream at the top of his lungs for everyone to get out, to get far, far away. Another part of him just wanted to run.

Instead, he had plastered a smile on his face and led Abraham up to the balcony, where they now sat opposite each other across the wobbly table. For the first time since seeing him standing outside the church, Gabriel took a good look at his visitor. It had been, what? Almost fourteen years? What was remarkable was how little Abraham had changed. He still wore his hair long; he still had the same relaxed, athletic build; he still had that smile. Gabriel remembered the first time he had seen it, all those years ago. He hadn't trusted it then, and he had been right not to. If only he had followed his instincts… Abraham's accent was that same unplaceable but personable drawl it had always been. They had met twenty-three years ago, and Gabriel still didn't have the first idea where the man came from.

"Father Gabriel," said Abraham with a broad smile, "thank you for taking the time to see me."

When it came right down to it, despite having had this conversation numerous times in his head, and having run it on a virtually constant loop for the last week, now that Abraham was sitting opposite him, Gabriel didn't have the first idea what to say.

Abraham spread his hands wide. "I love what you've done with the place. The people I represent are so excited at the opportunity to support your wonderful work."

The dread in Gabriel's stomach turned to anger. "Can we cut the shit, please?"

Abraham raised his eyebrows in mocking surprise. "Should you be using such language? What with you being a priest and all?"

Gabriel held his hands in his lap, resisting the urge to fidget. "I am sure you are upset."

The jovial tone slipped from Abraham's voice. "Upset? Why would I be upset? Oh, because I find out my son – who I thought died fourteen years ago, who I mourned – is alive and well and pretending to be a priest?"

"I am not your son."

"I raised you. That makes you my son. You are all my sons."

"And how many sons have you lost now?"

"It is a cruel world."

"Only because you make it so."

Abraham leaned forward. "Really? When I found you in that shithole favela in Rio, a scared little punk-ass eleven-year-old kid with nobody to look after him and nothing to look forward to but a life of pain and degradation, that was my fault, was it? I gave you a life."

"And what a life it was."

The older man gave Gabriel a searching look. "You liked it fine at the time. You got everything you wanted. Everything you needed. And let us not forget you were good at it, so very good at it. You were a warrior, Daniel."

"That is not my name."

Abraham gave a mocking laugh. "And Gabriel is?"

Gabriel turned his head and looked up at the roof of the church. They still hadn't found that accursed leak. The diocese had promised to get back to him about it but there had been nothing. Those damned spotlights still sat downstairs. A part of his mind entirely disconnected from his new reality made a note to ask Rosario to check on that.

"Gabriel is who I am now."

"Pretending to be a priest? It is obscene."

Gabriel turned back and shook his head. "I actually am a priest. I went through seminary and I have been ordained."

Abraham gave a humourless laugh. "Like what you truly are can be erased? Like what you have done can be forgotten?"

Gabriel shrugged. "The Catholic Church was founded by a man who spent his earlier life persecuting Christians."

"Oh, please, you are no saint."

"No," said Gabriel, "that I am not."

"Which brings us rather neatly to your 'Road to Damascus' moment, doesn't it?" Abraham fished a silver cigarette case out of the inside pocket of his suit. Gabriel recognised it. He had given it to him as a present.

"You cannot smoke here." He said it automatically.

Abraham smirked across at him. "Is that so, *Father*?" He laced the last word with bitterness. "So tell me, how did he do it?"

"I don't know what you're talking about."

"Please, do not play dumb, Daniel – you can't pull it off. How did Bishop Ramirez turn my son against me?"

Gabriel ran his fingers through his hair and leaned back in his seat. "Can you really only see it in those terms? He did nothing except offer me the chance to not be what I was. What you made me."

A shiver of recognition passed through Gabriel's body as Abraham squinted at him. It was a look that meant he was displeased. "You ungrateful bastard. What kind of man turns his back on his family?"

Gabriel looked away. "You have a very damaged view of what a family is."

Abraham looked at him as he pulled a cigarette out of the case and, producing a gold lighter from another pocket, lit it. Gabriel said nothing, deciding not to rise to the bait.

"He died begging for his life, you know."

"Who?"

"Your precious Bishop Ramirez."

Gabriel sighed. "No, no, he didn't."

"How would you know?"

"You forget – I have seen him face death before."

The scent of Abraham's smoke wafted across the table, releasing a torrent of sense memories in Gabriel's mind. He rolled them himself with tobacco you could only get from three shops in France. Abraham raised two of his fingers to his lips and pinched away a stray leaf of tobacco. "He gave you up. Told me where you'd be."

Gabriel shook his head again. "No, no, he didn't. My face appeared in the damn paper. That's how you knew where to find me. You killed him because, well…"

"Because," continued Abraham, "he stole from me."

Gabriel sighed. "You really have to see it in those terms, don't you? What is it in you that cannot accept I don't want to be what you want me to be? I was out. I was gone. Why couldn't you let me stay dead?"

Gabriel flinched as Abraham slammed his fist down onto the table. "Because you don't get to just betray me and walk away."

"Nobody gets to walk away though, do they?" Gabriel looked at the stained glass in the window, through which the last cold light of the day threw patterns on the wall, and he asked a question he didn't truly want an answer to. "How many sons have you lost now?"

"How many brothers have you betrayed, do you mean? How

many of those sons do you think might still be alive if you had been there?"

"Don't put your sins on me, Abraham. I have enough of my own to carry."

Abraham took another drag on his cigarette and the two men sat in silence as a world of history bore down on them.

Then, as if hearing a silent bell, Abraham stood and dropped his cigarette, crushing it beneath his leather shoe. He picked his cigarette case off the table, snapped it shut and placed it back into his pocket. "Well, it has been such fun catching up, but I must be going."

"Could you...?" Gabriel stopped, as he had no idea what he wanted to ask.

"What?"

Gabriel lowered his eyes to the floor. "I could just stay dead. That is in your power. You could leave me here. I... I think I am doing good work."

Abraham's voice was soft when he spoke. "It is a matter of principle."

Gabriel nodded. He had known it was a futile request even as he was making it. "Very well. All I ask is that you don't do it here."

"Do what?"

Gabriel raised his eyes at the honest tone of surprise in Abraham's voice.

"Kill me."

Abraham laughed. "I'm not going to kill you Daniel. No, no, no. I've decided that I am going to take you back."

Gabriel furrowed his brow. "What do you...? I will never go back."

"Oh, we'll see about that. This" – he waved a hand in the air – "is all an affectation. A phase. I know the real you. You are a warrior and a killer. I saw it in your eyes that first day, in that shitty little police station in Rio, and I still see it now. You can deny it all you want, but I know who you really are."

Gabriel shook his head. "No. I will never be that man again."

Abraham ran a hand over his suit, smoothing it. "You changed once; you will change again. I have always known how to motivate you. This will be like old times."

"Please don't..."

Abraham waved jovially as he descended the curving staircase, laughter in his voice. "This will be fun. I look forward to working with you again, *Father*."

CHAPTER TWENTY-NINE

Zoya opened another can of the energy drink she was supposed to be cutting back on with her left hand and moved the joystick with her right. She was curious, that was all. Curious. She had spent the day doing her work for the sisters and developing her new idea for a personal defence system. Rather than be reliant on somebody realising the danger in time and pressing some button, she was developing a jacket that could determine when somebody was being attacked and respond accordingly. Military aircraft had automatic defences that deployed when an attack was detected; why shouldn't a human being have the same? She had come up with the idea last night while watching a dreadful movie. Actually, that wasn't entirely true. The film had provided some of the inspiration, but she had also been spending quite a bit of time thinking about coats – one in particular.

It wasn't an invasion of privacy, because she wasn't trying to invade anyone's privacy. She knew that was weak logic, but it spoke to intent. She was just... curious. Jackson Diller seemed like a very nice guy who, despite having little to his name, went out of his way to help others. Zoya reasoned that such a person was deserving of her help. You couldn't help somebody while invading their privacy at the same time, could you? Those sounded like sort of opposite things. Still, Zoya was hoping she'd never have to explain why she had a camera outside Jackson Diller's home or why the new coat she had provided him with had a small but powerful tracker in it. Come to that, she wouldn't like to explain why she was currently using Birdie to follow him either.

She only did it at night, as Birdie would be too visible in the daylight – looking into that was on her to-do list. Still, it was proving to be an excellent test. Birdie had successfully homed in on the tracker and picked Diller up at a bicycle shop in Longwood. He had just acquired a new mountain bike – or rather, it was new to him. It was in pretty banged-up condition and in need of repairs, but he looked pleased with it. Birdie had followed him home, which was again an excellent test of how the autopilot software, programmed to avoid all obstructions, integrated with the tracking software while maintaining surveillance on a reasonably fast-moving target – because Jackson Diller was lightning on a bicycle.

He'd raced home to stash his new acquisition and then he had gone out to the store, having checked with Mrs James to see if she wanted anything. Zoya had done a bit of digging there – Mrs James was a 76-year-old lady who had lived in Hunts Point her whole life and had no living relatives. It seemed that Jackson Diller and his mother had taken her in, inasmuch as they didn't technically own the property they were living in. It had been condemned six years ago, as had all the houses on that street, but the city hadn't got around to doing anything about it yet. Zoya had also looked into Jackson Diller's mother, which was a more complicated story.

She watched as Diller left the store, three large grocery bags in his arms. He smiled and nodded at those he passed, and was greeted warmly in return. The man had a way with people that Zoya could not begin to understand. People scared Zoya. No, scared was the wrong word. And it wasn't that she hated people either. Uncomfortable? Yes, that was it: Zoya was uncomfortable around people. She didn't like people standing close to her, and she wasn't good at conversation. Sure, she could talk to Dionne, but that was different. She could also chat online, but again, not the same thing. Words on a screen were one crucial step removed. If it got awkward, you could just stop. No biggie. It wasn't that simple IRL – in real life.

Jackson Diller stopped as a motorbike suddenly pulled up on the sidewalk in front of him, blocking his path. Zoya cranked up the sound. A big man with a muscular build was riding it, with a short blonde woman hanging on to his back. The man pulled off the visorless helmet he was wearing.

"Hey, Diller, long time no see."

Jackson Diller smiled nervously. "Hey, Barksdale, how you been?"

The woman piped up. "He's been waiting for his money, that's how he's been."

"Hey, Carol," said Diller, "me and Barksdale worked all this out. We got a plan agreed, and I paid the money my mom owes for this month already. I can't give you what I don't got."

Barksdale put the kickstand down on the motorbike and they both climbed off it, moving closer to Diller.

"Is that right?" said Barksdale.

"C'mon, Barks, you know I've always been straight with you."

"Really?" said Carol, an undisguised edge of excitement in her voice. "Then how come you're out buying yourself fancy new coats?"

Zoya held her head in her hands. Unintended consequences. Why had she not considered something like this?

"Yeah," said Barksdale, "how come you out living large on my money?"

Zoya looked up as her PC pinged. The recognition software had picked up the licence plate on the bike. Someone had reported it stolen from Queens a day ago.

"Look," said Diller, "straight up – this was a present. I've been nothing but straight with you."

"Bullshit," said Carol. "I think it's time you send this punk-ass bitch a message."

Diller took a step backwards as Barksdale took a step forwards.

"Maybe I should. Maybe I should."

Zoya chewed on her nail and watched the screen, her heart racing. This was going badly – really badly.

"Look," said Diller, "this is all a big misunderstanding."

"Sure it is," said Barksdale, taking another step forward.

"Well then," said Carol, "how's about you give us that nice coat of yours?" She walloped Barksdale on the arm. "That'd fit Tito, and he got that birthday coming up."

"Yeah," said Barksdale with a nod. "How about we do that?"

Jackson Diller sighed. "I... I can't."

"What?!"

"It was a gift, I..."

"Let me get this straight—"

Barksdale didn't get the chance to get anything straight, as he was distracted by the searchlight in the sky that had just burst into life. He looked up, throwing his arm over his eyes. A female voice boomed, "NYPD. Move away from the stolen vehicle. Put your hands in the air. You are under arrest."

Diller placed his grocery bags neatly on the ground and raised his hands.

"Shit!" In their rush to get back on the bike, Barksdale and Carol got tangled up with each other and Barksdale accidentally kicked his girlfriend off the seat.

"Jesus, Barks!"

"C'mon!"

She hopped on behind him and Barksdale kicked the engine into life. In his panic to get out of there, he throttled it too soon, causing the bike to leap forward and slam into the wall.

"Damn it, Barks!"

"Shut up, Carol!"

He walked the bike backwards, kicked it into life again and raced off down the road, the engine screaming as he rocketed up through the gears. As they did so they passed old Willie Franks. Willie was the closest thing Hunts Point had to an institution. He'd been pushing the same shopping cart around for as long as Diller could remember, stopping to look in every trash can and dumpster. Right now, he was standing with his mouth open, gawping up at the air.

Diller also looked up into the air – at a light that disappeared as quickly as it had appeared. He stared into a sky notable for its lack of helicopters.

Willie wheeled his cart down the path towards Diller.

"I seen it, Diller, I seen it."

Diller, blinking his eyes to try to clear the spots left by the light, didn't look down. "Yeah, I saw it too, Willie. I'm just not sure what it was."

"I know. I know."

Diller lowered his head to look at Willie.

"Aliens!" said the older man excitedly.

"Really?" said Diller. "UFOs are working for the NYPD now?"

Willie nodded his head as emphatically as it was possible to do while allowing it to remain attached to his shoulders. "I telling ya, Dill, I seen 'em. You take my advice – you get out of here before they probe you."

"Right," said Diller, not really processing what had just happened.

"Aliens are all perverts," said Willie, grabbing his cart and pushing past. "Sticking things up a man's ass. Ain't right. Ain't right."

Diller bent down and picked up his bags. He watched Willie Franks scurrying down the uneven pavement as fast as his old legs would carry him. His shopping cart kept veering off course and banging into the wall, as he was steering it one-handed. The other hand was firmly clamped over his rear end.

CHAPTER THIRTY

Sitting outside the office, Emilio was a picture of sweaty-palmed terror.

Rosario popped her head out of the door. "Why you looking so frightened?" she said, doing nothing to make him any less frightened.

"Am I... in t... t... trouble?"

"No, you ain't in trouble. Where's Trey? He's supposed to be with you."

Emilio just gave his one-shouldered shrug.

"I don't think I ever seen you without either him or Bianca in tow. Three of you is thick as thieves. Thick as thieves! Come to that, where is she?"

Emilio shrugged again.

"I told Trey five o'clock," said Rosario. "Why is he not here? You gotta keep the right time if you're working for a living."

"He disappeared. Don't know." Emilio held his cell phone up. "I been t... t... texting."

The back door opened and Bunny stuck his head in. "Have you told him yet?"

"Trey ain't here."

"Where's Trey?"

Emilio shrugged again.

Rosario looked at her watch. "I gotta go now. I need to pick up my aunt at the thing. I was gonna wait for Father Gabriel, but he'll be in his meeting for a while. Will you tell him to ring me? You know he don't like the phone."

"He doesn't like the phone?" asked Bunny, walking in.

"When I tell him to ring me, he never does. I thought it was a Franciscan thing?"

Bunny shook his head. "We take a vow of chastity and poverty" – Bunny nudged Emilio's shoulder – "so I can't explain why he isn't using the phone, but I can explain why he's never asked you out to a fancy dinner."

"Brother!" said Rosario, looking scandalised. "Such talk from a man of God!"

Bunny waggled his eyebrows. "I'm only stating the facts. It's only a devotion to God that has you a single woman."

Rosario hoisted her wardrobe-sized handbag over one shoulder while flapping Bunny away with her free hand, failing to keep the smile from her lips. "I gotta go."

Bunny pointed at Emilio. "But we've not done the thing yet."

"Well, half the people ain't here!"

Bunny looked down at Emilio, who had moved from terror to annoyance at everyone talking obliquely over his head. "Wh... wh... what's going on?"

Bunny nodded to Rosario. "Well, go on then."

She shook her head. "You do it. I don't deliver good news well."

"What's that supposed to even mean?"

"I don't. Apparently, I sing 'Happy Birthday' wrong too – I been told."

Bunny gave Emilio a quizzical look. "Are you getting this?"

"C'mon," said Rosario, tapping her watch, "I'm running late, tell him!"

Bunny sighed theatrically. "Alright, fine. We're having this discussion tomorrow though. And I want to hear you sing 'Happy Birthday'. I bet it's like Marilyn Monroe."

Bunny smirked in Emilio's direction, but he returned only a blank look.

"Oh, for feck's sake, Google it when ye get home."

"Bunny?" said Rosario.

"Alright! I'm doing it!" He turned to Emilio. "Right, so – while you were working on the masterpiece outside, d'ye remember how Trey kept sloping off into the office?"

Emilio nodded.

"Well, he wasn't just in here enjoying Rosario's company. He set you up with your own website, full of pictures of all your – what do you call 'ems?"

"Pieces," said Rosario.

"Right," said Bunny. Emilio was looking tense again. "Jesus, lad, would you relax. 'Tis good news. Not only do they look great, but Madame here got a phone call today." Bunny pointed at Rosario. "You're doing this bit."

Rosario's cheeks flushed. "OK. Fine. This nice man from a company in SoHo – one of them advertising companies – wants to hire you to do a piece for them. Three thousand dollars!"

"See," said Bunny, "you told it grand!"

"You sure?" Rosario pointed at Emilio, who was doing a remarkably accurate impression of a landed fish gasping on the deck of a boat.

Bunny waved a hand in front of his face. "Oh Jesus, Rosario, you've broken yet another man."

"Hush now!"

"I... I been hired?"

"Yes," said Bunny. "To paint a whatchamacallit..."

"Piece," finished Rosario.

"One of them," agreed Bunny. "Jesus, it's lucky you're good at it, Picasso, as I'm starting to doubt your data processing skills. You're getting this is good news, right? Three thousand dollars. Do you fully understand they're paying you that and not vice versa?"

"You gotta go meet him after school tomorrow," said Rosario. "I already cleared it with your grandma." Rosario bit her lip. "Oh yeah, she knows you do graffiti now…"

Emilio looked like he might collapse.

"Don't worry," said Rosario quickly. "Father Gabriel talked to her, smoothed it all out. Convinced her it was sorta art, and you were doing it all respectful and none of that gang nonsense."

Emilio found his voice again. "I… I gotta go talk to s… somebody?"

Bunny clapped his hands together. "Christ on a Segway – yes, you do. Before you start freaking out about that, your business manager, aka Trey, is going with you. Don't worry, they know you're not much of a talker. Works perfect; gives you an air of mystery – the women go mad for that."

"So," said Rosario, "your grandma got you a loan of a suit from your cousin and Trey is gonna wear the one he got for his interview."

Bunny nodded. "So, you're all set. Congratulations – you're on your way to being the next Banksy."

"What's a Banksy?" asked Rosario.

"Some English fella – his walls go for millions."

"He must have a really nice house."

They both stopped and looked down at Emilio's stunned expression.

"Fecking hell," said Bunny, "I'm beginning to think we're both crap at delivering good news. Quick, Marilyn, cut to the song."

"Thank you," said Emilio, and he stood up and walked out the door in a daze.

"I dunno," said Bunny. "Millennials – they don't know they're born."

"He ain't a millennial."

Bunny shrugged. "To be honest, I don't know what it means. I call everyone younger than me a millennial. All I know about them is Han Solo used to fly a falcon named after one."

Rosario's eyebrows shot up her face. "Father!"

Bunny turned to see that Father Gabriel was now standing

behind them. His vacant expression was eerily reminiscent of Emilio's.

"Well?" said Rosario, failing to contain her excitement.

Gabriel gave her a blank look before glancing down at his watch. "I thought you were going to pick up your aunt?"

Rosario waved the question away. "The meeting! How did it go?" Her face fell. "Oh Lord, it was very fast. That's not good. Is it good? It isn't good, is it?" Rosario blessed herself. "We'll find something else."

"For the love of..." interjected Bunny. "Let the man speak, would ye?"

They both left a pause which Gabriel didn't fill. Belatedly sensing the eyes on him, he returned from wherever his mind had wandered.

Bunny clicked his fingers in front of him. "Earth to Padre. Come in, Padre."

"Sorry," said Gabriel, giving his head a slight shake. "What was the question?"

"The meeting, Father, the meeting!" barked Rosario in a near shout. "Is Mr Green going to support us?"

Gabriel's mind finally jumped back a few minutes, into a simpler world where that was what the meeting had been about. "Oh, right. He said nothing definite..."

Rosario's face fell.

"But he seems enthusiastic."

And then lit up again. "Enthusiastic? How enthusiastic?"

"Oh, pretty enthusiastic I think. I mean, he represents a lot of people, doesn't he? He probably has to go back to them and make the case for us."

"Right," said Rosario, biting on the knuckle of her middle finger. "But he was interested?"

"Yes. Definitely interested."

"How interested? Like on a scale of one to ten?"

Gabriel puffed his cheeks out. "I'd say... a seven, maybe? Or eight?"

"Is ten the good end or the bad end?"

Gabriel tilted his head, struggling to follow the conversation he was trapped in.

"Ten," repeated Rosario. "Is ten like the best or the worst on this scale?"

"Oh, right. Ten is the best."

Rosario clapped her hands together. "And we got an eight!"

"Now, I said seven, maybe an eight."

"Oh, Father, that's an eight!" She gave a little squeal of delight. "We have so much we could use the money for!"

"Those are some strong numbers," agreed Bunny.

Gabriel nodded.

Rosario gave him an awkward hug.

Bunny laughed. "Contain yourself, Señorita."

"Oh hush," she responded, before wagging a finger at Gabriel. "And this is all because of the thing in the paper. I told you we should do it."

Gabriel nodded and tried to force a smile. "Yes, yes you did."

Rosario blessed herself again and quickly kissed the cross around her neck. "I prayed to St Jude."

"Ah yeah," said Bunny, "he's the best one."

"I gotta go," said Rosario, looking at her watch. "I'm so late!"

She took off down the church, her heels clacking on the tiled floor.

Bunny turned back to Gabriel. "Well, you've made her happier than any priest should really be making a woman."

His words bounced off Father Gabriel, who walked into the office and sat heavily into his chair.

"Are you alright?" asked Bunny, following him in.

"I…" Gabriel started. He stared at the mountain of paperwork in his in tray.

"What?"

Gabriel waved his hand in the air. "It doesn't matter. Did you want to talk to me about something?"

"Well," said Bunny, "I figured I probably had a bollocking coming, so I thought I'd get it out of the way early."

"What?"

"I wanted to apologise for earlier."

Gabriel furrowed his brow.

"In the gym."

"Oh. Right. Yes. OK."

Bunny sat on the edge of the table. "Alright, what's up?"

"I don't know what you are talking about."

"Really? I walk in here not only expecting but probably deserving a right boot up the backside, and you don't give me one. In the time I've been here, that's the closest thing you've had to a hobby, so what's up? Was it that meeting? Was the eight overgenerous?"

"I never actually said eight. All I—"

They were interrupted by the sound of running feet in the church. "Father G! Father G!" It was Emilio.

Gabriel and Bunny rushed out of the office. The quip on Bunny's lips died when he saw Emilio, his gait painfully awkward as his scurried forward, his working arm holding the limp one. "F... Father."

"It's alright, Emilio. We're here. We're here."

The boy came to a stop in front of them, sweating profusely. Bunny putting his hand out to steady him.

"I was w... w... w... sta... started walking home. We... Trey..." His face contorted as the words he wanted wouldn't spill forth.

Gabriel reached out and placed his hands on his shoulders. "Emilio, it's OK. Take a deep breath. Relax. Whatever it is, we can fix it."

Bunny nodded agreement. "'Tis OK. Take your time."

Emilio took a moment to gather himself, gulping in air before continuing. "It's T... Trey."

Despite what he'd just said, Father Gabriel tightened his grip on Emilio's shoulders and involuntarily shook him. "Trey? Is Trey OK?"

Emilio's expression of consternation became more pronounced as his frustration built. "He's O... O... OK. He's OK. P... P... P..."

Such was Father Gabriel's concern, he broke the rule of what you should never do to someone with a stammer. "Pocket?"

Emilio nodded his head, grateful. Then, a thought striking him, he reached into his jeans and fished out his phone. He held it up to Father Gabriel, who read it and then closed his eyes and hung his head.

"What is it?" asked Bunny.

"Pocket," said Gabriel. "He's been shot."

CHAPTER THIRTY-ONE

Father Gabriel pushed through the swing doors, Bunny, Emilio and Rosario following in his wake. He knew his way around St Martin's Hospital – sadly all too well. They had caught Rosario before she'd driven off and then they'd all squeezed into her Ford Fiesta. It had taken them a painfully long time to determine which hospital Pocket was in – Trey wasn't answering his phone – but eventually one of Father Gabriel's hospital contacts had given them the information. They'd had to calm Rosario down as she drove, so that they didn't end up as patients themselves.

All the way over, Gabriel's mind raced in other directions. As he'd walked back from the meeting with Abraham, the choice had seemed simple: he had to run. Pick up his things and leave the parish. Disappear off the face of the Earth. It was the only way to protect those he loved. Abraham would never stop and anyone near him was a target now.

Then Pocket and Trey... It was always the way with Coopersville: whatever plan you had, the random, senseless violence laid waste to all in its path.

Gabriel got to the reception desk of the ER and saw Nurse

O'Mara. She seemed to work every night shift here, as far as Gabriel could see. She gave him a grim nod, born from the familiarity between two people who only see each other in the worst of circumstances.

"Nurse, do you have a John Darnold here?"

Technically, information could only be given to family, but Father Gabriel was known and exceptions made. She nodded grimly. "GSW to the chest and another in the leg. They rushed him into surgery about an hour ago. It's..." She glanced at the three people standing behind Gabriel. "It's not great, Father."

Gabriel nodded. "His brother is here somewhere?"

"Yes, there's a lot of them..." Her voice carried an undercurrent of disapproval. "They're up in waiting room three. We could do with less of them being here." A light flashed on a board behind her, indicating that someone needed assistance elsewhere. "You'll have to excuse me."

The nurse headed down the hall and Father Gabriel hurried in the opposite direction.

"It's just up here," said Gabriel.

As they rounded the corner, they nearly banged into a group of three men. It looked like the elder was giving his two young associates instructions. They all wore the New Bloods colours of red and black. The two younger men were not much more than boys when you looked closely, barely older than Emilio. One was overweight, with a goatee, and the other tall, wearing a baseball cap that shadowed most of his face. The eldest wore gold earrings in both ears and his body language displayed that he was the clear alpha of the group.

Gabriel went to step around them towards the door to waiting room three, but the alpha stepped into his path.

"This room is private."

Gabriel looked up at the man, who had a good eight inches in height advantage on him. He wore designer shades and, closer now, Gabriel could see the angry whirl of damaged skin that ran from the front of the man's neck up to his right cheek; scarring left by previous damage that had never fully healed.

Gabriel could sense Bunny tense behind him, and he raised his hand to still any action he might be tempted to take.

"I wish to speak to Trey. I am his and John's parish priest."

"I know who you are. It's family only."

Gabriel spoke calmly. "You are not his family."

The man straightened himself up. "We all family. Pocket is our brother. His bro is our bro."

The other men nodded.

"I see. What was their mother's name?"

"What?"

"If you are family to these two boys, you should know their mother's name."

"What's that got to—"

"She died almost three years ago – cancer. Her anniversary is Saturday, as it happens. I conducted the funeral mass."

"Whatever."

"I am their priest and I am going into that room to see Trey. The only way you can stop me is through force. How do you think that will go?"

The two men stood there in a frozen tableau for several moments before the younger took a step to the side. "Fine. I'll allow it. Only you though."

"You can—" Bunny was silenced by Gabriel turning to him and shaking his head. "It's fine."

Bunny mumbled something beneath his breath, but he took a step back.

Gabriel turned to the heavyset younger man. "And James, your grandmother's hip is getting worse. You should visit her."

The kid nodded mutely.

Gabriel put his hand on the door and then paused, looking up at the man who had stepped aside. "Karen. Her name was Karen. She was a very nice lady."

He looked away, as if Gabriel no longer existed in his world.

Gabriel went through the door.

It was the same as every waiting room in every hospital he had ever been in: the same nondescript furnishing, neutral paint and bland artwork which only had the function of filling a space on a wall. Members of the New Bloods sat around, talking quietly in twos and threes or just staring at their phones. Trey sat in the corner with a man Gabriel recognised as Ben "Ice" Redmond, the gang's leader. He had his arm wrapped around Trey's shoulders, talking softly into his ear.

Gabriel walked across and bent down in front of Trey. His face had a blank, almost numb, look to it that Gabriel recognised as the disbelief of the young when reality came crashing down around their ears. "Are you OK, Trey?"

Trey nodded.

"We came as soon as we heard. Have the doctors spoken to you?"

"Yeah, uh... a lady spoke to me. Said the bullet in his chest passed near his spine, so they gotta look at that and then, the other one in the leg, it hit near an artery and they gonna do something with that too."

Gabriel nodded. "This doctor, was it a lady called Doctor Chen?"

Trey nodded again.

"That's good. She is superb at her job. John is in the best hands possible."

"He better be," said Ice.

Gabriel glanced at him and then returned his attention to Trey. "How are you holding up, son?"

Trey shrugged.

"If you want, we can clear everyone else out and just you and I can wait here for news."

"'Scuse me?" said Ice, a note of indignation in his voice.

Gabriel ignored him. "Sometimes a bit of space is a good thing when dealing with these things."

Ice tightened his arm around Trey's shoulder, pulling him closer to him. "Pocket is my right hand, and his brother is my brother."

Gabriel tried to keep the irritation from his voice. "Trey is not in your world."

"You all in my world."

Gabriel dipped his head lower, to push himself into Trey's eyeline. "How about we go down to the chaplaincy? Emilio is outside in the hall; Rosario and Brother McGarry too. We could all go down and pray for John?"

Ice leaned forward. "You'd be better praying for the fools who shot him. They the ones who gonna die."

This was met with a murmur of assent from around the room. Ice stood, forcing Gabriel to shift backwards. "Thanks for dropping by, Father, but Trey cool hanging with us."

Gabriel stood upright and looked directly into Ice's eyes. As he did so, he was aware of a shift in the body language of the others in the room. "I have no interest in your wars and neither does this boy."

"Who do you think you are? Coming in here making demands, disrespecting me?"

"I have no interest in you. Just this boy and his brother."

"It's alright, Father," said Trey. "Honestly, I'll be OK. You head home."

"No, I'm staying here with you."

Trey stood. "Please, just go. Alright? Go. I'll talk to you tomorrow."

Gabriel opened his mouth to protest.

"Go. Please."

He bit his lip in frustration. "You have your phone?"

Trey nodded.

"Call me any time, day or night. I don't mind."

"OK."

"And... where are you going to stay?"

"We got that," said Ice.

"No, you don't. The boy is under sixteen and he needs to stay with a designated adult."

"It's cool," interjected Trey, before Ice could say anything. "I'll crash at Emilio's."

Gabriel paused for a moment and then nodded. He was out of moves.

"OK then. Call any time."

Trey nodded. "Yeah, I got it."

Ice patted him on the shoulder and guided Trey back down to the chair. "We got this. Be seeing you, Father."

With one last look at Trey, who was back to staring at the floor, Gabriel turned and exited the room.

CHAPTER THIRTY-TWO

Bunny's eyes opened; he knew this sensation. He was not what you would call a morning person, but sometimes he awoke instantly alert. It did not happen without reason, though. It was a peculiarity of the Bunny McGarry physiology that he could sleep through anything and yet sometimes be awoken by the slightest of sounds. It used to drive his old partner Gringo demented way back in the day. So much so that, to prove a point, Gringo had once broken into Bunny's house "in the name of science", as he'd grandly put it. This experiment had resulted in Gringo getting a proper wallop in the kisser, which even he admitted afterwards had been richly deserved. Bunny hadn't known who he was punching when the blow landed, but he didn't regret it once he realised that Gringo had been acting the maggot.

What so annoyed Gringo was that Bunny seemed capable of sleeping through ludicrously loud things – even snoozing on when an actual brass band passed them while they were on an unofficial stake-out. He was also capable of sleeping through his own percussive and occasionally downright explosive farts, which was the bit that really annoyed Gringo. And yet if Gringo attempted to pinch a biscuit out of the emergency pack of chocolate Hobnobs that Bunny kept in the glove compartment, he would instantly wake up. Through some evolutionary quirk, there appeared to be a part of Bunny's brain that stood sentry, processing background noise while the rest of him slept, deciding what did and didn't warrant waking him up. Bunny himself didn't understand it, but he had learned to trust it, which was why he lay there, unmoving – wondering what had triggered his sudden awakening.

It had not been a good night. They had returned from the hospital with Father Gabriel in a foul mood. From all Bunny had seen over the last week, the man genuinely cared about every single kid who passed through the doors of St Theresa's, but it was inevitable that he'd become closer to some than others. Trey was a special kid, as were Emilio and Bianca, and whatever had happened in that waiting room had wounded the priest. Gabriel had said almost nothing on the drive home, but from what little Rosario's questioning had gleaned, he'd gathered that Trey had sent him away. Bad enough that the poor lad's brother was touch and go to make it, now it seemed that Gabriel wasn't able to reach him. As soon as they'd returned, Gabriel had said he had paperwork to catch up on and locked himself away in the office.

Bunny had gone to help with the evening's training sessions in the gym. The kids had been full of talk about the latest developments in the gang war between Los Diablos Rojos and the New Bloods. The shooting of Pocket was front-page news; it seemed he was the power behind Ice's throne and there would be a reckoning. Bunny had done what he could to move the kids away from the topic. Bianca had been unusually quiet – clearly worried about her friend. She and Emilio had both been texting Trey but got little response.

When training had finished, Bunny had heated some of the food Rosario insisted on making them and delivered a plate of it to Gabriel in the office. He had found the priest sitting drumming his fingers on the table.

"The poor lad is in a lot of pain," said Bunny. "I wouldn't take it personally."

Gabriel shook his head. "I don't. I just... I've seen this before. These kids can go one of two ways in this situation. If they let it out, if they talk about it, it can be handled. But if they bottle it up..." Gabriel looked up at the ceiling as if searching for inspiration. "They bottle it up and it comes out somehow – never in a good way."

Bunny nodded. He'd dealt with enough young men back in Dublin to know the truth of what Gabriel was saying. It was hard to watch a kid you thought you'd reached slip away from you. Bunny could sympathise, not that it would do any good. Father Gabriel was a closed book. Every time Bunny attempted to engage with him, he shut down.

After that, Bunny had read for a while and then drifted off to sleep. The mattress in the storeroom wasn't exactly palatial, but he'd had worse. At some point, he was dimly aware of Father Gabriel passing through into his bedroom on the far side of the room.

According to the radio alarm clock that Bunny had rescued from a box of junk, it was 3:12am. Mind you, it was permanently stuck on a station that played nothing but eighties hair rock, so it couldn't be one hundred per cent trusted. Bunny didn't know why he was awake, but he was willing to bet there was a reason. He did a quick self-assessment. He didn't need to pee, which meant...

All those years ago when Gringo had got a proper thump, he had been trying to sneak into Bunny's bedroom to leave him a sarcastic note. Gringo had sworn blind he hadn't made any noise. While Bunny had pretended otherwise at the time, he'd believed him. To whatever little sentry stood guard in his mind, the most alarming sound was the entire absence of it. The kind of absence created by somebody deliberately attempting to not be heard. Bunny lay there unmoving and watched through lidded eyes while the figure in black moved silently across the room. It wasn't Father Gabriel, not unless he had taken to wearing a balaclava to go for a pee. The intruder slowly and deliberately opened the door to Gabriel's room, the hinges offering only the slightest of squeaks. As the figure slipped inside, Bunny silently rose from his bed and grabbed the item he had stashed under it. The other great peculiarity of the Bunny McGarry beast was how unnervingly quiet it could be when required.

As Bunny's eyes adjusted to the darkness, he could see the figure standing in the doorway more clearly. He guessed male, from the gait. The only source of light was a red Sacred Heart cruciform bulb on the far wall. The bed was all of six feet away, and in it lay the slumbering form of Father Gabriel, entirely oblivious. The intruder stood there, looking down at him for a moment. Just as he was taking a step forward, he stopped, as cold steel was pressed against his back.

"Move and you're dead," said Bunny.

He swore under his breath as the intruder spun around, barely dodging backwards in time to avoid the slashing blade, which picked up the faintest of glints from the red light as it ripped through the air.

Bunny lifted his weapon – a length of pipe – to shield himself. Experience had taught him that if you couldn't have a gun, it paid to have something that would feel a lot like a gun when jabbed into somebody's back. Of course, that approach assumed that the person you were jabbing with it wasn't suicidal. If it really had been a gun, this individual would now have the kind of ventilation that typically proved fatal to the human body.

Bunny moved backwards as quickly as he could, his attacker advancing with the blade in an alarmingly efficient manner. With nothing but a pipe, a string vest and a pair of boxer shorts for protection, he was suddenly feeling all kinds of naked.

Bunny swung the pipe at the knife held in his attacker's right hand, only to find it out of range as the heel of the intruder's left hand drove a blow into his solar plexus. Bunny sidestepped and a flash of pain bloomed in his upper left arm. The blade, which had been aimed at his chest, had struck his arm instead. He really hated knives, especially when the person who had one of them wasn't him.

He directed a kick at the area where his assailant's testicles would typically be found, but a boot met his naked foot. His yowl of pain was cut short by his other leg being swept from under him as he landed messily on the hard stone floor.

Before Bunny could swing his legs around in a desperate attempt to level his opponent and even the odds, the balaclava-clad figure crumpled to the ground beside him.

Bunny looked up to see Father Gabriel standing over him.

CHAPTER THIRTY-THREE

Father Gabriel flicked the light switch on and looked down at Bunny. "What on earth do you think you're doing?"

"What am I doing? Ye fecking ingrate, I was saving you from getting assassinated! If it wasn't for me, you'd…"

Bunny stopped talking as he looked toward Father Gabriel's bed and noticed that he still appeared to be asleep in it.

"You're shitting me?!"

"I was handling the situation," said Gabriel. "You did not need to interfere. You could've been killed. Look – you're bleeding."

Bunny looked at his left arm, down which blood was flowing from a wound a few inches below his shoulder. "Ah, 'tis just a scratch." He looked at the floor. "Feck it though, I'm going to have to mop this place again."

Bunny took off the string vest he was wearing and awkwardly wrapped it around the wound to make an improvised bandage.

The figure at Gabriel's feet stirred slightly.

"Come on," he said, "help me tie our visitor up and then we can deal with your arm properly."

Gabriel pulled some cord from the storage cupboard and together they tied the new arrival to the broken cast-iron radiator, stretching his arms out wide to make escape impossible. Only then did Bunny pull off the balaclava. "Jesus."

"Language," said Father Gabriel, almost on automatic.

"But he's like..." Bunny looked down at the assailant, who minutes before had been endeavouring to stab him through the heart. He was clean-shaven, Caucasian and... "He can't be more than – what? Seventeen?"

Gabriel shrugged. "I would imagine so."

"Flipping heck," said Bunny, trying to not further annoy Gabriel. "In the last couple of days I've been stabbed by a teenage boy and punched out by a teenage girl. I think I might be losing my edge."

"If it is any consolation, this boy is not exactly a typical teenager."

"D'ye know him?"

"No, but I know what he is." Gabriel finished patting him down and then stood up. "Damn it."

"What?"

"All he had on him was this knife." The priest held up the article in question. "A Strider with a four-inch drop-point, flat-ground, tiger-striped blade of CPM S30V steel."

"A what now?" asked Bunny.

"That means that this is his initiation."

"Alright," said Bunny, "that is it. Either you explain what in the hell is going on or I'm calling the police. This is insane."

Gabriel ran his hand across his brow. "Yes. I suppose it is time."

Bunny followed Gabriel up to the office. The church at night had an otherworldly quality to it, the pad of their bare feet oddly loud in the silence. Bunny felt his body shake, whether from the cold, the adrenalin or both, it was impossible to say. He sat at Rosario's desk and Gabriel pulled the first aid kit off the wall. Bunny watched him expertly disinfect, stitch and then bandage his wound. The cut wasn't too deep and looked much worse than it actually was. Bunny resisted the urge to ask questions. The priest had said he would come clean, and it made sense to let him get to the truth in his own time.

The arm properly bandaged, Gabriel leaned back on the desk, still holding a roll of medical tape in his hands.

Bunny watched the priest's eyes dart around, as if trying to find the point at which to start. Finally, he sighed. "The boy downstairs, he is part of an organisation that doesn't have a name, although its members refer to it as 'the family'. Do you remember the meeting I had yesterday, with the supposed gentleman from Wall Street?"

Bunny nodded.

"That was just a pretence. His way of getting to me. He goes by the name of Abraham and he is the head of the family. He set up the family I don't know how long ago, but if I was to guess, I would imagine maybe thirty years. The system is simple: he finds children, typically around the ten- to twelve-year-old range, and he 'adopts' them."

"He steals kids?"

Gabriel shook his head. "No. These children, they are not the kind that anyone misses. He takes them, educates them and then trains them."

"Does...?" Bunny stopped, unsure what question he wanted to ask.

Gabriel lowered his eyes. "No. The children are well treated, at least in the sense that they are well fed, looked after and safe. He used to operate out of a base in Panama – a large villa where around twenty people could comfortably live. The operation also worked out of the Philippines for a time, as well as a brief stint in Somalia. That did not end well."

"How did...?"

Gabriel shrugged. "A local warlord saw a rich man living with children and assumed an easy target. That proved to be a very costly assumption on his part."

"Jesus."

Gabriel looked down at his hands as he continued. "The children receive a good education. I would imagine that the boy downstairs can speak and write several languages."

"That's not all they're taught though, is it?" said Bunny, remembering how well the kid had wielded his knife.

"No," agreed Gabriel. "They also receive extensive combat training. Weapons, unarmed combat, survival – you name it. Abraham places a great emphasis on melee weapons. As odd as it might sound, he does not like guns."

The priest went quiet again.

"You keep saying 'they'," said Bunny.

"Yes," agreed Gabriel. He took a deep breath and looked at Bunny. "You are only the second person I have ever told about this."

"You were one of these kids?"

The priest just nodded.

"Jesus," said Bunny. This time, Gabriel let the blasphemy slide.

"I was eleven, I think."

"You think?"

Gabriel shrugged. "I was an orphan from a favela in Rio de Janeiro, living on the streets. My mother was... I didn't know her. Birthday parties weren't a big thing. I was alone early, relying on my wits and, occasionally, the kindness of strangers and... It was, let us say, not a nice place to live."

Bunny let that go by without prying further.

"The police arrested me, not for the first time. A man had been attempting to take... advantage of me..." The words came out in measured beats, as if each one came at a cost. "I had fought back." Gabriel gave a bitter smile. "All you need to know of that world is summed up by the fact that I was the one who was arrested."

Bunny noticed his own hands had formed into tight fists and the fingers were digging painfully into his palms. He relaxed his grip.

"The police put me in an interview room and a couple of minutes later they led in this man. He looked European, but he spoke Portuguese with no accent. He smelled nice. It is strange that I remember that, but I do. He was clean and smelled nice. I suppose that was maybe unusual in my world."

"Abraham?" asked Bunny.

"Abraham," confirmed Gabriel. "At first, I thought... Well, you can imagine."

Bunny nodded.

"A beating. Maybe much worse. I was prepared, tensed to defend myself. Surveying the room, looking for my options, for a means of escape.

"He looked at me and smiled. I'll always remember the first words he spoke to me: 'So, what are you thinking? Try to take me down fast and then get to that window?' There was a small window up near the ceiling. I watched him and then shook my head. I said, 'The glass is too thick. I'd kick the ventilation fan out of the far wall, try that way.' He nodded and sat down, then he took out a cigarette case and lit one. 'Yes,' he said, 'I would try the fan too. My name is Abraham. It is nice to meet you.'

"I said nothing. I was looking at him, waiting. He just sat there, smoking his cigarette. Then he asked, so casually, 'Do you want to kill him?' I asked who and he just laughed and said, 'You know who.' I remember thinking it might be a trap, but then I thought what do I care? I was already in so much trouble – a little more didn't matter. You see, the man – the man in question, the man I had... injured..."

Bunny nodded.

"He had been an important man. I was in all kinds of trouble. So I said yes, I wanted to kill him."

Gabriel gave a sad smile.

"Then Abraham picked up his cigarette case and put it back in his pocket and said, 'How would you like three meals a day, your own bed every night and nobody to ever touch you like that again?' I shook my head. I didn't believe those things existed, not for someone like me. He laughed. 'OK, how about this,' he said, 'three meals a day, your own bed and nobody will ever touch you again, plus, one day, you will get to kill that man.'"

Gabriel shrugged his shoulders. "To a boy who, right there and then, would have taken a quick death... I thought, why not? I did not believe it when Abraham called the officer back in, gave him a wad of money and then held the door open for me. Even as I followed

Abraham out of the station, I was looking for a way out. He led me to a yard where a van was parked. Inside it were three boys, all a couple of years older than me. In hindsight, it made sense. How do you get a child in that situation to trust you? Put him with other children who seem healthy and happy. One of the boys handed me a drink and a sandwich and welcomed me to the family."

"Jesus," said Bunny, puffing out his cheeks.

Gabriel nodded. "We flew out of Rio on a military plane and then I reached the compound in Panama. There was me and another new recruit."

"I don't understand," said Bunny. "Is this guy trying to build his own private army?"

"Oh, nothing so grand. Abraham has no political or ideological affiliation. However, if you have the money and you want someone discreetly and professionally killed, his is the number you call. He is a one-stop shop for all your killing needs. A source of untraceable death, just a phone call away. Of course, you don't actually call him; there are intermediaries. Businesses, governments, various criminal organisations – they will all occasionally find themselves in need of an efficient and deniable instrument of death. It is easy in this world to find someone who will kill for you. What you are paying Abraham for is invisibility and efficiency. It will not fail, and if it does, it will never come back to you, because the person doing the job has no idea who they are working for. You could try to find Abraham, but the family are very good at staying disappeared. And even if you did… Well, as the few relatives a certain Somali warlord has left will tell you, that would come at the most terrible cost."

"But they're children," said Bunny.

"No, the children are just the trainees. Abraham likes kids because they can be moulded. He prides himself on creating warriors in some ancient tradition – although he's really taking ideas from many places and fitting them into his own 'warrior code'. I trained every day in numerous weapons. It became my life. After a few months, it seemed it was all I had ever known. And honestly," he said with a shrug, "it was fun. All children like to play at being soldiers.

We were trained in systema, a martial art developed by the Russians, plus lerdrit, which is the Thai version, not to mention knife fighting, marksmanship, wilderness survival, as well as every weapon under the sun. That is not an exaggeration. Abraham collects melee weapons from all over the world.

"It was better than the life any of us had known before. There was an order to it. There was 'the seven' – they were the older members who had graduated. They had their own rooms at the villa and they would occasionally disappear with Abraham to go on missions. Sometimes they would not come back. We would have a meal in their honour and then Abraham would announce who was to be the next potential graduate, ready for their final examination."

"The initiation?" said Bunny.

Gabriel nodded. "We all wanted it so much."

"And you didn't question it?" Bunny winced; the question had come out wrong. "I don't mean it like..."

Gabriel waved his protestations away. "Honestly, no. We did not discuss where we had come from that much, but you quickly learned that you were in a safe place. Most of the kids were African, Southeast Asian or South American. There were a few from Eastern Europe too. In hindsight, he was building a stable. A face that would fit any situation. The one thing we had in common was that we had come from somewhere a lot worse. If you misbehaved, you were punished – but in the middle of a jungle, where would you run to? And honestly, you didn't want to. All any child wants is safety and family, and we had that."

"Fair enough," said Bunny.

"I was chosen for my initiation – my graduation ceremony, if you will – at fifteen. Apparently I was the youngest ever." Gabriel looked embarrassed. "I was never very big, but I was good with a blade and I was a very accurate shot. I also was the one who could fence the best against Abraham. I mean, I never won, but he enjoyed sparring with me the most." The priest looked suddenly embarrassed, like he had revealed something he didn't want to. He straightened his back. "Initiations," he said, "follow a ritual. You are given only a knife" –

Gabriel took the knife he had taken from the boy downstairs out of his pocket and held it up – "and then you are told who you have to go and kill. If you fail" – his voice dropped to a whisper – "you are dead."

"Holy fuck!"

Gabriel nodded. "It didn't even seem strange. To us, if you failed to do what you had been trained for, you might as well be dead. That was our world and Abraham was the leader, father, demigod in it. All any of us wanted to do was make him proud."

"So, what happened on yours?" asked Bunny.

"I killed a man. The man whose death I had been promised all those years before. I would like to tell you that a part of me was appalled. Horrified at what I had become. Honestly? I enjoyed it. I was good at it. Abraham made killers, and he called me his greatest success. The others were jealous. I was our father's favourite. All the most challenging missions came to me."

Gabriel's eyes were damp now, his face wet with tears. He turned to Bunny. "Ask the question."

Bunny didn't know what to say.

Gabriel looked away again. "Eighteen. In my life, I have killed eighteen people. Don't ask me their names; to my shame, I don't know them."

"You were..." started Bunny.

"What?"

"You were... he made you into that."

Gabriel shook his head. "I still had a choice. God gave us free will. I have blood on my hands."

He looked down at the knife he held.

"But—" said Bunny, only to be silenced by Gabriel raising his hand.

"Respectfully, Mr McGarry, I have not come to you for absolution. I am telling you what you need to know, seeing as you insist on being involved."

"Alright."

"Which brings us to how I got here. To give you the brief version, not unlike our young friend downstairs, I was sent to kill a priest. A simple job for someone of my expertise. And do you know what the man did? As he kneeled before me, waiting to die?" Gabriel turned around to look at Bunny again. "He forgave me." Gabriel nodded. "As stupid as it sounds, the man forgave me and then he offered to hear my confession. Father Ramirez – a simple Mexican priest who had upset some cartel or other. I don't know. I have run that night through so many times in my mind. Clearly, somewhere within me, deep down, I knew what I was doing was wrong. What I had become was… a monster. And somehow, this man had seen past that to the broken little boy within. I tried to turn the gun upon myself, but he wrestled it from me." Father Gabriel leaned across and straightened the pile of bills in his in tray. "The next day, the priest told a tale of a man who had come to kill him, who had slipped from a balcony and fallen into the sea, onto the rocks below. They never recovered the body. A man who never existed ceased to exist, and Father Ramirez sent me to live with some Franciscan monks in Venezuela."

"So," said Bunny, "you're not actually a priest?"

Gabriel gave a sad smile. "No, I am. I spent two years there, talking to the brothers, learning from them. Then I joined the seminary and became a priest after five more years."

"Oh, right."

"I don't think we can view my vocation in the same way as that of others. Most come because God calls them to Him. I came because I was desperately trying to wash my sins away." Gabriel held his hands out, the blade lying flat on his right palm. "This is what is at the core of me. How many good works, how many days in the Lord's service, what penance can ever be enough to wipe away those terrible, terrible sins? I have taken life." Gabriel pointed his finger at the outside world. "Men like we met today – Ice, those above him, those who deal in the death he sells – am I any better than them? Can I ever be? When I meet my Lord on the Day of Judgement, what will matter most?" Gabriel's voice cracked with emotion.

Bunny didn't know what to say. He scratched at his beard while Gabriel turned away, gathering himself.

But Bunny still needed answers. "Why now?"

"Excuse me?"

"Why has Abraham come looking for you now?"

Gabriel turned and offered a sad smile. "My picture was in the paper. Somehow, they must have seen it. He thought I was dead. What are the chances?"

"So he sent men to kill you?"

"No," said Gabriel. "That first team, the ones in the van, they were not the family. He used contractors. I think he just wanted to test me. Abraham has a very... particular way of thinking. He enjoys toying with people. It is hard to explain to someone who has not been around it. He is also a very patient man."

"And then, tonight, he sent that lad downstairs to kill you?"

Gabriel shook his head again. "I mean, technically yes, but not really. You see, 'initiations' have one sacrosanct rule. You succeed or you die trying. Back in those Panama days, my friend Simon failed and returned to us. Abraham shot him in the garden."

"Jesus Christ!" said Bunny.

"He is a man who is capable of anything. He didn't want that boy to kill me. He wanted me to stop him because then.... because then I would know that I had effectively taken the boy's life. Abraham doesn't want to kill me for betraying him; he wants to turn me back into what I once was. He wants to make me into a killer again."

CHAPTER THIRTY-FOUR

Bunny had very limited experience of one-night stands, but the next morning felt a lot like the aftermath of one of those. Father Gabriel had poured his heart out, and now there was a different kind of awkwardness between them. Bunny didn't know what to think – it was hard to reconcile the cold-blooded killer Gabriel had described with the man he now was. He looked more like a librarian than a soldier, but then, he supposed that was the point. He would blend effortlessly into any background. Gabriel seemed unable to look Bunny in the eye, weighed down with the shame of who he had been.

Bunny had always considered himself to be a reasonably moral person, but what Gabriel was and had been, and what it all meant, seemed too immense to untangle. Should he be in jail? Possibly. But how much could you blame the man for doing what the boy had been raised to do? The organisation seemed like a cult as much as anything. Even the name – "the family" – Charles Manson much? So now the killer had become a tortured soul looking for forgiveness and Bunny didn't know which directions were right and wrong.

Aside from all of that, the priest seemed trapped, with no way out. They had a trained assassin tied up in the basement and no idea what to do with him. If they released him, Gabriel assured Bunny that he would attempt to fulfil his mission and kill him. If they somehow sent him back, his failure was a death sentence. Gabriel had said they'd have to leave him tied up, and he would try to talk to him that evening when it was quiet. Bunny got the feeling the priest didn't think he'd be able to deprogramme the kid but felt he had to try. From what Bunny could see, the best of the bad options open to him was for Gabriel to run, and to hope he could disappear somewhere that a band of highly skilled killers wouldn't find him. That would also mean that the priest would have to pull himself away from all he had built here, which he seemed unwilling to do.

Gabriel had tried to ring Trey throughout the morning without success. He had been tetchy with everybody, even Rosario. He'd contacted Emilio and Bianca at school, but they hadn't heard from him either. According to the hospital, Pocket was out of surgery; they described his condition as critical. They were monitoring him closely to see if any internal bleeds would force them to operate again. He was being kept in a medically induced coma and the surgeon had told them that, honestly, it was touch and go. Father Gabriel had also spoken to the ward nurse, who had informed him that all the people waiting for news of Pocket had left, some escorted out by security. No one at the hospital had any idea where Trey was, but he wasn't there. He wasn't at school either, and Emilio said he had neither turned up to Emilio's grandma's apartment nor was he in his own. So, Gabriel paced around, made busywork and was in a foul temper for the whole day.

At around 4pm, Rosario called Bunny out of the gym. Emilio stood outside the office, looking about as uncomfortable as it was possible for a human being to look. He was wearing a brown suit that was too short in the leg and slightly too big in the body. Bunny guessed his cousin came from the squatter end of their gene pool. He was also wearing his Dolphins cap.

Rosario and Bianca stood on either side of the condemned man.

"Tell him he looks good," said Bianca.

Bunny nodded enthusiastically. "Very sharp, Emilio, very sharp."

"He got his meeting about that job and he don't want to wear the suit," said Rosario.

"Looks s... stupid," said Emilio glumly.

"Tell him to take off the hat," said Rosario. "It isn't professional."

Bunny looked from her to Bianca and back to Emilio, and got a handle on the situation. "I hear what you're saying, Rosario, but the hat – the hat is like Emilio's signature."

Emilio nodded.

"It ain't businesslike."

"No," conceded Bunny, "but remember, this isn't a typical job. They want to hire an artist." Bunny waved a hand up and down the suit. "This says, 'I'm all business. I'm a professional.'" Then he pointed at the hat. "This says, 'But I'm an artist' – which is exactly what they want." Bunny patted Emilio encouragingly on the shoulder. "The lad has an incredible eye. I'd have you redesign my wardrobe. What do you reckon – does this brown sack thing I got going on bring out my eyes?"

Emilio shook his head in response and gave the hint of a smirk.

Rosario muttered something under her breath and her jowls vibrated with disapproval. "OK, fine – he looks great. You two need to get going."

"No Trey news?" said Bunny.

"No," said Bianca. "He's still AWOL, so I'm gonna be E's hype man instead. I'm good at talking and shit."

Bunny tried to hide his wince, which was more than Rosario even attempted.

"That ain't no way for a young lady to talk."

"Right," said Bunny, clapping his hands together and then motioning Emilio and Bianca towards the door, keen to get them out before Rosario built up steam on the ladylike language talk. "Off you two pop. You'll do great. We'll all be telling our grandkids about this momentous day."

"You can't have kids," said Rosario.

"Figure of speech," said Bunny. He placed his hands on their shoulders as they moved down the aisle, lowering his voice. "She means well."

This was met with diplomatic silence.

"Remember," said Bunny, "these people came looking for you. It's a done deal. Emilio, you just look at the wall and nod. B, don't punch anybody and you'll be fine."

"Remember how I knocked you out cold?" said Bianca.

"No, loss of memory is one of the many advantages of being punched repeatedly in the head. Now off you go!"

Bunny watched as the duo walked the rest of the way down the church. As they reached the doors, he raised his voice again. "Remember what I said about punching people!"

He was shushed aggressively by a Chinese woman he was pretty sure was called Mrs Wu, who he hadn't noticed was kneeling in prayer in one of the far pews.

"Sorry, I'm, y'know, ministering to the flock. Apologies for—"

"BUNNY!"

He turned to see Gabriel standing at the door of the office, waving for him. He gave an apologetic wave to Mrs Wu and hurried to meet him.

"It's Trey," said Gabriel. "Jimmy Sands rang me. He said he met Trey coming out of a shop up on Bleacher about an hour ago. We have to find him."

"Alright," said Bunny.

"I'm going with Rosario. We need to split up. Ring your friend."

"OK, I..."

Rosario rushed by in a state of panic. "C'mon, Father. Come on."

Gabriel nodded and went to follow her out the door before he stopped and turned back to Bunny. "Jimmy said he'd bought a can of spray paint and a knife."

"Ah, bollocks."

CHAPTER THIRTY-FIVE

"I'll have to get gas soon," said Smithy.

"Right, yeah," replied Bunny distractedly, scanning left and right. They had been searching for Trey for an hour and a half with no success. He'd checked regularly with Gabriel and Rosario in the other car, but they'd had no luck either.

"Has this kid got any family?" said Smithy.

Bunny shook his head. "Only the brother who's in the St Martin's ICU. They'll ring us if he shows up there again."

Bunny felt his phone vibrate and answered it on the first ring. "Yes?"

It was Gabriel. "We checked the graveyard where his mother is buried. Nothing."

"Damn."

"I've spoken to the police again and I insisted on talking to a captain this time. I pointed out that if they did nothing to find an at-risk teen and something happened... So they're sending a couple of squad cars out."

"Right," said Bunny. "Well, unless you've any better ideas, I guess we'll start again and cover a ten-block radius around the church. It's getting dark, maybe he'll..." Bunny didn't know what else to say. That the kid might see sense and turn away from whatever path he was on seemed like a forlorn hope. Bunny had some idea of what it was like to be young and full of rage. From Trey's perspective, his whole world had collapsed around his ears – who knew where that would lead.

"Yes," said Gabriel. "You do that. I'm going to start ringing anyone I can think of. Somebody must have seen him."

Bunny and Smithy drove around for the best part of forty-five minutes more before stopping for gas. They were just on their way out of the gas station when the phone rang again. Gabriel. "Are you anywhere near the Philpott Projects?"

"No," said Bunny, "we're on..."

"Intersection of 142nd and Maybury," said Smithy.

"Intersection of 142nd and Maybury," repeated Bunny.

"Damn it," said Gabriel. "I just heard. Trey is over there and he's tagging."

"Right," said Bunny. "That's not so bad."

"Left! Left!" shouted Gabriel, presumably to Rosario, before returning to the call. "It is. That's Los Diablos Rojos territory. It's damn near suicide."

"Ah, shite! We're on our way."

"There."

Gabriel was out of Rosario's car before it stopped moving, running around the chain-link fence that enclosed the basketball court which sat at the centre of a ring of apartment blocks. He could see Trey on the far side. Some kids were on the court, but they weren't playing. They were hurling abuse at the hooded figure with the spray can who was daubing a large "NB" insignia onto the wall of the apartment block. NB was the New Bloods.

Gabriel hurried around the path of cracked concrete paving stones that enclosed the court.

"Trey! Trey!" Gabriel tripped over a tree root that had broken through the concrete and stumbled messily to the ground, scraping his hands and knees. Damned sandals. Gabriel picked himself up and resumed running, turning the corner. Only then did Trey look up, his face frozen in a death mask of determination.

"Get out of here, Father."

The jeering from the kids increased as Trey finally acknowledged someone else's existence.

Gabriel stopped, panting hard. He placed his hand on Trey's shoulder. "Son. Stop this. Come back to the church with me. Rosario is over there in the car."

Trey shook Gabriel's hand off angrily. "Leave me alone. I'm taking care of my business."

He moved a few feet down the wall and started a fresh NB logo.

"Trey, listen to me: Pocket wouldn't want this, son."

"Yeah, well, Pocket's in a coma and he doesn't get a say."

Gabriel noticed a change in the timbre of the jeering coming from the younger kids on the court. He turned to see a group of five men emerging from the door of the apartment block and heading towards them with a purpose.

"Trey, we have to go now!"

"I ain't—"

"Trey!"

"What the fuck we have here?"

Gabriel turned to face the five figures, placing himself between them and Trey. As they drew closer, he realised that he had met two of them before. It had been last week, and they had been flanking Santana on the steps of the church. Marcus and Sergio. Gabriel might not have been much good with people, but he could always remember names.

"We're leaving," said Gabriel. "This boy isn't in his right mind. We're leaving."

"The fuck you are," said Marcus, who, absent Santana's presence, was carrying himself like the leader. "You disrespected us last week and this young 'un is doing it right now. Payback is a bitch."

"Yeah," said Trey, "you want some payback? Come on then."

Gabriel could see Trey reaching for something in his back pocket.

It must be the knife. He threw his arms around the boy and started trying to drag him away.

"We're leaving."

"Get off me," said Trey, struggling to escape Gabriel's bear hug.

Marcus had his hand on the grip of the pistol stuck into his trousers. "Nah. You can leave; your boy's staying." He turned to the kids on the court. "You all get the fuck out of here."

Roused from their entranced watching of the unfolding drama, the group of kids moved away, one of the older boys pushing a couple of reticent ones who wanted to stay and watch.

The words "no witnesses" burned in Gabriel's mind.

"Get off me, Father," screamed Trey. "Get off me. I'm gonna handle this."

"No, you're not," said Gabriel, the desperation grabbing at his chest now. It took all his strength to hold the rabid animal that was Trey in check.

"C'mon, asshole," yelled Trey. "Let's go."

"He's Pocket's brother," said Gabriel, searching for anything that might avert the coming collision.

"Yeah?" said one of the other gang members. "Last I heard, Pocket's a dead man, and that *hijo de puta* shot my cousin." He pulled out his gun and two of the others followed suit. "This kid ain't protected by no one no more."

"I don't need protecting," screamed Trey, "I'll take you all on."

"No," hollered Gabriel, ducking his head to avoid Trey's elbow as he continued to struggle in his grip. The boy was now raging in the face of several guns pointed right at them.

"Please," said Gabriel. "This boy isn't involved. He's not..."

Marcus pointed at the logos on the wall. "He's involved now. He's gonna be a lesson. He's—"

"Howerya, lads!"

They all turned. Bunny stood about a hundred yards behind the five gang members, waving his hands. "Remember me? I slapped the shite out of two of you, then I stole your money and your drugs. Made you look like a pair of fecking eejits."

The shout would have probably been enough, but never one for half measures, Bunny pulled up the hem of his brown robes to reveal in no uncertain terms that Brother McGarry was travelling commando. "Or to put it in the Dublin vernacular, ye can ask me bollocks."

"Get him!" screamed Marcus.

"But," started one of the others, looking at Gabriel and Trey before running after the other four. Gabriel was dimly aware of Bunny disappearing around the corner of the building, but his attention was focused on Trey.

"Let me go!" screamed Trey.

"No," said Gabriel, "no, I won't. I'm not going to let you kill yourself."

"Let me go."

Desperate, Gabriel made a decision. He manoeuvred around Trey's flailing arms to apply a chokehold. Ten seconds later, Trey's eyes rolled back in his head and he was unconscious. Gabriel picked him up in a fireman's lift and carried him back toward Rosario's car.

Smithy sat in the front seat of the taxi and drummed his fingers nervously on the steering wheel. Bunny had been very clear, instructing him to wait right here with the engine running. Smithy didn't like waiting. He was double-parked around the back of an apartment block in the Philpott housing project, receiving admonishing honks from passing drivers, which he met with apologetic waves. A truck pulled up behind him and the driver lay on the horn hard. Smithy swore under his breath and lowered the window, waving at the driver to go around. There was room, but the guy seemed determined to get Smithy to move, which he wasn't going to do. After thirty seconds of continued honking and a couple of choice hand gestures in either direction, Smithy saw, in the side mirror, the door of the truck's cab opening.

"Great," muttered Smithy, "this is the last thing I need."

He watched the driver's beer belly, followed by his sour

expression, come marching towards him. Smithy turned and stuck his head out the window.

"I gotta stay here."

"The fuck you do!"

"Look," said Smithy, waving at the road beside him, "I'm sorry for the inconvenience, but there's plenty of room. Please go around."

"Bullshit. Assholes like you think you can park your cabs wherever you like. I ain't having it. Move."

The truck driver kicked the rear door of the taxi.

"Don't do that!" said Smithy. "I just got the paintwork fixed last week." It had taken every cent of the money Bunny had given him. Smithy had said he wasn't getting involved in any more of Bunny's nonsense, but when he'd called today, he had seemed so honestly worried about this kid that Smithy had come immediately, dropping a very unhappy fare off nowhere near where he'd wanted to go.

"Then move your frickin' taxi, faggot."

Smithy glowered at the guy. "I can't move – it's a matter of life and death. And shut up with your homophobic bullshit language."

The guy kicked the door again, this time hard enough to leave a dent.

"Quit it!"

"Make me, princess!"

"Oh, for…" Smithy unclipped his seat belt. He would keep his temper, but he was going to have to stop the guy damaging the vehicle. That was all. He opened the door and hopped out. The truck driver looked down at him and burst out laughing.

"Holy shit, where's the rest of you?"

"Hilarious."

The man's belly vibrated up and down under a T-shirt that had seen both better days and an owner about two sizes smaller. "This a fucking clown car? Are ten more of you gonna come out and then the doors fall off?"

Smithy pointed back at the truck. "Shut your cakehole, walrus-breath, and get back in your truck." He was doing really well in his efforts to de-escalate the situation.

"You waiting for your mommy to pick you up from school?"

Smithy pursed his lips. Stay calm. Stay calm. Stay calm.

The truck driver started dancing around on the spot and humming what he no doubt thought of as the circus theme tune. Smithy knew the song was actually called "Entrance of the Gladiators", which was very appropriate as this guy was about to get himself gladiated. Hard.

Smithy recognised the tingling sensation at the back of his mind. "Oh, come on!"

That last comment wasn't meant for the truck driver, but he took it as such, adding in some hand-waving to his dance and redoubling his efforts. It was possibly more exercise than the man had done in years.

As far as Smithy was concerned, the voice he occasionally heard in his head was a result of getting run over a couple of years ago. As far as the voice itself thought – and for that matter, Jackson Diller, who Smithy had made the mistake of telling about it – it was the voice of God.

IGNORE HIM.

"I'm trying to ignore him."

RISE ABOVE.

"Is that supposed to be funny?"

"Yeah, it is," said the dancing idiot. "What you gonna do 'bout it, munchkin?

"Seriously?"

IGNORE HIM.

"Don't hit the cab again."

The dancing idiot had now incorporated kicking the door into his dance routine.

RISE ABOVE.

"I'm gonna..." Smithy stopped; he'd heard a sound. He jumped up on the rim of the door and looked up the pedestrian walkway between the two buildings. Bunny was holding up the hem of his robes and running for all he was worth. A sandal flew off as his feet pumped furiously beneath him. The reason for this became clear as five youths rounded the corner at the far end. Wild shots were being fired at Bunny's back. Smithy heard a bullet whistle by overhead.

"START THE FECKING CAR!"

Smithy hopped back in. Bunny was still maybe two hundred feet away. To the side of the cab, the asshole truck driver was still dancing around, oblivious, too wrapped up in his own vigorous humming to notice the sound of gunshots.

SAVE HIM.

"You've got to be kidding!"

SAVE HIM.

Smithy stuck his head out the window. "Get out of here, you idiot."

"Run along, little fella." The driver, now working up a good sweat, seemed to be enjoying himself so much that it might well prove fatal.

SAVE HIM.

Ninety feet now. What kind of idiot didn't notice bullets?

SAVE HIM.

"Right. Fine."

Smithy hopped out of the door and delivered a life-saving punch to the truck driver's nether regions that sent him crashing to the ground and out of the immediate line of fire.

"You're welcome."

Smithy hopped back into the driver's seat and threw the car into drive.

Through the side window, he watched as Bunny hurtled straight for him, not slowing at all – like a big, sweaty, red-faced Irish meteor. A bullet pinged off the hood of the cab.

"Sssssshhhhhhhiiiiiitttttteeeeee," said Bunny.

Fifteen feet.

Ten feet.

Bunny threw his arms up and stumbled the last few feet. It dawned on Smithy that he probably should have opened the door or at least the window just as Bunny came barrelling through it, sending diamond chunks of tempered glass raining down around Smithy. "GO!"

Smithy floored it, with Bunny dangling half in and half out of the car.

Smithy held him in with his right hand as he threw the car around the corner, watching in the rear-view as the five men looked on, waving their guns in frustration. Behind them, a truck driver who'd just had a lifesaving right hook to the testicles gingerly crawled back to his truck.

Smithy decelerated sharply to get the car around the corner without losing control of either it or the passenger he didn't quite have.

"Whoa," said Smithy, "that was close."

"Close?" wailed Bunny. "Speak for yourself – I've been shot in the arse!"

CHAPTER THIRTY-SIX

"Arse. Feck. Shite. Bugger. Bugger. Bugger."

"Please, Brother McGarry," said Gabriel, "I know you're in some discomfort, but…"

Bunny was lying on Rosario's desk, the contents of which were now on the floor following his indelicate landing. He turned his head and looked over his shoulder. "Sorry, Father, didn't see you there. BOLLOCKS!"

Smithy was kneeling on Gabriel's desk, trying to be of assistance – or at least moral support. "To be fair, Padre, he's not in discomfort. He's been shot in the ass."

Attending to Bunny was Gina Marks, an emergency room nurse who also gave women's self-defence classes at the church. As it happened, she was due to take a class that night. Gabriel had rung and told her there was an emergency and begged her to come in early, not telling her the details until she got there. He knew more field medicine than most, but this situation required greater expertise. He didn't know any doctors personally, but he knew that, sadly, a New York emergency room nurse like Gina would be all too familiar with the treatment of gunshot wounds.

"SWEATY BOLLOCKS!"

"Sorry," said Gina. "Seriously" – she turned to Gabriel – "can't the brother go to a hospital with this?"

"No," said Bunny, "I can't."

"But—"

Gabriel put his hand on Gina's shoulder. "I'm sorry to ask you to do this, but please, do what you can."

Gina gave Gabriel a long, hard look before shaking her head. "Alright, but I could lose my job."

"That won't happen," said Gabriel.

"Yeah," agreed Bunny, "I'm not going to sue anyone. I might slap the good Father around the chops though."

Gabriel smiled awkwardly. "The brother has quite a sense of humour."

Smithy and Gina diplomatically did not comment.

"Well," said Gina, "we're lucky it's not too deep, but I need to sterilise it. All I have is your first aid kit and the pliers, Mr..."

"Call me Smithy."

"...gave me. I need something to clean the wound."

"Yes," said Bunny, "well, we're in luck there. Father Gabriel has my flask of seventy-proof alcohol. That should do the job."

Bunny and Gabriel locked eyes before Gabriel squeezed past Gina and slid his hand down the back of the filing cabinet, pulling the flask out.

Bunny shook his head. "Sneaky sod. Only place I didn't look."

"You were not supposed to be looking for it in the first place."

Gabriel handed it to Gina.

"For a man who got me shot in the arse, you're tremendously judgey."

Gabriel shifted awkwardly, and not just because he was crammed into the gap between the desk and the filing cabinet. "Thank you for your help with that, Brother."

"Wow," said Gina, pulling her nose away from the top of the flask. "Is this lighter fluid?"

Bunny raised his voice. "Would people please stop making

derogatory remarks about the poteen? What you're holding there is an Irish national treasure."

"Do you mean the booze or your ass?" asked Smithy.

Bunny turned his head to look at Smithy. "Are you enjoying this?"

"Of course not. Oh, and not to pile on, but there's a bullet hole in the passenger door of the taxi and a broken window you jumped through."

"Stick 'em on my TAB!" The last word was shouted as Gina began to sterilise the wound. "Shitting Nora!"

"Sorry," said Gina again.

"S'alright, Gina. I don't blame you." Bunny looked pointedly at Gabriel.

"Father, Father!" Rosario appeared in the doorway. "F... Ohh."

"Howerya, Rosario," said Bunny. "C'mon in. We might as well stick a picture of this on the church's Instagram account. See if we can get some likes for my perforated posterior."

"Nice alliteration," said Smithy. "Do you mind if I use that?"

"How is that going to come up?"

"Sorry," said Rosario. "Brother, Father, Trey has gone!"

Rosario looked in a state of panic. Gabriel was all too aware that today had brought up painful memories for Rosario of her son's death.

He held his hand out in a calming gesture. "It's OK, Rosario. The hospital rang. They said Pocket is regaining consciousness. He has gone there."

"Oh," she said, at least partially mollified. "OK."

"Maybe you could go over to the gym, make us all some coffee?"

She nodded. "Sure. OK. How is everything going?"

"Grand," said Bunny. "Actually, you're a good judge. As someone who regularly checks out my arse, which cheek did you think was my best – y'know, previously?"

Rosario smiled and flapped her hand at him. "You are a terrible man, Brother!"

"This from a woman who has me splayed out across her desk."

Rosario gave a smile. "Coffees." And she headed off, her heels click-clacking in the hall outside.

Bunny lowered his voice and looked at Gabriel. "Is she OK, what with...?"

Gabriel nodded. "I think so."

"Not that it's my business," said Gina, who was cleaning the area around the wound, prior to extraction. "But from what I've heard, maybe you should've restrained that boy? Made sure he stays out of trouble until he regains himself."

Gabriel shrugged. "We did what we could, but we can't take him prisoner."

Bunny said nothing, but he looked at Gabriel pointedly. One kid tied up in the basement was hard to explain; two would really look bad. "I take it the heart-to-heart didn't go well?"

Gabriel shook his head. "The only way I could get him out of there was by knocking him out with a chokehold. That's hard to come back from."

"I suppose."

"It's lucky the hospital called."

"Sorry to interrupt," said Gina, "but I'm about to remove the bullet. You might need to find something to bite down on."

"Hang on," said Bunny, "before we do that" – he extended his hand behind him – "I need to sterilise my throat."

Gina put the flask into Bunny's hand, and he swung it round to his lips. He looked up at Gabriel. "Say something, I dare ye! I fecking dare ye!"

Gabriel wisely said nothing.

"OK," said Gina, "Here goes."

"OK, just – CHRIST ON A SHITTING LILO!"

CHAPTER THIRTY-SEVEN

Diller looked up into the night sky. A couple of hours of persistent snow had given way to a temporary reprieve, though the forecast said there'd be heavy snowfall later in the night. The light pollution of the city meant that it was never ideal for stargazing, but up here, on the roof of his house, the view wasn't half bad if you got a clear sky. He and his mom used to sit up here sometimes in the summer and share a lemonade. You had to hold on to the good days.

Now it was too cold for sitting around, but that had not been his intention. It had taken him the best part of an hour, but he had gathered up all the snow and formed it into the shape he wanted. As a final touch, he took the package he had carefully wrapped and held it up to the sky, feeling rather stupid as he did so. Like he was presenting an offering to some benign god. Only in this case, it was really giving thanks, seeing as he had been rescued by whatever it was and, he assumed, received the gift of his new coat from it too. Diller wasn't sure exactly what was going on, but he had given his original coat away while standing opposite the base of operations of the Sisters of the Saint, and he assumed that wasn't a coincidence. He knew it was weird, but Diller had never minded weird. For a person who had spent his life feeling lonely, having someone looking out for him felt nice. He had also been raised to show appreciation, hence the gift. He had spent the last two nights carefully crafting it, and he hoped whoever it was would like it.

Once he'd placed the package down, Diller went to climb back into the hatch on the side of the roof, but first he stopped and offered a wave, feeling faintly ridiculous. Still, nobody could see him in the dark. At least, not from the ground.

Several miles away, Sister Zoya stared at her monitor. There, on the roof of Jackson Diller's house, were the words "THANK YOU", spelled out in huge snowy letters beside a similarly formed smiley face. She watched in silence, biting at her nails. Part of her knew she probably shouldn't. Technically, it could be a ruse. Birdie could descend to pick up whatever was in the package and be nabbed by some fiendish trap. Or the gift itself could be the trap. Or there could be some kind of monitoring device on the roof, designed to capture a picture of Birdie. The problem with having a devious mind, which Zoya definitely had, was that it was very hard not to see the multitude of angles in any supposedly innocent gesture. The thing was, Jackson Diller, who admittedly she had never actually met, didn't seem like the fiendish-trap sort. Zoya knew that while she was great with the devious, the intricate and the downright ingenious, she had never been very good when a human element was introduced into the equation. She didn't understand people, and that made her wary. Still, for all that, Jackson Diller didn't seem to have an ulterior motive.

Zoya took a deep breath. "OK, Birdie, let's see what we got."

CHAPTER THIRTY-EIGHT

The sound of "Ave Maria" being played through the speakers in the church above carried down into the basement. Gabriel had locked the doors and put up a sign saying they were closed for maintenance as soon as they'd brought Bunny back. He'd then put on the music to drown out the sounds of Bunny being attended to – and the loud and evocative swearing that accompanied it.

The bullet had been removed and Gina was bandaging the wound. Gabriel felt bad about asking her to get involved, but he had no other choice. It seemed that, increasingly, his life was about making the least worst choices in tough situations. And so, he would take the one option he had left.

Down in the basement, the boy who had been sent to kill him the night before was still tied to the broken radiator, his arms stretched out and his body bound to it in order to prevent escape. This had the unintended consequence of him looking not unlike Jesus on the cross – if the cross were an old cast-iron radiator and the nails tightly knotted cord. Bound and gagged as he was, Gabriel hadn't been able to give him any food or drink. Removing the gag had been too risky; his shouts could have brought unwanted attention.

Now, Gabriel held a tray containing a large glass of milk and a plate of Rosario's cookies. He looked at the boy, at his brown eyes and dark hair, and saw pure hate staring back at him. He placed the tray down, unfolded a chair and placed it in front of his captive.

"If I free one of your hands, can I trust you will behave yourself?"

The boy just stared back at him.

Gabriel shook his head but moved across and carefully released the boy's left hand from its binding. He attempted to grab Gabriel, but the move was expected, and he stepped easily back out of reach.

The boy pulled the gag out of his mouth and roared at the top of his lungs. "Help!"

Gabriel looked down calmly at him. "Are you done, or should I take the food away?"

The boy glanced at the milk and cookies, his tongue moving across his parched lips. He looked back up at Gabriel and nodded.

"Good," said Gabriel, pushing the tray within reach with his foot. The boy grabbed up the glass of milk and gulped it down. Gabriel sat in the chair and watched as he devoured the cookies too. They really were very nice, although he doubted his captive was even tasting them, such was the speed with which he wolfed them down. He had probably been too nervous to eat before his mission.

Only once he had finished did Gabriel speak again. "So, what is your name?"

The boy said nothing.

"Come on, you are allowed to tell me your name. Even soldiers are allowed to give name, rank and serial number."

The boy rolled his head around slightly on his neck before answering. "David."

Gabriel nodded. "I see. I once knew a David. The man who had that name before you."

This statement was met with a blank look that was eerily familiar. It was the same look he had received from many teenagers over the years, although none of them had tried to kill him.

"Do you have any idea why you were sent to kill me?"

The boy only smiled. Gabriel recognised the bravado for what it was.

"Yes, of course, you aren't going to say anything. Tell me: does he still bring in his friend Mr Wakefield to do the counter-interrogation training?"

The smile fell from the boy's lips, and despite his best attempts to disguise it, Gabriel saw a flash of real incomprehension. He would have been expecting many things, but that this priest could know anything of his world would have never occurred to the boy.

Wakefield was a sadist of the worst kind. Abraham let the man take his time, trying to extract information from each of the family members in turn. Gabriel still remembered that part of his training in his dreams. In hindsight, its purpose was less to teach resistance methods and more to instil firmly into the children the belief that death was a better option than capture.

"Don't worry," continued Gabriel, "I will not torture you. I don't even need to ask you any questions. I don't need to know who you are, because I used to be you."

The expression on the boy's face indicated that he didn't believe that.

Gabriel held up the knife he had taken from the boy. "A strider CPM S30V steel combat knife, considered by your leader to be the finest combat knife available. They armed you with it and only it because last night was your initiation. Abraham does so love knives. It is important to him that the first kill be up close and personal. He needs to know you have the stomach for it."

The boy's eyes widened.

"I had my initiation seventeen years ago."

"That's bullshit," said the boy, breaking his vow of silence.

"Really?" said Gabriel. It had been a while, but the training never really left you. Without looking, he tossed the knife and heard the thunk as it embedded itself into his bedroom door on the far side of the room. "I was OK with a knife, but my specialties were hand-to-hand, fencing and sniper. Is Martin still one of the seven?"

The boy said nothing, but there was a flash of recognition in his eyes.

"Yes. I was a better sniper than him. He has the technical skills but lacks the patience."

The boy's curiosity trumped his training. "What was your name then?"

"Daniel."

The boy shook his head. "Daniel is dead. His name is up on the wall."

"Ah," said Gabriel, "you still have that? The names of every family member who died on a mission. Paul. Mark. Connor. James. Simon. Matthew. Stephen. Then, there would be me, of course. I don't know who came after that."

The boy opened his mouth and closed it again.

Gabriel gave a sad smile. "You don't need to tell me. I would imagine there are several more now. Some I knew well; some I never met. Such a waste. You, of course, won't make that wall – failed initiates never do."

"If you are who you say you are," said the boy, "then you betrayed the family."

Gabriel shook his head. "Why? Because I escaped? Because I didn't spend my life killing on Abraham's command?"

"It's a better life than this."

"Do you think so?" said Gabriel. "Here I am helping people. In a small way, I am trying to make the world a better place. I am trying to atone for the sins of my life with the family. I killed eighteen people. Eighteen! That's eighteen lives stolen; eighteen families robbed. Eighteen marks against my soul. Do you have any idea how heavy a load that is to carry around?"

"It's a cruel world."

"And now, you're just parroting what Abraham says to you, over and over again. I remember it. You can't see it now, but you've been indoctrinated, brainwashed. He has made you his weapon. You don't have to be that. It's not too late for you – you still haven't taken a life. You can be someone else."

The kid sneered. "I seek only to fulfil my destiny."

Gabriel walked over to the door to his bedroom and pulled the knife from it, then he opened it slightly and took out a small rucksack he had packed the night before. "Your only ambition in life is to join the seven, isn't it?"

"It would be an honour."

Gabriel sighed. "I remember that feeling so well, I really do. Abraham has you so convinced that he has your best interests at heart."

"He is our loving father."

Gabriel turned away for a moment and then he marched across the room and kneeled down to look directly into the boy's eyes. "Are you the best?"

"What?"

"Of the current batch of initiates waiting for their chance to rise to join the seven. Are. You. The best?"

The boy said nothing, a peculiar look on his face.

"That's what I thought. You see, I am Daniel. Abraham likes to use the folklore of the family as part of his training. I bet you have heard stories of my missions."

The kid shook his head.

Gabriel gave a mirthless laugh. "Yes, you have. The general in Somalia who died of a heart attack while surrounded by his troops. The arms dealer in Dubai who was killed when his own prototype malfunctioned. I was very good at what I did."

"And?" said the boy.

"And," repeated Gabriel, looking directly into the boy's eyes, "I was very good at what I did. A cold-blooded killing machine. Abraham used to call me his finest creation. Why do you think he sent you, not even the best of his novices, to kill me?"

The boy's face was a mask of rage. "No."

"No what? Come on, I know he teaches you to think. To assess the situation. Assess it!"

The boy looked away.

"Yes," said Gabriel, making an effort to lower his voice again, to try and regain control over his emotions. "He didn't expect you to kill me. He doesn't want you as one of the seven. He is trying to force my hand. To force me to kill for him again. He wants me back. My leaving – my escaping – it wounds his all-consuming ego. He was willing to sacrifice you just to get to me."

The boy shook his head, but Gabriel could see the hint of wetness in his eyes.

"If Abraham is your loving father, then why did he send you to your death, just to try to prove a point?"

"Shut up!" screamed the boy, his tear-stained face making him less and less like the grown man he was trying to present to the world.

Gabriel leaned forward. "I know this hurts, but believe me, it is better than the alternative. Don't let that man turn you into a killer. It is not too late for you. You can still have a different life and save your soul. You can go to the authorities."

The boy straightened his back. "Never. My loyalty is to the family."

"But you failed. Look where you are; you have been captured. If you return to them now, you know what it will mean for you. He wanted me to either kill you or send you back, knowing it was the same thing. Why would you let such a man rule your life?"

Gabriel leaned further forward. "There is another way. I know some people. I can run and you can run with me. Together, we can try to find a new life."

"He'll find you," said the boy.

"Maybe not." Gabriel pointed at the bag sitting at his feet. "I'm going right now, and you can come with me. I can get you away from him."

The boy shook his head again. "He will find you. He found you the first time, when you were supposed to be dead. He will never stop."

"But you, you're still a young man. You can..."

Gabriel was so focused, he hadn't heard the door to the basement opening.

"Father."

"Please – not now, Bunny."

"Sorry, but... we've had a phone call."

Gabriel turned to look at him, only then seeing the ashen expression on Bunny's face.

"It's Emilio and Bianca..."

CHAPTER THIRTY-NINE

"What about them?" asked Gabriel.

Bunny didn't answer. He stared at the bag at Gabriel's feet.

"Bianca and Emilio? What about them?" He failed to keep the panic from his voice.

"Were you off somewhere, Padre?" Bunny pointed at the bag.

Gabriel moved towards Bunny. "Brother McGarry, what has happened to the two of them?"

Bunny looked directly into Gabriel's eyes. "The phone in the office rang. It was Emilio."

"Is he OK?"

Bunny snapped back. "Yeah, he's fine, that's why I came rushing down here, shot arse and all. I just wanted a chat."

Gabriel bit his tongue.

Bunny glanced at the boy, still tied to the radiator, and then back at Gabriel. "He didn't say much. I mean, he didn't answer me when I asked if he was OK. He sounded scared – I mean really scared. And what kind of sick bastard makes the kid with the stammer deliver the message, I mean—"

"What message?" Gabriel resisted the urge to grab Bunny and shake him.

"He said, 'Come for a family fun day,' and then the phone went dead."

Gabriel closed his eyes and turned away. He should have gone sooner. Before Abraham had the chance to take hostages. Why had he not gone sooner?

"I assume that means something to you?" asked Bunny.

Gabriel said nothing. He felt like he might throw up.

Bunny turned, startled, when the boy spoke. "It's the park."

"The what now?"

Gabriel turned around. "Every year, Abraham brought the family to America and we went to the same amusement park. It was a… tradition. He still does that?"

The boy shook his head. "Not for the last couple of years. It got shut down. Some people got hurt on one of the rollercoasters."

Gabriel nodded. The Wonderama Park was about an hour outside of the city. Even when he'd last been there, all of fifteen years ago now, the place had been a little run down. It was based around a TV series that had briefly been popular in the eighties, but which had long since faded from memory. It had survived by being the cheap option in a world of slick corporate entertainment for all the family; it had a sort of rustic charm to it. As weird as it sounded, every year Abraham brought a team of killers and killers-to-be for a day out. It was their most treasured occasion. It was the rarest of days: one where the children actually got to be children, and the family actually resembled one in its own messed-up way.

"So," said Bunny, "this Wonderama place – that's where he's holding Emilio and Bianca?"

Gabriel gave a tight nod.

"Right. Give us me gun back, I'll go get them."

Gabriel turned on his heel, his anger rising. "What are you talking about? You think you're going to just wander in there against a team of highly trained assassins?"

"I didn't say I liked my odds." Bunny looked down at Gabriel's bag. "I could also run, I suppose." The words came out laced with spite.

Gabriel took a step towards him. "You don't understand anything, do you? I was trying to get out of here because I feared he would…" Gabriel closed his eyes and lowered his head again. "He would do something like this. Damn it! Why didn't I leave sooner?"

"Well," replied Bunny, "you didn't, and you doing a bunk now isn't going to help. These people being who they are, I imagine that if we inform the authorities—"

"The kids will be dead and Abraham will be gone. There aren't many people in this life who could go toe to toe with the family, and believe me, none of them work for the police."

"In which case" – Bunny held his hand out – "I'm going to google the address for this place. Gimme me gun back and I'll take care of it."

"That's suicide."

Bunny shrugged. "After you've died the first time, you sorta get used to it."

"I don't have your gun. I flushed it."

Bunny placed his hands on his hips. "You what?"

"I broke it up and flushed it down the toilet. No guns in the church."

"Right," said Bunny. "Fantastic. So I'm up against a team of fecking psycho ninjas, I can barely walk, thanks to being shot in the arse, and now I've no gun. D'ye want to tie one of my hands behind my back too or do you think this is enough of a challenge already?"

"This isn't any of your concern."

It was purely on instinct that Gabriel pulled his head back quickly enough to avoid Bunny's swinging left fist. He attempted to follow it with a right, but his injury threw off his timing and Gabriel's deflection and hip check were enough to send Bunny stumbling messily to the floor.

Gabriel stepped back as Bunny swung a leg, hoping to knock him off his feet. "Calm down, Brother."

"Stop fecking calling me that, you sanctimonious prick. These kids are in danger."

"I know that," said Gabriel. "But there's nothing I can do. I swore

I'd never kill again. That's what Abraham wants. Don't you see? He wants me to go in there and kill to get them back. He wants me to prove that I'm not any better than he is. This is all about his power trip."

"Whatever," said Bunny. "I don't have time for this souped-up Charlie Manson or your crisis of conscience. They're a couple of good kids and they're caught up in other people's bullshit, and I'm going to go get 'em. End of story. They're expecting you; they're not expecting me."

"What chance do you have?" said Gabriel, holding his hands out. "I mean, look at you."

Bunny glared up at him from the floor. "I'm a bit rusty. I'm sure I'll get my mojo back."

Gabriel shook his head. "You are so pig-headed. Do you have any idea what these people are capable of?"

Bunny grabbed a chair and messily pulled himself up to his feet. "I do, yeah, but they've no idea what I'm capable of. That's an advantage."

"It's the only one you have."

They both turned, at the sound of a throat being cleared, to see Smithy standing at the bottom of the stairs. He was looking at the boy tied to the radiator. "Sorry to interrupt whatever the hell this is, but... No, actually, what the hell is this?"

"It's not what it looks like," said Bunny. "The kid was sent here to kill him."

"Right," said Smithy, looking far from convinced by this explanation. "Well, on a related note, a couple of cars just pulled up outside. If I was guessing, I'd say those Diablos Rojos dudes have come to get back that bullet they shot into your ass."

CHAPTER FORTY

Zoya smoothed the paper and stood back to once more admire the gift she had received. She gazed up at it with a near reverence as she chewed on her bottom lip. Jackson Diller had a wonderful eye. Yes, it was unusual – 'quirky' was probably the word Dionne would use – but Zoya thought it was possibly the coolest thing she had ever seen. Drawn on a simple sheet of poster-sizes paper was an image based on the iconic cover of the Beatles' second album *With the Beatles*. Zoya had googled it, as she didn't know much about them, but even she recognised the image. It was the one where their faces were half in light and half in darkness. Not that Jackson Diller had drawn the Beatles though. No, he had recreated the exact image but replaced them with four chimps, complete with moptop hairdos. Zoya loved it. She giggled and hugged herself a little. It was the coolest present she had ever received, and she had hung it pride of place in front of her workstation. Maybe she should buy a frame? Make sure it was preserved for posterity.

Zoya jumped as there was a sharp knock on her door. Dionne entered. Zoya stood there feeling somehow guilty.

"Hey Zoya," said Dionne, "sorry to bother you, but..." She noticed the drawing. "Is that the Beatles as monkeys?"

Zoya shrugged in a way she hoped projected nonchalance. "Yeah, I s'pose."

Dionne nodded. "Hmm, quirky."

Zoya suppressed a smile – and then didn't need to when she noticed the look on Dionne's face.

"I need you to come downstairs."

"What is it?"

"It's Sisters Bernadette and Assumpta. We've received a videotape."

Zoya didn't need to ask if it was good news. Inexpert as she was at judging human emotions, the pain was writ large across Dionne's whole demeanour.

Five minutes later, Zoya was standing in Dorothy's office as she, Dionne and Dorothy looked at the old VCR and TV combo that stood on a trolley. Dionne puffed out her cheeks, the control jiggling in her hand.

"OK, I should warn you – this is pretty upsetting."

Dorothy nodded. "You've already warned us, Sister – just press play. We need to see this for ourselves."

Dionne nodded and pressed the button. The screen was filled with a snowstorm of static before an image appeared. Someone was holding up a newspaper in front of the camera. It was a copy of *El Universal* newspaper and it showed yesterday's date.

Then it was pulled away and a room came into focus. Zoya gasped. Bernadette and Assumpta were sitting tied to chairs. Assumpta had swelling around her left eye, but otherwise they looked unharmed.

Bernadette glared at the camera with such intensity that Zoya found it hard to look directly at her. "It's..." started Zoya, "it is possible that this is fake. I mean..."

She stopped as a male voice from behind the camera spoke. "OK, Sister, time for you to deliver the message."

Bernadette raised her chin defiantly, in a way that anyone who knew her would instantly recognise. "Deliver your own message, you pathetic excuse of a man."

Zoya's heart sank. You couldn't fake that.

"Do it," said the voice, "or you'll regret it."

"I'm not afraid of you."

The voice laughed. "No? But tell me, are you afraid of what might happen to your fat friend?"

Assumpta didn't look at the speaker or at Bernadette. As was her way, she appeared to be more interested in staring at somewhere entirely different in the room. Bernadette glanced at her and then looked back at the camera.

In a slow, steady voice, devoid of all emotion, she delivered the message. Then the video cut off.

Dionne, Dorothy and Zoya watched it again in silence.

And again.

Finally, Dionne turned it off.

A heavy silence descended upon the room.

Dionne cleared her throat before she spoke. "They're asking for the impossible."

Dorothy nodded. "Yes. Yes, they are."

"So what do we do?" asked Dionne.

Dorothy tapped her fingers on the wooden desktop for about ten seconds. "We have no choice. We do the impossible."

CHAPTER FORTY-ONE

Father Gabriel stood in the centre of the church and scanned all around him. He held in his hands a broom.

"Right," said Bunny, "we need a plan. They're probably just checking the perimeter, but they'll be in here in a minute."

"I can't believe I'm the one saying this," said Smithy, "but shouldn't we call the police?"

"Yeah," said Bunny, "and the best of luck explaining the kid in the basement. Right, here's what we're going to do..."

"No," said Gabriel, his voice calm. "I will handle this."

"But—" said Bunny.

"No buts," replied Gabriel. "Remember our agreement: my church, my rules."

"No offence, Father," said Smithy, "but these guys are packing serious heat. I'm not sure a stern talking-to will cut it."

"Go and get our guest and bring him up behind the altar so we know where he is. All I need you two to do is press some buttons." With a quick jab of his foot, Gabriel broke the head off the broom. "I will handle the rest."

· · ·

Santana looked around at the snow, which was now coming down hard. Snow could make anywhere look clean, even Coopersville – at least for a little while. It was beautiful, if that was your kind of thing. "Looks like that blizzard they were talking about is finally hitting." He looked around at the trio of his men, standing in front of the large wooden doors to St Theresa's Church. "Y'all should ring your moms after this, check they're OK."

They greeted this advice with unenthusiastic nods. Santana guessed they were trying to psych themselves up for what was about to happen. Santana wasn't wild about this either, but the reality was that after what had happened over at Philpott, the word was out there that some Irish priest dude was making Los Diablos Rojos look like fools, and they couldn't afford that right now. With Pocket out of the picture, the Diablos were primed to make a move on New Bloods territory, and the last thing they needed was anything that compromised their power. It was just business, and this guy was just some guy – his Friar Tuck get-up didn't change that. Santana was out money and dope; this was always going to have to be dealt with – but the incident earlier in the day had made it priority number one.

Father Gabriel had miscalculated. He thought his associate being a priest, or whatever he called him, made him untouchable because of the attention it would bring. Heat from the cops was bad, sure, but being made to look like fools was way worse in the math of Coopersville.

Marcus reappeared from the side of the building, a baseball bat resting on his shoulder.

"Well?"

He nodded. "All handled, boss. The gym is empty and locked up tight. I chained up the side door of the church. Ain't nobody getting out of there and there ain't no other way out but this one."

Santana gave a curt nod and withdrew the Colt .45 pistol from inside his jacket. His men mirrored his actions, giving their weapons one final check. Trip had brought the Kalashnikov.

"You sure you know how to use that?"

"No doubt," replied Trip.

"Yeah," said Santana. "Still though, stay in front of me. Alright, this is gonna be smooth. Everyone just do what I say. The sooner we handle this, the sooner we can get back to business." He pointedly looked at Marcus. "Nobody shoots until I say."

Marcus was looking down at his gun.

"Marcus?"

"Sure. Whatever you say, boss."

"OK. Let's go."

Santana slipped in through the doors and stood to the side, the four others following him in. The stained-glass windows threw weak pools of patterned light over the rows of pews that stretched up to the front, the falling snow outside creating a rippling effect. There was also some diffused red light above the altar, illuminating the large crucifix that hung over it. Santana looked up at the face of Jesus – it had been a while since he'd been inside a church. He'd given up attending funeral services. You didn't retain a position like his for as long as he had by letting people know where you'd be. He didn't like getting his hands dirty much these days, but with a war on the horizon, he needed to send a message to his own troops as much as anyone else.

Santana touched his finger to each man's chest in turn and pointed, sending Trip up one side of the church and Dex up the other, keeping Marcus in the middle aisle so that he could keep an eye on him. Marcus was becoming a problem, but again, with a war coming, a hothead was less of a liability than in normal circumstances. Such men had the ability to cause a lot of damage before inevitably ending up in a box themselves.

Santana left Sergio to guard the door because he was dependable, and he didn't seem to have much stomach for the nasty stuff. It was all good man management, knowing who fit which role best. They'd had a kid positioned outside all week, so they knew the priests were in here. He just needed to make sure they didn't get out until what needed to be done was done. Santana didn't want to drop a body unless absolutely necessary. A message could be sent without a fatality. Fear spread could be more powerful than a life extinguished. Ultimately, everything was a business decision. What happened next would all depend on what answer they received, and Santana was prepared to back up the question with as much force as necessary.

They moved up the church in line, slowly. They had reached just shy of halfway when the head of someone Santana didn't recognise popped up from behind the altar.

"Howerya, lads. If you're here to confess your sins, I'm afraid we're closed."

"We ain't," replied Santana. "Come out nice and easy."

"No, thanks. I've already got shot once today, and I didn't care for the experience."

"You must be the Irishman. It's you we've come to see."

"I'm touched. By the way – fair warning – I've got a hostage."

Santana looked around and back, checking all of his men were in place. "What?"

"I mean, you don't know him, so he's not a hostage so much as an innocent bystander. I just didn't want any of you lads to be racked with guilt at shooting an innocent teenager while you were attempting to shoot a man of God. He's behind the altar here, tied up. It's a long story."

"Shut the fuck up," said Marcus. "Or we're going to blow you to pieces."

Santana glowered at Marcus in the dim light. "What did we talk about?"

Marcus shifted awkwardly. "Sorry, boss."

"Is that Marcus?" said the Irishman. "I've not seen you since you tried to mug me. How's it going, fella?"

Santana held his finger to his lips to silence Marcus's response. "My name is Santana. You have something that belongs to me. This is your last chance to come out and play nice."

"Ah, Mr Santana. What've you lost? Your book on copyright law?"

"OK, enough of this."

"I agree," said the Irishman. "This is *your* last chance. Leave now and there won't be any trouble."

Santana laughed. "Funny man. You won't be laughing in a minute." He pointed at Marcus. "Go get him."

"Hold on," said the Irishman, standing up. "Calm down, lads. I'm coming out. Try not to shoot at the altar. You'd want to be real confident in your atheism to do that."

Santana watched as a figure emerged in the dim light and stood with his arms outstretched.

"This?" said Santana, turning to Marcus. "You were caused all that trouble by this fat fuck?"

"Hey," said Bunny, "for the last time, 'tis the portion sizes." He waved his hands. "Can everyone see me clearly?"

"Yeah."

"Grand. In that case... Hallelujah!"

On the word hallelujah, a lot of things happened at once.

Bunny dived out of the way a split second before dazzling lights positioned around the altar burst into painful, blinding life. Simultaneously, the church's PA system, cranked up to a deafening volume, belted out the "Hallelujah" chorus. This unexpected turn of events was surprising to everyone except Sergio. That was because, five seconds previously, a black-clad figure in a balaclava had dropped down from the ceiling beneath the choir balcony and delivered a neck chop made popular by the US Marines, which resulted in him losing consciousness and then his gun, in that order.

As quickly as they'd come on, the spotlights died – leaving Santana with close to zero vision in the darkness.

He heard a thump to his left. "Trip, you OK?"

Santana crouched behind one of the pews, with Marcus hunkered down before him. "Trip?"

"I can't see a fucking thing," said Marcus.

Santana turned at a scream from his right.

"Dex?"

A yowl of pain issued from where Dex had been. "My knee!"

"Fuck this," said Marcus, standing up beside Santana. He got off one shot before he collapsed into a heap on the ground. Santana's own rising gun hand was met with a sharp blow from some kind of wooden object which shattered bone and caused him to release his grip. Then a fist smashed full force into his face, quickly followed by a foot slamming into his knee with a sickening crack. Before Santana could crumple to the floor, a hand grabbed him by the right shoulder. The sensation of flying was with him briefly before his body somersaulted in the air and landed full force on top of the supine Marcus.

And then, all of fifteen seconds after it had begun, the music stopped, and the floodlights came back on.

Santana's attempt at crawling towards the doors was cut short by a heel slamming firmly into his neck, sending his face crashing down to meet the marble floor. His mouth filled with blood, and as he gasped for air, he felt his two front teeth tumbling out from between his bloodied lips.

He lay there struggling to breathe, his body trying to decide whether losing consciousness was a good idea. Pain screamed from several places at once. Around him, the groans and expletives of those of his men who were still conscious mingled with the sound of footsteps coming down the church towards him at a casual pace, accompanied by the cheerfully hummed melody of "Hallelujah".

"'Tis a cracking tune, that."

A hand grabbed Santana by the hair and pulled him upright. He held onto the side of a pew to steady himself, as his shattered right knee meant standing on that leg was impossible.

"Mr Santana – Bunny McGarry, at your service. Lovely to make your acquaintance. I've got all your albums."

Santana tried to form words, but his semi-concussed state and his shattered mouth were making it difficult. "Fuck..."

"Now now, has nobody told you not to swear in church? If I was you, I'd watch your manners. Your hand isn't the strongest."

Bunny turned Santana painfully around so he could see the rest of the room. His men lay crumpled or unconscious on the floor, all taken out with ruthless efficiency.

When Santana was turned back around, he saw a man in a balaclava standing behind Bunny. Calm eyes stared at Santana through the eyeholes. Later, Santana would wonder if he had imagined that. Certainly, the memory of a dwarf appearing beside the figure must have been from a fevered dream. The most disconcerting part was how the man in the balaclava wasn't even out of breath. He held in his hand what appeared to be a broomstick.

"Who the...?"

Bunny glanced over his shoulder. "Oh, what? Him? Funny you should ask. This gentleman is Mr Roy Keane. He is a lawyer for Manchester United Football Club. He has come to inform you that any unauthorised use of the brand 'The Red Devils' is strictly prohibited."

Santana tried to focus on McGarry's face. "What are you talking about?"

"Oh, never mind. Time for your nap."

Something hit him hard. Santana was unconscious before he hit the ground.

Twenty minutes later, Santana regained consciousness with an EMT and a cop standing over him. He and his men were Mirandized and charged with breaking and entering before being loaded into two ambulances. They had to double and triple up, as the snow was coming down hard now and no other crews would reach them. Santana was in no state to argue. Luckily, there were no gun charges, as their guns had all disappeared – along with the Irishman, the dwarf and whatever demon they had conjured up to wreak their vengeance.

CHAPTER FORTY-TWO

Zoya sat in her seat and Dionne stood behind her, a phone pressed to her ear.

"Damn it," said Dionne, "there's still no answer from either Father Gabriel or the number Bunny left with us."

Zoya was scrolling through the day's surveillance footage from the cameras she had placed around the church. She had done this every night for the last week. Outside of a rather exciting bit when three heavy-looking dudes had turned up and had an intense-looking chat with Father Gabriel on the steps of the church, it had just been a lot of normal comings and goings. An incredibly dull watch.

Zoya slowed the footage to real time when a taxi pulled up beside the side door and the dwarf who had assisted Bunny in his ill-fated break-in attempt – Smithy, he had called himself – leaped out, ran around the car and assisted Bunny in getting out. There were bloodstains on the bottom half of his robes.

"What is that?" asked Dionne.

Zoya shrugged.

Five minutes later, Father Gabriel and the woman who worked there appeared, with a truculent-looking teenager in tow, and went inside too.

"I wish we had cameras inside," said Zoya.

"Don't worry about that now. Just see if Gabriel and McGarry leave again at any point."

Zoya scrolled forward, seeing another lady arrive at the side door and enter. Then the kid left, followed by the two women.

Zoya went back to normal speed when five men walked up the front steps. One of them had a baseball bat resting on his shoulder. Zoya and Dionne watched in silence as the baseball bat guy went around to the church's side door and chained it closed.

"Oh hell," said Dionne. "How long ago was this?"

"About forty-five minutes ago."

They watched as the man rejoined his colleagues and then they all pulled out weapons and entered the church.

"Oh Lord," said Dionne. "Who's in there now?"

"Far as I can tell, the priest, the Irish guy and the little dude."

They looked at both screens as nothing happened.

"This is torture," said Dionne. "Wind it forward."

They wound it forward fourteen minutes and stopped at the first sign of life. Smithy returned to the taxi parked at the side of the building. He looked at the door, then went to his trunk, took out some bolt cutters and removed the chains. The door opened and Father Gabriel and Bunny, both having abandoned their Franciscan garb for ordinary street clothes, came out and looked around.

Zoya let go of a breath she hadn't realised she was holding.

"Thank God," said Dionne. "They're OK."

Smithy cleared some stuff out of the trunk and placed it in the back seat. Bunny and Gabriel went back inside and re-emerged a few seconds later with what appeared to be a bound and gagged teenage boy, who they shoved into the trunk.

"What in the hell?" said Dionne.

"Who is that guy?" asked Zoya. "He's not one of the guys who just went in. And where are those guys? Damn, we really need cameras inside. This is insane!"

Bunny went back inside again and came out carrying a duffle bag which appeared to contain a few bulky objects. The handle of a baseball bat stuck out of the top of it.

"How did those three...?" started Zoya.

"I don't know," said Dionne. "But we know McGarry is resourceful, and Father Gabriel..."

"What is his deal?"

"I don't know. Dorothy just told me he had a complicated past."

They watched in silence as Gabriel opened the trunk and checked on their prisoner, then he closed it and got in the car, and they drove off.

"Complicated past?" echoed Zoya. "It sure looks like his present and future are going to be a tad colourful too. I mean – what in the what?"

"Well," said Dionne, "wherever they're going, they're apparently not answering calls. I'd better go tell Dorothy. She is not going to be happy."

Zoya started typing furiously. "Give me the numbers."

"What?"

"Their cell numbers. I can track them."

"Really?"

Zoya rolled her eyes at Dionne, who immediately gave her the numbers.

CHAPTER FORTY-THREE

If it wasn't the most surreal drive of Smithy's life, it had to be right up there. Through the heavy snow, he'd taken them out of the city and north onto the I-95 while Bunny – who was sitting in the passenger seat, perched on a cushion to take some of the pressure off his wounded buttock – explained who the priest in the back really was and why they had a teenage boy tied up in the trunk. He was driving with gloves on because the car was freezing, thanks to the trash bag that was doing a dreadful job filling in for a passenger-side window. All of this, and they were on their way to Wonderama, a deserted theme park, which a quick Google had revealed was scheduled for redevelopment but was currently stuck in stasis due to a series of legal disputes involving owners, former owners, the IRS, property developers and an organisation representing the rights of wading birds.

It would have been an hour's drive out of the city in normal conditions, but these weren't normal conditions. The police were advising against undertaking unnecessary journeys and the snow was coming down so hard that it would soon be impossible to make any kind of journey, necessary or otherwise. In an hour, even the interstate would be the exclusive preserve of the foolhardy or hard-pressed. The whole eastern seaboard would be snowed in by morning. Normally, Smithy wouldn't drive in such conditions, but Bunny had asked, and, well, the man had asked. Smithy didn't owe him anything, but you did for friends. Still, he kept his eyes on the road, only occasionally lifting them to look in the rear-view mirror and glance at the priest, who sat wordlessly in the back seat, staring out the window, lost in thought. He sure didn't look like the killer that Bunny described, but from his position as switch-flicker back in the church, Smithy had seen the destruction the man had wrought, taking out five armed assailants with brutal efficiency and a broomstick. Smithy had collected up the weapons, which now sat in a gym bag in the back seat beside the priest. The five unconscious or otherwise incapacitated thugs would be keeping orthopaedic surgeons busy for a while, assuming that Los Diablos Rojos had a good healthcare plan.

"So," said Smithy, "I get that this Abraham dude has a hard-on for the padre, but why has he taken these two kids hostage?"

Gabriel spoke before Bunny could formulate a response. "Because he is forcing me to try to save them. He doesn't just want me dead; he wants everything I became after I left him to truly die. He wants me to kill again, because he wants me to go back to being, in his words, the 'warrior' he raised."

"Even if who you kill is him?"

Gabriel nodded. "Yes, although I doubt that is his first choice. He will not be alone – of that I have no doubt. He will have some of the family with him."

"That is fucked up."

Gabriel nodded. "It is hard to disagree with that assessment. All that matters now is getting Bianca and Emilio back safely. This is nothing to do with them."

"How many of the members of this family do you expect to be there?"

"I don't know," said Gabriel. "At a guess, he may have all of the seven with him."

"Wait a sec," said Bunny. "The bowsey in the boot?"

"The what?" said Smithy.

"Sorry, the lad in the trunk, trying to kill you. It was his whatchamacallit – initiation?"

"Yes," said Gabriel, and then he raised an eyebrow, the closest thing to emotion Smithy had seen from him. "I see your point. That means there is an opening in the seven. So, there's that."

"Yeah," said Bunny, "so it might only be – what? Six plus Abraham against two?"

"Three," said Smithy.

Bunny shook his head emphatically. "Feck no, Smithy. I mean, I appreciate the offer, but this isn't your fight."

"Since when has that mattered? You're in this; I am in this."

"No way," said Bunny. "The other times were... This is just different."

"We are going in against some of the most skilled killers on the planet," said Gabriel, "in a situation they have set up and with almost every advantage on their side. This is a suicide mission, and it is one I will undertake alone."

"Bollocks!" said Bunny. "I said I was helping with your situation, and I am. End of."

"I'm sure Sister Dorothy didn't mean—"

"Regardless," said Bunny, "I know them kids. I can't walk away now. I'm in this until the bitter end."

"And where he goes..." said Smithy.

"No," said Gabriel. "Absolutely not. I am not bringing another innocent into this."

"He's right," said Bunny.

Smithy pulled the car over to the side of the road, coming to an abrupt enough stop that it skidded on the snow. He turned to face Bunny. "And what am I supposed to do? You're forgetting" – he jabbed a finger at his own temple – "I have the voice in my head."

There was a moment's pause before Gabriel spoke. "I'm sorry, you have what?"

Bunny answered. "He hears the voice of God in his head."

"Respectfully," said Gabriel, "no, he doesn't."

TELL HIM HE'S WRONG.

"Oh God," said Smithy. "Not now."

"Sorry?" said Gabriel.

"I wasn't talking to you," said Smithy. "Alright, maybe it is the voice of God, or maybe it's just some form of really awkward mental illness – whatever. It doesn't change the facts. How do you think it will feel about me letting an actual priest and one of my best friends go to their deaths?"

"All we need is a lift," said Bunny. "That's already a massive ask."

"But—"

"Besides," said Gabriel, raising his voice. "I need you to do something else for me."

Smithy turned and glared at him. "What?"

"I need you to live, because I need the boy in the trunk to live. He's a young man who has known nothing but the family for most of his life, and they have programmed him to feel that his sole purpose is to kill. In particular, to kill me – otherwise he has failed. That's why we had to take him with us. If we'd released him back in Coopersville, he would have stolen a car and followed us, all in the hope of killing me. If we let him out here – same. If we'd left him in the basement, there was a very real chance he'd kill whoever found him and then attempt to find me. Similarly, if we let him out at our destination, he will endeavour to kill me. There is only one solution: I need you to drop us off and then take him far enough away that he has no chance at killing me and then release him. Please, God, at that point he might see that his only choice is to disappear and start a new life." Gabriel took a brown envelope out of his coat pocket and raised his voice. "Seeing as he can no doubt hear me, I might as well explain this. This envelope contains four hundred dollars and the name of a man in New Jersey who will get him out of the country, no questions asked. All he has to do is tell him my name."

No noise came from the trunk.

Gabriel pointed at Smithy. "So, you see, I need you to help me give the boy a second chance at life."

Smithy and Gabriel locked eyes and looked at each other for a long moment.

DO WHAT THE PRIEST SAYS.

"Really?" screamed Smithy, before punching the steering wheel. He closed his eyes and counted to ten, breathing steadily.

"Is he alright?" asked Gabriel.

"Just give him a minute," said Bunny in a soft voice.

Smithy threw on his signal and pulled back out onto the road. When he finally spoke, it was mainly to himself. "Making me take someone and release them miles away. It's what Cheryl makes me do with a damn mouse!"

A frosty silence descended on the car, save for the *thunk-thunk, thunk-thunk* of the windscreen wipers battling against the never-ending snow.

After a couple of minutes, Bunny finally spoke. "I don't know if it's any comfort, but..." He smiled over at Smithy. "You're definitely going to win the bet. Whatever happens next, it is going to involve some serious fecking violence."

CHAPTER FORTY-FOUR

It occurred to Emilio that, technically, this was the closest contact he had ever had with a girl in his entire fifteen years on this earth. Technically, he could theoretically claim to have reached second base, not that he ever would – first, because he was a gentleman and second, because there was a very good chance he was going to die before he ever got the chance.

Emilio laughed.

Bianca moved her head to look at him. "What is so funny? I'm freezing my ass off here."

"S... Sorry."

They were sitting in the front car of a rollercoaster, cable ties around their wrists, the safety bar securely locking them into the seat. The term "safety bar" seemed entirely inappropriate though, given the circumstances. Their arms were wrapped around each other because they were in the middle of freezing to death. They had started hugging after Emilio had remembered a documentary he'd seen about surviving in the extreme cold; they were trying to conserve their body heat as efficiently as possible. Also, while Emilio had left this part out, it made him feel slightly less terrified. To be honest, as ways to die went, Emilio didn't think it was the worst.

A thought struck him. "Damn!"

"What?"

"Th... the pigeons. Who's gonna look after my pigeons?"

"Really? We go to a meeting for you to become this hotshot artist only to have some douchebags pull guns on us and now we're trapped at the top of a rollercoaster, and you're worried about them damned racist pigeons? If they're as smart as you say, they'd have rescued us by now."

"G... give them time. We a long way from Coopersville."

"Yeah," said Bianca, "like that's the problem. Where the hell are we anyway?"

"Dunno," replied Emilio. "The v... view is kinda cool though. D... don't you think, B?"

"Yeah. It's fantastic. Just a shame it's gonna kill us."

They sat there, arms around each other, while all around them snow fell onto the skeletal remains of the abandoned theme park. Emilio thought it looked kinda awesome in a post-apoc sort of way. He would have liked to walk around it. Of course, that would mean getting off this rollercoaster, which didn't seem too likely.

It had been one hell of a day. And to think, that morning he had been worried because he had to wear a suit and go to a meeting. He still had the suit on. He laughed again.

"What's so funny now?" said Bianca.

"I was just thinking. I w... wish my cousin Lorenzo was fatter. I'd be warmer now."

Bianca shook her head and rubbed her hands up and down his back, inside his coat. "You're an idiot, you know that?" But she said it in a nice way. You had to know Bianca to understand. Emilio did.

"Yeah."

Bianca lowered her voice to a whisper. "You think we can move this bar? I could climb over and knock this fool out."

The fool in question was sitting in a car about five seats back, wearing an all-white camouflage jacket that Emilio thought looked wonderfully warm. He was letting a covering of snow rest on him, which made him look like a snowman with a serious grudge. He wasn't looking at them. He had his eye to the scope of the sniper rifle he had trained on the amusement park below. From what Emilio had seen of him as they'd been loaded into and then out of the van, the dude was maybe six-three and he had a thick red beard. His right eye was also developing an impressive shiner – Bianca wasn't the "go quietly" type. He spoke without taking his eye from the scope. "I'd like to see you try, you little bitch. You and the retard aren't any good at whispering either."

Bianca raised her voice. "Fuck you, you Grizzly Adams-wannabe douchebag. How about you put your gun down and we finish what we started?"

"Shut up."

"You gonna make me, you limp-dicked shit-show? Need a gun to make you feel like a man?"

The limp-dicked shit-show didn't move his eye from the rifle's sights, but he pulled a handgun from his holster and pointed it directly at Bianca. "Two guns, actually. I'm pretty sure we only need one living hostage."

Emilio, as much as was possible, tried to move his body to cover Bianca while putting his hand over her mouth. "Sh... she'll be quiet. I promise, sir. I p... p... promise."

The snowman placed the handgun back in his holster in one fluid motion and then spoke in a mocking voice, "O... O... OK th... th... th... then."

"Ouch," said Emilio, pulling his hand back. The palm of it had just been bitten.

"You ever put your hand over my mouth again," whispered Bianca, "I'll bite the whole thing off."

"Sorry. I was trying to make s... sure you didn't get shot."

"At least I wouldn't be cold anymore."

"Yeah," said Emilio, "b... but I would. After death, the human body loses 1.5 degrees in temperature an... n... n... hour. And all your muscles would relax, so your hug wouldn't be as nice."

Bianca nodded. "Good to know."

"Plus, all those muscles relaxing – you'd probably sh... shit your pants."

"Ugh. Well, you sure ruined that moment."

Emilio smiled and rubbed his hands up and down Bianca's back.

"How come you stutter less when you talk to me?"

The question came out of nowhere. Emilio guessed she'd wanted to ask it for a while. He attempted a shrug, which didn't really work in his current circumstance. "I find you easier to t... talk to than anybody else."

"Oh. OK."

Emilio looked over Bianca's shoulder and watched the snow falling silently behind her. "I'm sorry a... about all of this," he said softly.

"Don't be. Ain't your fault. Hell, I've no idea what this is about" – she raised her voice– "and seeing as none of these shitnozzles will tell us" – she lowered it again – "I probably never will. But I'm sure it ain't your fault."

"Y... yeah, but if I was braver or s... smarter, maybe I'd..."

"Hold up," said Bianca, pushing Emilio away slightly so she could look at the side of his face as she talked. "What the hell are you talking about, E? You have a stutter, an arm that don't work and a more messed-up start in life than anybody I know, and that's really saying something. You get shit from everybody and you never back down. Hell, you get shit from life. Most people in your shoes would be bitching and moaning. You just go out and do – and you still found a way to be great. You got your art. After all that, you stood up and said this is me. You are the bravest guy I know. That's brave. That's real brave. Brave ain't being some asshole with a gun."

"She d... didn't mean that."

"The fuck I didn't."

Emilio pulled Bianca closer again. "Could you stop trying to g... get shot for one minute, please."

Bianca said nothing, clearly not willing to commit to that concept.

Emilio lowered his voice and tried to summon his courage. "I'm sorry about the oth... other thing too."

"What other thing?" asked Bianca.

"The mural on the wall of you... I'm... I'm sorry you didn't like it."

There was a long pause, and Emilio felt Bianca's breath on his ear. "What? Who said I didn't like it?"

"Well..."

"I'm..." Bianca's voice, stripped of all its faux aggression and bravado, was softer now. "I just... It was the nicest thing anyone's ever done for me. I guess... I didn't know how to react, but... I love it."

Emilio took a deep breath and then tried to gather his courage. Aw hell, they were going to die soon anyway. He moved his head back and his lips found hers. The kiss was awkward, with his cap getting in the way and teeth banging against each other, and they had no idea where noses were supposed to fit. It was also, by a considerable distance, the most wonderful moment of his life.

"Pathetic," said the ginger-bearded snowman.

They disengaged from the kiss and Bianca gave Emilio a big smile, then she turned to their chaperone. "I swear you're going to get your head knocked clean off, you micro-penised, ass-munching—"

The snowman reached for his handgun again and Emilio all but threw himself on top of Bianca. "She didn't mean it! She didn't mean it!"

"One more word." He took his hand off the grip of his sidearm.

Emilio relaxed slightly and spoke in his softest voice. "You t... trying to scar me for life? First girl I kiss, and she gets her head blown off ten sec... seconds later?"

Bianca smiled at him. "First?"

"I was holding out for B... Beyoncé, but it's looking like that might not happen."

She slapped him gently on the back of the head and then kissed him again. The second one was even better. The trick with the nose thing was that everyone leaned to their right, apparently.

Technical second base and one hundred per cent verified first base. This was a big day for Emilio. They disconnected lips and leaned against each other. It felt somehow different now.

Behind them, Emilio heard a radio beep.

"Confirmed. Target has arrived."

CHAPTER FORTY-FIVE

Smithy pulled the taxi over to the side of the road. At least, he thought he did. Since they'd left the I-95, the roads were so covered in snow it was impossible to see any markings. He was using the GPS as his primary method of figuring out where the road might be, which wasn't the greatest of driving techniques. He couldn't see much outside of the snow-filled beams of the car's headlights, so he knew nothing of the area they were in except that there didn't appear to be anyone else on the roads. The taxi's wheels had been ploughing through a crisp covering of unsullied snow that was getting steadily deeper.

"OK," said Smithy, "I think this is as far as I can take you and have any realistic shot at getting back onto the interstate. Welcome to sunny Connecticut."

"Grand," said Bunny, "appreciate the effort."

"No problem. That'll be 186 bucks."

Bunny gave a sad smile. "Put it on my tab."

Father Gabriel was going through the sports bag. "I'm taking the Glock; do you want the Sig and the spare clip?"

Bunny looked at Smithy and nodded towards the back seat. "He's not big on goodbyes."

"Oh," said Gabriel, shifting awkwardly. "Sorry."

"Don't worry about it. Yes, the Sig, and I'll take the baseball bat too."

"Really?" said Gabriel.

"It's not my sport, but I'm a bit of a demon with a stick. It's sort of my signature move."

Gabriel nodded and then looked at Smithy. "Thank you for the ride and for taking care of our friend in the trunk."

Smithy nodded.

HE IS WELCOME.

"I will…" Gabriel looked around and then got out of the car. "Take your time."

Bunny watched the door close behind him. "I think he thinks we're going to kiss or something."

"I had a hot dog with extra onions for lunch, so…"

Bunny tutted. "Story of my life." He looked at the windscreen, which already had a light covering of snow on it. "Tell Cheryl I apologise for making you late for dinner. And, y'know, keep an eye on Diller. He's a good lad."

"He is," said Smithy with a nod.

"Thanks for everything. And take care of yourself too. Don't get into any scraps you can't win."

Smithy looked out the window and nodded. "Yeah. You too. If you want, I can…"

"No," said Bunny, "you promised you were going home."

"After I release the mouse."

Bunny laughed. "Yeah."

"If you die, I will never forgive you."

"If I do, I promise to haunt you."

"Thanks."

"I mean it. At really awkward times too. Every time you're about to get it on with the missus, I'll be chucking cups in the kitchen."

"Cock-blocking from beyond the grave. That is so you."

Bunny held out his hand. "It's been fun, ye annoying little short-arse."

"Likewise, you drunken Irish prick."

They shook and then Bunny stepped out into the snow.

"If my calculations are correct," said Gabriel, "the entrance to the park is just at the end of this road."

They trudged on side by side through the snow. No light could be seen except for the faint illumination of a town off in the distance to their right and faraway headlights on the interstate, bouncing off the clouds. It would have been slow going even if Bunny hadn't been hampered by a gunshot wound to his left buttock. They walked in silence through the darkness. Gabriel checked his gun for the third time.

"Y'know," said Bunny, "the first time I died was in the snow too."

"What does that mean?"

"Ah, tis a long story. We don't have that kind of time.

Gabriel nodded. "Probably not."

"And to think, as a young fella, I used to bloody love when it snowed. This is Ireland, mind – we could go years without getting a proper snowfall. One time a bad one closed the whole country down – nearly brought down a government."

"Is that so?"

"Yeah. Poor old Michael O'Leary never recovered. Got known as the minister for snow. Good Cork man in the wrong place at the wrong time. Kinda know how he feels."

"It's not too late to back out of this, you know."

"I could say the same."

"This isn't your fight."

"Now that's a fecking shitty thing to say. Those are good kids; I'm not the type to live with the memory of waving them off as they went to meet their doom. I even told Bianca not to punch anybody. Jesus, I really hope she didn't take that advice. Everyone deserves to get one good shot in."

Gabriel checked the spare clip he held in the side pocket of his trousers. "You are a strange man, Brother McGarry."

"I could say the same, Padre."

They walked on, Bunny swinging the baseball bat in his left hand. "Jesus, I'd say this thing pops a fair old wallop."

"I sincerely hope you get the chance to find out."

"You really don't think we stand a chance here, do you?"

Gabriel shrugged. "No."

Bunny laughed. "Well, thanks for the inspirational speech, Captain."

"Sorry," said Gabriel. "I... I've never known the right things to say. I try, but... I guess all that time spent learning the different ways to end a life was when I should have been learning the basics of social interaction."

"Ah," said Bunny, with a wave of his hand, "talking is overrated. For what it's worth, I don't know if you can ever even out what you've done and what you were, but, well, what you did at St Theresa's, that's pretty special. It should count for something."

"Thank you."

Bunny stopped walking and pointed with the bat. "What in the shitting hell is that?"

Gabriel looked at where he was pointing. "That's the front gates of the park."

"What's that over it?"

Gabriel looked at the outline and memory filled in the blanks. "That's the – I don't know what you'd call it – mascot for the Wonderama park? It's Waldor the Clown."

"Ara, shit on a shitty stick, I fecking hate clowns."

"Excuse me?"

"Clowns. Hate them. Creepy bastards."

"I see."

"Coulrophobia. It's a real thing. A proper phobia."

"Right."

Bunny turned around in a circle, doing a weird hop on the spot as he did so. "Ahh feck it, feck it, feck it. Fucking hate clowns."

Bunny put his hands on his knees and started taking deep breaths.

At first, he wasn't sure what the noise was – it sounded like Father Gabriel might be having some form of attack of his own. Bunny turned around and looked at him. The priest had a weirdly giddy look in his eyes.

"Are you... laughing?"

"Sorry. Sorry," said the priest, around increasingly high-pitched, wheezing hysterics.

"What in the fecking hell is so funny?"

The priest struggled to regain control of himself, bent double, his whole body shaking now. "Sorry, I..."

Bunny stood up straight and glowered at him. "I'll tell you what this is, 'tis unprofessional! Man in your position."

Gabriel straightened himself up and waved an apologetic hand. "I apologise. It's just, we're facing near certain death, impossible odds, and... you're afraid of clowns!"

"I never fecking liked you," said Bunny, marching off purposefully towards the gates, Gabriel following in his wake.

"I'm sorry, I—"

They both stopped as the lights came on, the park suddenly dazzling in the gloom. Multicoloured arrays of bulbs sprang into life behind the fences, as if someone had turned the entire park on in one go. Bunny stared as the Ferris wheel, carousels, waltzers and all other manner of rides sprang into life.

The two men gawped in disbelief. "You have got to be fecking kidding."

Despite himself, Bunny jumped as the clown over the gate started to move, its head bobbing up and down hellishly as it laughed.

"Shitting Nora on a lilo!"

With a squeal, the park's PA system came to life.

"Welcome, fun-seekers, to Wonderama, where dreams come true. I'm your host, Abraham. It seems we have more guests than we expected."

They looked at each other and then, feeling slightly foolish, Gabriel shouted back, "This is Brother McGarry. He's just here to make sure the kids get back OK."

"I'm sorry," said Abraham, "it's strictly family only."

Gabriel looked at Bunny, who held his hand up and took a step forward, clearing his throat theatrically. "You can go fuck yourself, you psycho donkey-gobbler. I'll go where the feck I like."

Bunny took a step back as a bullet sliced into the snow a couple of feet in front of him.

"That's Martin," responded Abraham. "He says hello. He has a high-powered sniper rifle and a low tolerance for foul language."

"Yeah, well he can kiss—"

Gabriel stepped in front of Bunny to stop him talking. "Look, you wanted me here – I'm here. Let the kids go with Brother McGarry. This doesn't need to involve them."

"Oh no," said Abraham. "We need them to make sure you really put in your maximum effort for the forthcoming battle. Can't have you not putting up a good show now, can we? If you want them, you'll have to come and get them."

A large spotlight sprang into life and illuminated a rollercoaster at the back of the park. Its cars sat at the apex of one of the ride's peaks. In the front car, Bunny could make out something – possibly just a pile of coats.

He cupped his hands around his mouth in an effort to make his shout somehow carry further. "Are you two alright?"

Through the cold air, Bianca's voice carried back. "I knocked some asshole out."

Bunny grinned and turned to Gabriel. "Oh yeah, that's her, alright. Bloody love that girl!"

"No fighting outside of the ring," shouted back Gabriel.

Bunny shook his head and muttered, "If there was ever a situation that was the exception to that rule."

Abraham's voice, sounding slightly irritated, came over the PA. "I hate to interrupt this reunion, but the park's two security guards are slowly freezing to death in a shed, not to mention our two guests on the rollercoaster. We should move this along. The rules are very simple: you can retrieve your young friends by getting through the park to reach me. I am, to put it in terms the kids might understand, the big boss at the end of the level."

"Asshat," came Bianca's voice.

Somewhere in the distance, there was a ping of a bullet ricocheting off metal.

"Bianca?" shouted Gabriel.

"She is fine," replied Abraham. "That was merely a reminder that children should be seen and not heard. Now, before we go any further – you know how I feel about guns. Please drop any you have brought with you."

There was a moment's pause where nothing happened.

"Please drop any guns," repeated Abraham, "or Martin will shoot you where you stand."

Gabriel took the gun out of his pocket and dropped it on the ground.

"And your friend?"

Bunny shook his head. "You've got a fecking sniper," he roared.

This time the sniper's shot hit close enough that snow bounced up and hit the leg of Bunny's jeans.

"I do not like the foul-mouthed Scotsman."

Gabriel turned and grabbed Bunny. "Don't. Don't."

"The next words he speaks," continued Abraham, "I assure you will be his last. Has he got a gun?"

Gabriel turned. "No. He's just a simple priest. He's only here to escort the children to safety."

"Very well. I will allow him to come in, merely as I think I will enjoy seeing him die."

"Likewise," said Bunny, under his breath.

"We must have trust," said Abraham, "so I will trust neither of you have any other firearms about your person. I am a very fair man, though, so I will make it simple: the first person on either team who fires a gun, Martin shall end their life. Does that seem fair?"

Bunny spoke under his breath. "Was this prick always this gaga or is it a recent thing?"

Gabriel shushed Bunny and then raised his voice to shout again: "Agreed. Do we get to know who else is playing?"

Abraham's laugh sounded weirdly robotic due to the distortion from the PA system. "Adam sends his apologies; he is currently observing the Bolivian elections. If the wrong person wins, it will be a brief victory."

"That's good for us," said Gabriel in a hushed voice.

"If not for Bolivia," replied Bunny.

"But the rest of us are eager to get introduced or reacquainted."

Gabriel's face fell. "That is very bad."

"Jesus," said Bunny. "If you ever fancy giving the priest thing a rest, you've a great future writing them inspirational posters. Y'know, the ones with cats dangling off branches and shite like that."

"I won't tell you the names of the five members of the seven who await you," continued Abraham. "Martin you know, but let's leave the other four as a fun surprise. Some new faces, some old friends. They are dotted around the park, eager to say hello."

Gabriel raised his voice again. "And if we win, you will let the two children go?"

"Of course," came Abraham's cheerful reply. "I'm not a monster. And unlike some people, I keep my word. Are we clear on the rules? No guns, just fun, fun, fun!"

Gabriel nodded and started to walk towards the gates. As they got closer, the mass of lights became more individual, and Bunny could more clearly see the various rides and attractions. Garish clown faces seemed to leer from every corner. He took a deep breath and tried to focus.

"Excellent!" said Abraham. Another brief squeal from the PA system was followed by a cloyingly cheerful tune. Bunny only had to hear fifteen seconds of it to know he really hated it.

"Alright," said Gabriel, standing before the open gates. "We should split up."

"Agreed," said Bunny.

"I can't work effectively if I'm trying to protect you."

"You really do have a way with words, you silver-tongued devil."

Gabriel pointed. "North or south?"

"What?"

"Do you want to go up the left or right side?"

"I'll take left."

"That's north."

Gabriel gave a curt nod and then, amidst the falling snow, he went down on one knee and bent his head. "Dear God, I don't know what plan you have that brought me here, but I pray I can do what is necessary to protect the innocent and to not take another life."

Bunny nodded and then looked up into the sky. "Howerya, God, Bunny here. I'm also hoping to do that, although – fair warning – I am going to kill any of these pricks that get in my way."

Gabriel blessed himself, stood and without another word, he moved off to the right.

The PA squealed again. "Let the games begin!"

CHAPTER FORTY-SIX

Zoya and Dionne sat before the monitor and watched the two dots on the map. The blue one was Birdie; the green one was – well, it was Father Gabriel's phone, which they were assuming he still had on his person.

"How far—?" started Dionne.

"About a hundred yards. We should see them soon."

They watched Birdie's camera feed in silence. All they could see was near darkness and the suggestion of falling snow.

Zoya and Dionne simultaneously leaned backwards as the monitor sprung into dazzling life.

"What on Earth?" started Dionne.

"You have got to be kidding me!" responded Zoya.

As the camera refocused from dealing with near darkness to an explosion of garish neon light, what they were looking at came into focus.

"It's a funfair or something," said Dionne.

"Amusement park," said Zoya, "at least according to the map. It's closed though. If we're to follow the Scooby Doo model for investigation, then they should definitely check out the old caretaker first."

"What?" ask Dionne.

Zoya tutted. "You really need to brush up on your cartoons, Dionne."

"Yeah, I'll get right on that."

The picture faded in and out again.

"Is there anything you can do about that?"

Zoya shook her head. "I've already boosted the signal as much as I can. We're pushing my little Birdie past anything she's done before."

Birdie wasn't designed to fly as far as this. They were now in Connecticut; Birdie had passed the point of no return at about the same time as they'd crossed the state border. That meant that whatever happened, Dionne was going to have to get into the old Dodge van the sisters used for transportation and pick Birdie up, as she wasn't making it home under her own steam.

"That's them, there." Zoya pointed up at the screen. Dionne could make out the silhouettes of two figures standing before the gates.

"What are they...?"

Dionne stopped talking as a voice came over the park's PA system. They listened in silence, Zoya moving Birdie forward just enough to pick up the voices of Bunny and Gabriel too.

Dionne only spoke after Bunny and Gabriel moved towards the gates of the park. "OK, we need to find those kids."

"Right," said Zoya, sounding distracted as she typed away. "Oh no, no, no!"

Birdie's camera feed started to wobble backwards and forwards.

"What is it? I thought you said she had another forty minutes of juice?"

"I thought she would. I think it's the snow – it's gathering on top of her and I can't... She's not designed for..."

Zoya gave out a plaintive whine as the picture started to spin around in a sickening blur. There was a brief image of the rapidly approaching ground and then the screen went black.

Zoya held her head in her hands. Dionne placed a consoling hand on her shoulder.

wrong when to his relief the kid sat up and looked at him. His hands were tied behind his back and his mouth was gagged.

"Hi," said Smithy, waving with his right hand, which contained the gun. He'd had a lot of stuff left in the cab since he started driving it; the sports bag containing two handguns and an Uzi, left by Bunny and the padre, wasn't even the weirdest. That would be the plaster of Paris cast of what Smithy was ninety-five per cent sure was a certain part of a gentleman's anatomy. He'd told Cheryl about it, and then she'd gone and made it weirder by suggesting that maybe the man had left it there deliberately.

The boy looked at him, making no effort to move.

"So, I'm Smithy – we didn't really meet properly. I assume you heard the chat I had with Father Gabriel about you."

The kid nodded.

"I get that there's a lot of... whatever between you and him. You're supposed to kill him or – actually, y'know what? I don't really get it, but I'm guessing we don't have that kind of time. It sounds like more of a 'three years of intensive therapy' type deal. Still, here's the situation. As you no doubt felt, we sorta crashed into a snowbank."

The kid leaned out of the trunk and looked at the side of the car.

"Yeah," said Smithy, "we're screwed. Well, I'm screwed. What happens next comes down to what you want, I guess. You can help me push the car onto the interstate, I can get you to the guy in Jersey and you can take that shot at a new life or..." Smithy looked around again. "Or I guess we hang out here until someone starts asking awkward questions that neither of us will have good answers to. I mean, I'm technically part of a kidnapping plot, but you'll have to explain who you are, which might also be tricky. So I guess that's the situation."

The kid just looked at Smithy some more. To be fair, gagged and bound, he had limited methods of self-expression open to him.

"So," said Smithy. "Do you want to take option A and, y'know, go to Jersey et cetera, et cetera?"

The kid nodded emphatically.

"OK," said Smithy, a little relieved. He hoped the kid meant it, but he wasn't naïve enough to simply believe him.

"So, I'm gonna untie you then." Smithy waggled the gun in the air to remind David he still had it, then he slipped his switchblade from his pocket, hacked through two cords of rope and stepped quickly back. David brought his hands around and rubbed them. Smithy could see the rope burns from where he'd been trying to get out, same as anyone would. Then he ripped the gag from his mouth and commenced a spluttering coughing fit.

Smithy held up the can of soda he kept in the glove compartment for emergencies not quite like this one. "Do you want this?"

"Yes," he said in a hoarse voice.

Smithy tossed him the can. David opened it and then quickly put it to his lips to catch the spouting fluid, gulping it down. He finished the can.

"So," said Smithy, "we good?"

David nodded. "I… I'd like to go to New Jersey, please."

"OK," said Smithy. He'd never heard those words in that order before. Nobody liked to go to New Jersey. This really was a strange day.

David moved to get out of the trunk – first looking at Smithy, who nodded his assent. David threw his leg over the side and lowered himself down. Then he stood there, stretching his back out.

"Sorry about all of… y'know, that," said Smithy, feeling awkward. "I'm sure it was uncomfortable but, y'know, Padre meant the best for you."

David shrugged, and it hit Smithy just how young the guy was. He may have been an assassin, but on some level he was still an awkward teenager, same as Smithy and, well, everyone had been.

"Right," said Smithy, "I'll throw it in drive and then you and me are going to try to push it out, OK?"

David nodded again.

Smithy got into the front seat and released the brake, turning the wheel as much as possible so that the thing had the best chance of moving. He got out, shoved the gun into the back of his jeans and joined David at the back of the car.

They both braced against it.

"OK. On three. One... two... th—"

Smithy came around a few seconds later. The kid hadn't hit him that hard, but it had been perfectly timed. Smithy lay there, dazed, on the snowbank. He turned to look down the incline and saw the faint figure of David in the darkness, running back the way they had come. It was then he realised that the kid had taken the gun too. "Fuck it!"

He stood up and watched as the kid's outline faded to nothing. He had zero hope of catching him. He raised his voice. "I was... we were just trying to help you."

Smithy kicked the back tyre of the cab, which did little to aid his predicament, mood or the state of his toes. "Goddamn teenagers!"

CHAPTER FORTY-EIGHT

Emilio looked at the neon winter wonderland spread out beneath them. The snow was still falling steadily, so it was hard to make out much detail. This day was only getting weirder. His heart had leaped when they'd heard first Gabriel and then Bunny, shouting from somewhere out in the darkness. He'd been trying to cling on to hope ever since the two men in SoHo had shown them through to a loading dock and then calmly pulled guns on them. Since then, his world had consisted of terror with occasional making out. From the moment Bianca had delivered a right hook to one of their captors, he'd been living in fear of his own death and, worse still, hers. She wasn't one to go quietly, but whoever these people were, one lucky punch aside, they knew what they were doing. They'd told them nothing about what was going on, but with Gabriel and Bunny showing up, they seemed to have something to do with it. Weirder still, it was Gabriel they appeared to be interested in. Emilio liked Bunny, but it wasn't hard to see how he could piss somebody off. Father Gabriel on the other hand? All the man did was grind away, trying to do right.

Behind them, the sniper – called Martin, apparently, at least if the voice over the PA system could be trusted – was watching what was going on through his scope. Emilio didn't know much about guns, but he knew some had infrared sensors. This one must have, as Martin appeared to be reporting back to his boss.

"Target is proceeding up the south side, coming into Jonah's area. The other guy is moving up the north side. Confirm – I should not take shot?"

Emilio couldn't hear what Martin was being told through his earpiece, but he saw the man wince.

"Alright, alright – just confirming. Seems pointless having me up here, but fine. Target has reached Jonah's area. Engaged."

Emilio watched as Martin shifted his position slightly. "I... Jonah is down. Confirm Jonah is down. What? What does...? Alright. I have... Correction. Jonah is alive but appears incapacitated... I don't know."

"Oh dear," said Bianca loudly, "is it not going well?"

Martin pulled his eye away from the scope and looked at Bianca. "Just for that, the worst things you can imagine will happen to you before you die."

Bianca glared back defiantly. "That's assuming your guys win."

Martin smiled at her. "Win? Regardless of what happens down there, you're up here with me. There is no way out of this for you."

Martin turned back to the scope. "Confirmed. Secondary target is entering Pascal's area. This should be quick."

Normally Bunny was good at sneaking. It was one of his skills. Normally, though, he wasn't limping due to a wounded arse, and he wasn't trying to make his way through four inches of snow. Sneaking was tricky in the snow, it being impossible to tread lightly when your feet were sinking into the ground. So, instead, he was limping at a steady pace, using the baseball bat as an occasional walking stick and making no attempt at concealment. He headed in the direction of the rollercoaster. He had no dog in this fight other than wanting to get Bianca and Emilio out of there.

He passed a merry-go-round. All the horses had clown faces.

Bunny watched as they circled round and round under the garish lights, bobbing up and down. What kind of messed-up mind even thought of something like that? Coming from all directions, he could hear automated demented laughter, along with hoots, hollers, bells and whistles. Maybe if the park had been full of people on a sunny day it might have added to the "atmosphere", but mostly deserted in the middle of a snowstorm, it gave the place an even creepier feel. He swore to himself that if he ever got out of this, he would track down the person who designed this nightmarish place and give them a piece of his mind. It was like Stephen King's *It* mixed with *Charlie and the Chocolate Factory*. He'd passed a line of fat animatronic clowns cancan dancing a minute ago. That was the kind of thing that would haunt his dreams – assuming he ever got to have any more. Bunny was feeling too old, too wounded and too cold to put up with this crap. One part of that he could do something about. He pulled his thermos flask out of his coat pocket and took the cup off. It had been one of the two things he'd quickly grabbed before they'd left the church.

"Howerya," he said, raising his voice. "I can see you there, standing in the shadows behind that booth. I'm more than happy to get to the kicking-the-shit-out-of-each-other bit in a minute, but any chance I could have a spot of soup first?"

The man stepped forward. He had dark, Mediterranean-looking skin and was dressed all in black. In his left hand, he was casually tossing a knife up in the air and catching it after two rotations.

"Jesus," said Bunny. "No offence, but you lot really do take the whole assassin image thing seriously, don't ye? Still, cuts down on washing, I suppose."

The man gave him a smile. "I am disappointed."

"How's that?"

"I was hoping you'd be Daniel. I've heard so much about him."

"What? The padre? Ah yeah, he's great. Not much of a conversationalist though. I'm Bunny. And you are?"

"The last person you'll see before you die."

Bunny raised his cup in salute. "Good line. I bet you're feeling proud of yourself. I'm going to call you Mack the Knife."

"As you wish."

Bunny slurped some soup. "Jesus! Hot! Hot!" He waved a hand in front of his lips before he bent down, picked up a handful of snow and shoved it in his mouth.

"Fecking hell. Sorry about that, Mack. Tell ye what though, these flasks are the dog's bollocks. I made that this morning. Still boiling hot. Incredible."

"Fascinating."

"So," said Bunny, placing the flask down on the ground in front of him and picking up the baseball bat, "have I understood this correctly? We're not allowed to shoot each other, and if we do, your sniper fella shoots us?"

"Apparently so."

"I tell ye, I'm really starting to miss when people used to try to kill me the old-fashioned way. You knew where you were with that. I don't suppose I could interest you in a snowball fight? Best of three. Standard one-point deduction for a head shot and no sticking stones in – someone could lose an eye."

"You talk a lot, fat man."

"Oh," said Bunny. "I see we're at the name-calling stage now, are we? For the last time, it's the portion sizes. I'm telling everybody."

"I'm bored with this."

"Fair enough," said Bunny, raising up the baseball bat. "Come at me. I'm too tired to chase you."

"No, thanks."

The blur of hand movement and the flash of metal were so fast, Bunny could only really process what had occurred when the blade dug into the flesh of his left thigh. "Fuck!"

He dropped the bat and stumbled backwards, his hands around the wound, and another blade thunked into his right thigh, in an almost identical position. "Ohhh…"

Bunny collapsed backwards onto the snow-covered ground, blood seeping from both wounds and turning his jeans red. He had a hand on each leg, and hot, wet blood was slipping through his fingers. He yowled in agony.

After a couple of moments, the face of his attacker came into view above him. "It hurts, doesn't it?"

Bunny spoke through gritted teeth. "Cheating bastard. Same. As. Shooting."

"No. Nobody said anything about throwing knives."

"Arsevent."

"I don't know if you're in any position to throw insults around."

"I'm dying..." Bunny panted. "I'll say what I like."

The man shrugged. "Hard to argue against that." He reached down and pulled the knife out of Bunny's left leg, giving it a twist as he did so. Bunny screamed and lashed out with his hand, but the man effortlessly batted him away.

He pulled the knife out of the right leg in a similar manner. Bunny clenched his eyes shut, tears rolling down his cheeks.

Bunny tried to pull the Sig out of his coat pocket, but a blade descended and jabbed into his upper left arm as he attempted to do so. "Ara fuck!" This stab wound was about an inch above where he had been stabbed the night before. His voice came out in a whine. "You are such a prick."

"Now now," said the man, as he reached into Bunny's pocket and took the gun, throwing it onto the ground a few feet away. "Sticks and stones will break my bones..."

Bunny lay back on the snow, his breaths short and shallow now. He looked up and watched the snow falling. He could taste blood in his mouth. Somewhere along the line, he must have bitten something. He laughed, causing blood-red saliva to bubble messily out of his mouth.

"Is something funny?"

"Weirdest sense of déjà vu."

"Enjoy it while you can."

Bunny spread his arms wide and raised his voice to the sky. "Feck it. Just do it."

"Aw, nothing to say? Are you out of witty repartee?"

Bunny closed his eyes.

"Have it your own way."

"Wait," gasped Bunny.

The man looked down.

"Have I told you that you're a prick?"

"Yes."

"Grand. Fire away."

The man flipped the knife in his hand again. "I've always wanted to try this. I call it death from above. Don't move or we'll have to do it again." He threw the blade high into the air, and he and Bunny watched it disappear into the darkness.

"What goes up, must come—"

Mack was interrupted by the *pop-pop-pop-pop* of the tendons at the back of his right knee being sliced through, causing him to scream and collapse forward onto Bunny. The knife in Bunny's hand was a Strider CPM S30V steel combat knife – namely, the one used the night before by David. It was the other thing Bunny had taken with him from the church, because not liking knives and not thinking you might need one were two very different things.

Mack's scream was animalistic – equal parts agony and rage. Bunny hugged him with all the strength his desperation could summon, like he was a friend returned after a half a lifetime away.

Mack scrabbled for the other knife that was holstered on his belt, but he didn't make it. As he looked into Bunny's eyes, his own blade descended from the sky and buried itself deep in his back. Bunny held him there for a moment and watched the light fade in his eyes, then he fell back to the ground, the dead weight on top of him.

Bunny sucked in a few deep breaths and felt his eyelids growing heavy. Starting to close. He just needed to rest for a second. Just a second and he'd be fine.

Just a second…

He jabbed his own finger into the knife wound on his left leg, which had the desired effect. He screamed, and with a rush of frantic energy, he heaved his assailant off him and struggled messily to his feet, grabbing up the baseball bat and the Sig as he did so. He staggered forward, trying to ignore the feeling of blood running down both of his legs, causing his jeans to cling to him. Pain seemed to issue from every part of his body now. He screamed into the night.

"Did you see that? You shower of donkey-knobbing nutjobs? He's dead! Ha – dead! I'd say it was the irony that killed him... but it was definitely the knife."

He moved forward, dragging his feet through the snow. He couldn't stop. Whatever energy was holding him up, he sensed its edges. Falling down again would mean never getting back up. He had to keep moving. Focus.

"I'm coming. Emilio and... Bianca. I'm coming. Hang on..."

He rounded the corner of the booth and screamed. Waldor the Clown, dressed as a cowboy, stood before him. Bunny swung the bat at its face on instinct, smashing fibreglass in a way that would probably get him banned from future visits. He staggered on. He was on some kind of thoroughfare, lights blinking from stalls on either side. Ducks in shooting galleries swam by and buckets were waiting for things to be thrown into them; basketball hoops too. And the noise. Pinging, bells ringing and the clown's mocking laughter provided a cacophonous backdrop. The rollercoaster was maybe a hundred meters in front of him now, going in and out of focus. "Fecking clowns. Clowns and assassins. Feck the lot of you."

He was light-headed. There was a dizzy, giddy edge to everything now. The colours seemed somehow brighter even as the shapes blurred.

"I'm... coming."

Seventy meters.

Sixty.

Fifty.

Forty.

A figure stepped out from behind one of the stalls and stood in his path. He had long blond hair and a thick muscular build.

Bunny staggered towards him. He didn't have the energy to go around.

He watched as the man smiled at him, and then something

dropped from his hands. Although Bunny couldn't put it into words at that moment, he knew he had seen these things before, on TV. On one of the cable shows that you only find when trawling through channels late at night. He'd watched it at two in the morning, scuttering drunk, with kebab down his shirt, too tired to make it upstairs to bed. They were known as Chinese whips – nine-link metal chains with a spike on the end. The lad on the telly had said they were the hardest weapon in all the martial arts to master. The man standing in front of him seemed to have managed it. The whips twirled around him in a dizzying whirl, sending snow flying up from the ground as they did so. He spun them around his neck and legs at intervals. While it looked insane, it was all intended to build up more and more momentum. The man on the TV had explained it all. The whole effect was mesmerising. It was like the man had his very own dry ice machine.

Bunny kept walking.

He couldn't stop walking.

It'd be like walking straight into the rotating blades of a propeller plane. The man moved forward to meet him.

"Very impressive," hollered Bunny, his voice giddy with excitement, his eyes blinking constantly as they filled with water.

The whirling whips were nearly in range now.

"Have ye seen *Raiders of the Lost Ark*?"

Bunny took out his gun and shot the man straight through the chest. One of the whips went flying over Bunny's head into the darkness.

"Sorry, but the last lad didn't play f—"

The shot from the sniper spun Bunny around, and he landed face down in the snow.

CHAPTER FORTY-NINE

Emilio and Bianca stared at the sniper as the echo of his shot reverberated around them.

"What did you do?" said Bianca in a quiet voice, afraid of the answer.

Martin ignored her, pulled the bolt back to chamber another round and pressed the comms unit on his ear. "Secondary target shot Marsellus. Both men are now down."

"No!" screamed Bianca.

She knew the metal bar trapped her in the car, but she still struggled to get out. "I'll kill you, motherfucker! I'm gonna kill you!"

He took his eye from the sights and smiled over at her. "Your fat friend is dead, bitch."

Emilio held Bianca awkwardly as she struggled, tears rolling down her cheeks. "You're gonna get your head knocked clean off your shoulders, you monster. You hear me? Clean off. So help me, God."

Martin smiled a wide smile. "Your God didn't help him and he's not going to help you."

Bianca struggled some more. "You're a no-good piece of shit, you know that? What kind of a weak-assed pussy has to shoot people from afar?"

"Shut up, I'm tired of your little girl tantrum."

"That little girl p... punched you out," said Emilio.

Martin sneered at him. "One lucky shot."

"Face-to-face ain't your thing," said Emilio, in a calm voice.

"He ain't got the balls to stand up and fight."

Martin placed his hand on the grip of his handgun. "I'm fucking tired of being a babysitter for you two whining brats. Maybe I..."

He stopped and put his finger to the comms unit again. "No, sir, he is..."

Martin shifted the sights. "He... I don't. Steffon appears to be down. I... Trying to reacquire primary now."

One hundred yards away, at the other end of the comms link, Abraham stood on the raised platform where, back when the park was open, acrobatic tumbling had been performed six times a day to entertain customers.

He looked down at the man standing in front of him. "Don't bother. He is here."

CHAPTER FIFTY

"Hello, Daniel."

"That is not my name."

Abraham gave a broad smile. The other man stood down on the ground in front of the stage – his audience of one. There appeared to be a red stain on his black jumper: a slow-bleeding wound or perhaps someone else's blood. "Are you telling me that a priest just killed two of my men?"

"I did not kill anyone. Jonah has a broken ankle and a shattered collarbone. Steffon has a broken leg. You should send them assistance."

Abraham pushed his long hair back behind his ears. "I did not raise any of you to need assistance."

Gabriel shrugged. "If you don't, their deaths are on you."

"Out of curiosity, how did you get by Steffon so quickly?"

"I was trying to go around him without engaging when he was distracted by the sound of gunfire. I saw an opening."

Abraham shook his head. "Sloppy. I noticed it on his last mission too. I'm wondering if his heart is in it anymore." He clenched both of his fists together. "He was such a force to be reckoned with in his prime."

"Maybe we all tire of death eventually," said Gabriel.

"I haven't," said Abraham. "Although I really consider myself to be in the business of life." He spread his arms out wide. "Without me, without your family, you'd have wound up dead in a gutter in that stinking favela I found you in. Not only do you turn your back on us, but now you fight against us. You kill us."

"I haven't killed anyone."

"Oh no?" said Abraham. "I believe Pascal and Marsellus are both now dead. That gunfire you heard was your friend."

Gabriel shrugged. "He is only here to save the two children you took as bait in your sick little game."

"Game?" said Abraham. "This is no game. I am trying to take back what was stolen from me."

"And it has resulted in two deaths and two of your men being incapacitated. Haven't you seen enough of this madness?"

"No. I consider this a valuable exercise. Frankly, if they cannot handle a couple of turbulent priests, then the seven requires an injection of fresh blood." Abraham looked up at the sky, watching the snow falling. "Shows no sign of stopping, does it?" He looked down, a thought occurring to him. "Oh, and you mean three. Three deaths. Your annoying friend is no longer with us."

"I am sorry to hear that," said Gabriel. "Sadly, I don't think we can call the man my friend. Being raised by you, I don't think I have the capacity to truly have friends."

"You had something better than that. You had a family."

Gabriel sighed, suddenly feeling all kinds of weary. "Can we not end this now? There need not be more bloodshed."

Abraham stepped forward to the front of the stage. "But we're just getting to the best part! It is time for you to truly embrace who you are."

"Who I was."

"And who you can be again." Abraham bent down and picked up what was lying at the edge of the stage. Gabriel had known they would be there: two fencing swords. "This was always meant to be, don't you think? The master takes on the student; there is a certain poetry to it. You kill me and become your true self, or you die a heroic death in battle, like the warrior you always were."

"Let's not pretend I live either way." Gabriel pointed at the sky. "I imagine I am in Martin's sights right now. He will be itching to kill me."

"Ah," said Abraham. "Sibling rivalry. It always saddened me that the two of you never got along."

"He is a psychopath."

"Now now, there's no need for name calling. I respect your objection though, which is why there is a sniper rifle behind the stage. If you kill me, you and Martin can work out your differences once and for all."

"Even if it is there, my chances of reaching it will be slim."

Abraham tutted. "So negative." He raised his arms to the sky and hollered out in a mocking tone, "All you need do is ask, and the good Lord shall provide."

He tossed one of the fencing blades towards Gabriel, who neatly stepped aside and caught it by the hilt.

Abraham jumped down from the stage. "*En garde!*"

"What are they doing?" asked Bianca, whose position gave her no view of the area below and to the right of the rollercoaster.

"They're f... fencing."

"They're doing what now?"

"'Hello. My n... name is Inigo Montoya. You killed my father. Prepare to die.'"

"What?"

"Never mind. It's y... y'know, with swords."

Bianca pulled at the bar yet again. "You are killing me. Father G is having a sword fight down there and I'm missing it?"

"Sorry."

"This sucks."

"Wow!"

"What?"

"Nothing."

"Emilio!"

"The guy, like, went at Father G, and Father G j... jumped over his sword. It was cool."

"Enjoy it while you can," said Martin. "If your so-called priest looks like he is getting the upper hand, I'm under orders to shoot him in the back of the head. You don't think the boss will actually let him win, do you? He just wants to prove a point."

"Scumbag!" spat Bianca.

"She's a real princess," said Martin, looking at Emilio. "It's a shame you will not get to enjoy your shitty life with your eight welfare babies in that ghetto you come from."

"Coopersville," said Emilio. "Coopersville ain't got much. Kn... know what it does have? Real family. Not like yours."

He laughed. "Please!"

"Hey, asshole," said Emilio. "Big man with a gun. I... I'm not a... afraid of you. L... look me in the e... eye."

Martin looked over at him. "What?"

"Thank you."

"What for, retard?"

"Being d... d... d... d..."

Martin mimicked him. "D... d... d... de man who is going to kill you and your girlfriend?"

Emilio shook his head and gave him a big grin. "Distracted."

"What's that supposed to—?"

Martin's thought was interrupted by the rollercoaster jerking into movement.

Gabriel was losing blood from cuts on his upper right arm and lower left leg. He was out of practice and it was going to kill him.

"Dear, oh dear," said Abraham. "You are very rusty, Daniel."

Gabriel parried a blow and counter-attacked, forcing Abraham to move backwards. "That. Is not. My. Name."

Abraham was toying with him. Gabriel felt like a mouse under a cat's paw. Abraham wasn't hungry, so he was enjoying the sport until he got bored.

"You are what I named you because you are who I made you."

Abraham's feint was well judged and Gabriel overcorrected, leaving his face open. His cheek stung as the blade sliced through the skin. He moved back. Blood was flowing freely; he could feel it run down onto his neck. Abraham lowered his blade and smiled at Gabriel.

"Getting angry, aren't you, Daniel? Doesn't this feel good? Being who you were meant to be."

Gabriel remembered the smile. It had always been there, every time they had fenced throughout his life. Through a child's eyes, he had seen it to be encouraging. Charming. Now, looking at Abraham from a world away, he saw it for what it really was: a smile that hid a sneer.

"Of course," said Gabriel, "this is quite a rarity for you, isn't it? Being in the action. I mean, normally you just send others to do your dirty work."

There was a flash of something behind Abraham's eyes. "That is the burden of command."

"Yes," said Gabriel. "How many sons have you sent to their deaths now?"

"It's a cruel world."

"It's interesting… You know, for all the talk of the family members and what they achieved in the field, your past is still a mystery."

Abraham resumed his fighting stance. "Is now the time for this chat?" He swung his rapier through the air, a whooshing sound accompanying the movement as it parted the falling snow.

"You always implied that you were some great, accomplished field operative. I wonder though…"

Abraham laughed. "Doubting your master?"

"What is it they say? Those that can't, teach."

Abraham darted forward and launched a volley of blows which Gabriel parried. Interesting. Abraham normally preferred to defend and counter. That was his technique.

Gabriel, the blood flowing down his face in a steady stream now, moved forward onto the balls of his feet. Somehow, his old balance felt like it was returning to him. "Is that it?" said Gabriel. "You set about to create something you could not be? Because you weren't good enough?"

"I didn't come here for one of your sermons, Father." Abraham almost spat the last word. There it was, the snarl.

Gabriel laughed. "Oh, good God, that's what this is, isn't it? The whole reason for the family. You lacked any power in the real world, so you created a fake one where you could play God. Train children up and then watch them die."

"It's a—"

"Cruel world," finished Gabriel with a laugh. "Yes, yes, you said. It was cruel to you, wasn't it? You never made it. You were a failure and you went to these great lengths, dedicated your life to creating the family, just to feel what it was like to be powerful. A small man, turning children into killers."

Abraham's assault sent Gabriel rocking back, the precision replaced with violence. Keeping his footing in the snow was difficult. He stumbled and... Abraham raised his blade to deliver a slashing blow.

There! Even as he fell, the gap revealed itself. Gabriel's blade lashed out, his aim true. Abraham screamed. The tip of the blade sliced through his right wrist. Abraham dropped his sword and pulled his hand back, spurting blood darkening his jacket.

Gabriel rolled and regained his footing, surging forward immediately.

Abraham moved quickly backwards, a false smile on his face. Trying to feign composure. "Superb, Daniel. I'd applaud, only..."

Gabriel passed Abraham's sword, lying useless in the snow. "You've lost."

Abraham shrugged and raised his finger to his ear. "Take the shot!"

Gabriel dived onto the ground. He scanned around him, looking for cover to sprint to, his body tensed for the shot he knew was coming. If he could only...

He glanced upwards. Then he risked a longer look, to confirm what he had seen. Then Gabriel stood and looked at Abraham, who was now staring up at the rollercoaster too. Or rather, at the empty piece of track where the train had been.

"Martin!" shouted Abraham.

"This is a terrible thing for a priest to say, but it appears that, for you, there is no man upstairs."

"FUUUUUUCCCCCCKKKKKK!" screamed Emilio. He'd never been on a rollercoaster before. His grandma had forbidden it. She'd said that, because of his useless arm and his neck, it was too dangerous. He didn't know if that was true, but he was pretty sure that this particular rollercoaster was too dangerous for anyone. His brain could be a grade-A dick sometimes. Case in point, the thought had popped into it, as the rollercoaster had gone down and around the first bend, that it probably wasn't supposed to run on frozen tracks covered in snow.

As they reached a relatively straight bit, Emilio glanced back. The one consolation was that even if he wasn't enjoying the ride, someone was enjoying it a lot less. At least he and Bianca were held in their seats by a bar. Martin wasn't.

"Stop! Stop!" came the scream from behind Emilio. "Who the fuck started this?"

Bianca smiled over at Emilio. Oh God, the crazy girl was enjoying this. She held her hands in the air. "Wooo!"

Emilio's first thought upon hearing the popping sound was that the tracks were coming apart, but on the second one, he saw a puff of stuffing as the bullet sliced through the material on the shoulder of Bianca's coat. She screamed a different scream. Martin had found a focus for his anger.

They huddled down, Emilio trying to put his good arm over Bianca's shoulder to offer what protection he could, useless though it was. The seats were designed for holding people in, and as hard as they tried to lean forward and give Martin less to aim at, the G-force kept pushing them back. At least the ride also made it difficult for Martin to find a clean shot. Still, their luck couldn't hold forever.

The rollercoaster hurtled around a hairpin bend and Emilio felt his stomach drop. His Dolphins cap flew off his head and he could feel the snow beating against his face as the car hurtled on. He closed his eyes for a second and then forced them open again. Whatever was coming, it was better to see it. He felt another bullet whoosh by overhead and heard Martin laughing dementedly.

Emilio glanced back. Martin stood in the back car, gripping the bar with one hand, his sidearm in the other. "Dying time!" he screamed.

Emilio's eyes widened and he gripped onto Bianca tightly.

She screamed again. Not with joy this time. Not with fear either.

Sometimes you roar into the darkness to show it you are unafraid.

Sometimes you scream at the injustice at it all.

And sometimes, just sometimes, life gives you a moment of pure justice and you holler in delight.

And sometimes it gives you a mad, blood-soaked, half-dead Irishman with a baseball bat standing by the tracks.

Years later, they'd both swear they felt the bat whooshing through the air over their heads, and they would always remember the sound. The sound of a man's head being hit clean out of the park, or at least off his shoulders, isn't something you're ever likely to forget.

CHAPTER FIFTY-ONE

Abraham slumped down onto the snow, his wounded wrist held to his chest, blood pumping from it.

"Let me look at that," said Gabriel. "You need help."

"Shut up," said Abraham. The man's charm had finally left him. He awkwardly crossed his left hand over to his right ankle and took out the gun that was strapped there. He pointed it at Gabriel.

"I thought you didn't like guns?"

"You think you're better than me. You're not better than me."

"OK," said Gabriel, "but there's no need for any more killing. Put the gun down and I can help you."

"Trying to bargain your way out, Father? Now you're staring down the barrel at death?"

Gabriel dropped his sword and raised his hands. "I've faced death a lot lately. Don't forget, you sent David to kill me."

"Oh, please!" said Abraham. "That was just a hello. Something to let you get your eye in. On your worst day, I knew you could handle him."

Gabriel ran his hand over his cheek and took it away, looking at the blood. "I'm truly sorry."

Abraham let out a laugh devoid of any humour. "It's a little late to apologise now."

He shook his head. "It wasn't you I was apologising to."

Gabriel averted his eyes as the shot rang out. One clean shot to the chest. He could hear Abraham slumping over in the snow.

When Gabriel opened his eyes again, he looked at David, standing on the far side of the clearing, the smoking gun still in his hand. They locked eyes for a moment and then David dropped the gun and walked away, disappearing into the night.

Gabriel moved over to where Abraham lay, his blood turning the snow red all around him. His eyes were wild with desperation and he was unable to breathe, drowning in his own life. Gabriel held his hand with his left hand and made the cross on his forehead with his right, unintentionally marking him with his own blood. "Through this holy unction, may the Lord pardon thee whatever sins or faults thou has committed…"

Father Gabriel looked at the controls of the rollercoaster and then, for want of any other ideas, hit the big red button. This turned out to be the emergency brake, which caused it to screech to a halt. Emilio was pleasantly surprised when they didn't come off the tracks. The bar disengaged, and he climbed down the ten or so feet to the ground with Bianca's help. He avoided looking at whatever was left in the car behind them. Some images you didn't need.

They found the father standing on the platform, leaning over Bunny's body, the shattered baseball bat by his side. Bunny was a colour Emilio had only ever seen at funerals.

"Is he gonna be OK?" asked Bianca.

Gabriel held two fingers to Bunny's throat. "He has a pulse, but it's weak. He's lost a lot of blood." Gabriel pointed at a dark patch on the left side of Bunny's abdomen. "The bullet went right through him, which is good, assuming it avoided hitting anything too important, but we have to get him medical help." Gabriel looked around, panicked. "I don't... they must have had a car or van. How did you get here?"

Before Emilio or Bianca could answer, they all looked up at the sound of something crashing through a fence. Unable to find the gate, and figuring that time was of the essence, Smithy had driven a snowplough he had technically hijacked straight through the fencing. He took out a multicoloured shooting stall and kept ploughing onwards. He was struggling to steer while holding a gun in one hand and looking for someone to shoot. He drove towards the rollercoaster.

"Is everything OK?" he hollered.

"We need to get Bunny to a hospital," Gabriel shouted back.

"Shit," hollered Smithy. "OK."

He looked down at the breeze block that was currently holding the gas pedal down. "Hang on, I'm gonna find something soft to crash into!"

CHAPTER FIFTY-TWO

Trey looked down again at the gun in his hand. They said it would be easy. All you had to do was just point and shoot. The guy would be coming out of the hospital by a back entrance – they had been given a tip-off. The hospital had metal detectors, so neither Santana nor any of his crew would be armed. The man was on crutches too. It would be easy. That's what they'd all said: easy.

Ice had told him that he would be taking out the man who'd ordered the hit on Pocket. It would be vengeance and it would be righteous.

Now, Trey was standing in the shadows of an alley across the street. He was trying to control his breathing. He felt like throwing up. He kept moving the gun from hand to hand as his palms were so sweaty. It had surprised him, when they'd given it to him, how light the gun had felt, but now... now it felt heavy.

He almost jumped out of his skin when the voice came from behind him. "I was sorry to hear about Pocket."

He turned to see Father Gabriel standing there, a large white bandage covering half of his face.

"How did you know I was here?"

Gabriel held his arm out, palm down. "Doesn't matter. I'm so sorry for your loss, Trey. I know you loved him, and I know he loved you."

"You shouldn't be here."

"It's a free country," said Gabriel. He tried to smile, but the bandaging on his face meant it was impossible. "So, let me guess: they told you that you had the chance to kill the man who killed Pocket?"

"This is none of your concern, Father."

"I'm afraid it is. I owe it to you to make it my concern. Not to mention your mother and Pocket."

Trey had tears in his eyes now. "I'm doing this for Pocket. This asshole killed my brother."

Gabriel sighed and leaned back against the wall. "Y'know, all the time I have been a priest, every day I wake up and think, if only I could find the words. Better words than what I had. The right words that could make people see things differently. To help take people's pain away. To make life seem worth living. The words to bring light to the darkness. Maybe if I had your skills with the language, Trey, maybe then I could change something."

Gabriel glanced at an alley cat that was prowling around in the gloomy light behind them. She stared back at him, her eyes bright in the darkness, before turning away, deciding they were not a threat.

Gabriel pushed himself off the wall and stood up again. "Do you know what I've only recently realised, Trey? Those words don't exist. Words can spark ideas, but it is actions that define the world around us."

"I'm taking action," said Trey quietly.

"Yes, you are," said Gabriel. "All I can do is ask you to consider the result of those actions. If you kill this man, you'll just be leaving more brothers, mothers, sisters and sons angry at the world and at the man with a gun who took their loved one. Trust me, it doesn't end, son. It doesn't end unless you end it. Sometimes the hardest action is deciding to be the one to walk away."

"I gotta get justice!"

"There is no justice. There's just the living and the dead. Lord knows Pocket and I didn't see eye to eye on much, but we agreed on one thing: you should have a better life than this."

"But I..."

"Look at my face, son."

Trey stared at the ground.

"Trey."

He looked up reluctantly.

"I know more about death than any man should, and believe me, Trey, none of this is going to make it feel any better. It won't stop the pain. It won't bring Pocket back. All it means is that any time a memory of the good times you shared pops into your head, it will be soiled, because your mind will come back to the moment you took a life and ruined your own. A life Pocket fought so hard for you to have. One man didn't kill him, son; Coopersville did – or at least what the gangs and the violence and the drugs have turned it into. If the violence is the problem, how can violence be the answer? This will make no difference. You will just be feeding the machine. You know I'm telling you the truth."

"I gotta..."

Gabriel held his hand out. "Give me the gun, Trey."

"But I..."

"Give me the gun. Emilio and Bianca are waiting to see you. There's an entire world out there for the three of you. Don't ruin it now. You've all worked so hard. Be more than this. The world doesn't need another broken man with a gun, believe me. Give it to me, son."

Trey stood there for the longest moment, his fingers flexing around the gun's grip, his eyes fixed on the ground.

His body sagged forward, and he held the gun out to Gabriel, who gently took it from him. Trey leaned his head on Gabriel's shoulder and tears poured out of him as his body shook. Gabriel held him there. "That's it. Let it out. Let it out."

EPILOGUE

Bunny opened his eyes and stared up at the ceiling. He didn't recognise it. He also had no idea how he'd come to be in a position to be looking up at it. He wasn't dead – at least, no more than he had been before all of this started – though he was admittedly basing that on the idea that death wouldn't be this bloody uncomfortable. His mind was groggy, he felt like his tongue had been replaced with a sponge and almost every area of his body was sending signals that, when the drugs wore off, this was going to hurt like hell.

An angelic face swam into view above him.

His voice came out as a parched croak. "Is this... heaven?"

Sister Dionne smiled down at him. "No, Mr McGarry, this is Brooklyn."

With a whirr, he felt his bed slowly rise up to place him in a more or less seated position. Sun was streaming through the windows. There was nothing that qualified as an actual view, because the bottom half of the window was that kind of translucent glass that educational institutions of a certain era specialised in, designed to let light in but not allow any young imaginations out.

Dionne held a glass with a straw out in front of him. "Here, drink this."

He did. He'd never have believed that water, just water, could taste so good. "How did I get here?"

"Well now," said Dionne, putting the glass down, "that's quite a long story. I believe you passed out at a fairground after doing something rather gruesome that involved a baseball bat and a man losing his head."

"Prick had it coming."

"I'm glad to hear it, as if that was your idea of a warning..."

"How are—?"

Dionne held her hand up. "Everyone is fine. Father Gabriel and the children are all OK. They and your friend Mr Smith managed to get you to a hospital."

"Mr Smith?" said Bunny, honestly confused. "Oh, you mean Smithy?"

Dionne nodded. "Yes. Technically, Connecticut police are looking for a man of... reduced stature who hijacked a snowplough at gunpoint but, as it happens, we know somebody in their highway patrol. Let's just say that the investigation is going poorly, and authorities are not optimistic."

"Right," said Bunny. "Hang on, I ended up at a hospital? But..."

"Yes," said Dionne. "The cops were very interested in you, and were keen to speak with you when you came around. Your injuries were both extensive and inexplicable. I have been told that if it hadn't been for some very good work by some very gifted surgeons, you really would be dead now."

"But..." said Bunny. "I know I'm just coming out of a coma... How long was I out?"

"Six days."

"Jesus. Six days. But I'm not in a hospital now."

Dionne shook her head. "No. You are back in the headquarters of the Sisters of the Saint."

"And how did I get here?"

"We busted you out. The police are even more interested in you now, but, sadly, all they have to go on from the guard on duty, who got knocked out, is that the nurse's shift changed and when he came to, you were gone – bed and all." Dionne patted it. "When you're better, we will of course drop it back with a note of apology."

"But..."

"Apparently when they checked the CCTV recordings at the hospital, all they found were pirated copies of the film *Sister Act 2* on each one. Sister Zoya does have a rather quirky sense of humour."

"Right," said Bunny. "I see." He didn't. "I think I'm missing something here. Last time we spoke, the Sisters of the Saint wanted nothing to do with me. Now you're going to great lengths to help me and you're nursing me back to health?"

Dionne was about to say something, but she was interrupted by the door of the room banging open. Sister Dorothy whirred in on her electric wheelchair.

"He is awake?" she said.

"Yes," confirmed Dionne.

"Is he making much sense?"

Dionne oscillated her hand in the air. "About the usual."

"Have you told him yet?"

"I was coming around to it."

"Time is of the essence," said Dorothy.

"Well, yes, but respectfully, Sister, it's not like he's in any fit state to get started now."

"We can't wait too long or—"

Bunny cleared his throat loudly. "Excuse me. Sorry to interrupt, but is there any chance somebody would like to tell me what in the fecking hell is going on?"

Dorothy looked directly at him for the first time. "You want to help your lady friend?"

"Simone," said Bunny. "Yes, of course I do. That's why I'm here."

"Good," said Dorothy. "Well, the only person who would know where she is, or at least might have a way of contacting her, is Sister Bernadette. As you know, she was missing."

"Wait," said Bunny, wincing as he attempted to sit further up. "Was – you said was. She's back?"

Sister Dorothy shook her head. "No. But we now at least know where she is. That is the one and only piece of good news in that regard. The situation is... complicated." Dorothy shifted uncomfortably. "We need your help."

Bunny smiled. "I'm sorry, what was that, Sister? I think I heard you wrong there. Could you repeat what you just said?"

Dorothy's face became even sterner, something Bunny wouldn't have thought possible. "You heard me."

"No, I don't think I did. I've been stabbed and shot and God knows what else; I think my hearing must be buggered to Belgium too. Could you repeat it for me again, please?"

Dorothy parsed the words out, as though speaking each one aloud was causing her pain. "I said, we need your help."

"That's what I thought you said." Bunny looked up towards Dionne, who was standing there with her arms folded. "That's what I thought she said. But that can't be right, because I offered that before and you said no. You were very definite about it."

"Yes, yes," said Dorothy.

"You did a whole bit. You asked if I speak Spanish. I said no. Did I know anyone in South America? I said I'd once won sixty quid betting on Peru in the World Cup."

"If you are quite finished," said Dorothy.

"You asked if I could dance the flamenco," continued Bunny, who was nowhere near quite finished. "I said no, but I could do you a pretty good foxtrot and my waltz was to die for."

"Bunny," said Dionne, her raised eyebrow possibly warning that he might push this too far.

Bunny looked back at Dorothy. "What was that Latin motto ye had again?"

She paused, looked up at Dionne and then back at Bunny, with the kind of look an Easter Island statue would consider unyielding. "If you're quite finished, Mr McGarry. To your advantage, we find ourselves in need of an alliance of sorts. It just so happens that we seem to have discovered the one and only situation where the Sisters of the Saint need the assistance of a man."

Bunny nodded and then yawned expansively. "Alright, I'm in."

"But you don't know what it is yet," said Dorothy.

"It doesn't matter," he replied, closing his eyes. "When I said I'd do anything, I meant it. I'm in. But I'm also shattered. Ye can explain it to me in the morning."

"But..."

Bunny fell back into what appeared to be a deep sleep.

Dionne and Dorothy stayed there, looking at him for a good minute. It didn't appear he was waking up any time soon.

"He really is quite something," said Dionne.

"That is one way of putting it."

"I mean, you can't doubt his resourcefulness or his determination. You heard Father Gabriel's description of—"

"Yes," said Dorothy. "Still, with this situation, I can't help feeling something terrible is coming our way."

Just then, something did – as Bunny farted loudly.

Dorothy turned her chair in disgust and proceeded out of the room without looking back. "Good God, open a window."

Dionne smiled. "Aren't you worried he'll escape?"

"That's exactly what I'm counting on."

FREE BOOK

Hi there reader-person,

I hope you enjoyed the book, thanks for taking the time to read it. If you've not already had the pleasure, then the Dublin Trilogy books are packed full of Bunny McGarry mayhem as is *Disaster Inc*, the first book in this spin-off series. The details of all of them are on the next page. If you've already read them all, then rest assured that Bunny will be back in 2020. In the meantime, if you'd like to get my short fiction collection called **How To Send A Message**, which features several Bunny stories go to my website:

www.WhiteHairedIrishman.com

.

The paperback costs \$10.99/£7.99 in the shops but you can get the e-book for free just by signing up to my monthly newsletter.

Cheers muchly,

Caimh

ALSO BY CAIMH MCDONNELL

THE DUBLIN TRILOGY (FEATURING BUNNY MCGARRY)

A Man With One of Those Faces (Book 1)

The Day That Never Comes (Book 2)

Angels in the Moonlight (A prequel that we're calling Book 3 as it needs to be read before...)

Last Orders (Book 4)

MCGARRY STATESIDE

Disaster Inc (Book 1)

I Have Sinned (Book 2)